Touchstone

Carol Donati - Hertle

ISBN

978-1-950621-33-0 (ebook)

978-1-950621-32-3 (print)

About The Author

Carol DeMaria Donati Hertle was born September 5th, 1931 in San Francisco, California. Her parents, John and Margarita Donati, were Italian immigrants. Carol is a first-generation "born in America" Italian who is very proud of her heritage. She was raised in San Francisco and North Beach immersed herself in the lifestyle of the Italian immigrants. While growing up she spent time on her uncle's ranch in the Carmel Valley where she fell in love with horses and ranch life. In 1952, she married and moved to Modesto, California. There she began her new life as a farm wife, mother, and rancher.

As an empty nester, Carol wrote this book. It is a fictional novel that encompasses portions of her life as a first-generation immigrant. The writing of this book brought her peace through some tough times.

Carol's dear friend, Mary Ruggieri, heartfully supported the writing of this book by editing and typing endless successive drafts. May Mary rest in peace knowing it has been published 40 years later.

Carol is now 90 years old, in good health, and keeps very busy with painting, traveling, church activities, and her dog. Keeping up with the lives of her family is a full-time adventure. Carol's 4 children have graced her with 6 grandchildren, 5 step-grandchildren, and 14 great-grandchildren.

Carol's 4 children are very proud of this book. They surprised her by having the book published for her 90th birthday celebration.

CHAPTER ONE

"Lead the soul of Eduardo Joseph Dante into paradise and free him from the pains of purgatory." Closing the prayer book, father Michael sprinkled holy water upon the pine casket.

Silently, village men shoveled damp clumps of Italian soil into the grave. Rosa, her head bowed, eyes blurred with tears, mourned for the man who had been her husband and the father of her twin children. Buried deep within her grief was the pain of knowing hers was not the only bed in the village that would miss Eduardo.

"Two husbands already, she will marry again," the village women whispered, "She has that same look at twenty-nine she had when she came to the village at fourteen. A woman like Rosa will soon take another man."

Walking with an elegance born not of peasant stock, Rosa held tightly to the small hands of her young children. Behind her, two older sons – not yet grown to full manhood – walked in silence and in grief.

Rosa and her children made their way down the narrow path, the early morning stillness broken only by the clatter of the empty hearse going back to the village.

Standing the child beside her, Nina stood, "I am Signora Orso, this is my niece, Rosa DeMarco."

Nina and the nun shook hands above Rosa's head.

"We have been expecting you, Signora."

Trying to hide herself in the folds of Nina's skirt, the child pushed her body ever closer. Head bowed, holding Nina's hand as tightly as she could, only her eyes moved as she glanced up at the nun.

Gently, yet firmly, Nina tried to push Rosa forward toward the nun's extended hand. Rosa buried her face deeper into the folds of Mama Nina's skirt. She would not take the hand. Nina knelt beside the trembling child. "I love you, bambina mia, never forget that. I will send for you." She kissed Rosa, their tears melding together as one.

"I must go now, bambina mia, I must go. Come and wave goodbye to your Uncle Anthony." But Rosa's arms remained locked around her Mama Nina's neck.

The nun pried the small arms free. The moment of separation came. Rosa wanted to kick, to bite, to yell, anything to get free from the strong hold, but she knew she must not for Mama Nina would not be proud of her.

The nun instructed, "Come, walk at my side, child."

A tight grip on Rosa's hand, she guided her out of the room and into the long corridor. Rosa prayed to the Madonna that Nina would follow her. She looked back and saw Nina start to take a step toward her, then stop.

Tears falling down her face, Nina called, "I will send for you, bambina Mia, I will." Rosa felt herself being drawn around the corridor of the hall, until she could no longer see her Mama Nina.

Rosa was pulled along with the strong, heavy stride of Sister Lucia. Suspended from the nun's waist was a heavy silver crucifix which swayed from side to side slapping against the child's bare leg. Large wooden rosary beads hanging from sister's belt clacked rhythmically against each other.

"Here we are," the nun said, urging the small child through the doorway of a large gray dormitory. Wood frame beds covered with earth colored blankets were lined up against the two long sidewalls.

Over each bed, the body of Christ hung on a wooden crucifix. On one wall, a long narrow horizontal window allowed a slim sliver of light into the stark room. At the end of the middle aisle, a narrow tiled shelf held twelve washbasins, a single white towel hung against the stone wall.

"This will be your bed, child." Sister Lucia said pointing to a straw mattress folded back above simple wooden slats. The nun handed Rosa a pile of bedding and a neatly folded blue jumper.

Instructing her to put the uniform on, she patted the top of Rosa's head with a heavy hand, "I will be back with the girls in a short while."

The small solitary figure stood before the wooden bed.

A lonely shiver went up her spine. The only sound was that of a light rain hitting the tile roof.

Climbing onto the edge of the bed she looked out the high window and saw Sister Lucia leading a group of girls across the wet brick courtyard below. All different sizes and shapes, the girls marched in unison, permitting neither pace nor posture to be affected by the falling rain.

As the heavy steps of Sister Lucia approached, Rosa jumped down from the bed and wiped her eyes on the empty sleeve of the dress she had just taken off. Hurrying to get the course wool uniform over her head, she squirmed.

Sister Lucia took one step into the room and stepping aside permitted the girls to march in front of her. Each girl stood at the foot of her bed at attention. Rosa's eyes darted from one to the other, finally stopping at the girl at the door of the bed next to her's.

Taller than most, she wore a white square bib apron over her wool jumper, a reward for excellent scholarship. She had dark deep-set black eyes, and long silky curls which hung loosely around her face. When their eyes met she smiled at Rosa.

"Now children," the stern voice of Sister Lucia broke the silence, "Wash quickly so you will be ready when I come back to lead you to the dining hall."

The minute the sister left the room the girls gathered around Rosa, telling her their names, chattering all at once. The dark-eyed girls said, "I am Angelina. Do not be afraid, I will help you."

Guiding her to the end of the room, Angelina showed Rosa which basin to use and added, "There are many rules to obey, you'll soon learn them," her voice was soft and kind.

"What are the rules?" Rosa asked, wondering if she had already broken them.

A voice from across the room shouted, "Rules! that is all they have here, it is a school of rules."

"Don't do this- don't do that," a skinny little pug faced girl added. Placing the white towel around her face like a wimple, she pulled her lips tight over her teeth and, frowning, walked up and down the aisle mocking the heavy step of Sister Lucia.

"Don't let them scare you." The beautiful face of Rosa's newfound friend was smiling. "My bed is next to you, so don't be frightened. We will be together."

"The important rule you must learn, Rosa," Angelina's face grew grave, "is to answer the bells. One bell we must get up, two bells we must eat, three bells we must kneel, it is time for prayers. Sister Lucia always has that bell cupped in her hand, ready to ring. You must answer the bells immediately, any time, any hour."

The chatter of the girls was stopped by Sister Lucia's reappearance. Again they stood at the foot of their beds, this time hands held out, palms up.

Angelina motioned Rosa to do the same.

Rosa wiped her hands hurriedly on the back of her skirt and tried to edge closer to Angelina.

Sister Lucia walked between the two rows of hands nodding her approval.

She stopped in front of a slim blonde girl at the far end of the row. Rapping the outstretched hands, "Francesca," she screamed, "these hands are not clean! This is a founding home. When will you learn that we are not dirty street beggars? We must be clean in body and thought. We are temples of God!"

Head bowed, Francesca hurried to the basin. The nun turned to address the others, her voice projecting across the room, "Now our soup will be cold, all of us will have to eat cold soup because Francesca was so inconsiderate!"

Frozen in one spot, Rosa dared not take a breath until the nun passed by her and nodded approval. Angelina smiled reassuringly.

Waiting until the errant Francesca had presented her with a pair of clean hands, the nun rang her bell and the girls lined up two by two.

Angelina took Rosa's hand, "Make sure your hands and face are clean before meals," she whispered. "When the sisters speak to you, bow your head and curtsy."

Angelina squeezed her hand, "If you want to study your lessons and say your prayers, you will not have any trouble. You will grow to love the nuns as I do. I pray all the time that I will someday be chosen."

"Chosen for what?" Rosa whispered.

"To be a nun, of course."

"Oh," Rosa said, tears filled her eyes, she wanted only to be with her Mama Nina.

They walked silently, Rosa staying close to her new friend. When they approached the dining hall Sister Lucia rang her bell. With military precision, the formation of girls stopped and waited while groups of first older and then younger girls entered the hall before them.

In the dining room, rows of blue clad girls stood, heads bowed, before the long narrow tables, a nun stationed at the end. Sister Lucia led her girls in grace and not until she rang her bell again did they sit. "Now remember, you are young ladies, sit up straight and do not gulp your food."

The silence of the dining hall was broken only by the clatter of spoons against thick white soup bowls. In the back of the room, Francesca knelt before a low bench, drinking her soup and making faces behind the nuns' backs.

That night, lying awake in the strange bed, the child Rosa remembered Mama Nina and Anthony arguing:

"We cannot take her with us to America. She can stay at the convent in Lucca." His voice sharp and dictatorial, "She is not ours, her

Mama is dead, and even her father abandoned her." When Rosa asked Mama Nina what "abandoned" meant, she said, "When a person doesn't want something anymore they throw it away- they abandon it."

Rosa lay on the unyielding straw mattress. Body coiled up like an infant, with tears pouring across her cheeks, she was remembering a sad little rag doll abandoned in the streets of Lucca.

When she reached to pick it up out of the gutter, Mama Nina told her, "Leave it, it is dirty, even the child who once loved her has thrown it away, it is worth nothing."

"Abandoned"- once no more than a word- now sent icy chills up the child's spine. Was she, like that doll, worth nothing?

As months and years went by, Rosa became a model student. She studied very hard and like Angelina, earned the coveted white apron. She excelled in English and in history and loved writing about her achievements in the weekly letters she wrote to her Mama Nina.

The nuns saw that she got the best education they had to offer, the kind usually reserved for children of wealthy merchants or noble families. But always, strong in Rosa's heart, there remained the longing for her Mama Nina. Faithfully she wrote every week, and with each letter that arrived from America, she prayed to the Madonna that that would be the one- the one telling her to come- to come to her Mama Nina.

It was only her love for Angelina which made the convent life bearable for Rosa. On Sundays when the tinkle of Sister Lucia's bell was silent and only the great bells from the Cathedral of St. Martin could be heard, Rosa would walk with Angelina.

Free to visit the town nearby, the two best friends talked and laughed and shared girlhood secrets. They loved to look in the store windows at the beautiful clothes. "Look at the silk, Angelina, someday I want to have a dress like that, so long and full and with bone buttons." Rosa pointed to a long blue silk gown with a bustle.

The girls watched the shiny horses, in heavy brass and leather harnesses, trotting proudly up the streets pulling fine buggies behind them. The rich ladies of Lucca, dressed in colorful silks, sat straight and erect, holding matching parasols to protect their white skin from the sun.

One pleasant Sunday afternoon in the park, while Rosa and Angelina were watching beautiful ladies walk by, Rosa asked, "Angelina, do you think I will ever have breasts like that pretty lady?" Angelina reassured the younger girl that she would and then Rosa added, "Do nuns have breasts, Angelina?"

"Of course they have breasts," Angelina answered quickly, then giggling she added, "Anyhow, I suppose they do, Rosa."

"Well I cannot see them," Rosa answered firmly, "their habits are as flat up here as the priests," she patted her own still flat chest.

"Don't be silly, Rosa, even the Madonna has breasts, she had to nurse our Dear Savior."

"But she was not a nun, and nuns do not have to nurse bambini," Rosa argued. "All the sisters are flat, even fat Sister Martha is flat. What happened to their breasts?"

Angelina shrugged her shoulder and Rosa continued, "You have breasts, Angelina, maybe you will not be chosen because you have breasts?"

Rosa prayed that her own body would soon develop. She did not want to be chosen, she wanted only to be with her Mama Nina.

One winter day five years after mama Nina left her at the convent, Rosa sat on the edge of her bed holding an unopened letter from America. Angelina had been called to Sister Superior's office and

Rosa was worried. Angelina never did anything wrong to be called into the dreaded office. A sense of doom filled Rosa's heart and shivers ran down her back.

Angelina burst into the dormitory, grabbing Rosa around the waist she danced her across the floor, "I have been chosen, I have been chosen!" She danced a wide circle in and out through beds, "The headmistress just told me, that is why I was called into the office." Angelina hugged Rosa close, "You will be chosen soon, too, my beautiful friend." She kissed her lightly on the forehead, "You will soon follow me. You are so good, I know they will take you too."

Rosa turned her head away. She did not want her to see her tears. It would be selfish not to want Angelina to follow her calling. But she did not want her friend to leave her.

"I must leave now. But I will come back to see you as soon as I can," Angelina said. Rosa watched her beloved friend gather her meager belongings, pull the blankets from her bed and fold back the straw mattress.

"I love you, Rosa, my dear friend," she said as they embraced one last time. Angelina ran from the room, her beautiful long silky hair bouncing as she ran. Rosa felt a terrible sinking inside her, something she had felt before. She remembered the letter from Mama Nina- maybe this time…

June 10, 1865

San Francisco

My Dear Rosa,

You will soon be ten years old, how I remember holding you in my arms, the night when you were born, the night your dear mother died. It seems so long ago, but my thoughts and my prayers are with you always. We are now in San Francisco, Anthony did not like New York.

He said there were too many Italians, too many foreigners. He wanted to meet Americans. He spent all our money on a boat, and now all we do is fish all the time. All the time we work, there is never enough money....

Rosa could no longer see the words on the paper; the tears she held back now fell freely down her face. She stared at the empty bed beside her. She was alone- empty- and one day more abandoned. She fell to her knees, holding the crumpled letter up to the ever-watching crucifix above her bed, pleaded, "Mama Nina, please, I do not want to stay here. Please take me with you."

CHAPTER TWO

"Come on girls, it is time to go to the chapel." In the distance, the bells of the cathedral tolled, while inside the stone walled convent, Sister Lucia's bell echoed.

With hands in prayer position, twelve-year-old Rosa took her place in the silent column of blue- clad girls. Two by two, heads bowed, they marched out from the dormitory.

Flickering candles cast a golden glow on the altar and on the white flowers symbolizing purity. With rosary beads wove through her fingers, Rosa knelt. She tried to pray, but excitement and anticipation could not be stilled.

The organ sounded a strong chord, the bishop entered, and the chapel of kneeling girls rose as one.

In his gold beaded, heavy satin vestments, he walked down the aisle, the candle light reflecting on the gold threads of his miter. Reaching the altar the bishop genuflected, the heavy embroidered satin vestments unbending as the body inside knelt. Piously he turned, crosier in hand, to await the bride of God.

Dressed in virginal white, a tight fitting bodice accentuating her full breasts, Angelina entered, the most beautiful bride Rosa had ever seen.

Even as beautiful as her Mama Nina had been at her wedding. Angelina's head bowed, the white veil touched the prayer book in her hand. Her long black hair, softened by the delicate lace, hung down her back in gentle curls. Rosa could hear the rustle of the silk wedding dress, and she wanted to reach out and touch this angel gliding past her, this beautiful bride for God.

Angelina knelt before the bishop. When she had repeated her vows, he lifted the veil from her face and placed the secret wafer in her mouth. Two altar boys stood side by side. One accepted the prayer book Angelina held out. The other stood motionless, in his hand a gold plate on which lay a single wedding band. The bishop slipped the gold ring on Angelina's finger.

Removing the veil from her head, the priest turned to the altar and placed it before the chalice. Genuflecting once more, he bowed and kissed the altar cloth. When he turned back to Angelina, he was holding a pair of scissors– shears of the shepherd to shear the sheep of God.

Towering above the kneeling child, the bishop paused for but a second. He picked up a large handful of black hair from the head of the girl, and, holding his hand up high, he stretched the hair taut. The blades of the scissors snapped together as the hair fell from the scalp. Abandoned, the fallen curls lay at the feet of the bishop.

Rosa watched in horror. Angelina's beautiful hair! Why did the bishop do that to her? Rosa put a trembling hand over her mouth. Her stomach lurched. Transfixed, she was unaware when her rosary beads slipped from her hand.

Frightened, yet fascinated, Rosa forced herself to watch as the bishop picked up yet another handful of hair– the snap of the scissors even closer to Angelina's scalp. One more jagged cut. The beautiful black hair now lifeless, a few small wisps of curls clung

14

desperately to her wedding dress. Head bowed, Angelina's bare white neck was lost in the whiteness of her wedding dress.

Rosa closed her eyes tight so that she could not see Angelina. But in the blackness of her mind, the picture of that hairless head remained vivid. Her stomach cramped; she felt the urge to run.

There was the Russell of silk, and Rosa opened her eyes. The shorn angel was standing before the prelate. He lowered a stiff white wimple onto her head. Two nuns silently stepped forward. Stretching a course robe between them, they blanketed in black the delicate white bride. The heavy material covered her white wedding dress, silencing forever the silk.

Sister Lucia led the girls in song: "Save the handmaiden, oh Lord, for in thee_ is her hope. Let her be good and humble. Let her be exalted by obedience. Let her be bound to peace. Let her be constant in prayer. Lastly, oh Lord, we beg- thee to receive graciously her offerings…"

Rosa stood motionless, the fallen rosary unnoticed at her feet. Tears fell down her face. She moved her lips but no sound came. The black-robed figure turned to face the chapel- it was a stranger, not her beautiful Angelina. As this person walked down the aisle, the black robe lay flat across her chest, there were no breasts.

When Rosa was fourteen, she was summoned to the office of Sister Superior.

Rosa remembered when Angelina had been summoned, and she remembered that day in the chapel, the day Angelina was wedded to God.

"Sister, I do not have the calling," Rosa's head bowed, her voice barely audible.

"Sister Lucia demanded, "What is wrong with you, child?"

"Sister I fear I do not have the true faith that Angelina had."

Fists planted firmly on her hip bones, the nun demanded, "And what do you want to do?" Heart pounding in her chest, eyes cast downward, Rosa said, "I do not know."

Sister Lucia turned her back, "You do not know?" You have been groomed for this, and now you are saying that you do not want to be a nun? I cannot believe this!"

Rosa trembled, her eyes welled up with tears. Hardly knowing what to think, she answered, "Sister, please do not be angry with me. Please give me time to think."

"Time? You've had nine years, and you want more time? How dare you ask for more time, you ungrateful child!"

Sister Superior stormed out of the room.

Rosa ran to her bed and fell to her knees. She buried her head in her hands and prayed for forgiveness. Apologizing to God, she begged him to understand why she could not give herself to him.

The following morning after Mass, Rosa returned to the dormitory and found her bedding ripped from her bed. The mattress was folded back, and on the bare wooden slats was her string bag containing the few belongings Mama Nina had left with her nine years ago.

From the doorway of the deserted dormitory, Sister Lucia spoke; "Rosa," she said, "the wagon is waiting to take you."

"Where to?" Rosa asked.

"To a place where you will have time to think. Hurry. Follow me."

Bewildered, the girl picked up her sack and took her place beside the nun. Once again Rosa DeMarco silently followed Sister Lucia down the king corridor- rosary beads clacking together, crucifix slapping against her leg,

"Sister, where am I going?" Rosa asked.

"You're being sent to Viareggio to work in the church house for Father Joseph."

"Father Joseph?" Rosa repeated, uncomprehending. From the darkened hallway, Sister opened the heavy wooden door and said,

"You will have time there to think, you ungrateful child," She turned and went back into the convent.

Numb and unfeeling, as if watching from outside herself, Rosa observed a lone figure, feet dangling over the back edge of a crude wooden wagon, clutching a faded string bag to her breast.

This figure- half child, half woman- kept her eyes upon the convent and the town of Lucca until the curve of the road took them from view. No tears fell from those eyes.

Her thoughts silenced and spirit deadened, Rosa's body swayed with the rolling of the crude wooden wheels upon the country road. Throughout the long morning hours, while the horses labored up and down rolling foothills, Rosa sat unseeing. The summer sun was directly overhead when the wagon stopped near a grove of evergreens.

The driver, an old man who did not speak, handed Rosa a water bucket and beckoned her to follow him down to a small stream. The horses watered, he offered her a bit of bread and cheese. Their silent meal done, the old man arranged for her to lie down, and the rocking of the wagon soon put her to sleep. When she awoke, it was mid-afternoon, and there was the smell of the sea in the air. The hillsides were green and covered with small shrubs and grasses. The horses' slow, steady plodding took them downward

17

nearer the sea, closer to the small village of Viareggio. Rosa sensed a feeling of freedom.

Alongside the road small, stone houses dotted the crest of the last hill, Rosa could see below her the clear blue water of the Tyrrhenian Sea.

The smell of salt strong in the air, Rosa smiled as she felt the brief chill of the sea breeze.

The Church, a solitary stone building, looked down protectively upon the cluster of small houses woven together with stone lined paths. When the wagon rolled to a stop in front of the church house, Father Joseph stood waiting, his white hair blowing in the gentle breeze from the sea.

"Welcome, Rosa, your room is ready, I have been waiting for you," he put his arm around her shoulder, his hand moving slowly down across her back. When Rosa looked up into his face, his eyes smiled and made her feel safe.

She was at last living in a real home, and anxious to please, Rosa worked hard. She knew nothing about baking or cooking or cleaning, or mending, but the village women, always happy to be close to the inner workings of the church, became her willing teachers. Rosa learned quickly and was soon doing as well as any full-grown woman.

Father Joseph became the father Rosa had never known, and when her housework was done, she loved listening to his stories. He often took her with him on his walks, and although his prayer book was always open in his hand, she never saw him read from it.

He would walk with his arm resting on her shoulders, and sometimes stop to view the blue sea from the hill, or to watch a songbird in the pine tree.

With his arms circled around her, and body pressed close to her, Father Joseph would explain to Rosa how birds gathered twigs to make their nests.

The Summer turned to fall and in that brief space of time, Rosa became aware that her body was changing. The beauty of her Italian heritage became more evident in her white alabaster skin, deep dark eyes, and high full breasts.

Whenever she went down into the village for water she knew the young men were watching her move, and she had strange feelings inside of her, feelings which alarmed her. When the young men tried to talk to her she became frightened and hurried back to the safety of the church. At night, alone in her room, she liked to look at herself naked in the mirror, and admired her womanly beauty, with the smooth skin and graceful curving lines. But she had been taught that it was sinful to admire her body.

"Your body is a temple of God," the nuns told her. Every week she would say her confession to Father Joseph and ask him for absolution of these evil, sinful thoughts.

In the lengthening winter evenings, Rosa looked forward to the time when her work was done. She would take Father Joseph a glass of wine and sit with him before the fire.

A parish priest for many years, he loves to tell her stories of a strange sight he had seen and the places he had visited in his youth. Their evenings in front of the fire began to stretch further into the night, with the old priest often becoming drowsy from the wine and falling asleep in his chair. Removing his slippers, and putting a blanket over him, Rosa would tiptoe out of the room.

Sometimes Rosa would look up and notice Father Joseph watching her. He told her how beautiful she was becoming, and, and unused to compliments Rosa would feel her cheeks grow warm.

Many times he kissed her good night, and said, "You have become so beautiful, my saintly Rosa."

She enjoyed the kind of praise she had never heard before.

It was late November, Rosa had been at the church house for six months.

"Come sit here, by the fire, Rosa," Father Joseph said, "the winds are already cold."

Taking her place on a small footstool, Rosa felt warm and safe before the crackling fire. Father Joseph sipped his wine and spoke of his younger years, "I was once in love with a beautiful girl, Rosa. She was so beautiful! But I was expected to become a priest as you were expected to become a nun. I did what I was told."

He sat back in his chair and looked at Rosa, she felt his eyes penetrate her.

"You remind me so much of that girl I left so many years ago. Her name was Beatrice, she came from Firenze. I wonder whatever happened to her." Rosa saw a longing in his eyes that she had never seen before.

"She had white skin, long silky coal-black hair, and a beautiful body."

"You look so beautiful tonight, Rosa," Father Joseph said.

"Sitting there before the fire, you look almost saintly, a glow from the fire is forming a halo around your head."

"Rosa was glad the lights were dim so that he could not see her reddening cheeks. "How lucky some village man will be to have you for his bride."

Rosa hung her head, and looked down at her folded hands.

"No, no, Father, I will never marry. I will never leave you, I will stay with you forever."

Setting his empty wine glass on the table, he leaned over and stroked her hand, "Rosa have you become a woman yet?" he asked. The kindly, fatherly eyes she loved so much had changed. They had a frightening glare.

Afraid to meet his gaze, she bowed her head, "I must go now, Father. It is late, I must go."

When Rosa stood to leave, Father Joseph took hold of her arm.

"Do not leave yet, Beatrice" he said as he pushed her back down onto the footstool.

Kneeling at her side, he rested his hand on her lap and fingered the material of her dress.

His face was so close to hers that she could smell the stale wine on his warm breath.

"Beatrice," he murmured.

Rosa's body rigid with fear, she tried to pull away from him but the heat of the fire stopped her.

He gripped her leg with one hand and his other hand slipped under her skirt.

"My dear Beatrice," he said over and over. Rosa began to tremble. She could not believe this was happening. She wanted to run but was afraid to.

"I am not Beatrice, Father, I am Rosa." She tried to push his hand away, "You are a priest, stop! stop! You are a priest!" Rosa was screaming.

"I am a man now, Beatrice, a man. I will not hurt you, my beautiful Beatrice," his speech was slurred. "I have always loved you, I have always wanted you, now you will be my bride!"

"Father stop it, stop it, you're hurting me. What are you doing? This is wrong, Father stop please!"

Rosa stood and he grabbed her ankle. She tried to take a step. He held tight.

He pulled her to the floor, and releasing her ankle, crawled on top of her. He tore at her clothes.

She screamed. He put his hand over her mouth. He mumbled, "Beatrice, Beatrice," and buried his face on her breast. "Be nice to me, I will not hurt you. I love you so."

He tore the buttons loose from her blouse. He fondled her breast, and his other hand slipped under her dress.

"Be good to me, I love you. I will not hurt you, my young virgin. You are so beautiful, my Beatrice, my Beatrice, I have wanted you for so long."

He squeezed her right breast with such force that Rosa screamed in pain. "Be quiet," his voice was now angry, beads of sweat on his forehead, and the stale wine sour on his breath.

He grabbed at her skirt and there was the sound of tearing cloth.

"Holy Mother, make him stop, oh please make him stop." Rosa prayed, her heart beating in her rib cage so loud that it echoed in her head.

"Better me than some dumb village man. I will appreciate you." He buried his face, his mouth on her breast.

"His fingers digging into her flesh, "Dear God please help me," she cried. She grabbed a handful of hair from the back of his head, and pulled with all her strength.

Arching his back, he cried out in pain. The priest let loose of her for a moment. She kicked free and rolled over.

Crawling, she tried to get up but stumbled on the torn hem of her skirt.

She regained her balance and got to her feet. Father Joseph reached out and grabbed her skirt, and she heard the cloth tear.

Her legs weak with fright, she got to the door, and pushed it open, and ran from the church house. The cold wind bit into the wetness of her cheeks. She turned and saw the black figure of the priest, half standing, half kneeling on the steps, his body silhouetted in the light from the open door.

His arm stretched out, he held a torn piece of her skirt.

Running down the hill, she clutched what was left of her clothing to her body. She ran past the well and down the narrow cobblestone street. The night wind bit into her bare shoulders. She could smell the faint odor of spent fires in houses. "Dear Mother of Mary, please help me," she cried as she stumbled and fell.

When she reached the water's edge, no one was at the pier to help her. She stopped to catch her breath.

But when she tried to take a deep breath, her lungs felt like thousands of stabbing knives and they refused to fill. She shivered in the cold.

The darkness of the night was broken only by a sliver of moon and the faint light shining from the widow Dante's window.

Her vision clouded with tears, unaware of her bleeding knees, Rosa ran toward the light. She banged on the heavy wood door with her first.

The door opened and Rosa collapsed at the feet of Giovanni, the widow Dante's eldest son. Rosa woke to little stabs of pain as Mama Dante dabbed at the dried blood on her knees. Realizing she was naked, Rosa clutched the covers tighter around her body.

"You are alright, child, you are safe, don't be frightened," Mama Dante gently patted her arm.

"You are Rosa, the girl from the parish house? What happened child, what happened to you?"

The short gray-haired woman put the basin of water on the floor and gently covering Rosa's knees, took her hand, and said, "Tell me…"

Rosa pulled the covers higher, half burying her face, only her eyes showed. She was afraid to tell, no one would believe that Father Joseph would do such a thing. Even she could not believe it.

"Nothing happened, Signora," Rosa sobbed, "nothing."

"Something happened child, tell me," Mama Dante insisted. Sitting beside her on the bed, the widow Dante held Rosa in her arms and stroked her back.

"Tell me, Rosa, do not be afraid." Finally, in between sobs, Rosa told Mama Dante the whole story.

"Did father Joseph make you bleed?" The old woman asked.

"No, Signora," she whispered.

Rosa could not stop crying, "I should have become a nun. Oh, Signora, God is angry with me. He made this happen to me."

"Sh-sh-sh, sh-sh-sh, child, it is not your fault."

"Father Joseph called me his child. What made him act like that? How could he do that?" Rosa sobbed.

"Because he is a lecherous, drunken old man hiding behind the cloak of a priest. He is a vigliacco! I knew something would happen like this! He was always too eager to have the orphaned young girls take care of him." Signora Dante used words Rosa had never heard before.

She brought Rosa a cup of warm wine, "here, drink some of this, it will help you sleep," she put the glass to Rosa's lips.

The smell of wine made Rosa remember the stench of Father Joseph's sour breath on her face, and she pushed the glass away.

Miss Dante tucked the covers gently around Rosa and brushed the matted hair from her face. "Alright, my child, everything will be alright. You will stay right here with me and my two sons, we are family. Mama Dante will take care of you, sleep now, sleep."

When Rosa closed her eyes, the memory of Father Joseph, his sour breath, the sweat on his forehead, the fingers digging into her flesh, his mouth touching the skin of her breasts, leaped up at her.

The tighter she closed her eyes, the more vivid the memories became. Clenching her teeth, she tried to bury her cries in her pillow.

She felt Mama Dante's soft gentle touch on her hand and heard the quiet soothing sound of her voice. She drifted off to sleep. As she slept a gold bishop came and stood over her bed, his figure a stone cold statue. Over his chiseled head he held not a sword, but a pair of scissors with blood dripping from their blades onto the bald head of a white-clad girl figure below.

25

Through her tormented dreams she was once more in the chapel, where candles heavy with wax, dripped onto the forgotten rosary beads. Black flowers hung dead from the altar.

An empty silk wedding dress, black curls clinging to the material, lay abandoned on the ground. There was no golden glow, but a foggy mess and a white-haired priest standing smiling, his eyes piercing her heart with icy stabs. His white hair wild, he stripped off his embroidered stole and lurched toward a naked girl clutching a string bag to her breast, her black silky hair held by a floating golden hand. "You will be my bride," he shouted at her, "my bride."

Rosa sat upright in her bed, perspiration dripped down her face, her body trembled and she pulled the covers close, her pulse pounded in her temples. She put her hands in prayer, "Forgive me Father in heaven, have I sinned?"

Early the next morning, when Rosa woke her belongings were at the foot of the bed. The following Sunday, mass was said by the new priest, Father Michael, and old widow Bellini are moved into the church house to care for him.

CHAPTER THREE

Rosa remained at the Dante home. The widow and her sons, Giovanni and Eduardo, were simple, gentle people who took Rosa to their hearts. But it was many months, all through the long winter, before Rosa could close her eyes at night without knowing again the nightmare of Father Joseph.

Even after spring flowers colored the rugged Italian countryside, there remained deep in Rosa's heart, an uncomfortable feeling that had she become a nun, God would not have abandoned her.

In the weekly letters she wrote to Mama Nina in America, Rosa never once mentioned that terrible night at the church house- if her Mama Nina knew, she might not love her.

Giovanni and Eduardo, strong bodied, good looking Italian men, were as different as two brothers could be. Giovanni, the elder, seldom spoke. He was a stocky man, with dark serious eyes, and a mind set upon business.

Eduardo, the younger, had a lean lithe body made for dancing, and in his eyes was a merriment few things could dampen. They worked side by side on the fishing boats, from before sun-up until nightfall, and always they watched out for each other.

For Mama Dante, as everyone in the village called her, the sun rose and set upon her two sons.

The small, pleasant Dante home was built of stone from the nearby Apuane Alps, and the timbers which supported the pink terracotta roof were the strong hard wood of the native Umbrella Pine. The narrow windows were bordered with wood shutters, closed only when storms blew in from the sea. On the seaside of the house was attached a three sided wooden shed which Paisano, the horse, shared with the fish wagon.

In the yard, white leghorn chickens roamed around picking at the olive pits and dry pine branches stored to fuel Mama Dante's stone ovens where she baked her famous bread.

In the summer months, the gentle sea breezes of Viareggio made it a haven for travelers from the hot inland cities, and Mama Dante's sourdough bread was much sought after.

A widow since Eduardo was a baby, Mama Dante had supported herself and her babies by selling the bread baked from her guarded secret recipe.

Papa Dante's father had built the house as one large square room, and a bedroom had been added for each new generation. The front door opened into the large kitchen, where the floor of hand-cut planks, had long ago been scrubbed and worn smooth and dull. There was a narrow wood table at one end, and at the other, a massive stone fireplace served to cook the meals and warm the three room house.

Mama Dante's chair rocked on a small hooked rag rug in front of the fireplace.

"This is my family album," she said, bending her full bulk and pointing to a particular portion, "this piece, here, was Papa Dante's wedding shirt."

28

She smiled, "And this was part of Giovanni's Holy Communion jacket."

On Sunday mornings the whole village made their way up the hill to the church for Mass, but on Saturday nights, they danced.

"Come with me tomorrow night, Rosa," Giovanni said after supper one evening when Rosa was fifteen.

Rosa shook her head no.

"You go! You will look so beautiful together," Mama Dante said, "My son will be the most handsome man there, and you will be the prettiest girl."

Giovanni smiled shyly at Rosa.

"But Giovanni, I do not know how to dance. I have never been to a dance."

Mama Dante laughed, "All Italians know how to dance, Rosa, even when there is no music, Italians dance."

"Not Italian girls who go to the convent," Rosa sighed.

"I will teach you, and Giovanni will teach you, and Eduardo, you too will teach! Come, my sons, we will dance."

Mama Dante put her hand out to her younger son, "Come, Eduardo, we will show Rosa how to dance! Move the table, Giovanni!"

Mother and son danced a fast polka around and around the kitchen until panting for breath, they stopped.

With hands resting on her round belly, Mama Dante said, "See how easy that is!" She reached for Rosa's hand, and leading her to the middle of the kitchen floor, asked,

"Can you count to three Rosa?"

"Yes, Mama Dante."

"Well, then you can dance."

"Now follow me, uno, due, tre," she counted, her short stout legs taking giant steps. Mama Dante pushed and pulled Rosa around the kitchen to a tune Eduardo sang.

"Now Giovanni, you take her to the dance, she will learn. No more excuses now, Rosa, and I will make you a new dress."

Mama Dante went to her sewing chest. Holding up a piece of material, studying Rosa, she looked back down at the cloth, she squinted her eyes like a great artist viewing a model, then, discarded it, and searched for another.

She repeated the whole process time and time again until finally holding up a length of soft jade-green cotton she said, "This is just the right color, good, you will look beautiful, Rosa."

When Saturday night arrived Rosa felt special. The expert needle of Mama Dante had created a dress to fit snugly over the womanly curves of her body. When she walked, the material rustled and made her skin feel alive.

With a matching ribbon in her hair, Rosa looked at herself in the mirror. She liked what she saw.

Giovanni was in his Sunday suit, skin scrubbed, curly hair combed flat, he waited nervously for her.

"You do make a handsome couple, " Mama Dante said, "just like your dear Papa and me when we were young.

"You two should get married, you both come from the same region, you are both Tuscans."

She opened the door for them, "Hurry now, or you will miss a dance."

Giovanni bent his elbow toward Rosa, she placed her hand lightly on his sleeve, and together they walked out the door.

One, two, three, she repeated to herself as they made their way through the village streets to the cafe. Giovanni and Rosa danced. At first, they moved slowly. He counted, "one, two, three that's it, Rosa, one, two, three .. you are doing fine, good, that's good."

Rosa relaxed, her feet obeyed and soon her body flowed with the rhythm of the music. Her head filled with excitement, Rosa felt the eyes of the village boys upon her.

Each young man waited his turn to dance with her. She had never been happier. She did not notice Giovanni who stood back, one foot braced against the wall, hands thrust deep into his pockets, watching as she twirled around the dance floor.

Tapping a young man's shoulder, Giovanni cut in and said, "This is my girl."

They finished the dance and when the music stopped, he took her arm, "Come on," he said, "let's go for a walk, before I lose you to another man."

Rosa's cheeks were flushed, her eyes sparkling, "Can we do this again, Giovanni? I've never had such fun."

His voice serious, Giovanni answered, "Mama said it, we could dance together until we get too old to dance. We do make a handsome couple, Rosa."

In silence, they walked down to the sea. The only sound was of the waves washing onto the

beach. Giovanni took her hand.

"Look at you, " he said, "The moon dances in your hair. You are so lovely."

31

He stopped and kissed the top of her head. Instinctively she drew away, until she remembered this was not Father Joseph, but the good Giovanni.

Smiling at him, she permitted her body to remain close to his. They walked along the water's edge, and in the distance, Rosa could hear the wagons filled with voices of young people going home from the dance.

Giovanni stopped before a row of fishing boats rocking gently with the tide.

"Someday I will have a boat of my own ..." he hesitated, "maybe you and I, Rosa, we could own our own boat together?"

Giovanni slipped his arm awkwardly around her waist.

Drawing her close, he stammered "Rosa, it is time- I mean ... Rosa .."

"Time for what, Giovanni?"

"Well, Rosa, I was thinking ... we should be ... ah- we should get. . .

"What is it?"

Staring intently down into the water, Giovanni said, "If we bought a boat together .. maybe ... I mean ..."

He looked up, put his hands on her upper arms.

"Rosa," he almost shouted, "will you ... would you ... can we get married?"

All of the villagers came. Rosa was a beautiful bride in Mama Dante's wedding dress, her long black hair a striking contrast against the white silk. Rosa smiled and accepted the many prayers for a long and fruitful life. Giovanni was a good man, Rosa knew. He would keep her safe, but she also knew that marrying a fisherman in Viareggio, she would never get to America to see her Mama Nina again.

At the wedding celebration, Rosa's new mother-in-law was queen. She danced with the groom, with Eduardo, and with every man and boy of the village.

"If only my dear husband could be here for this happy day," she said looking to the heavens making a quick sign of the cross. Happy tears fell on her round cheeks, she laughed, she cried, she prayed, and thoroughly enjoyed her eldest son's wedding day.

She hugged Rosa, "Now I have a daughter! Every woman should have a daughter. At last, now I shall have many grandchildren."

Rosa went to her wedding bed knowing that something secret happened after marriage, but she was not sure what. At school, in private times when nuns could not hear, Rosa and the other girls had whispered and giggled about boys. The priests repeatedly warned them about "sinfulness" and about being alone with boys. And now, in the darkness of their bedroom, she was alone with a man-her husband. The thought of Father Joseph flashed into her mind, and once again she felt the terror of that night. She trembled.

Giovanni lit the lamp. His back to her, he removed his coat and his tie. He pulled the tail of his shirt out from his trousers and undid each button. His chest bared, he stood before her.

Silently he took her in his strong gentle hands and

held her close to him. "'Rosa, do not be frightened. I will be gentle."

He unfastened the buttons on the back of her dress, slipped it off her shoulders, and watched it fall from her hips. Draped in a sheer chemise, the outline of Rosa's young body was silhouetted against the light. Giovanni took her in his arm, and again the vision of Father Joseph came before her.

She tried to draw away, but he held her close, "Rosa, you are my wife now, do not pull away from me."

He took the pins from her hair, "When I first saw you-not the night you came here-but when I saw you in the village, you were so beautiful, so gentle. I watched you for such a long time, and on Sundays at church, instead of praying, I stared at the back of your head, just waiting for you to turn so I could see more of you. That is when I first wanted you, but I never dreamed that you would be mine."

He lifted her in his arms and carried her to the bed. He kissed her face, her neck, "You may think the things men do to women are strange, but they are necessary," He kissed, "you will soon get used to it…" He kissed her now with more intensity and stroking her thighs, spread her legs.

"I will be gentle Rosa," he kept repeating- until the moment of passion took hold of him.

Rosa screamed. He thrust and thrust at her again until his needs were

satisfied.

"It will not be so bad for you next time, my Rosa," Giovanni said as he rolled over onto his back.

Tears drying on her cheeks, she lay silently next to this man, her husband. Soon his deep breathing was the only sound in the room. She slipped out of the bed, he did not move.

More tears fell down her cheeks. Was this the great passion that writers and poets wrote about?

Victor was born three days after their first wedding anniversary.

Mama Dante was consumed with happiness! At last a male heir to keep alive the tradition of the Dante fishermen. Named for his grandfather, the baby was taken every morning to the well in the center of the village where the proud Nona graciously accepted smiles and praise from the women.

Running plump fingers lovingly over the arm of the rocking chair her dear husband had made for her, Mama Dante told Rosa, "You nurse your baby in this chair. Three generations of Dantes' have been rocked in this chair."

She showed her daughter-in-law how to care for the few treasured pieces of furniture and taught her all the things a mother would.

She taught her how to care for the baby, how to hold him, and how to comfort him when he had the colic.

A cook without equal, Mama Dante taught Rosa how she made the sauces for pasta and how she prepared the polenta and squid and other special dishes Giovanni and Eduardo loved.

She shared with Rosa her ways of making the traditional celebration cakes and showed her how to turn sometimes meager supplies into delicacies.

When Rosa was not nursing the baby, she cooked, washed clothes, cleaned the house, mended, and made new dresses for the baby.

During the warm weather, Mama Dante made her sourdough bread to sell to the cafes. On days when the old woman's knees were aching too much, she let Rosa put some bread into the cart and take it to the innkeepers.

Sometimes she would let Rosa help make the bread, but never while she was making the dough, "I will let you know when you can help," she would say, keeping Rosa away until the bread was shaped and ready to go into the ovens.

The secret of Mama Dante's famous bread, coveted for years by all the women in the village, was a secret Mama Dante would not share with anyone, not even her daughter-in-law,

"In this house," Mama Dante said, "I make the bread!"

CHAPTER FOUR

Mama Dante died soon after her second grandchild, Dino, was born. The secret of the sourdough bread died with her.

Rosa and Giovanni moved into the main bedroom. They slept in the same iron post bed where Giovanni and Eduardo were born and where Mama Dante died. Eduardo's cot was moved from behind the kitchen stove to the small back room.

The Dante brothers loved each other. Giovanni, the serious, hard-working, firstborn, was the stable bow of the ship. Eduardo- the sail that billowed in the wind- brought joy and laughter into their home. Both men had the same muscled upper arms and backs, and a strength which came from dragging heavy fishnets from the sea.

They had the ruddy complexion of the northern Italian and the black curly hair of the southern Italian.

Giovanni's black eyes were deep and serious, but in Edoardo's eyes there danced a mischief that could not be tamed. He was not married, not because he could not find a suitable wife, but because he enjoyed being the bachelor of the small village, sought after by all the girls. He took meals with his brother's family, but in the evenings spent his time at the café, or, it was rumored, in the arms of every pretty girl in the village.

This is the way Eduardo was. They called him Viareggio's "Casanova of the fishing fleet."

Together they fished, and saved their money, and dreamed of owning their own boat. Together at the kitchen table, the bottle of dark red wine in the middle, they counted their money and talked of their dreams.

Rosa was proud of her family and she worked long and hard taking care of the four men in her life.

In the village, she was begrudgingly considered a cook "second only to Mama Dante." Her house was spotless, and never would she permit any of "her men" to be seen without freshly washed clothes. Victor and Dino grew healthy and active. The older son, a solid stocky boy grew more like his father every day- serious and quiet. Dino, whose outward appearance favored his uncle Eduardo, was a thoughtful, sensitive child. He loved to look at the books Mama Nina sent him from America, and when he closed the cover, had dozens of questions.

The village women shunned Rosa. Because she had not come to the village until she was 14, they were suspicious of her as an outsider.

In the mornings when she took the jugs to the well for water, they smiled at her and then, turning their backs, put their heads close together and whispered. They thought her stately walk meant she considered herself better than everyone. Only fat old Maria, Mama Dante's closest friend and neighbor, came to pass time of day with Rosa and to tell her the local gossip. Rosa pretended that she was not hurt by their slight, but often alone at night after Giovanni had fallen asleep, she thought about Angelina and wondered where she was and what she was doing. Rosa longed for that wonderful close childhood friendship they had shared, the friendship that had made those years in the convent bearable.

The peasant women made fun of Rosa for teaching her children American words, and with a finger under their nose, pushed the tip upward in a gesture of contempt. But Rosa did not want to forget the English she had learned in the convent, and over and over again in her head, she recited the poems they taught her. In the evenings, before the fire, she read aloud to the boys from the English books Mama Nina sent and dreamed of someday seeing her again.

And always she tried to find the secret of the sourdough bread that Mama Dante had been famous for and of the coins she could save if she could make that famous bread and sell it to the innkeepers. The bread she baked was never quite right.

"It's good but it doesn't have that special something that Mama's had," Giovanni and Eduardo told her.

During the holidays the house smelled of the sweet scent of cakes. Rosa baked all the special breads and cakes her mother-in-law had taught her. But during the rest of the year, she skimped and saved every penny she could, for the secret dream she cherished within her bosom that someday she would sail to America to see her Mama Nina again. In the spring she grew most of the food they ate in what she secretly called "her America Garden. "

It was a beautiful day in the spring of the year that Victor was 5 years old. Rosa noticed both boys acting strangely, and by noon they had been back and forth from the house to the dock a dozen times.

"The men will not return for hours yet," Rosa said.

"Yes, yes, we know, Mama," Victor said.

He took up a post on the front doorstep and for a long time sat motionless staring at the sea. Dino danced around the stone ovens in the yard, chasing the chickens until Rosa, fearful of having no eggs for the table, put a stop to it. "What is the matter with my boys today?" She asked, more of the sky than of her children who were already down at the water's edge again.

Rosa was experimenting with still another batch of bread dough and was just about to place it in the oven when she saw Giovanni and Eduardo coming toward the house.

"What is wrong, husband?" Rosa demanded as she ran toward them.

"Why are you home with so many hours of daylight left?"

They sloughed off her questions with little more than a casual wave of the hand, but her fears were quieted when she saw the unmistakable glimmer of mischief in Eduardo's eyes.

Dino flitted about and Victor stood solemnly by the front door trying hard to look serious. The men silently washed up and when they reappeared, they were dressed in their good clothes.

Dino spit on his fingers and slicked his hair down and stood alongside the two men, a smile trying hard to break through the serious frown on his face. Giovanni said, "Come, Rosa, you must come with us now."

The four of them surrounded Rosa and led her out of the house.

"What is it?" "Where are we going?" Rosa kept asking, but no one would satisfy her curiosity, "Be patient," one would say, and the other add, "You will see." The boys no longer struggling to keep the smiles from their faces, ran first far ahead, only to return and encircle the group as it made its way toward the water.

As they neared the waterfront, Giovanni took hold of Rosa's arm, "close your eyes, Rosa, we will guide you." One on each side of her, the Dante brothers whisked Rosa along, her feet barely touched the cobblestone road beneath her.

"We must be certain you don't see too soon." Taking the scarf from around his neck, he wrapped it across her eyes, "this must be a total surprise," he added.

Each holding one arm, Eduardo and Giovanni guided Rosa out on the pier. She could hear the boys running about and laughing, and then, suddenly everything became quiet. Even the water seemed to stop its constant lapping against the wooden pier.

Giovanni untied the blindfold. Rosa blinked in the bright sunlight. Then she saw the reason for their excitement. Tied to the dock was a new, sleek azure blue boat. Its lateen sails snugly tied to the single mast. On the bow, in large dark blue letters, was written Rosa I.

Muffling a shriek with her hand, Rosa threw her arms around Giovanni's neck and kissed him. Victor and Dino danced up and down asking her over and over again, "Are you surprised?" "Do you like it?" She hugged Eduardo and Giovanni both. Victor and Dino joined in and together the five of them danced happily to the music of the sea. Tears flowed down Rosa's cheeks.

"Why the tears Rosa?" Giovanni asked, a look of concern on his face.

"Tears of happiness, my husband- tears of happiness." She danced with excitement, the tears rolling down her face. "Never in my life have I been so happy. I will run home and get our best wine to christen the Rosa I."

"No", Eduardo said, "it will not hurt us to use the everyday wine to christen the boat. We have some in the cabin below." He said as he jumped on board. "We will drink the aged Chianti, Rosa and I will not care, but we will long remember the taste of the wine we drank this day."

Giovanni brought the bottle of wine across the bow of the boat, and everyone cheered as the glass shattered and red liquid flowed in rivulets over the light blue hull.

Giovanni held the bottle, first for victor and then for Dino to take a sip of the wine and join in the toast. Rosa's heart was bursting with happiness.

"And now a toast," Giovanni said, "Vito the Rosa I, soon to be followed by the Rosa II and maybe someday the Rosa III."

"Wait," Rosa stayed the bottle of wine from his lips, "should we not first say a prayer of thanks to God for such bounty?"

"God's bounty?" Eduardo asked, "it was work- damn hard work that made this boat possible."

"Well brother, God never said he'd refuse the help of a hard-working man." Everyone agreeing, they drank their toast.

The dawn was overcast with clouds, the air too cold, the December sun too timid to rise. "Don't go out today, Giovanni, it's going to storm. Look at that sky," Rosa said.

"We have to go, how else will we pay for the boat?" Giovanni said. "If we worked only on sunny days, we would never have enough fish to sell." He paused in the doorway, "do not worry Rosa, it will clear up, the storm is just passing over us. Do not worry." As he closed the door behind him, Rosa felt a chill run down her spine.

By mid-morning, the storm had unleashed a terrible fury. Rosa braved the storm to ferret out from her garden the last of the potatoes to be sure the men would have enough to eat when they returned.

She bolted the shutters right across the tiny windows and threw more olive pits onto the fire. Putting on a large pot of soup to boil, she set the bowls out on the table. She checked and rechecked the men's work clothes, mending the tiniest tears she could find.

She sat down next to the fire with Victor and Dino to read to them. But all she could hear was the whine of the wind and the pounding of rain on the tile roof.

The day dragged on into evening and still, the Dante men did not return. The sky became dark as a moonless midnight. Rosa sat staring at the heavy wooden door. It opened.

She jumped up. She stopped. Eduardo stood alone. Hands hung limply at his sides. His black hair clung to his face. One long black strand stuck to his wet cheek. Face red from the cold, his eyes were grey with despair.

"Where's Giovanni?" Rosa asked, her heart racing. "Where is he?" She screamed again, running towards Eduardo.

"Oh Rosa, Rosa," he sobbed.

"What happened? Where's Giovanni? Where's Giovanni?"

"Rosa, there's been an accident- a terrible accident." He held his arms out to her. Rosa knew only that someone was speaking, "... overboard... the sea so high... could not hold the boat... bounced like a piece of driftwood." Her head reeled.

"Lashing the sail... suddenly gone... circled and circled... waves so high... no one could survive... forced back to shore," Eduardo sobbed.

"My God, my dear God!" Rosa could see only a vague form standing in front of her. Body numb, her legs no longer in front of her, her head and body seemed not to be one. Eduardo's face blurred before her- a twinge of pain- she reached out toward him and sank to the floor. Kneeling, he took her in his arms.

"We searched for him until the storm forced us back. Oh Rosa," he cried, "our Giovanni is lost." Tears rolled down his face, "Oh Rosa, we have lost our Giovanni, we have lost our Giovanni."

Victor and Dino threw themselves sobbing into the anguished forms of their mother and uncle. Arms intertwined, each of them united by grief.

When finally Rosa stirred, she asked, "could he have been found by another boat?"

"No Rosa, no, all the other boats are in."

"How is it possible," she cried holding Dino close to her, "one minute you have your life, and then it is gone?"

Victor tried awkwardly to pat his mother's hand. "Why does God do this to me? Why does he keep punishing me- why?"

Rosa spent the days desperately searching the beach, and the nights she spent in prayer that Giovanni would be returned to her. She could not believe that he was gone- there was no body, no final parting, no last moment of life- there was nothing. She could not believe that he was dead- that she was once again abandoned.

Two weeks after that dreadful night, father Michael said mass for the repose of Giovanni's soul. And as they had done for centuries before, the fishermen of Viareggio and their wives and their children walked to the cemetery to place flowers upon the grave for which there was no body.

"I must write to Mama Nina," Rosa said aloud to herself as if speaking to an errant child.

"She will worry- it has been weeks, she will know something is wrong, terribly wrong." The words came painfully from her pen, the telling of Giovanni's loss so painful, her worries about the future so hard to put into words. The daylight was beginning to fade before Rosa finished.

What lay ahead for her and her children in this tiny fishing village? What would she do... what would happen to her and her sons? Rosa blotted the last bit of ink into the paper and prayed to the Madonna that Mama Nina would tell her to come to her, to come to the comfort of a mother's love.

But for the time being, Nina knew they were safe. Eduardo was staying near her and the children. With Old Guido to help him, he fished every day and shared his catch with them. In the evenings, he stayed at home and tried to comfort her, and sometimes, if the days were calm, he took the boys with him on the boat.

But for a man like Eduardo, this could not last. He was too full of the love of life and excitement and there were too many girls in the village with their caps set for him. When one caught him she and her sons would have no one to care for them.

Just like Mama Dante- a widow with two sons to provide for, and Rosa was afraid. Mama Dante had fed her boys by selling her bread to the hotels and inns, and now Rosa tried even harder to discover her mother-in-law's secret recipe.

Up before dawn, she worked throughout the day, trying dozens of combinations, and still, nothing worked- nothing tasted like Mama Dante's famous sourdough bread. If she could not unlock the secret, what would she do?

Rosa saw Maria approaching the house. She knew the old woman was coming to tell her again how the village women were talking about "how shameful" it was for her to live in a house with a man, not her husband.

Maria was sixty, a widow, a short, round, lumpy woman with a heart as big as her zest for gossip. Maria had been there when she married

Giovanni, with her when Victor and Dino were born. Maria was willing to help and to be her friend. Rosa loved her but had long since wearied of hearing her say every day that she should find a husband and have someone to take care of her and the boys.

To Maria, her Viareggio was the world, she knew nothing of the world outside the tiny little fishing village.

Rosa poured the old woman a cup of strong black coffee and asked, "why did Mama Dante take the secret of the bread to the grave with her?" Didn't she know how much it would mean to us all someday?" Rosa pleaded with Maria for some kind of explanation.

She used to tell me," Maria said, fussing with her loose thread on the sleeve of her dress, "that her bread- she always called it "her bread"- was the only thing in the world that was all hers. It was like," Maria went on, "she believed that if the secret of the bread died with her, she would be immortal."

Rosa looked out the window, the fields were green with early morning grass.

"I used the same starter, I let the dough sour as Mama had. I spend hours stoking the stove ovens. I build the fire with a mixture of pine branches and olive pits. I oil the bricks with olive oil, I throw cornmeal on the bricks to test the heat… but nothing has ever unlocked Mama Dante's secret. I even brought the rocking chair out and sat in front of the oven and rocked and waited for the bread to bake."

"What is to become of me and my two fatherless children?"

Sitting down at the kitchen table next to Maria, Rosa became aware of a beam of light shining across its surface. A cloud had moved away from the hot summer sun, and a beam of sunlight penetrating an empty bottle in the window ledge, cast a rainbow of colors on

46

a white bowl sitting on the table. Rosa stared for a moment at the colors, emerald green faded into hues of yellow.

Following the shaft of light to the window, she saw it was Mama Dante's bottle the sun traveled through. Rosa remembered the bottle, always there when Mama Dante baked, now left forgotten on the shelf since she died.

"What did Mama Dante use this bottle for?" Rosa asked Maria. "I don't know," Maria said, "it was one of her secrets, she never would tell me what she did with it!"

Maria took the bottle from Rosa, and holding it up to her face, wrinkled up her nose and scoffed, "ugh, it even smells bad!" Maria struggled to raise her bulk from the chair and went back to her own house.

That evening when Eduardo came home Rosa showed him the bottle and asked, "what did Mama use this for?"

"I don't know," Eduardo answered, "she'd ask us to fill it with seawater for her- not from the shallow but from the deep. She never said why. I just brought it, never asked why."

"Tomorrow then," Rosa said, "please fill this with seawater for me, from the deepest part of the sea you sail to." Eduardo took the bottle, and he said nothing. Rosa smiled.

The next night she could hardly sleep, and the following morning she had the ovens fired up before Guido came by to get a cup of coffee and walk Eduardo to the boat as he did now every morning.

At supper, Rosa placed a long loaf of golden brown bread on the table. She carefully cut it into slices and watched Eduardo taste it.

He raised his wine glass and asked, "how did you ever do it, Rosa?"

"Never mind," she replied, "in this house, I bake the bread."

47

Rosa took her bread to the innkeeper and waited fearfully while old Mr, Franco Romolo examined it. He cradled a loaf in his hands and gently tossing it up, measured its weight, then, breaking a loaf in the middle, held it to his nose and inhaled deeply, he pulled off a piece of crust and measured its strength with his bony fingers, finally he placed a piece of bread in his mouth, and moved it slowly about with his tongue evaluating each subtle change of taste.

Finally, he smiled. "Bravo Bravo!" He said, "you have done it, it is just like dear Mama Dante used to make!"

Rosa walked effortlessly along thinking about the coins she would earn by selling her bread. Without knowing how she got there, she found herself at the church. Kneeling before the Madonna she recited ten Hail Mary's, and making the sign of the cross, lit a candle. She whispered, "thank you, mother Mary, for letting me find the bread recipe, for giving me the way to provide for my babies." Outside she stood for a moment on the wide marble step of the church, looking down upon the tiny village, her thoughts turned to Mama Dante.

She was a good woman who served God well, and in return, he took care of her and protected her. Rosa felt safe. Her steps were light and swift as she made her way down the hall.

Eduardo was becoming restless. In the last few months, he was not spending his nights in the cafe dancing and flirting with the girls as he had done before. Rosa feared that soon he would be back to his old ways.

She took care to see that he had a good dinner, and afterward encouraged the boys to crawl up into his lap. They loved their uncle Eduardo, and he was becoming like a father to them. He liked to show them tricks and tell them stories of the sea.

On a Saturday night when he seemed more restless than usual, Rosa suggested he ask his friends to the house to play cards.

"Alright, Rosa, if you can put up with us, I will have Umberto and Mario and the bunch over. We will play cards."

"I will clear everything that is breakable." Rosa smiled, she knew Eduardo needed his paisano's but worried that if a fight broke out her few treasures would be broken.

"Don't worry Rosa," Eduardo said, "we are not fighters, we fight only with words. The real fighters all left Italy, like your father to fight with Garibaldi, to fight another country's war. All we have left are fishermen and cowards." He laughed. "Believe me, your furniture is safe."

Rosa sent the children off to bed and cleared the kitchen table. She knew the men would first play cards, drink great quantities of wine, and argue politics. They would get angry and yell and threaten each other, and when the wine was finally gone- the state of Italy's government would still remain unsettled.

The men arrived and sat around the kitchen in the middle of the table and dealt out the cards. Rosa sat in her rocking chair by the fireplace, and with her sewing on her lap, she listened to the bluster of men. She never spoke.

As they played out their hands, the air grew heavy with cigar smoke, the wine in the bottles sank lower, their speech became slurred, and their voices loud.

Eduardo slammed his cards down upon the table and with a wild look of victory said: "There, I win! I got you by the balls the way the church has Italy by the balls!" He glanced quickly at Rosa. She did not look at him. She was afraid for him, for his blasphemy.

Giuseppe stood up, shook his fist, and shouted, "For Christ's sake, Eduardo, the only Italy by the balls are the Italians." He wiped the dripping wine from his mustache with his sleeve and sat down amid the hearty approval of others.

Mario said, "Nobody has ever had Italy by the balls because no one was ever strong enough to get all the people to unite under one flag!"

"Vittorio Emanuele did in '61 when he became king!" Umberto yelled, waving his arms so vigorously that he almost fell off his chair.

"Jesus, dear Jesus! How stupid you are, my friend!" Eduardo jumped up, with his hands on his hips, proclaimed, "The pope is the only one who has the power, not the people, not Emanuele, no one! The pope makes the rules, and we all jump and obey!"

As he spoke, Eduardo snapped his fingers and hopped up onto his chair. Staring down upon the open-mouthed Umberto, he went on.

"And then if we want to be sure to get into heaven, the pope will arrange that too- for a slight fee of course!"

Staring steadily at his spellbound audience, Eduardo stepped from the chair. He spoke right at Umberto's face, "The priests and the nuns take a vow of poverty, but it's us dumb peasants who are poor! They take the vow of chastity and we all know that!"

Eduardo paused while the men mumbled agreement. "They take a vow of obedience and we are the obedient ones! We are all a bunch of damn puppets."

Eduardo jumped around the room pumping his arms like a puppet on a string. Then he stopped. Pointing his finger at the men he waited until they were all looking at him, eyes welling with tears, he spoke with great sorrow in his voice, "Garibaldi said it, the Vatican has a dagger in the heart of Italy."

He sat back down in his chair and drained the wine from his glass. For a moment no one spoke. Then Mario slammed his first down upon the table, knocking over his wine glass.

"Eduardo you sound like Machiavelli, you think all the national ills have been caused by the church. If Italians would unite, the church wouldn't have the power it does." He ran his hand over the spilled wine and licked his fingers.

"He is right, Eduardo," Umberto said. "The Italians used the church- king- anything at all to prevent unification, and now that we have unification what do we do? We let the church undermine it! So what use is it?"

"It has only been a year since unification, give it a chance," Mario answered.

"If you want my opinion," Umberto spoke solemnly, "unification is a joke. Just to say we are unified does not mean a damn thing! The Tuscans can't unify their own province, how do they expect all of Italy to unify? Every province thinks they are their own empire."

Eduardo leaned forward, the veins on his forehead bulging. "The church has kept us under lords and popes, the church supports the invaders, that way the church keeps the power. If the church would leave us alone, Italy would unify."

Rosa's heart seemed to stop beating as the angry words of her brother-in-law fell upon her ears. Could he be right? Could the church be capable of self-serving evil? Could it be that the pope was not the voice of God?

"Oh, Basta! Basta Eduardo," Umberto said, "Vittorio Emanuele freed land so that the people could buy it."

"Yes he did, but who bought the land… not the port peasants, the church and the rich men did, they were the only ones who could afford to. Little good that did for the peasants. And that is why so many good men leave and go to American or Argentina. They leave their families, go to make money, come back and buy land."

"At least we do not have to buy the sea we fish. If the church could think of how they could tax the sea to us they would." Mario laughed.

"The church would control Italy, the sea, they would have everything… but not me," Eduardo said, "I am not going to obey their damn rules."

"You are a stubborn son of a bitch, Eduardo. I am going home. I have drunk all your wine, and you are the one who is drunk." He pointed a finger at Eduardo and then slapped him on the shoulder, and said, "See you in church in the morning."

They tipped their caps to Rosa, and patting each other on the back, they shuffled out the door- still friends until their next meeting when the arguments would start again.

Rosa watched the men make their uncertain way out the door and wondered if Eduardo was right. Could the pope- the church- do evil? Father Joseph, a spokesman for God, and… the remembrance made her shiver. Perhaps the church rules were not the rules of God? She thought then of the bells, the bells that rang in the convent all those years, and the sudden knot in her stomach reminded her that disobeying the rules of the church was disobeying God.

She cleared away the wine glasses and washed the cigar ashes from the table, aware of a growing heaviness upon her. Why did God let people suffer so much- men lost at sea, the old people of the village, sick children, motherless babies? Why did God take my mother from me? My father too, and even Mama Nina went to

52

America, and now God has taken Giovanni from me. Why does he make us suffer so?

She picked up the playing cards left scattered about on the table, for a woman alone in Italy life would be hard, even for a woman who could bake Mama Dante's famous sourdough bread and sell it to the innkeepers.

For a woman with children, it was even worse. What kind of life can I make for my two fatherless boys? What does the future hold for them? I have nothing but a few meager possessions and a recipe for sourdough bread.

Even the boat- the boat Rosa I- is not mine. Under Italy's laws it belongs to Eduardo, even the house I was married in and bore my children in is not mine. I inherit nothing from my husband- only his brother- but no, not another marriage.

For now, I have a place to sleep, a house to bed, my two babies, down in, and for now, Eduardo is here to help, but what if...? What if one of those girls Eduardo teased, and danced with, got him to the altar? I would have no home, no roof between me and the sky.

Even now, as the surviving son, he could make claim to his house. A new wife would know this, and I have nothing. Oh, most blessed Virgin Mary, she prayed, help me. Help me to take care of my two sons.

CHAPTER FIVE

After a full year of mourning, Rosa's spirit remained heavy. The kindness the village women showed her after Giovanni's death, had long since dwindled away. When she walked to the well for water or passed them in the street, she could hear them saying evil things about her living with Eduardo. Once again the feeling of loneliness and abandonment overtook Rosa.

During the long winter days, she baked what little bread could be sold to the town's infrequent off-season visitors. She cooked for Eduardo and the boys, washed and mended their clothes, and cleaned their house. But for Rosa, there was no joy in the doing.

Was this to be the rest of her life? She lived only for the day when she would hear from America. In the meantime, she and her sons ate the food Eduardo provided... but they could not stay much longer in the same house together.

Rosa spent long hours walking alone in the hills above the village, her thoughts often turning to God and the church. Angelina came frequently to her mind and heard again the convent bells and the often repeated message that goodness and purity in this life would be rewarded with such eternal peace after death. But why did he put such pain and sorrow upon his children? Would he punish them for the heresy Eduardo spoke of? Could there be any truth in his accusations against the church and their meddling in the ways of the state?

Rosa looked down upon Viareggio and the sea below, and her heart cried out in pain and an anger against God for taking Giovanni from her- leaving her a widow with two fatherless children.

At times she hated the sea, and yet at other times – when she took her lonely walks – it seemed to be her only friend. In the late afternoons she watched for the courier from Genova who brought goods and sometimes letters from great ships, but each day she walked home empty handed.

The gray dismal days of winter passed one after the other. When December neared and still there was no word from America, Rosa fixed her hopes onto Nina's Christmas letter.

At the time when her spirit was near to heartbreak, she held doggedly onto the glimmer of hope for the future, she prayed to the Madonna that the letter would bring her a new life for herself and her sons.

Soon it would be Epiphany, the day celebrating the coming of the Three Wise Men to Bethlehem.

12 days after Christmas, it was the day when all the children received small gifts from La Bafana. With material Maria gave her, Rosa made matching wool jackets for her two sons, fashioning them as best she could remember to the coats the gentleman and Lucca wore.

For Edoardo, she used a piece of heavy wool and made him a coat to protect him from the cold Seawind. And because he had been so kind to her and her fatherless children, she added a double row of brass buttons down the front.

When they were finished she had them safely away in the bottom of the bedroom cupboard. When she turned to walk out of the bedroom, she caught a glimpse of her solemn black figure in the mirror. She ran her hand down her body, and felt the coarse weave of her heavy black morning dress, this is a dress of grieving for the past, not of looking forward to the future.

She searched for a piece of Venetian lace mama Dante had given her many years ago. She cut the sleeves out of the dress and removed the yoke. Working with the delicate lace she replaced the sleeves and fashioned a new bodice.

When the dress was finished she studied herself in the mirror. Untying her long black hair, she watched it glisten in the candlelight, and felt an almost forgotten feeling of joy.

On the eve of the Epiphany, Edoardo went to the Pine Forest and brought back a large Yuletide log, and placed it on the slate hearth. In the sunset, they ate bowls of steaming polenta covered with warm sweet wine.

"Come, let's make our wishes to La Befana," Eduardo said, gulping down the last of his wine and handing the boys their pine wish sticks.

He twirled the two blindfolded boys in a circle and turned them free to find their way to the log. Rosa stood back out of reach of the flailing sticks. Eduardo stood at the sometimes tangled boys and teasing, and sent them in the wrong directions.

When Victor rumpled over the footstool, the younger boy reached the log first, and tapping it victoriously, made his silent Christmas wish.

When Victor finally found the log, he struck it forcefully many times, ordering La Befana to grant his wish.

"Mama, Mama," Dino shouted, thrusting his stick into his mother's hand, "make a wish too, La Befana is a Lady witch so she will surely grant your wishes."

Taking Rosa by the shoulders, Eduardo twirled her in the circle, "Keep your eyes closed now, no peeking." He said and turned her loose.

"Don't peek, mama or your wish will not come true," Victor advised.

When in spite of a barrage of misleading hints, Rosa reached a log, the children laughed and cheered.

"Now it is your turn, Uncle," Victor said, standing on tiptoes trying to get the blindfold in place. Together the boys pushed Eduardo in a circle one way, and then twirled him in the opposite direction. They turned him loose and squealed with delight as he flapped his arms like a disjointed rag doll.

Eduardo moved towards the door, and the boys shouted false directions to him as Rosa ran to open it.

"That's right Uncle," Victor giggled.

"You're doing it right," Dino said, his hand over his mouth to muffle his laughter.

"Now wait a minute, you are sending me out to sea." he pulled the blindfold from his eyes and affectionately wrestled the two to the floor. He tapped the log many times and when he made his silent secret wish, stole a furtive glance at Rosa.

The boys hung their stockings and made one last wish before Eduardo put the Yuletide log in the fire.

"It will burn all night, or our wishes will not come true," Dino said, "Will you keep it burning, Uncle?"

"Yes Dino, I will guard the fire with my life- now both of you go to bed."

Victor and Dino kissed their mother and started to leave. Stopping, they turned back and throwing their arms around Eduardo's neck, hugged him. As this handsome fisherman embraced her two sons, Rosa prayed they would not get too fond of him.

"Sleep well, boys," Eduardo said, patting them on their bottoms, "And I will keep an eye out for La Befana."

Rosa filled the stocking with nuts and oranges, and all the time she felt Eduardo's eyes following her.

"Come, come, sit by the fire. We do not often have the luxury of burning the pine log. It smells so sweet, so much better than the olive pits."

He extended his hand for Rosa to sit next to him, "And I have orders to make sure it burns all night. Must I sit here by myself?"

Uncomfortably aware of the way he was looking at her, she said, "I will sit with you for a few minutes Eduardo."

"I am a happy man tonight," he said, "the men are at the cafe, and look at me, here I sit, making wishes to the Yuletide log like a child. You know, if they could see me now, this Casanova would be the laughing stock of the village." He reached for her hand.

"Your secret will be safe with me," and shifting to the edge of her chair, she added, "it is time for me to go to bed."

"Wait Rosa, do not be in such a hurry." Pulling her toward him he said, "before you go, loosen your hair, please, let it fall free."

He took the pin from her hair. Pulling her hand skillfully from his, she stood up and said, "for just a moment." The coiled hair released and fell softly around her face.

"Oh, that's better, Rosa," he said, "You are very beautiful. I think my brother picked the prettiest girl in the village."

He leaned back in his chair to take a full view of her. His eyes were not those of a man looking at his sister-in-law.

She kissed him lightly on the cheek, and said "Felice Natale, Eduardo. The log will burn all night tonight." She hurried from the room.

Only the closing of the door shielded her from Eduardo's eyes, and she felt an unwelcome twinge of excitement stirring up inside her.

On her knees, looking up at the crucifix above her bed, she prayed to have strength over her body, and she asked the Madonna to send Nina's letters quickly from America.

In the morning, on the first light of day crept over the mountains, Rosa heard the boys searching through the treats in their stockings.

This was the one morning of the year the whole village went to communion, even uncle Eduardo who would join Rosa and the boys at church.

Dressing with special care for the Epiphany mass, Rosa tied a small piece of lace in her hair. She knew she would have to cover it with her shawl as soon as she left the house, for this moment her hair was free.

Eduardo was wearing his only suit, the same one he had won the day he and Giovanni blindfolded her and christened the Rosa I. The memory sent a sudden stab of pain through Rosa's breast, but she must permit herself to think only of the future.

"You look lovely, Rosa. La Befana gave you a new dress?" Eduardo asked.

"This is not new, I added some of your mother's lace to my mourning dress." She straightened Eduardo's tie and said, "You look handsome this morning." Turning quickly away from him she called to the boys to hurry, it was time for church.

"But, Rosa, you cannot wear such a dress to church, if the old women see that they will know you are headed straight for hell. A widow is expected to wear black for a decent mourning period. There is no need to get their tongues wagging again."

"Yes, Eduardo," Rosa shrugged, "it will be covered by my shawl, no one will see I am wearing a pretty dress, but I will know. My spirit needs a bit of cheer."

"After mass, they stopped to speak to Father Michael, and hovering nervously about her, Eduardo pulled her shawl up around her neck.

Why was Eduardo, who took delight in shocking the elders of the village with his behavior, so concerned about hers? Does a man care so much what people say about his sister-in-law? Or does he care more for what they say about a wife?

If only the letter would come before his patience runs out – before it's too late. In the wagon on the way home, Eduardo said, "Our boys must have been good this year. I see that La Befana did not leave them buckets of ashes." He winked at Rosa, "I saw her go by last night."

"Did you really see her?" Dino asked, eyes wide.

"Yes sir… I sure did. She was riding her broom and carrying a bucket of ashes with her in case she found any children who were bad. I even heard her twinkle her silver bell."

Eduardo turned his head away to hide his smile. Rosa served the traditional breakfast of hot milk, coffee, and panettone she had prepared with dried fruit and sprinkles of cinnamon.

Victor and Dino, although too young to go to communion, had fasted before mass, and now could hardly wait for breakfast. When they had their fill, they sat on the edge of their chairs, waiting impatiently for their uncle to finish.

When he finished eating, Rosa went to the bedroom to get three coats she had made for their gifts. Dino ripped the wrapping from his gift and working his arm into the sleeve of his new coat, said, "I feel like the captain of the fleet," he reached to give her a light kiss on her cheek.

"Now it is my turn to play La Befana," Eduardo said as he returned from his room. "A gift for each of you; here, Victor, here, Dino."

The boys excitedly pulled the paper free without untying the string. In each package was a wooden boat complete with lateen sails.

"I carved them myself out of umbrella pine from the mountain." Eduardo's eyes danced with as much excitement as the boys.

"Now we can pretend that we sail with you on the Rosa I." Victor hugged him.

"And look," Eduardo said, "they are named." He pointed to the dark blue hulls, "see, the Rosa I and the Rosa II."

The two boys settled down near the hearth to play in an imaginary sea, and Eduardo turned to Rosa, "and this is for you," he held out a small package in the palm of his hand.

"When Rosa saw the tiny package, her excitement darkened with a fear of what might be inside. She carefully unwrapped the cloth around it, and when the last layer was turned back, she saw a carved tortoiseshell comb.

Relieved, Rosa threw her arms around his neck and kissed him on the cheek. "Thank you, thank you, it is beautiful, Eduardo, where did you ever find such a beautiful comb?"

Returning her kiss more ardently than a brother-in-law should, he said, "from the little village near Vecchiano it came. Every time I took the fish cart to sell there, I searched the street merchants for the most skillful craftsman I could find."

He has been working on it for many weeks. I sent Mario's boy there yesterday to pick it up for my beautiful sister-in-law. And oh," he added, "he brought back a letter for you – it is from America, from your mama Nina."

All the strength went out of Rosa's body. She took the letter, and conscious that Eduardo was staring at her, sat down in the rocking chair before trying to open the letter. Fingers trembling, eyes fixed upon the single sheet of paper, she was unaware of anything else in the world.

"My dear child," Nina wrote, "how I grieved for you and the loss of your husband, Giovanni. How I long to have you here with me and your two little bambinos that I've never seen. But Anthony says..."

Rose fell at the altar rail, a tiny figure huddled beneath the outstretched arms of Jesus Christ on the cross. Red blood oozed from the wound in his side, straining to fall down upon her and bury her in a sea of red despair.

She lowered her eyes, and deep in prayer, did not notice Father Michael come into the church. When she stopped at the holy waterfront to bless herself, he came forward, "My child, forgive me, but I cannot help but notice how long it has been that you grieve for your lost husband. Life must go on, you know, even the Virgin Mary..."

In a voice hardly audible, Rosa answered, "Yes, you are right, Father." The tears which had flowed secretly from eyes lowered in prayer, now rolled unashamedly down her upturned face.

"Come, my child, come to the rectory with me. I will give you a warming cup of coffee, and we will talk." Obediently she followed.

Mrs. Balenie came in carrying a tray. She made her way slowly painfully across the room, set out the cups, and hobbled to the fireplace to poke at the fire. The coffee warmed Rosa's body and Father Michael's kindly voice made her feel again secure in the certainty of the Catholic Church.

"You know, Rosa, it has been over a year since…"

"Yes, Father, it has been."

"Some of the villagers…"

"Yes, I know, they talk."

"Foolish, of course. I know you would never…"

Rosa raised the cup slowly to her lips and wondered what the priest believed.

"What are your plans- for the future- for your sons?"

"I have no plans – not anymore." Ignoring the questioning look on his face, she went on, "what is there for a widow with two children to do?"

"Do you still sell your bread to the inns?"

"Yes Father, but in the wintertime, it is so little…"

The priest got up, and placing another log on the fire, said, "What you need is a husband."

A chill went through her, she saw herself, an old woman like Mrs. Bellini, widowed for more than forty years, wandering aimlessly through a meaningless life. She became aware that Father Michael was talking.

63

"... a strong healthy young woman like yourself..."

"Excuse me Father, what were you saying?"

"I said that you must marry again, there are many more good years for you to have babies- a healthy young woman like yourself... How old are you now, Rosa, 21, 22?"

Rosa's head was spinning, the heat from the fire burned the skin on her face, moisture trickled down her neck. She braced her arm on the edge of the table, struggling to get to her feet, "pardon me, father, I do not feel well, I must get some fresh air."

Disregarding his protestations and Mrs. Bellini's suggestions that she sit down and put her head between her knees, Rosa walked out of the house of the priest.

Dear God is that all that is meant for me in this life? Rosa tossed the last handful of meal to the chickens who frantically plucked the tiny seeds from the earth. She leaned against the cold stone oven, and watching a waste of cloud flow past the barely warm winter sun, wondered how many more winters she would stand in the same yard like this feeding chickens.

She saw Eduardo coming toward her. He had the same worried look on his face that had been there every time he looked at her, ever since Epiphany. He approached cautiously, stopped in front of her, and taking a small Chamois pouch from his pocket said, "Open it, it's for you."

She felt him watching her. Standing up she cupped the package in her hand. "Go ahead, Rosa please."

She untied the drawstring and withdrew a small bundle wrapped in scraps of yellow tissue. Carefully parting the layers of paper, she found a wide gold ring.

"Oh, Eduardo this is your mother's ring."

"She gave it to me just before she died."

"It is- it is- so beautiful." Around the outside of the band were carved angels, worn smooth by the years. Looking more closely, Rosa saw that they were not angels, but small, delicate Della Robbia cherubs in flight, the tips of their fingers touching.

"I want you to have it, Rosa. You have been so sad. I want to see you smile again."

"I do not know what to say."

"Well, you see, Rosa, the eldest brother always inherits the house, and the youngest son gets nothing. My mother gave me her ring so that I would have something to give the girl…" taking the ring from her gently, he slipped it on her finger. "Rosa, will you marry me?"

"Marry you, Eduardo?"

"Yes, you know that I love Victor and Dino as if they were my own. Living here as your brother-in-law, I feel only frustration. I have needs. It's about time for me to settle down and become a husband and father. What do you say, Rosa?"

"Yes, Eduardo, I will be your wife."

She lowered her eyes, God denied her wish to go to Mama Nina in America. He wanted her to remain in Viareggio, to be the wife of another fisherman. Rosa prayed for the faith to follow the Lord's wishes.

Early the next morning, Eduardo took Rosa up the hill. Father Michael had just finished mass.

"Good morning, good morning, you are very early today," he called out to them, "late for mass perhaps, but early for a walk."

"I am a working man, Father," Eduardo blurted out, no smile softening his meaning.

"We came here to see you on another matter," Rosa added quickly.

Father Michael hurried them in the direction of the rectory. "Come, let us get out of the cold. What can I do for you, Eduardo?"

"We have happy news, Father," Eduardo said, hurrying to keep up with the priest. "I wish to marry Rosa."

Father Michael stopped. He turned to face them. Eduardo, smiling confidently down at Rosa, did not notice the startled look on the priest's face.

Rosa felt a terrible sickening in her stomach.

"Father, what is it? What is wrong?"

"Wrong? Is something wrong?" Eduardo spoke as if dazed.

"Come inside, children." Rubbing his hands together and cupping them to his mouth, Father Michael warmed his hands with his breath.

"It is too cold out here... come inside where there is a fire and hot coffee."

Rosa followed Eduardo and the priest walking briskly into the church house. The smell of fresh coffee soon filled the room.

"Well," Eduardo said, unable to hold his tongue any longer, "well, what is it? What is wrong- I want to marry Rosa, that is all."

"Yes, yes, I know, Eduardo, you want to marry Rosa. But, you see, there is a problem..."

"A problem? What kind of problem?" Eduardo's face was red, the veins on his forehead prominent.

"Please, Eduardo," Rosa pleaded wordlessly, "let Father Michael tell us. Please, Eduardo."

Father Michael appeared deep in thought as he poured coffee slowly into their cups. "There is a rule. A very old rule…"

"What kind of rule?" There was anger in the younger man's every word.

Rosa reached forward as if to stay Eduardo's hand and then leaned back in the chair.

"Church law forbids relatives from marrying…"

"Relatives?" Eduardo interrupted.

"Yes, the law was meant to keep blood relatives from intermarrying."

"But we are not blood relatives," Eduardo said, "Rosa married to my dead brother does not make her my blood relative!"

"Yes yes of course you are right. But you see, a rule is a rule."

"Rules! You see Rosa? Rules again! I tell you…!"

"Now now my son, calm down, sometimes it is possible to get a dispensation." Father Michael sipped his coffee, "yes, I think that is what we will do."

He turned to speak directly to Eduardo.

"These rules are intended for cases where the priest does not know the families, but of course, I know your family."

Father Michael went to an old wooden desk in the corner of the room and searched through the heavy bottom drawer.

"Yes, here it is!" Holding up a small book, he thumbed through the pages, and said, "Yes, this tells how to write it up."

He sat at the desk and picking up a pen said, "and you will both have to sign this statement. Then I will send it to the Bishop in Lucca."

"Send it to Lucca, Father? No, I do not intend to wait that long, and besides, we cannot trust such matters to some dolt messenger boy. I will take it there myself!"

They drank their coffee while Father Michael prepared the paper for them to sign. He looked up and smiling privately at Rosa said, "you will not be sorry, my child, God will be pleased."

He laced their coffee with a dab of Brandy. "Salute! God bless you both." Father Michael blotted and folded the papers carefully.

"I will see that these get to the bishop, and if we get his approval, you can post the banns." He walked to the door with them.

"I will be there to baptize the children."

As he walked out the door, back to the priest, Eduardo mumbled, "Well, at least the pope does not have to get involved in this one."

Starting down the hill, Rosa said, "You should not talk like that about the pope."

"Father Michael didn't hear me," Eduardo answered.

"Your faith in the church is stronger than mine. And I get damn tired of the church always running our lives, always telling us what we can do and what we can't do."

"You are not being fair to God." Eduardo stopped, he turned to her, "Rosa, I'm not talking about God, I am talking about the church. Rules, rules, rules, it is nothing more than a religion of rules. If the church stayed out of what is none of their business, Italy would be better off."

"You cannot blame the church for all of Italy's problems."

"I blame the church and the pope, their powers to greet the pope stay in Rome in the Vatican. He has enough to do to manage the church. Let Italy rule itself."

Eduardo's voice was tinged with anger, his breathing deep and heavy.

"The idea of the pope declaring himself infallible! He s just a man. No better than me. He is so damn afraid to lose his power that the Italian people will end up losing Italy."

Rosa walked on in silence. He followed. "That is what the Risorgimento was all about, Rosa, the struggle for unification- a free Italy."

With the toe of his boot, Eduardo kicked fiercely at a stone in the path. He walked the rest of the way down the hill in silence.

When they reached flatland, Eduardo's breathing was once again quiet.

He looked around. No one was looking. He kissed Rosa quickly on the cheek. "Rosa, I love your God, it's his servants I do not agree with."

He turned and bounded down to the waiting Rosa I.

Maria came out of her house, "Rosa, Rosa," she called, "come I have a good hot fire to warm you."

Rosa smiled at her friend's obvious curiosity. Her deep brown eyes were wide with anticipation, Maria hurried Rosa into the kitchen. Pouring her a small glass of wine, she said: "you were up at the church very early this morning, and everyone knows Eduardo only goes to mass when he has to."

Full of questions, Maria hovered over Rosa, fussing constantly. Rosa teased the old woman with her silence. Maria sat down next to her. She rubbed her knees and groaned, "Povera me, poor me, my poor sore knees. Tell me, Rosa, enough is enough."

"Eduardo wants me to marry me."

"I knew it, Rosa, that's exactly what I thought."

Maria jumped up, not a pain in her body.

"I knew it!" She poured more wine into Rosa's untouched glass.

"Ah, that will shut up all the old tongue waggers. You said 'yes' didn't you? Eduardo is a good fisherman. He will provide for you."

Her hands clasped together as if in prayer, she looks skyward, "God takes care of his own. Now Victor and Dino will have a man – a papa – that is good, and there will be more babies."

Maria sat down and reaching for Rosa's hand asked, "How soon will the wedding be? I will cook, I will make the cake for the wedding."

Although no one else was in the room, she leaned close to Rosa and whispered, "Does anyone else know?"

"No, Maria, and no one else must know yet, not for a while."

"Why is that?" Maria said, looking worried as if she might cry with disappointment.

"We must get a special dispensation from the bishop- before we can marry…"

"Dispensation?"

"Yes, the church considers us relatives."

"Then will they let you marry?"

" I think they will, but it will take time. You must promise me not to mention this to anyone. Promise?"

"Not even one person?"

"No."

Maria wadded up her apron, and pressing it to her mouth, "Rosa, oh, Rosa, oh you ask so much of me."

"But you must promise."

" Oh, my Rosa, you ask so much of an old woman!" The spring had gone out of Maria's step and once again she sat down and rubbed her knees, back-and-forth.

"No one must know until we hear from Father Michael."

"All right! I swear upon the grave of my dead husband that not one word will pass these lips…"

Rosa put her arms around the old woman, "You will be the first to know. I promise."

Maria smiled weakly.

Rosa went home.

For the next two weeks, Maria kept a steady lookout on Rosas coming and going. On the morning that Father Michael came to talk to Eduardo and Rosa, Maria was waiting.

Eduardo had the priest barely out the door before Maria came in, "I can see from your face that everything is alright. It is, Rosa, isn't it all right?"

"Yes, Maria, everything is alright. Father Michael will post the banns next Sunday and we will be married."

With tears in her eyes, Maria kissed Rosa, "You haven't told anyone else have you?"

But before Rosa could answer her, Maria jumped up, "I have to get you some water!"

Putting her shawl around her shoulders, she started out the door, "You stay Rosa, I will be back. Don't leave. Drink some coffee, have a cake." Maria slammed the door shut with a thud, and trotted down the street.

Her little fat knees and bending body swinging from side to side, the old woman moved with short quick steps.

She carried the empty water pitcher toward the group of women gathered at the well. There was a sense of great importance about her.

Rosa smiled, by the side of the stove, she had two clay pots, each full of water. She laughed, the women at the well would have all the news, and she would have all the water she needed.

That night when Eduardo returned from his days fishing, he tossed his hat onto the hook and announced, "The whole village is buzzing with the news. Umberto met me as I came off the boat, saying, 'you've finally been caught, paisano.' He asked what kind of net had been used to catch the fish."

"Yes." Rosa said, "today at the well, Maria was the queen, and we have enough water for many days."

On a brisk sunny winter day in late January, Maria and Guido, Victor and Dino, all in their best clothes, followed Rosa and Eduardo up the hill to the church. Father Michael said mass and offered holy communion.

Mrs. Bellini watched from the first row as Guido, self-conscious in his position of authority, awkwardly gave the bride away.

That evening, the villages came to celebrate. True to her word, Maria had baked 'enough to feed Garibaldi's army' as Eduardo would put it.

Their long wooden table seemed to sag under the weight of the dishes the village women brought. "How can you invite these women here to come and drink our wine? Now they smile sweetly," Eduardo said, "and only yesterday they were saying unkind things about us?"

"Maybe so, husband, but what better way do you know how to sweeten their tongues, than to treat them with sugar?"

As the wine drinking increased so did the intensity of the political arguments. And in every corner of the room, small clusters of men vented their anger and frustration against the politics of church and state.

Only when Eduardo announced, "friends, we are here to celebrate, not to argue. Now let us have music and dancing, and no more arguments."

The table was moved up against the wall, guitars were brought out and soon there was dancing.

Victor and Dino found a comfortable spot under the table, and when the dancers left their half-filled wine glasses behind, the boys reached up and took them below. Although they had been weaned from mothers' milk to wine, this night they're young bodies had more than they could handle.

Maria came running over, "look at your boys, Rosa." She pointed a fat finger towards the front yard.

Victor and Dino were stretched out over the woodpile throwing up.

"They will be sick in the morning," Maria said, "Don't worry, I will take them home with me, and see that they do not find any more wine to drink tonight." Maria laughed.

"Don't worry, Rosa, I will watch them."

When all the guests were gone and the last lantern blown out, Eduardo took Rosa by the arm, "Come, wife," he said.

Eduardo made love as he loved his wife: forcefully, robustly, and fast.

Rosa had always been told by the nuns that the marriage bed was to bring babies into the world. But why, she wondered, on her second wedding night, did men get all the pleasure?

CHAPTER SIX

During the calm autumn weather, Victor and Dino rose early each morning, dressed quickly, and prayed to be permitted to go out on the Rosa I. Eduardo and Guido taught them the ways of the fisherman and had endless stories of the sea to tell them. Proud to be part of the Dante family's fishing tradition, the boys returned home at night full of excitement and adventure to tell their mother. While Rosa listened to their happy chatter, her thoughts were on another child– the child growing inside her.

The weeks went by and Rosa became larger and larger, Eduardo would kiss her and pat her belly asking "how is my son doing today?"

"I want a baby sister for Mama," Victor shouted, "Mama needs a girl, she needs help. You have two boys to help you Eduardo, I mean Papa. Mama needs a girl, she needs help."

Dino said little. He drew close to Eduardo whenever anyone suggested the baby could be a boy.

"But boys," Eduardo answered, "we need more help fishing. Another fisherman is what we need. Then maybe we could buy another boat- the Rose II." Eduardo winked at Rosa and tussled Dino's hair.

"Me and Victor are good fishermen now Papa. We learn fast. We're all the help you need!"

Eduardo drew the boys close to him, "God will give us what he thinks we need," he said, "and there is nothing we can do about it."

Rosa watched the three men in her life, their happiness warming her heart. With a sense of sorrow for her fatherless firstborn children, she tried to reassure them, "Even if we have ten more boys, you are both my special children, my first sons."

It was September, soon to be the festival of the Volto Santo, the day the miraculous crucifix was brought to Lucca. All of Viareggio was preparing for the celebration of the joyful day. Festivities would start at dusk with the villagers carrying lighted candles on pilgrimage to the church. After mass, there would be a great feast and dancing.

The day before the holy day, Victor and Dino did not go out fishing. The talk that evening at supper time was not about the sea, but about the next day's celebration. After dinner, they gathered in front of the fire.

Eduardo lifted Dino up onto his lap and said, "Tomorrow we celebrate Volto Santo- do you know why we do that?"

"No, papa, please tell us."

"Well, many many years ago, our own Italian Bishop Gualfredo, went on a pilgrimage to the holy land, and there he came into possession of a beautiful crucifix with the figure of Jesus carved on it.

"It turned out that this was the cross Nicodemus carved after the crucifixion of Christ. The bishop had never seen anything so beautiful in all his life, so he took the cross and set out alone on a

76

boat. He wasn't much of a sailor, and there was no one on board to help him.

"He didn't even have any sails. So it wasn't long before he washed ashore. He landed right near there on the beach by Luni.

"Well, when the people heard about the boat washing ashore with just one man and a great cross in it, they came from everywhere to see.

"An argument started between the people of Luni and Lucca. Each village thought they should have this holy crucifix for their church.

"And while they were standing around arguing, the bishop of Lucca got somebody to put the cross in an ox cart for him, he took it off to the Cathedral of St. Martin in Lucca."

"And while I was a little girl going to the convent in Lucca, I used to pray before that cross," Rosa added.

Victor stood up and said, "and that's why we celebrate the festival of Volto Santo on this day, the 13th of September, right papa?"

"Right."

On the feast day morning, Rosa sent the boys off with the men to fish and started her preparations for the festival meal.

She had not been sleeping well, the baby was so large she couldn't get comfortable at night. Quick sharp pains jabbed at her.

She mixed up a batch of dough and then had to sit down to rest, her face warm, her hands clammy, she became concerned.

Looking down at her protruding belly, she patted and said, "Settle down, little one, settle down. It is not time for you, you must wait another whole month."

Rosa leaned back, put her feet up on a chair, and tried to rest. She closed her eyes but could not sleep for the stabbing pains in her back.

She tried to sit straight in the chair, but that did not help. She lay down and stretched her body the full length of the bed, but the pain grew worse. Then a much stronger pain grabbed her.

Dear Madonna! The baby. Is the baby coming? Could it be? It is too early. The baby will be too small. Dear God, send me a healthy baby. Madonna, please!

Well it was nearing noon and the pains had not stopped, Rosa lifted herself from the bed and walked in labor to Maria's house. When she opened the door, Maria turned toward her and, dropping the dish from her hands, screamed, "Rosa, what is it?"

"The baby, is the baby coming?" Maria pulled the chair over and slid it under Rosa's sagging body.

Another pain started. Rosa arched her body and pressed her hand into her lower back. "The pains, they're not like the other children." She groaned. "Maybe you better get the midwife. Hurry! I'm worried. The baby! You better get help. Get the midwife! Get Sophie."

Maria wrapped her shawl around Rosa. "First I will take you home."

"No, I will be alright, just go get Sophie. The pains are coming. I'll take myself home, you go get Sophie- go!"

By the time Rosa lay down in her own bed, the pains were intense. Would Maria be able to find the midwife when everyone was busy getting ready for the feast of the Volto Santo? Would she find her in time? Would this child come without anyone to help?

Again, the long-hidden terror flared up inside, her mother died in childbirth, father had gone off to fight with Garibaldi's army, and then – even her mama Nina went away. All alone Rosa's pains increased.

Madonna, help me do not let me die. Let me live. Another pain, stronger than the last, stabbed at her. Rosa pressed her rosary beads to her breast, "Oh, my god, I'm heartily sorry for having offended thee.."

A sudden rush of water. Another pain.

She tried not to cry out, "Dear Madonna," she whispered, "send help, please- send someone."

Drawing her knees up close to her chest she rolled over on her side. The pain, more intense, held longer than the others, she pushed her legs out straight.

When finally the pain lessened, she rolled onto her back, and, opening her eyes, stared at the wood-beamed ceiling. She lay very still lest the slightest movement brings her pain.

"Rosa, we are here!" Maria called. The door was thrust open and Sophie was there at her side.

Throwing the sheets aside, she spread Rosa's legs. "Your waters broke. The baby is close, Rosa, it is close."

"It is too soon Sophie, much too soon." Rosa cried out, tears flowing freely.

"God knows when to send his children, and he knows how to count. By your size, you are ready."

Sophie spoke in a strong commanding voice. Aside to Maria she said, "It's a good thing you found me when you did."

Maria wiped Rosa's face with a wet cloth and brushed a small strand of damp hair from her face.

Soon the contractions were only minutes apart, and with each one, Rosa prayed for strength to bear the pain.

"Push, Rosa, push... now push again! I see the head... push again!" Sophie ordered sternly. "You are ready, push."

Rosa grabbed the iron posts on the bed.

"Push, do it, Rosa... push... "

"The head is out... now..."

A brief pause.

"Push... the shoulders... push!..."

Rosa screamed out in pain and then she felt the hot burning brush between her legs.

"It's a boy, Rosa," Sophie said.

Maria muffled a cry, "but he's so tiny!"

"Shut up," Sophie shot a warning look at Maria.

Turning away from Rosa, she held the infant up by his feet and spanked his backside until he let out a thready cry. Sophie laid the boy child on his mother's stomach and tied the cord. Rosa reached out to touch the tiny infant. Another contraction.

"What is wrong?" Sophie asked.

"Another pain," Rosa said. "It's the afterbirth..."

Again, a pain, Rosa cried out.

"... or it might be another baby! Here, Maria, take the baby... keep him warm."

Sophie kneaded Rosa's stomach. "There is another," she said, "that's why you're so huge, Rosa. That's why… that's why they're early."

"Santa Maria! Holy Mary! Mother of God!" Holding the infant in her arms, Maria took her eyes from Sophie, who turned and ordered, "Rub him! rub him, keep him warm!"

Eduardo threw open the door and rushed to Rosa's side. "They told me at the dock…" Sophie pushed in front of him. "Maria, here, give Eduardo the baby and come here," Without turning toward him, she ordered, "and you rub him well, keep him warm, he's tiny."

"You have to keep his blood moving," then to Maria, "Quick, I need your help. Hurry before she closes. The child is breech."

"Oh my God," Rosa groaned.

"Calm down, Rosa, relax until I tell you to push. Then you push!"

Eduardo moved to the back of the room. He stood silent. Holding the tiny bundle close to his breast, he awkwardly rubbed his hand back and forth over the fragile flesh.

Rosa let out a deep groan, "He's breech?" She whispered. "Sh- h- h, sh- h- h. push! That's good, good, you are doing fine, Rosa. I've delivered many twins before. Do not worry. You do your job, I do mine." Sophie spoke with authority.

"The feet are out, Rosa, now hurry, push… push… push!" Sophie pulled the tiny feet.

"It's a girl!" Maria screamed. "There, the shoulders, push Rosa… ah- h- h-h… a tiny girl with blonde curly hair."

Rosa felt the passage of the baby. Sweat poured down her face. Her hands released the post and fell to the bed. The rosary beads dropped to the floor. Slipping out of consciousness, Rosa heard Maria whisper, "Holy Mary mother of God…"

She awoke, aware that something was wrong. At the far side of the room, Maria and Sophie, backs turned toward her, huddled together whispering.

Eduardo entered the room carrying a basin, and headed directly toward the two women. "Here's the cold water you wanted."

"All right, all right. Now go find me some whiskey."

"Whiskey?" Eduardo asked, watching Sophie take the smallest infant out of the basin of warm water and submerge it in cold water.

"Yes, whiskey!" She answered never taking her eyes off the tiny body in her hands. "Don't stand there asking stupid questions, go get me the whiskey!"

Leaving the room, Eduardo glanced toward Rosa. When she reached out her hand toward him, he did not stop.

He returned almost immediately. Maria took the brown bottle from his hand and pushed against him, "now, go to the church," Her voice urgent, she added, "get him here quick!"

Sophie twisted a piece of clean white cloth into a point, pushed it into the neck of the whiskey bottle. She put the soft cloth into the tiny mouth.

Tickling the baby's cheeks she waited until she saw the beginning of the sucking motion.

Rosa cried out, "What is the matter? Where are my babies? Where are they?" Maria came over and wiping Rosa's face, smiled down at her.

"Now, now dear, you try to sleep, everything is fine. You need your rest."

"Eduardo, where did you send him?" Rosa watched the changing expression on Maria's face, and screamed, "Where has he gone? What is wrong?"

"Nothing is wrong, Rosa, he'll be right back."

"The priest, he went to get the priest! My babies, are they…?"

"Now, now, the babies are alive, just a little small, they are breathing better now, their color is better…"

"Why is he getting the priest?" Rosa insisted, trying to rise onto her elbows.

The door opened and two village women, carrying blankets, rushed in, and went straight for Sophie, "Warm blankets.. " one said, and the other picked up a basin of water and hurried out.

"What are they doing?" Rosa tried to swing her feet to the floor.

Maria pushed her back down to the bed. "Now, don't you worry, dear, they are just here to help."

"Two babies. That is why you were so big. That is why they came early. Twins can run out of room."

"Sophie!" Rosa called out over Maria's head, "tell me what is wrong? What are you doing? Tell me!"

The village women came back in carrying a basin of hot water. The other one was holding out the warm blanket to Sophie. The only sound was that of water hitting the edge of the tin basin, "there!" Sophie said, her back still to Rosa. Turning, she wrapped the baby in the blanket, and drying her hands on the apron said

"There! That did the trick, she will be all right now."

The midwife turned to the village woman, "Wrap her tightly, keep her warm!"

Watching white with wide eyes, Maria made the sign of the cross and fell to her knees. Burying her head in Rosa's quilt, she chanted, "Blessed be the name of Mary..."

Sophie came to Rosa. "There now, child, rest, they will be alright now."

"But the priest?"

"You know how excited Maria gets about everything. The babies are small, she wants to get them baptized right away, she believes they will get strength from God to make them grow big and strong if they get baptized right away."

"Yes, Rosa, that is it," Maria said, raising her tear stained face from the bed, "I am a silly old woman – that is all – a silly old woman, they are fine – strong- yes, fine..."

"Bring my babies to me, I want to see them."

Sophie said, "Now, now, little mother, you need your rest. There will be plenty of time for you to see them."

" Don't put me off like that," Rosa said, "I want to see them now."

"All right, all right, if you must." Sophie nodded to the two women holding the twins. "Here is your son," she said, placing him carefully in his mother's arms.

"They will get strength from their mother's milk. That is what they need," Rosa said. "Look at that! I think he is already rooting around for something to eat." Rosa helped the baby find the nipple, and when after a few attempts at suckling, he fell asleep, her eyes filled with tears.

Sophie took the baby boy and Maria handed Rosa the girl.

"Oh my God, how tiny she is!" Rosa felt a terrible fear inside of her.

"Yes but don't fret," the older village woman said, "girls are always smaller than boys."

The girl baby showed no interest in nursing, and Sophie gently took her away. She said, "Now, lie back, try to sleep," and leaning down, she whispered in Rosa's ear, "do not worry, you know how you get excited."

With a gentle pat on the forehead, Sophie tucked the covers in around Rosa.

"The procession has started," Maria said, and moving toward the window, she added, "they are walking up the hill to the church – silhouetted against the night sky – their lit candles look like a stream of marching fire."

"These will be very special children, dear Rosa, to be born on the night of Volto Santo." Coming to the bedside, Maria leaned down and placed a tender kiss on Rosa's forehead, "And they are of good Italian stock."

Rosa smiled up at her dear friend, "Bring Victor and Dino in, so they can meet their brother and sister."

The boys came in silently to the room, walking as they might enter a sacred place. "There are two babies, mama? Two?" Dino asked as if hoping to be wrong.

"Yes, my sons, God has sent us a double blessing, he has given us twins."

"But mama, Maria said one was a boy and the other was a girl, they can't be twins, twins are supposed to look alike, aren't they?"

85

"Not all twins have to look alike. But because they are born at the same time, they are twins. This way we get one boy and one girl."

Sophie listened to this conversation from the back of the room and picking up one baby nodded to Maria. They carried the infants to the bed and held them down low for the boys to see.

"Get closer, sons, they will not bite," Rosa said, "look at how beautiful they are. One boy and one girl."

Victor said, "Ugh, mama, they are so ugly! They look like newborn pigs. They are so tiny, so ugly."

Dino gave a look of disgust, "Mother, were we this ugly?"

Rosa smiled. Maria frowned. Sophie reassured them, "Yes they are not very pretty right now, but they will grow beautiful and handsome like you."

Victor and Dino were ushered out of the room. "At least we got half our wish, Dino, we could have got two boys." The older brother shrugged and, looking in the mirror at his own face, said, "Nothing that ugly will ever grow up to look anything like me."

"Mama says they will, but I can't see how they could ever look human." Dino agreed. "But maybe God fixes them up after they are born."

"Pigs are ugly when they are born, and they don't get any prettier when they get older." Victor said. "They both look like little pigs and I don't think they'll ever look any better."

The kitchen door opened and Eduardo came rushing through, Father Michael right behind him struggling to keep up. The boys stood up to greet the priest, but he brushed past them and followed Eduardo into the bedroom.

"See," Victor said, "no one will ever notice us anymore."

The two boys followed the men back into the bedroom, and Dino whispered, "When I grow up, I'm sure not going to have any babies."

Father Michael went directly to Rosa's side. "My dear child, two babies! God has surely blessed this house. Eduardo dragged me away from the procession," he said, standing at the foot of Rosa's bed. "He said the babies were so small I must baptize them immediately."

"Yes, father, they came too early." Suddenly seized with panic, Rosa tried to get out of bed to go to her babies.

Instantly Sophie was at her side gently pushing her back down into the bed. "There, there, everything is taken care of, we have done everything…" she said.

Eduardo moved in and taking Rosa's hand from the midwife, said, "There, there, little mother."

Maria grabbed hold of the priest's arm and turned him toward her. "Father, the sacrament! They must have the sacrament right now!"

She lit candles on the small wooden table she had placed before the bed.

Father Michael spread a white linen cloth and arranged the holy oil and water on the table. "Alright," he said, putting on his vestment, "bring me the firstborn. What is his name?" He asked Eduardo.

"We shall call him Giovanni Eduardo Dante. He shall carry my brother's name and my name."

Huddled together in the shadows at the far side of the room, Dino whispered to Victor, "Why should he get my father's name? He weighs less than a suckling pig, I will not call him by my father's name!"

Victor stated simply, "His name should be 'Porko'."

Rosa was saying, "I would like Victor and Maria to be his godparents."

"Oh bless you, Rosa," Maria said, possessively snatching her godchild from the arms of the priest.

Hanging his head, Victor whispered to Dino, "Now I am to be the godfather of Porko!"

Maria pulled victor to her side in front of the table and held the small infant as Father Michael anointed him with holy oil and poured holy water over his head. "With these words, Giovanni Eduardo Dante, I baptize you, in the name of the Father, and of the Son, and of the Holy Ghost."

As the priest spoke the holy words aloud, Victor mouthed his own words, "I baptize you, 'Porko Dante' in the name of the Father, and of the Son, and of the Holy Ghost, amen."

Sophie handed the baby girl to the priest.

Looking at the new father he asked, "What is her name to be?"

"I should like to call her 'Rosa'."

"No, no," Rosa protested, "we will have too many 'Rosas'. We have me, the Rosa I, and someday the Rosa II. No, husband, I wish to name her 'Angelina', after my dearest friend."

"A beautiful name," Maria said quietly.

Wondering if she saw a hint of disappointment in her old friend's face, Rosa went on, "Angelina was very special to me when I was a child, and our daughter born on the day of Volto Santo should have a holy name. I would like to call her Angelina."

"So be it," said Eduardo.

"But her middle name must be 'Maria'," Rosa continued. "Sophie, would you be her godmother?"

"Angelina Maria!" Maria cried, and Sophie smiled as she accepted the child in her arms. "Dino," Rosa continued, "would you be our little angel's godfather?"

Dino nodded at his mother, then turning toward victor, he muttered, "she doesn't look like an angel."

But when he took his place next to Sophie and looked down at the tiny infant, a tender smile crept across his face.

After the baptism, Eduardo said, "Sophie, could the boys hold the babies for a minute?"

"Well, just for a bit," the midwife answered, "they are not playthings, you know."

"Would you like to hold your brother and sister and your godchildren?" Eduardo asked.

Reluctantly- awkwardly- the boys held out their arms and permitted the tiny bundles to be placed in them. Victor looked at his new tiny brother and under his breath said, "Porko- Porko."

CHAPTER SEVEN

The next evening Eduardo sat by the fire watching Victor and Dino play with their boats, when there was a quiet knock at the door.

"Come in, come in," he said, opening the door wide for Father Michael.

"Have you come to see my babies?" Eduardo asked, placing two glasses on the table and filling them with wine.

"Sophie is still here, she wants to watch the babies, to be sure they are all right. They are so tiny – it doesn't seem possible that anything that small…" Eduardo shook his head ever so slightly forcing the worry out of his voice, then asked, "did you see the dimples? Did you see them last night? They each have one of Rosa's dimples… one, only one." he laughed. "Can you believe it, each just one dimple!"

The priest remained silent while Eduardo put out bread and cheese and rattled on. "Maria found another cradle, she went all over the village looking for it. She didn't want her godchild to have to share his sleeping quarters any longer," he said. Urging the priest to eat, he continued, "she said he'd already been kicked by his sister long enough."

Father Michael fingered his wine glass thoughtfully and occasionally glanced at the two boys catching imaginary fish in a make-believe sea.

He drew close to Edoardo, and spoke in a low voice, "There is something unpleasant I must tell you."

"Oh?"

"The village people are talking."

"What are they talking about now, Father?" Eduardo said, sipping his wine.

"The old ladies and all your girlfriends are having a great time counting on their fingers."

"What about?"

"Most of them can't read or write their own names but they can count to nine very quickly."

"So they can count. What's the problem?"

Glancing in the direction of the boys, Father Michael leaned closer,

"You were married right after New Year of '75 and the babies were born September 13th."

Leaning back in his chair, the priest continued,

"They are saying the Casanova of Viareggio has two little bastards."

Spitting out the half-chewed bread he had in his mouth, Eduardo said, "My children bastards?"

"Those damn people, have they nothing better to do but gossip?"

Father Michael gently patted Eduardo's arm. "Now, now, Eduardo, don't get mad at your friends. This will pass like all the other village gossip does."

Pulling his arm away from the priest, Eduardo banged a clenched fist against the table, "I can't believe this, Father!"

"What's wrong papa?" Victor asked, looking up from his play.

"Nothing, nothing, play with your boats."

Eduardo returned his attention to the priest and lowered his voice.

"You know it's not true, father. You saw our little Angelina- as frail as a butterfly, and little Giovanni- hardly bigger than a minnow. You even had to leave the procession of Volto Santo to baptize them because Maria was afraid they were going to die."

Eduardo's voice grew almost to a whisper. "The people who are doing the talking should see the babies."

"Maybe that is the answer," Father Michael said.

"Well, I'm not going to have the whole town tramping through my house," Eduardo's jaw thrust forward.

"Well, I suppose you could take the babies to church on Sunday. The village people would see for themselves how tiny they are."

"That is impossible! I cannot take the babies from Rosa." Eduardo took a long drag on his cigar. "It is getting cold, they should stay home. We cannot take chances with them."

Father Michael said, "Then they will continue to talk. I see no other way."

"Let them talk, what do I care? I know it's a lie and that's all that's important." Eduardo cut another slice of cheese, forcing the knife downward as if it were an executioner's blade.

Father Michael stood. "Think it over, just think about it." He nodded to the children and left.

Eduardo remained at the table. Tearing a piece of bread from the loaf, he wiped it around the inside of his glass and used it to soak up the last drops of wine. He could not put the priest's words out of his mind.

Maybe he was right. Yes, maybe he was. Sunday, I will take the babies to church!

Eduardo went into the bedroom and told Rosa of the gossip and the decision he had made.

"Dear God in heaven," Maria muttered, shaking her head and wagging her finger above the bed.

"Why must they say such things?" Rosa asked holding her hand out to Eduardo.

"Because they have nothing better to think about than to meddle in other's affairs. And that is why I am going to take the babies to church, then they will see!"

"No, Eduardo, it is better to just go on as if we hear none of it. Soon they will forget all about it- as soon as they find something else to talk about."

Eduardo sat on the edge of the bed. "I cannot do that! They have insulted me and my family!"

Pacing around the room, he said, "Oh, those jackasses! I'd like just one of them to say that to my face!"

"But, you and I know we have not sinned, so let us not give them the satisfaction of getting upset about their talk."

"Maybe that is the way… but I don't know."

"Please Eduardo, for me, do not pay any attention to the evil words of idle tongues. Please, as the mother of your two precious babies, I beg of you."

"How could I refuse?" He knelt down by the side of the bed, and holding Rosa's hand said, "Alright, mother of my children, I will hold my tongue."

"Tomorrow you take the boat out, you will see, a day at sea always makes you feel better- it will all blow over soon- just idle tongues."

Eduardo went wordlessly through the kitchen, past Maria and the boys, and out into the night. Dino looked up as if to say something to Eduardo, but seeing his face, remained silent until Maria came to check the fire.

"You both look grim," Maria said, "is something the matter?"

"Nothing is wrong, Nona Maria."

"What do you think of your new little brother and sister?" She asked.

"Oh, they are too little, they don't even do anything."

"That is true, but they will soon enough."

Studying Dino's expression, Maria said, "There is something on your mind?"

"Yes, well, we had a question, but we don't have to bother you if you're busy."

"I'm not busy," she said sitting at the table. "What is your question?"

"Well, we were just wondering- what is a bastard?"

Maria quickly lowered her eyes. "Where did you ever hear such a terrible word like that? Don't ever let me hear you use such language again, do you hear me?"

"Yes, Nona, but we were just…"

"Nonsense! It is a bad word, you shouldn't listen to the garbage those fishermen talk, go now, leave me alone, and don't bother your mother with such silly questions."

Saturday night, pleased with the day's catch, Eduardo hurried toward Giuseppes for an evening of wine and card playing with old friends.

When he arrived, the cafe was already crowded. The air, filled with smoke from twisted black cigars, was heavy with the dank smell of old wine barrels. Filled with a sense of pride at having fathered not one- but two babies, Eduardo entered the cafe.

Puzzled by the sudden silence, Eduardo watched the eyes that were watching him. Nodding to Giuseppe, he walked the full length of the room and sat alone at the long table near the bar.

A loud voice called from the middle of the cafe, "Here's the Cassanova of the fishing fleet!"

Eduardo ignored the remark.

Giuseppe brought him his wine and cautioned, "Don't pay any attention to these guys, they are half drunk already."

At a table across the room, Umberto pushed his chair back and struggled to his feet.

Steadying himself on the tables he headed toward Eduardo. His glass raised in a toast, he said, "Let us drink to Eduardo, Viareggio's own Cassanova. He did not even let his brother's bed cool."

Eduardo started to get up but felt the push of Giuseppe's hand on his shoulder. "Ignore him, ignore him, Eduardo!"

"Shut up, Umberto, you're drunk," another voice called out.

With mocking tears, Umberto continued, "Oh what that poor, sweet Rosa has had to endure!"

Eduardo pushed his body from the wood bench and stood.

Holding him, Giuseppe called out, "Shut up you drunken fool!"

Umberto staggered closer. "Let's drink to poor Rosa and the two little bastards."

Another voice jeered, "He was just keeping Rosa in training."

Eduardo's body tensed, his black eyes narrowed. Pulling against Giuseppe's grasp, he said, "I didn't expect this from my friends. You're no better than the old women at the well."

"You had a damn good deal, you lucky bastard! You had Rosa, and then you got a special dispensation to do it with the pope's blessing. How much did you have to pay the pope for that one?"

Umberto stood, swaying before Edoardo.

Eye to eye with his tormentor. "Goddamn big mouth!" Eduardo cursed, anger spewing drop spit onto the coarse hairs of Umberto's head.

"What'd you care Eduardo? You had all the fun and now two little bastards too."

Eduardo lunged at Umberto. He hit him a strong blow across the mouth knocking the glass from his hand. Umberto fell to the floor.

Eduardo spat and turned away from his fallen foe. "He's coming for you!" a voice called out.

Eduardo turned.

On one knee, his head down, Umberto reached up for the lip of the bar, he lunged like a charging bull, his head rammed squarely into Eduardo's belly.

The two went to the floor.

Onlookers edged backward and cheered.

"Hit him, Eduardo, hit him!" A voice yelled.

"Hit him, Umberto, hit him!"

The two rolled over and over, a tangle of flailing arms and legs.

First, Umberto on top.

Then Eduardo on top.

Voices cheered the man on top.

"Kick him!" "Jab em!" "Kill him!" "Hit the son of a bitch!"

Men's voices melted into a frenzy of excitement. Umberto was on top. Breathing heavily, his soft belly heaving, he pounded his fists, again and again, tearing into the flesh of Eduardos face. Blood gushed from a deep gash on his victim's cheekbone. Umberto's fists slid through red liquid.

Mustering all his strength, Eduardo thrust his knee into Umberto's groin.

His opponent off balance, he rolled on top and buried his head and chest in Umberto's abdomen immobilizing him. Punching anywhere his fists would land. "Call my babies bastards, you son of bitch!" He pounded harder and faster, forgetting all else but his anger.

Giuseppe grabbed Eduardos kerchief. Pulling it right against his throat cutting off his breath.

"Basta, basta that's enough," he said, "you'll kill the poor fool!"

Two others helped Umberto to his feet. Giuseppe yelled to them, "Take that guy home, get him out of here before he tears up my cafe."

Letting go of Eduardo's shirt, Giuseppe said, "Go on now, get on home! Enough is enough." He steered him toward the door.

His torn cheek throbbing, Eduardo walked down the dark cobblestone street deep in angry thoughts.

I'll make those damn people eat their words! Those babies are going to be in church tomorrow morning! I am the man of the house, I am the one who decides what we do! What must be done!

He didn't hear the clatter of the horse-drawn cart until it was almost upon him. With barely time to jump out of the way, he cursed the driver and shook his fist at the wagon as it sped away.

Eduardo entered the sun kitchen and Maria jumped and reached for a cloth. "Holy Mary, mother of god, what happened to you?"

Eye swollen, cheek bleeding, his shirt was smeared with dry blood.

"Just a fight down at the tavern," Eduardo said, taking the dipper from the kitchen nail and sloshing water around his mouth.

Maria dabbed at his face trying to wipe away the dried blood. Spitting into the slop bucket. "Leave me alone," he said, "leave me alone Maria. I have to talk to Rosa."

"You clean up, or you will scare her to death. Sit down here and let me take care of that cut. I know why you were fighting tonight."

Maria finished doctoring Eduardos face. "You have to tell Rosa, she's bound to find out that the men are talking too." She handed him a clean shirt.

Rosa was sitting up in bed, Angelina to her breast, Giovanni tucked snugly beside her. "Dear God in heaven, what happened to you?"

After she heard the story Rosa held her hands out to Eduardo. "Why must people spoil our happiness with such talk?" She asked.

"I don't know, but that's why I must take the babies to church tomorrow. Small-minded peasants, all they know how to do is talk."

Eduardo's shoulders slumped forward, his head bowed.

"All right," she said, her voice becoming strong, "tomorrow we will both go to church. We will take all of our family with us. You'll have Victor by the hand and I'll hold Dino, and we will carry our babies in our arms. We will walk all the way down the aisle to the front pew so everybody will see us!" Eduardo looked up at her.

"We're not going to hide! After mass, they'll have to find something else to talk about."

"Rosa you can't go to church. It's too soon after the babies are born. You might bleed. It is too dangerous."

"No Eduardo. I will go."

Early Sunday morning Eduardo went to the shed behind the house.

"Sorry Paisano, but there will be no Sunday rest for you today." Eduardo filled the feed bag with grain and slipped it over his ears.

"You're a good old horse, my friend, but Rosa cannot walk to church today, we must help her."

He brushed Paisano's thickening coat and ran the comb through his long back tail. "Sometimes, Paisano, I think you are a better friend than all those jackasses at the cafe. At least you do not cut my face to ribbons, do you?"

Paisano looked up and snorted as if he understood.

Maria and Sophie were just leaving the house. "You'd better hurry up, Eduardo, Rosa and the babies are all dressed."

The two women, kerchiefs around their hair, shawls across their ample bodies, took off at a fast pace toward the church.

Rosa took a last look in the mirror, pulled her body up as straight as she could, and pinched her pale cheeks.

Stand up straight, walk tall!

Studying her reflection, Rosa remembered Sister Lucia's commandment, "Young ladies of breeding must stand and sit tall and erect."

She prayed to the Madonna for strength on this Sunday.

Eduardo helped Rosa up into the wagon. He wrapped a blanket lightly around her and putting Victor and Dino on the floor of the wagon, entrusted each with a lightly wrapped infant. "Come on, Paisano," he urged, "let's get this family to church!"

Maria was waiting for them on the church steps. She took Angelina from Dino and hurried toward the church steps. Eduardo called, "Maria wait, I will carry both of my babies."

"I will help," she argued, "I will carry one."

"No maria, I will carry both of my babies." Eduardo shaped his arms like a cradle, and Maria reluctantly placed Angelina in the bend of his left arm while Sophie put Giovanni Eduardo in the other.

Refusing help, Rosa climbed the church steps alone. With Victor and Dino at her sides, she followed Eduardo down the center aisle, looking neither to the right nor the left.

Her forehead was cold and her heart thumped against her rib cage. Focusing her eyes on Father Michael waiting at the first pew, she prayed she would not faint.

Rosa took her place beside her husband. She felt the eyes of the village people on her back and shivered from the coldness of their stares.

The priest celebrated the mass. Each motion, each prayer, each ritual, was accomplished in an agony of slow motion.

Finally, when the prayer part of the mass was done, Father Michael turned to face the congregation. He opened the Bible. "From the epistle of St James: 'Behold, even the ships, great steered by a small rudder wherever the touch of the steersman pleases. So the tongue also is a little member, but it boasts mightily.'"

Watching the tiny infants sleeping in Eduardo's arms, Rosa became aware that the priest was still reading: "... but the tongue no man can tame- a restless evil, full of deadly poison.'"

When Father Michael closed the book, he stared silently down upon the parishioners.

"We are all born with sin," he said solemnly, "the sin that can only be washed away with baptism. Our dear Jesus died so that we might be bathed infant to the father, he gestured toward heaven with both hands, "but their souls are pure! More pure than any man here in this church."

His voice stern, he shook his fingers at the congregation. "Let no man among you soil such purity with evil words."

The minute mass was over, Maria plucked her godson from Eduardo's arms and marched proudly down the aisle.

The villagers, their heads lowered, remained in their seats as Rosa and Eduardo, followed by Sophie and the two boys left the church. Some of the village women lifted their eyes and smiled tentatively, but Rosa did not meet their glances.

Once outside, Rosa took a deep breath of the sweet-smelling sea air.

"Father Michaels words went right to the point." Eduardo said. "Did you notice the women giving us those sheepish smiles?"

101

Rosa took her husband's arm, "Brining the babies to church was the best thing to do."

Eduardo leaned down and brushed her cheek with a kiss, "Come, we must get you home. Why are you laughing, Rosa?"

"I'm laughing at you, at your poor battered face. It's good you didn't have that big cut and that black eye the day we were married. The people would have said, 'there goes Rosa, dragging poor Eduardo to the altar.'"

He started to laugh, but grimaced with pain when the cut on his lip broke open.

"I feel good enough to walk home," Rosa said.

"Oh no, and have people say that I mistreat you? No, wife, you will ride with me behind Paisano."

Paisano lurched forward. Just then Umberto stepped out from a small crowd of people hovering at the foot of the church steps. Hat in hand, Eduardo gathered up the reins in one hand and shook Umberto's hand. No words were spoken, nothing needed to be said.

CHAPTER EIGHT

Sliding her knuckles against the wood with a token knock, Maria flung open Rosa's door and sailed into the kitchen.

Giovanni Eduardo, who had been sitting quietly in the middle of the floor, shrieked and held his chubby arms up to Maria.

"You have spoiled them, the miniature Giovanni Eduardo sees you, he wants his sugar titty." Rosa was feeding Angelina her breakfast and watched Maria chip off a lump of sugar, center it in a small square of gauze, and tie it with a piece of string to form a nipple.

"Here, my little man," Maria said as she picked up the child, cradled him in her arms, and placed the sweet gauze nipple into his open mouth. Watching Maria's every move, Angelina clamped her mouth shut, refused another spoonful of the soft mush, and held her arms out to Maria.

When both babies were finally quieted, Maria asked, "Where are Victor and Dino?"

"Eduardo took them out on the boat. They begged to go with him, and when they call him 'papa' he can't resist. It is good for them to spend time alone with him. Helping on the boat makes the boys feel important, especially now since they must share him with babies."

"They accept Angelina, but there's a little jealousy toward Giovanni Eduardo. Victor calls him 'Porko' when he thinks I'm not listening. Dino calls him 'Gio.' I like 'Gio,'- 'Giovanni Eduardo' is a mouthful," Rosa said, smiling down on the happy baby.

"What kind of name is 'Gio'?" Maria sputtered. "You gave the boy a good respected Italian name, now you want to change it to some dumb shortcut!"

"The trouble is, Maria, that Victor was named after a grandfather he didn't even know, and this baby comes along and gets the honor of bearing the name of Victor's father."

"Every family has jealousy like that, Rosa. So what? That's no reason to change the poor baby's name."

"Now, now Maria, we wouldn't really be changing his name, just making it a little bit easier for everyone."

"It's just not right. You gave the child a good Christian name, that's what his name is!"

"But at least Gio is better than 'Porko'."

"Humph!" Maria snorted. Picking up the baby and wiping his mouth, "here, Giovanni Eduardo," she said, "Maria will take care of you."

Before Rosa could say anything, there was a loud knocking at the door.

"I'll get it," she said. A dark-haired young man, clumsily snatching the Fisherman's cap from his head, thrust a hand out toward Rosa.

"It's for you, signora." Not until the messenger put his cap back onto his head, turned, and started down the path, did Rosa comprehend that he had handed her a letter.

"From Mama Nina..." she said, more to herself than to Maria.

Drying her hands on her apron, Maria said, "Mama Nina indeed! She should be with you instead of tramping all over the world with that Tony Orso she married up with. She's your only family, she should be here to help you."

"I have you, Maria," Rosa said as she turned her chair toward the light from the window and opened the letter.

4- January- 1876

Mia Bella bambino Rosa, San Francisco

How my heart cried when I left you so many years ago that I forgot. Now, you have duo more bambini, and I am a Nona again.

My heart prays for one look at your babies. Victor and Dino how proud they must be.

Your letters I read are so beautiful to all in San Francisco. I go to church and the letter I put in front of our dear Madonna. She will watch over you and your beautiful babies. I ask for you the protection of the Madonna.

Now that Tony buy the boarding house, he gots more boats for fishing but he works many longer hours. Many hours I must spend alone now that he is so busy, cook for the fishermen, but at night, I am alone. I am happy Rosa that you have your family close to you.

I still pray that someday I can send for you. You would like San Francisco. The bay, the fishing boats, the hard work is like Italy, even the fish taste the same.

I say prayer for you always for you are my child. I pray that God keep you and your beautiful babies well. Write me. Letters bring your Mama Nina molto joy.

Sempre con molto affetto e amore,

Mama Nina.

The house was quiet, Maria went home, and the twins were sleeping.

Rosa folded the letter and slipped it into the envelope. She went into her bedroom and opening her black enamel tin box fingered the bundle of letters tied with blue ribbon.

Every letter Mama Nina had sent her from America was in that box. Rosa re-read the letters often, and always, she longed to see her Mama Nina.

Many nights she fell asleep dreaming of going to her in America.

Rosa held the letters up against her cheek and spoke to them.

How I have missed you through the years, my dear Mama Nina.

In the six years that followed, Victor and Dino grew to the threshold of manhood. The twins were no longer babies, and with each month the bundle of ribbon-tied letters in Rosa's tin box grew. With each new word from America, the longing within Rosa grew.

The summers had brought many travelers to the beach and the hotels, and Rosa's bread had become as famous as Mama Dante's. With each passing season, more of the innkeepers asked her to bake for them all year round.

"I must bake some bread for old Mr. Romolo this morning," Rosa said to Maria, "this is the day he pays me for all the loaves he has eaten."

"I suppose you want me to go to my house so that I do not see how you make the bread?" Maria's voice sounded hurt, but Rosa knew it was more curiosity.

"No, no, Maria, no need for you to leave. The dough was made, all I have to do is bake it."

"Rosa Dante! You are the most hard-headed 'testa dura' woman I know. Me, your good friend, you do not even tell me the recipe."

Rosa smiled pleasantly as she formed the long loaves of bread and placed them to bake in her outside stone ovens.

"Besides," Maria said, "baking bread in January in outside ovens is foolish! All you do is burn good fuel and for what? For a few pennies!"

"A few pennies, perhaps, but to keep my customers happy for next summer, that is important, too," Rosa said.

When Mr. Romolo's bread was delivered, Rosa returned home to find that Maria had fed the family some of her special soup and was washing the dinner dishes.

The twins were playing on the floor, and Eduardo and the boys had gathered around the fire. "We did not have a good day today," Eduardo said, "I hope your luck was better Rosa."

"Yes, Eduardo, I had a good day," Rosa jingled the coins in her pocket, "and I bought us a new book."

"I hope it is an English, mama," Dino said.

"Read it to us, mama," Gio pleaded.

"Here, Rosa," Maria shoved a large bowl of soup in front of her, "before you do any reading, you have to get something hot inside of you. This is good nourishing soup. Now, eat, do you hear?"

"Sit down with us, Maria," Eduardo said, "stay and hear our latest book from America."

"Umph!" Maria snorted. "I have better things to do than to listen to the crazy words those foreigners use. What's the matter with Italian? Isn't it good enough for you?"

Maria left and Rosa asked, "Now, Eduardo, why do you tease her so, you know she thinks I waste my time teaching our children English."

107

Eduardo averted his eyes and said nothing.

"I know how you feel about the government and the Vatican, Eduardo, surely you must see that they like to keep the peasants ignorant."

"Only the rich receive education," She had told him when the twins were born, "we must teach our children because there is no one else in the village to do it."

"Father Michael teaches them religion – they know the rules of the church – but they don't know anything about the history or the world around them."

"Come on, read to us, mama," Angelina said, "read from our new book."

"Yes, mama," Eduardo imitated, cupping her chin and chipping her face forward, "read to us, mama," he joked and winked at her.

Angelina climbed up onto her father's knee and Gio onto the other.

"You two are getting too big for this," Eduardo said, readjusting them on his lap.

"We are almost six now, huh, papa? We are big."

"Pretty soon you will have to find another lap to sit on," Eduardo said smiling.

Victor and Dino spread out on the floor and Rosa read from James Fenimore Cooper's The Pioneers. When the chapter was finished and she closed the book, Gio and Angelina were fast asleep in their father's arms.

Rosa handed the book to Dino. "There are nice pictures," she said and carried the sleeping Angelina to bed.

Eduardo followed with Gio.

"When you go to bed, Victor, Dino," Eduardo called, "be sure to close the shutters tight and turn down the lamp!" Eduardo closed the bedroom door.

Rosa stood before the dresser, Eduardo came behind her and kissed her neck, and cupped his hands over her breasts.

He unbuttoned the back buttons of her dress and slipped it from her body. He watched her as she brushed her hair. Eduardo lay in bed, propped up on one elbow. "Come to bed Rosa, you have teased me enough," and held out his bare arm to her.

At first tender and flirtatious, once his passion took hold, he satisfied his hunger, kissed her, and rolled over.

She closed her eyes, and for a long time lay there listening to his rhythmic heartbeat.

Rosa woke coughing, her throat dry and burning.

"Eduardo I smell something." She stumbled out of bed. "Oh my god- smoke!" Ed- Eduardo, wake up!" She ran to the door. "Fire, oh god! Fire!"

Struggling to pull on his pants, Eduardo yelled, "The twins, the window! Quick, put them out the window."

The twins woke up coughing and crying. "Hurry, hurry, Rosa!"

Hopping to the door, one leg in his pants, one out, he yelled, "Victor, Dino! Wake up!"

He opened the door, a cloud of smoke poured in.

On his hands and knees, Eduardo crawled toward the boys' bedroom. The wall of the kitchen was ablaze, the window blown open, the lantern was swinging frantically back and forth.

"Papa, papa, where are you?" Eduardo bumped into a crawling figure.

"Come, go through your bedroom, help your mother with the babies! Hurry, hurry!"

Eduardo grabbed at the figure crawling next to him and thrust him forward. "Dino, where are you?"

"Here, papa, I cannot see..." he was coughing, Eduardo disappeared into the smoke.

Rosa was trying to lift the screaming Angelina up to the window when Dino got to his feet beside her.

"Quick, Dino, go first, so you can catch the babies."

Like a sleek leopard, he was out the window, calling to her. Victor had Angelina, lifting her up into the window he lowered her to his brother.

Rosa felt through the smoke for Gio, but Victor already had the boy in his arms. "Go, mama, go, I will take care of Gio."

"No!" She screamed, terrified, "put Gio out, then you go!"

She was pushing against him as if to force him through the narrow opening.

Eduardo was calling to them from the outside. "Rosa, Rosa, where are you? Hurry!"

Rosa pushed on Victor's feet as she slipped through the narrow opening and she pulled herself up into the window. Strong hands took hold of her arms and she fell to the ground on top of Eduardo.

She screamed, my babies, where are my babies? Eduardo grabbed her roughly, "Rosa, Rosa, they are all right, we are safe!"

"Holy Mary mother of God!" Rosa felt herself sinking to the ground.

"Fire, fire!" Eduardo cupped his hands to his mouth. "Bell! Hurry, and Dino, take the twins to Maria. Hurry, hurry, tell her to get out of her house. If we don't get this under control, her house will be next."

Rosa was on her feet. "Buckets! We need buckets!"

"I'll get them, you get help!" Eduardo ran toward the back of the house.

Rosa raced down the narrow street. "Fire! Fire!" She screamed, the cold wind burning her face.

People in their nightshirts pulling clothes around them, dashed out of their houses, carrying buckets, water jugs, or pots to the well.

The narrow street was soon lined with men, women, and children passing buckets of water from the well to the burning house.

Panting and out of breath, Umberto reached the house. "Is anyone left inside?" He asked.

"No, we're all out safe," Eduardo answered. "Hurry, get the water."

Fanned by a cold wind from the sea, the flames grew tall and angry. As water splashed onto the burning house, wisps of wind came to fan the embers back into tongues of fire.

Licking upward, the fire was on its way through the roof and raged as if to burn the very heavens.

Soon all that remained were stone walls guarding the angry fire raging in its belly.

Hardly knowing what her hands were doing, Rosa stood in the line passing one bucket after another. Maria stood across the road in a group of women huddled against the cold.

She was holding onto Angelina, and another woman, too old to be any help in the line, was holding Gio. Victor and Dino were at the head of the line working shoulder to shoulder with the grown men, throwing water into their burning home.

Where was Eduardo? She started to break out of the line, but another bucket was thrust into her hands.

Someone was yelling, "No, no, don't be stupid! Get away from the shed. Eduardo, god damnit, stay away. Oh, Jesus Christ!"

Breaking from the line, Rosa ran toward the shed when she heard Umberto yell, "Come back, Eduardo, come back, leave the damn horse!"

Rosa saw Eduardo dart into the shed, flames already leaping around the wood timber's holding up the roof. She screamed, "Eduardo, Eduardo... come back, come back!"

Barely able to make his figure through the smoke and flames, she thought he was at his horse's head, he seemed to be stiffening with the rope that tied him.

A terrifying crackling noise! The horse bolted free. A burning timber fell. Eduardo pinned to the ground.

She ran toward him, the scorched ground burned the soles of her feet. Umberto grabbed at her. She pulled free. She ran until a wall of flame stopped her.

"Eduardo! Eduardo!" She screamed. All she could see was the outline of his body with the burning timber crucifixion. Snake-like coils of fire circling the fallen timber.

Rosa started to fall dreamlike to the ground. Her legs were of rubber, the world turned black.

Someone caught her and carried her back across the road. "Take care of her," the voice said as he placed her on the ground in front of the women. "Keep her here," he shouted over his shoulder as he ran back to the fire."

Rosa struggled to get up, an old woman bent over her wiping her face. "Oh Rosa," she wailed, "he is gone- he is dead."

"Eduardo, my Eduardo!" She yelled, "Oh god, not again!" Rosa struggled to her feet.

"Don't, Rosa, you can't go over there," Maria pleaded, her fingers digging into Rosa's arm.

Rosa broke free and ran to the shed.

Umberto was standing near Eduardo's body, he turned and put out his arms to block her. "Don't come in here, don't look, Rosa. Rosa, don't."

Rosa pushed into him almost knocking him to the ground. He held her.

"Oh, god!" She sobbed. Holding Rosa close to his chest, Umberto turned her away from the burnt body of her second husband. Someone threw a blanket over the dead man.

"My god, my god," Rosa wept. Gagging and choking on the smell of burning flesh, she struggled for breath.

Umberto lowered her gently to the ground. On her knees, Rosa wretched. On her knees, Rosa wept.

Umberto knelt beside her. "Rosa, come with me. You can do nothing. Let us take care of things, go to your children, they need to know."

The wind had died down, the fire was out. People had stopped passing the buckets of water, and only one by one they walked past the remains of Rosa's home, and then they went to their own houses.

Rosa got to her feet. "That cursed horse!" Rosa screamed, "Where is that worthless animal?"

"He ran away," Umberto replied gently, his hand under her elbow steadying her, "last time I saw him, he was running free... up the hill. For all I know he is still running. Come Rosa, come."

Rosa turned to look toward the body.

Blocking her view with his shoulder, Umberto urged, "Don't, Rosa, don't look at him." Holding her by the arms, he moved her slowly away.

"My house? My house?" She sobbed.

"Sh-h-h, sh-h-h, the fire is out now, come on Rosa, come."

He led her to Maria's.

Crying uncontrollably now, she could barely walk.

Her body started to shake. Someone called for a blanket. "She's almost frozen," a voice said.

"The priest! Where's the priest?" Rosas legs wouldn't move.

Her whole body shook. "Extreme unction! He has to get the last right," she screamed.

They picked her up, she struggled to be free, then a wave of warmth rushed through her, and she lay quiet.

"Some wine, quick," Umberto called as he hurried to Maria's, "where can I put her? Give her some wine, she's almost frozen."

"Oh my lord, her feet, they are cut to ribbons. Put her on the bed."

Rosa felt something warm flowing down inside her body. She tried to open her eyes but could only make out vague shapes moving around the bed.

The room was shaking. Figures surrounded her, rubbing her hands. A soft gentle voice spoke to her, and as the shaking stopped, Rosa began to feel warm again.

CHAPTER NINE

"Lead the soul of Eduardo Joseph Dante into paradise and free him from the pains of purgatory." Closing the prayer book, Father Michael sprinkled holy water upon the pine casket.

Silently, the village men shoveled damp clumps of Italian soil into the grave. Rosa, her head bowed, eyes blurred with tears, mourned for the man who had been her husband and the father of her twin children.

Deep into the earth, Eduardo's body would rest alongside the remains of his father and his mother. For Giovanni, his body lost to the sea, only his name carved in granite above the grave would unite him with his family in death.

Rosa held tightly the small hands of her young children; behind her, two older sons – not yet grown into full manhood – walked in silence and in grief.

Rosa and her children made their way down the narrow path, the early morning stillness broken only by the rattle of the empty hearse going back to the village.

For endless hours the villagers came to pay their respects, the women brought dishes of food and cried with Rosa. The men with shovels tipped their hats, muttered what words they could think of, and went outside to work. The tile roof of the house had collapsed, only the stone walls remain.

Mama Dantes outside ovens, chard and ugly ash black, were covered with ash and twisted pieces of chicken wire. The village men drew their rakes through the ashes, while Rosa watched from the window, her mind struggling to comprehend what had happened to her life.

Through the long, treacherous night, Rosa fought with dreams and nightmares that would not leave her be. Waking up alone into a strange bed, she shook with a sudden surge of terror. A dream, oh God, a terrible dream. She brushed her hair from her face and smelled the smoke cling to her skin… "Dear God, it was no dream!" She cried. "The children, where are they?" Screaming, she ran into the kitchen.

"Rosa, Rosa, it is alright," Maria spoke gently.

Wiping her wet hands on her apron, she put her shawl around Rosa's bare shoulders. "I sent them down to the boat. They should go out today, the sea will help them." She guided Rosa into a chair.

"Yes, Maria, that will be good," Rosa said breathing deep to try to calm her breathing.

"Here, drink this," Maria set a cup of hot coffee with brandy before Rosa. "Guido will look for them, do not worry. It is good to keep them busy."

The hot liquid warmed Rosa, and she smiled when Angelina said, "I am busy too, mama, I have been helping Maria." Angelina climbed up on her lap and Rosa hugged her close.

"My poor babies," she cried, burying her face in Angelina's black curls. "Dear God, the smell of smoke is even in Angelina's hair. Everything smells of death."

"When I woke up this morning, Maria, I thought it was a bad dream- that nothing had happened- but this smell, it keeps reminding me. Maria, will I ever forget the smell of death?"

Rosa's eyes were red and swollen when she finished her solitary prayers and left the church. The winter sun low across the horizon, she walked down the hill, her thoughts drifting in and out of the years of memories she had shared with Eduardo, memories of pain and of happiness.

Always her thoughts came back to that one terrifying instant so deeply carved in her mind-the moment the fiery beam crashed down top of him pinning his body to the ground.

Dear saints in heaven, help me! She walked slowly along the narrow street. Pausing near the stone where the door of her house and been, she whispered a prayer to the Madonna, but only the silence of death answered her.

At her feet a blackened hinge clung by one nail to a burnt board, a crushed iron pot lay alone on the kitchen floor. An unburned corner of the kitchen table rose up on one leg amid the rubble.

Rosa paused at the threshold of her bedroom, her stomach pulled into a knot, beads of sweat rolled down her temple. She stared at the grotesquely twisted iron bedstead and at the clumps of her scorched mattress bulging through the springs. Her body pulled back.

"My tin box…. my letters… my money!"

All she could find of the old bedroom chest of drawers were pieces of metal rims on top of a heap of charred wood. With a half-burned stick, she dug through the pile of ashes until, at the bottom, she heard the sound of metal and found her tin box. Warped from the heat and charred, it had not been burned.

Rosa tucked it under her arm, and as she left, her steps caused a flurry of movement in the lightly piled ashes.

Something red appeared. It was a piece of cloth, cloth with a red stripe. She snatched it up as though someone might beat her to it.

Searching through the rubble, she could find no more. Rosa wept. She knew what it was. It was a small scrap of Eduardo's kerchief – the one he blindfolded her with the day they christened the Rosa I.

She placed the cloth in her tin box and walked on.

Maria's kitchen was warm and safe, full of the love and kindness of an old friend. The scent of garlic and a big kettle of soup simmering on the woodstove flooded Rosa with happy memories. For just a moment, she forgot tragedy and felt only the warmth.

"Good nourishing minestrone for you and my babies Rosa."

The twins ran to their mother and she knelt down on the floor and hugged them both to her. They were too big for her to pick up.

'You will soon have to find another lap to sit on,' Eduardo had said to them. She hugged her babies tight. "Miei poveri bambini, my poor babies. How will you understand what has happened? What must you be thinking?"

Holding them close to her, she rocked them back and forth.

After dinner, Rosa sat by the fire, wondering what was to become of her and the children. She fingered her rosary beads and wondered if God had abandoned her.

"Good night, Rosa," Maria said and went into the bedroom. Rosa watched the old woman stop at the foot of the bed. With one hand on her hip, she looked up at the crucifix and shook her finger.

"Now what have you done?" She scolded. "This time you have made a mistake! Taking Eduardo from this poor family!"

Shaking her finger at the cross as she would scold a bad child, Maria continued, "He was a good man, now what is poor Rosa to do? You were asleep doing this one!"

Rosa smiled, thinking how Eduardo called her old friend 'Ave Maria' because of the way she talked to god.

Even Father Michael knew of Maria's special relationship with the heavens. She seldom went to him to confess because, as she explained, "I go directly to the top man!"

That night as Rosa waited for sleep to bring her peace, she looked at her body and almost for the first time realized that the only clothing she owned was her nightgown – the gown she'd been wearing that night in bed with Eduardo.

She thought of the way he made love to her, the way he held her in his arms just a few nights ago. That would never happen again… She would have only her memories- that is all of him she had left- memories and his children.

Maria saw to it that they all had plenty of good hot soup, and she especially liked to fuss over Victor and Dino, for, as she said, "They worked like men, they had to be fed like men."

Watching her sons eat their supper, Rosa knew Maria was right.

Angelina, who had been playing with a dog, came over and stood by Dino until he lifted her up onto his lap. Seeing this, Gio tried to scoot up onto Victor's lap.

"Pick Porko up, Victor, huh?" Victor smiled at the sound of the nickname, his black eyes darting toward his mother.

Rosa laughed and the moment of release felt good. "See Victor?" She teased, "he knows that is your special name for him. You tagged him with that name, he will not forget that."

"Come here then, Victor will share his soup with you, but don't be a porko and eat it all."

Rosa smiled, the things we think are so important turn out to not be very important after all.

She watched Victor and Dino, their youth had been taken from them by the fire. Victor, Victor, my firstborn. You are now 13, and still hot-headed.

You have Eduardo's nature more than your father's. Your walk is a swagger, yes, how much you are like Eduardo, and you already have an eye for girls. She looked at her younger son. He was holding Angelina on his lap, stroking her black curls. Dino, who are you like? You are my dreamer.

You stand on the bow of the boat watching clouds instead of counting fish. You are the gentle one, you grieve for the bird with the broken wing.

Rosa lifted her tin box from the table next to her: the letters from Nina, the money she had saved from all those loaves of bread she had baked and sold, and the piece of Eduardo's scarf.

He wore it around his neck that Sunday morning more than six years ago when we carried the babies to church. "All the villagers must see my babies," he said.

They had been so proud carrying those tiny infants down the aisle.

"Dear God," she prayed, "grant me the strength and the courage to walk tall and straight, and the wisdom to know which path to follow."

She kissed the cross on her rosary beads.

CHAPTER TEN

Rosa stood at the water's edge watching her children play in their forts of sand. Her long, black skirt billowing in the February breeze, she inhaled deeply of the sea air.

She lifted her eyes to the heavens, and drew her shawl around her shoulders, in the wool there lingered the scent of fire. Dear God, when will you let me forget the smell of death?

Shuddering, Rosa turned from the water, three weeks since the fire, and still the terror. I have been orphaned, abandoned, and widowed, so many I loved have deserted me.

Will there never be anyone I can depend on?

Rosa turned to watch the twins: Angelina's fingers marched through the sand- soldiers assaulting sand castles- while Gio's finger- army fought to drive invaders back from the gates.

"Mama, I have to go pee pee," Gio said, his legs squeezed tight, his body squirming.

"Pee in the sea," she answered and watched her six-year-old son at the water's edge.

His pants hung down around his boney knees, his back arched, his bare bottom dimpled and tight.

Yes, my son, pee far into the sea, we shall follow it to its destination. But what will our destination be?

He sprayed out as far as his young body could push the stream, but managed only to get his shoes wet in the tide.

"I am sorry, mama," he looked first at her and then down at his shoes.

"It's only water, piccolino," she said.

Angelina ran up to her mother, "Mama, read to me…" she said, "I am tired of playing red shirts."

Sitting on an abandoned fishing boat, Rosa took the child in her lap. "Our books are burned."

"Will papa bring us more when he comes back?"

Rosa fought the lump forming in her throat. "Papa is not coming back. He has gone to God." Rosa hugged her daughter close.

"Can we go visit him?"

"No, Angelina, all you can do is pray for him."

"But if he is with god, why do we have to pray for him?"

"So that he'll know we love him." She kissed Angelina on the top of her head, and the child squirmed free and ran back to her brother and the sand.

In a voice lost to the sea, Rosa added, "We pray that your papa will ask God to tell me what to do."

Warmed by the late afternoon sun, Rosa leaned against the forgotten fishing boat and studied the deep blue waters. How many sailors slept, she wondered, at the bottom of the Ligurian Sea, and how many widows did they leave behind?

Tiny fishing boats bobbed up and down, their patched colored sails pitching from side to side. What was left for her here, on the shores of this sea which turned wives into widows?

Another marriage for survival? She shuddered. Have more babies and be abandoned again? Go to Lucca to work in the silk factory? No, women alone in the big cities are lost to poverty, their children left to beg.

I have so little left, the stone walls of my house, the boat, and my bread money. "Pee in the ocean and we shall follow it to its destination," she repeated aloud.

"Perhaps, that is my answer."

She brushed the sand from her skirt and called to the children, "We have to go now, the boats will be in soon." She held Angelina's hand as they walked up to the long cobblestone street which separated the village from the beach.

The street was full of empty horse-drawn wagons bouncing and clattering toward the pier. In front of the sun-bleached stone houses lining the street, old men sat warming in the afternoon sun. Sometimes they looked up, sometimes they tipped their caps.

Gio pulled on his mother's sleeve. "Are we going to sleep at Ave Maria's house tonight?"

"You must not call Nona, 'ave Maria'," Rosa scolded.

"Papa did."

"That was his little joke, but you are not old enough or make such jokes about grown-ups. You will hurt Maria's feelings."

"But are we, mama, are we going to Nona Maria's?"

"Yes but first I must go to the boat and give your brothers their supper."

Running to the edge of the pier waving, Angelina called, "Mama, here comes the boat."

With Guido at the helm, the Rosa I nosed into the dock. Dino pulled the heavy rope surrounding the bell and Victor waved from the bow.

The bow butted against the pier and Victor, black curls sticking out from under his knit cap, jumped to secure the lines. The lines lashed securely, Victor saved the last wrap for Gio.

"Good boy, Porko, good boy," Victor said swinging his little half-brother onto the boat. Angelina held her arms up for her turn to be swung in the air and set down on the runway.

Victor held out his hand to Rosa as she stepped onto the boat.

"I see you had a good catch," Rosa said to Guido who was feeding the nets out to Dino on the dock.

Guido grunted but did not look up from his work. No one knew how old Guido was.

When Rosa was sixteen, he had looked old to her, and still he looked the same. Bent over the nets, only his back could be seen and the familiar black knit cap.

In weather hot or cold, he was never without his wool cap.

The only time Rosa ever saw his full grey mane was one of his rare visits to church.

Hired to help after Giovanni's death, Guido had lived in the boat, going ashore only for supplies. Although Rosa invited him to their home for Christmas and festival time, he would only bow, and say "Grazie, Grazie."

A true man of the sea, he never strayed far from the water.

Rosa went below to put a pot of soup on the small oil stove and sliced bread and cheese.

When Victor came below he lifted the lid. "Smells good. I am hungry."

"We will eat soon," Rosa said to him, then turned to the twins,

"Now both of you go to Maria's. After I feed your brothers I will come and tell you a story. Run now before it gets dark. Maria is waiting for you."

"Come, Angelina," Gio said, then looking at his mother with a smile, added, "we must go to Ave Maria's."

"Gio, what did I tell you?" Rosa said, trying to control a smile.

"Just teasing, mama," he giggled and climbed up on the deck.

"He is just like his papa," Victor said pulling the bench out from the wall and taking his place at the table. "He will grow to be a good fisherman, I think."

Dino entered and winked at his mother. "He might even get to be as good as us, someday."

The meal was eaten in silence, and as Rosa watched her two sons, she felt a surge of pride that had been born of her body.

That evening, walking back to Maria's house, she wondered if Gio would be a fisherman too, and what life would be like for Angelina here in this tiny fishing village.

Listening to the rhythm of Maria's heavy breathing, Rosa waiting in vain for sleep.

She was filled with fearful visions of the future for her and her children. She said a rosary, but still, her mind could find no peace.

She slipped quietly out of bed, a blanket around her shoulders, poured herself a glass of red wine. As she waited for it to bring her forgetfulness to sleep, she looked out at the charred ruins and suddenly knew this was no longer her home.

A fleeting sense of peace passed over her.

The following morning, the winter sun barely showing, Rosa tied her scarf around her head, and paused to answer Maria's questioning look,

"I must take communion this morning." She hurried out the door. The air was full of the scent of pine trees damp with morning dew, and the brisk breeze from the sea quickly reddened her cheeks.

"Come in my child, come in. Father Michael will be here soon. Sit down, I will bring you some coffee." Signora Bellini wore a long, shapeless dress covered by a white apron spiked at the corner from frequent wipes of her hand.

In flat gray slippers, the backs turned down, she slid her feet from step to step, never lifting them off the floor. "How are you and your two little ones, Rosa?" She asked, placing a cup of hot coffee on the table.

She looked at Rosa with sad deep-set eyes. "I know how hard it is to lose a husband," She wrung her hands, "and you have two little ones. My two boys – they left. When their papa died, they left. They went to work in the big city. I never see them, Rosa- never."

She looked up to the heavens and said, "I thank my dear Savior that I have this job. But Rosa, you are young and so pretty, you have the face of our dear Madonna. You will find someone to take care of you," she cupped Rosa's face tenderly in her worn hands.

127

Rosa walked around the room, the cold marble of the mantle felt the same as it had 15 years ago, and the painting of Christ still hung crooked on its velvet cord. She straightened the picture.

Nothing has really changed. In the same spot before the fireplace was Father Joseph's plush chair, starched white doilies on its arms and back. But for Rosa, nothing could give that chair respectability.

A rush of panic, which the years had barely dimmed – the worn burgundy velvet footstool, the fireplace, everything is still the same.

If I do not leave, I will end up an old widow taking care of a priest just like I did when I was a young girl. Oh God, do not let my life come around full circle, do not let me end up like Signoria Bellini.

Father Michael came into the room rubbing his hands together. "Good morning, Rosa, what brings you out so early on this cold day? I trust nothing is the matter?"

"Good morning, Father, I have come to ask your help."

"The church is always here to help you, my child."

Taking the chair by the fireplace, he motioned Rosa to sit down.

"Father, I want to take my children and go to America."

"America? Rosa, you can't do this! A woman alone?"

"Father, please, I have thought of little else since the fire and Eduardo's death. I am going to take my children and go to my aunt in America."

"You have an aunt in America?"

" My mother's sister, she took care of me until she married and went to America with her husband."

"Oh, Rosa, you cannot be serious!" Father Michael got up and stood with his back to the fireplace. "Oh, no, Rosa a beautiful young woman like you? America? No, you can't be serious!"

"I am serious, very serious."

"You are still grieving, but soon, when the sun shines again and the wildflowers bloom and the birds sing on the mountainside, you will see, yes, you will remarry. Believe me, Rosa, that is what God would want you to do."

"Remarry, have more children, and bury another husband? Is that what your God has in store for women? No, thank you, and we will go to America, with or without your help."

"But Rosa, my dear child, even if you could go to America, what would you use for money? Five of you going to America is going to cost…"

"Father, please listen to me and try to understand what I am saying to you. I have a little money saved, and I have the fishing boat. If I sell the Rosa I, and with my savings, I think I have enough."

"You think, you think! Rosa, I think you are still in shock. You cannot possibly do this. Travel halfway around the world, with four children? Rosa, you are not Christopher Columbus!"

Tears started to pour down Rosa's face.

"Now, now, Rosa. I am sorry for being so cross with you, but you have to realize that this is a foolhardy decision you are making. Now stop crying and let us say a rosary. You are still in mourning. It has only been a few weeks since Eduardo died."

"Father, I do not have the luxury of a year of mourning. In a year, I would have nothing left, the money would be gone."

Rosa got up and, walking around the room, said, "No! I will never have this opportunity again. Mourning is for the rich, and for the very poor. I cannot spend my days wringing my hands in despair, crying 'poor me, poor me'."

Looking toward the outside door, she felt the young Rosa running from the room as she had done so many years ago.

"Father, I am not crying for sorrow, but from frustration. I came to ask for your help, I did not ask for advice, only your help."

Her face lost its pallor. Her voice became stronger. "If you can't help me, I will do it alone."

Why do priests always let me down? What is the church if you cannot go to it in time of need?

Eyes wide, voice quavering, she started toward the door, "If you cannot help me, then there is nothing more to talk. You just stay here and pray for the repose of my soul and I will do the rest. I will prepare for the rest of my life, you prepare for my death."

"Wait Rosa. Please calm down. Sit, sit, please, let us talk. I will help you…" Father Michael said, "… if I can. What do you need from me?"

"Oh, Father, thank you! I need someone to sell the Rosa I for me. A woman would not get a fair price. Will you act for me?"

"They only want new boats now, boats with all the fancy rigging on them. Selling that boat won't buy you tickets to America. You won't have enough money."

"I'll find the money somehow. Will you do it? Will you try to sell it for me?"

"I will try."

"I must have full payment so we can leave soon after Easter."

"I will do my best. There's something else?" He asked.

"There are many things I have to know. When do the boats leave Genova, and do any of them go to San Francisco? That is where my Mama Nina is."

"Rosa, oh, Rosa, the boat trip is bad enough, but crossing America is even worse! It is wild country, trains are attacked all the time."

"I'm sure it is a long trip, but tell me, Father, how does the church get its nuns to America?"

Father Michael silently filled Rosa's coffee cup and laced it with a splash of brandy from the green straw-bound bottle that stood on the floor near his chair.

"Does God drop them from the sky? If the nuns can survive a trip to America, I certainly can." Rosa pushed the potent coffee.

"Father, all I am asking is for you to get me the information I need."

The priest sat back in his chair, holding his coffee cup on his knee. "All right, what do you want to know, Rosa?"

"There is so much- about the ships- when do they leave- how long does it take- what is the best route- should I go to New York– around the Horn?- what papers do I need- how much will it cost?"

"You can take a breath Rosa, I will not interrupt you", he smiled, "I am listening."

Rosa's hands relaxed, she smiled. "I would like some English books, all my books were burned."

The priest stood up. Hands clasped behind his back and in a pontifical pose, he paced back and forth. "Rosa, do you remember the English you learned in the convent?"

131

"Yes, father, I had an English book, and every night before the fire, I read a chapter aloud to the family. I wish I had someone to talk to in English, I read it better than I can talk it."

"Father," she laughed, "you spoke to me in English! I didn't know you knew the language."

"... Si, un poco," he said, "when I studied for the priesthood in Rome, there was a young Irishman there too- Father O' Malley. I helped him with his Latin and Italian, and he helped me with English."

"We had great plans, we were going to be in the same parish and serve God together. He is still a good friend. He has a lively sense of humor- always joking- it sometimes got him into trouble in our younger days.

"But he was sent back to New York and I was sent here. I still get letters from him, he longs to come to Italy and I long to go to America."

"Oh, now I see Father," Rosa said, "you do not want me to go to America, but you want to go yourself." Rosa tasted the coffee. "I will make this trip for the both of us."

"Tomorrow I go to Genova. I am to take care of a few matters for the church, I will go down to the port and find out everything I can for you."

Father Michael looked at the calendar on his desk: "Easter is March 28, 1880. It is early this year. I will see what ships leave early in April."

"I thank you Father, for myself, and for my children."

He walked with her to the door. Lifting her hand in his he said, "I will find out what I can, and I'll try to find a buyer for the boat. But it cost very dearly to sail to America. Maybe for now, it would be better for you to stay here and try to save your money and go in a few years- after the twins are older. Please, promise me you will think about it, Rosa."

"Yes, Father, I promise. But if the boat does not bring enough money, I will find it somehow." She started out the door then turned, "Father, one more thing…"

"Something else I am to find out for you?" He teased.

"No, it's Maria, I don't want her to find out from someone else, her feelings would be hurt. Please don't speak of this to anyone. I must tell her myself."

Rosa stopped at the graveyard and rubbed her fingers across Eduardo's name so freshly cut into the stone.

"Dear husband, if only you could speak and tell me if I have made the right decision. Pray for your family."

Angelina was waiting for her mother. "Look, mama," she called when Rosa came through the door, "Maria helped me sew it," holding up three little scraps of material stitched together, she said, "I am going to make you a new dress."

"Oh, thank you, Angelina, how pretty I will be."

Maria set bread and mush on the table. She poured coffee and said, "Well, what was it that would not keep, that you had to go out so early in the morning?"

"It was nothing, Maria, I just wanted to spend some time alone with God, that's all."

"Well, while you were gone, Giovanni Eduardo went to the ashes. He was covered with dirt and then he sat down in the middle and started crying."

Maria sat down at the table. "Poor Bambino, he misses his papa so."

"I know he does, poor lamb, but let him cry, it's good for him to cry for his papa. When there is no one left to mourn, we'll all be together in heaven."

"The children cry because their lives are upset and confused. It is time now to think about putting our lives in order."

"I must write to Mama Nina, do you have paper?"

Maria let a small sheet of paper float from her hand to the table then hobbled back to her sewing. She rubbed her knees as she sat, "you are always writing to that one in America."

Rosa smiled at Maria and wrote:

Dear Mama Nina, 3, February, 1880

By now you have received my letters about the fire. The twins and I have been staying with Maria, and Victor and Dino work with Guido and live on the boat. Life here without Eduardo is bleak, there is nothing left here for me in Viareggio.

The house is nothing but burnt timbers, charred tiles and stone, and twisted melted iron bed. Old furniture burned, the only thing I have left is my tin box you gave me when I was a child. It's charred and warped, but it's still my most precious treasure. I have made up my mind to come to America. My hope is that after all these years, you will welcome me.

Rosa put her pen down and went to the window. She studied the gray overcast sky and the sea dotted with white caps. "Dear God," she whispered, "am I mad?" She looked at the remains of her house, and a tiny wave of strength rose within her, she took upon her pen:

134

The priest has gone to Genova to get information about boats, and I hope we can get on a boat at Easter time. I will have enough money for the journey and when I arrive in San Francisco I promise not to be a burden to you or to Uncle Anthony. You have often written about opportunities in America for a woman not afraid of work. I have built up a good business selling my bread to the inns for their summer visitors. I hope to have the same success in San Francisco.

Here in Viareggio I am lonely and frightened about the future. I understand now how desperate the village widows feel, I know what makes them sell their hair for a few extra pennies. The desperation of such poverty frightens me.

Dear Mama Nina, now that I have made the decision, I feel a burden has been lifted and the future seems brighter. With God's loving hand and your prayers, we will arrive safely.

My love always, your child,

Rosa

Maria bent down to stir the soup simmering in the black iron pot over the open fire. "What did you tell Nina, Rosa? What did you write to her this time?"

"I told her that you are spoiling us, with all your good soup." Kissing Maria on the cheek, Rosa added, "I must take this letter down to the dock, then I will wait till the Rosa I comes in."

"Tell the boys and Guido to come up here and eat," Maria said, tasting the soup, "there is no need for them to be hermits. I can at least feed them."

"Tomorrow night, Maria, tonight I must talk to them."

CHAPTER ELEVEN

"I have something to tell you," Rosa said when she had fed Guido and her sons their supper.

Guido got up. "I go topside," he said.

"No, stay, Guido, this concerns you too."

Frowning, he sat back down, his bushy eyebrows connecting into one heavy gray line across his forehead.

"Ever since the fire I have been trying to think of what we should do, what would be best for the twins – for all of us. We can't go on forever living with Maria."

"We will rebuild the house for you, Mama," Victor said.

"The house is only part of our problem."

Rosa took her string sack down from a hook on the wall and opened her black tin box. She took out two small piles of paper money and a handful of coins. Spreading the money out of the table, she said, "All we have left in the world is this little bit of money, the shell of a house, and our boat."

Hearing her own words, the reality of what she was about to say, gathered into a knot in her stomach. Drawing in a deep breath for courage, she clasped her hands in front of her on the table.

"I have decided that we will all go to America- to San Francisco- to be with Mama Nina."

"But, mama…" Victor said.

"Mama, we can't just pick up and leave just like that," Dino blurted out.

"Let me finish, sit down, please. I know this is sudden…" She reached out to touch Dino's hand. "We can sell the Rosa I and have money…"

"No, mama, you cannot!" Victor yelled. He stood up. "This is Eduardo's boat."

"Victor please, it is the only thing we have of any value, we must sell it." Rosa's voice became sharp.

"Mama, you can't do this."

"Dino, this may be our only chance to better our lives. In America the twins can get a good education, you boys can have a choice of the kind of work you want to do."

Studying the tough wooden table in front of her, she added, "For me it might be a chance at something better than always waiting for a fishing boat to come in, wondering if my men are safe or if they are lost at sea."

"You could marry again, mama, you are very beautiful," Victor said.

"No, Victor, twice widowed is enough, I won't marry again. Don't you see, in America the future could be better for all of us, for all five of us." She shivered when she heard herself say "the five of us", it had always been "the six of us".

"You don't know anything about going to America!" Victor said, corners of his mouth turning down.

I've learned much from Mama Nina, and from the agents who come to the village to get men to go there to work.

"You're not going to sign up with an agent, are you mama?" Dino asked.

"No, I won't. Agents are for people who don't have enough money for the trip."

"I've spoken with Father Michael, he's going to Genova tomorrow, and he'll find out for us how much passage will cost."

"You talked to Father Michael before you asked us?" Victor slammed his fist down on the table.

"Yes, Victor, we can't postpone this decision any longer. We can't waste any more time, if we do, the little money we have will be spent. This fishing boat won't support all of us now that Eduardo is gone. And Guido can't go on working for nothing."

Guido cleared his throat, "Signora, I work for very little, I need very little. The boys- they already know the sea- we can manage. Then when little Giovanni grows up, he will help too."

"No." Rosa snapped, "we have to do more than just manage!" She banged her hand on the table, "this is our chance to better our lives."

"But, mama," Victor pleaded, "I don't want to go anywhere. We can fish, and I will be the man of the house. I can do it, mama."

"But what of your brother and sister, and what of me? Shall I sit and wait for old age, wait for you and Dino to marry, and then live with you and your wives? Must our whole lives be spent just scraping by?"

"Alright, mama." Victor crossed his arms across his chest, "I'll buy the boat." His black eyes narrowed, face sullen.

"Do you have enough money, son?" Rosa asked quietly.

Lowering his eyes, Victor slumped in his chair.

Dino leaned closer to Rosa, his hand on hers, and said, "Mama, all the Dante men have been fishermen, it's the family tradition. It's our life, it's all we know!"

"This is all you know now, but you are only twelve. You have so many years ahead of you. There are so many things you could do besides fishing, you have a brain! You could be a merchant, even a student, or a teacher. You have tried nothing but fishing, there is a whole other world out there, past the horizon." Making a broad gesture, she continued, "America has opportunities for us all".

Victor stood up. "You can go, I will not, I will stay here. You can't force me to go!"

"Victor," Rosa said, "you're not the only one to be considered here, there are the twins, a chance to make something of their lives. And I have to think a little of myself too."

"I don't want to live the rest of my life just barely scraping by. A life like that is deadly! I want to use my energy to build a better life for myself and my children."

Rosa's voice trailed off to a whisper, "There is nothing left for us here, there is nothing left to do."

"Oh, mama," Dino said, "we will take care of you- I promise."

"You are a good boy Dino, and you too Victor, I know you would do everything you could, but unless you have a better plan, then all we can do is go to America, make a new life for ourselves."

She kissed Dino. "We have talked enough, it is late, go to bed, now, we will talk again."

She bent down to kiss Victor, his body remained rigid.

"I will bring breakfast in the morning," she said. Drawing in her breath, her arms pressed tight against her ribs, she went topside.

Holding onto the railing, her strength spent, she began to sob. Why was Victor angry? Dino so stubborn? Unable to understand, she was frightened. She had made the decision and now the thought of what lay ahead filled her with terror.

She heard footsteps. "Signora, prego, I speak to you?"

"What is it, Guido?" She asked without turning.

"Rosa, don't do this terrible thing, do not take my boys to America. It's a terrible voyage, people are lost at sea- are never heard from again.

"Great ships disappear in storms, oil lamps shatter and burn the ship. Even a good sailor like me, I would never make such a voyage."

"Guido, it is the only thing I can do. I have made my decision," she stared out at the horizon.

"The sail from Italy to America means going halfway around the earth. Do not do this, please I beg of you. Victor and Dino are the sons I never had. The Rosa I is my home."

"Guido, I know, I am sorry, but what else can I do?"

Guido lowered his eyes, and with a shrug of his shoulder, turned and went below.

Rosa walked slowly along the wooden pier, the moon casting a long shadow in front of her. A solitary seagull perched on the edge of the wharf, his bill tucked under his wings, stood up and stretched.

Rosa watched as he effortlessly glided up into the air and flying free disappeared into the night sky.

I wonder if he knows how free he is, does he treasure his freedom as I yearn for my own?

One by one, lights in the small houses went out as families made ready for bed.

With each house she passed, Rosa thought of the women inside, the widows still young in years caring for children alone, the women old before their young bodies ready.

The dark street silent, Rosa's lonely footsteps echoed from the cobblestones.

Maria's tiny house was dark. Quietly, Rosa crept in and made her way across the room by the glow of the fire.

Maria and the twins were asleep in the big bed. Clinging to the edge, Maria's breathing was deep and rhythmic, a snore escaped with each breath she exhaled. Rosa covered the children and kissed them both gently.

They are best friends, when one is hurt, they both cry, when one is happy, they both laugh. Theirs is a magical bond. How nice it must be to have a special friend to talk to, someone who has the same feelings, someone who understands.

She tiptoed out of the bedroom and poured herself a glass of wine. Standing by the fire, she undressed slowly, letting her clothes fall around her feet. The fire's glow danced over her naked body.

Alone, mesmerized by the dancing flame, she drew her arms around her naked body, and hugged herself, drinking in the warmth of the fire and from her own touch.

In the freedom of the warm air, Rosa felt a fleeting sense of strength. Dear Madonna, she prayed, am I doing the right thing?

Sleep came slowly as thoughts of ships vanishing off the edge of a flat world filled her head. Visions of a faceless stranger on the edge of a distant shore reaching out to her, trying to reach, to touch, but the ship sailing passed- their fingers never touching.

Early the next morning Rosa packed food for her boys and reached the pier as the sun was beginning to light the village.

The dock was busy with sailors loading their nets, preparing for a day at sea. Guido and the two boys were huddled at the rail.

"What is wrong, you are not ready to leave?" Rosa asked.

"Signora," Guido called, "we must talk signora, please."

"Come below, mama," Dino urged.

"It is time to go out," Rosa said, "I have brought you breakfast."

"Eat with us mama, we must talk."

She put the food on the table before the three silent fishermen. "Maria said that last night's soup was your last supper, from now on she wants you all to come to the house to eat," Rosa said.

"Next she will want us to sleep there." Guido growled, without raising his head from the bowl.

"She cooks better than you, Guido. You will have to admit that," Dino said, "and if we're going to be partners, I vote we eat at Maria's."

"Partners?" Rosa said, "What are you talking about?" Victor and Dino looked at each other and busied themselves eating.

Guido pushed his empty dish to one side. "Rosa, have you changed your mind about selling the Rosa I and going to America?"

"No, I haven't."

The old fisherman walked to the bunk and pulled back the corner of the thin mattress. He took out a paper-wrapped package tied with twine and set it on the table.

First clearing his throat and running his fingers through his hair, he cut the twine and carefully folded back the wrinkled brown paper to reveal four neatly tied stacks of money.

"Signoria, this is my life savings." With his gnarled hands, he patted the package like it was an adored wife.

" I saved it, so someday I could buy my own boat, but then the Rosa I became my home."

"Dear God in heaven, all that money?" Rosa gasped.

" It is mine, don't worry, I no steal it."

"My needs are simple, I sleep on the boat, one pair of shoes, one suit is all I need, no wife, no family. No one ever asked me for money because they think, 'poor Guido, is so poor,' so I save."

"My brothers and sisters live in Florence, so they never come to see me."

Guido pushed the package in front of Rosa and pulled his hands away. "I want to buy the Rosa I," he blurted out. "Is this enough money?"

Rosa picked up one stack of money, and bedding back a corner let the bills flutter past her thumb. "Guido, this is more money than we paid for the boat. This is more than enough," she padded the money.

"The Rosa I is a good boat. I want this boat." Guido bowed his head and pulled his lips tight, "I don't want you to sell it to anyone else."

Rosa looked over at Victor and Dino, who sat silent, their faces serious, they waited for a verdict.

"Rosa, I ask you again. Is this enough money for the Rosa I? Will you sell it to me."

"Guido, dear man, it is more than enough money…"

"Well? Well? What is your answer then?"

"Yes, all right, Guido, the boat is yours. Eduardo would have been happy for this, but I will not take all this money, it is too much."

"No, no," Guido insisted, pushing the stacks of money closer to Rosa, "you must take it all, you must have enough for a safe trip to America – you must!"

Rosa looked at her sons, their eyes gave her their answer.

"All right, Guido, as God is my witness, you are a good man. I will take it if that is what you ask."

"And now what I ask would also make Eduardo happy", Guido said.

"There is more?"

"I will not buy the boat…"

"What?" Interrupted Rosa, "you just said that you would…"

"Please wait, Signoria, I cannot buy the boat unless I have help. I can't do everything."

"There are always men on the dock willing to help…" Rosa said.

"…. No, Signoria. I want Victor and Dino to work with me on the Rose I."

"What Guido? You mean my sons to stay here?"

"The boys, that is what they want."

"Leave my sons here? I cannot," Rosa cried.

"I will go topside, you talk," Guido muttered.

"Stay Guido, help us," Dino said.

"No. You are men now, you can handle this yourselves." He rolled down the sleeves of his plaid shirt and pulled his knit cap down over his ears and left the cabin.

Fighting the chill creeping along her spine, Rosa folded her hands in front of her and waited.

"Mama," Victor said laying his hands on hers, "we don't want to go to America".

Dino chimed in, "We think that if you want to go to America, you should go, but you should let us stay."

"Yes, mama," Victor said, his eyes bright and powerful, "Guido wants to buy the boat and he needs us to help him."

"Let us stay. We want a chance to show you we are not children, we are men. We will make you proud of us, mama."

Rosa's eyes filled with moisture.

"We will miss you, mama, but you are right, it would be better for the twins, they should have a good start in life, they have no papa to show them."

She looked at the faces of her sons- faces which had lived through sorrow. They were no longer boys – they were young men. They were no longer her babies. Tragedy had made men of them.

"I feel sadness at this moment, but I also feel pride. I don't know which possesses me more. I want to reach out and cradle you in my arms as I did when you were babies, and I also want to stand up and shake your hands for I feel such pride in you. But the mother in me is sad."

"You know you don't have to always be fishermen. You are not locked into it, no one has ever said you had to do what your ancestors did. In America, there would be many opportunities." She searched their faces, hoping that she had somehow changed their minds.

"Mama, we understand, but we don't want to leave here," Victor said.

He took a piece of paper from his pocket and flattened it out onto the table. "Look, mama, Dino and I figured this out."

Dino added, "We will help Guido on his boat, and we have many ideas about selling the fish. We will take the train as far north as Chavari, will go south to Pisa, and even to Lucca, we'll get our fish there faster on my horse and cart, so it will be fresher."

Rosa tried to keep the tears back, but she could not.

"Do not cry mama, be happy for us. This is the first time in a long while we have felt hope. Please be happy for us, do not cry."

"If I say you can stay, and in a year it doesn't work out, will you promise me that you will come to America then?"

Without needing time to consider, the boys spoke in unison, "It will work out, mama, it will." Victor said.

"Yes, mama, we promise, but it will work, I know it will," Dino assured her.

"My thoughts will be with you all the time. Are you well, are you happy? All the thoughts any mother would have about her sons in another town, and we will be separated by an ocean. I will be in another world."

Rosa hugged Dino, "My love for you has never been greater, and Victor, my young businessman," she reached over and brought him closer to her.

Arms entwined, she held her sons close. "You stay in Italy, if that is truly what you want."

She squeezed them both to her, "You have a year", she said and buried her head in Victor's shoulder. "I give you my blessing." And to herself, she added, "I pray you are ready to fly free – I pray your wings are as strong as the wings of a gull."

On deck, Rosa took a long slow breath of air and stopped to watch Guido who was sitting on a canvas stool whittling a piece of pine. "Guido," she said, "the three of you planned this well."

"Signoria," he folded his knife and put it into his pocket, "your boys, they are men, eh?"

"Men? Yes, I suppose they are almost men, but they are still my babies."

" Do I have a boat or no?"

" Yes, Guido, you have a boat, and you have a crew," the words came painfully.

"Did they show you all the figures they put together? They did that, not me, I can't read or write. Their ideas are good. They may never have this chance again. You cannot break their spirit. You must let them stay."

"Yes, yes, Guido, it is all right, I'll have already told them they can stay."

"Oh, Signoria, you will see, you will not be sorry. I take good care of them, I'd be like their papa, you see."

"I just pray to heaven it is the right decision – but for you, Guido, to put every cent you have into this and to set out with two green boys – is that right, is that the right thing for you?"

"Yes, yes Signora, it is right for me. Do you think I have to buy the Rosa I to get a job? No, there are many fishermen that have already asked me if I was going to stay and work for a woman.

"I tell them nothing. It is none of their damn business what I do. I buy it for your boys and for the memory of Eduardo, and for me. Don't fear, they will have to work and work very hard, but they will be good fishermen."

Guido took his knife out and started working again on the slim pine stick.

"I was the youngest of 12 children, but the rest of them are all lazy and do not like to work, so piss on them!

"My father and mother were farmers and when they died my sisters married and moved away, and my brothers left the farm to rot. The beautiful grapes produced no more. They drank and fought and soon they lost the farm.

"That is why I left. I do not even like to go to Lucca to see the land, it makes my heart sick. The beautiful Chianti grapes are all dead."

In all the year's Rosa had known Guido, she had never heard so many words come out of his mouth.

"So, I don't want anyone to know the boat is mine. Only Victor and Dino will know and when I die, the Rosa I will be theirs. I sign a paper for you so there won't be any trouble when I die."

"Eduardo and Giovanni must both be smiling down upon you, Guido."

"Victor and Dino are my family now. They have the spirit of men who love the sea."

Rosa looked up at the mast and felt the salt stiffened lines which held it fast. "Last night," she said, "everything seemed so easy. Just sell the boat, pack my suitcase, take my children and go. But now, I must leave my sons, and that is like leaving a part of myself."

"Guido, there is something I must ask of you." The old man looked up from his whittling and waited.

"The boys have promised me if at the end of the year, things are not going well, they will come to America. Will you promise me that if that happens, you will send them to me?"

Guido paused, eyes scanning the horizon, "Yes, Rosa, I guess that is fair enough."

"And if," she went on, " if they will not come because they will not leave you, then you will come with them? Guido, will you promise me that?"

"Come to America? I don't know…"

"I am giving up my sons, you can do this much."

"All right. Yes, I will promise you that, as God is my savior," he made the sign of the cross.

Rosa patted him on the arm. "Thank you, Guido, may he keep you all safe."

Rosas' eyes searched the sky, and running her hand over the smooth worn railing, she tried to comprehend the decision she had just made.

"Dear God, protect my sons from the sea that took their father," she turned toward the water, drew her shawl around her shoulders, "and if the sea is not to be their life, show them the way."

Guido went below. The two boys waited silently for him to speak. "Partners," he said, extending his hand first to Victor and then to Dino, "we are partners now. Let's fish, or we will be out of business before we start!"

"You're the boss," Victor said.

"You're damn right I am the boss, and don't forget it, and another thing," he said, pulling on his black rubber boots. "I think Maria's cooking is pretty good, maybe it would be a good idea to eat at Maria's. I'm tired of my own cooking. Besides when your mama leaves Maria will be lonely, we better help out that old lady."

"What do you mean, old lady, Guido?" Dino said, "she is younger than you."

"Nah... Dino, I think maybe we are the same age."

"But you two fight all the time," Victor said.

"We don't fight, Victor, we just argue but we don't fight; there is a difference."

"You're not going to get sweet on Maria, are you Guido?" Dino teased.

"For Christ sake boys, you have a lot to learn. After your mama leaves, a real meal will taste good, I'm going to Maria's for your sake, not mine. I promised your mama that I would look out for you."

CHAPTER TWELVE

Following Sunday mass, Father Michael motioned to Rosa, and in English said, "I have something for you."

"What did he say, Rosa?" Maria asked, her eyes squinting suspiciously.

"Father is just practicing his English, Maria."

"Dear God in heaven! She has been teaching poor children English, and for what? It is like speaking Italian was going to be outlawed. Now she is doing it to you, Father. Next thing I know, she will have you saying mass in English."

Maria shook her hand at Father Michael. Her wrist moving, her fingers tight together, she shook her head back-and-forth. "We have to watch her, Father, next she'll try to teach me English."

Maria reached for the twins' hands, "I go feed my babies, you come after you finish with your English."

In his office, Father Michael pulled a chair up to the table and said, "I have an English dictionary for you, Rosa." He handed her four small books, "I also got three primers that the nuns used to teach English. They're worn but good enough." Unfolding a large map that covered most of the table, he said, "and here's a map of America, all of America!"

"Dear, God," Rosa exclaimed, "what a big country!" Putting one finger on New York she said, "all I have to worry about is here, and..." She searched across the map, "and here", her other hand pointing to San Francisco. "At least I don't have to worry about all that country in the middle."

"That's a lot of country not to worry about, Rosa. You may get stuck in..." Moving his hand randomly above the map, Father Michael squinted down at the letters his index finger landed on, "you might get stuck in OH- MA- HA, what a name!"

The priest moved to the easy chair in front of the fireplace and lighting his pipe said, "I did get some information about ships sailing out of Genova. They have a new kind of ship now, they say they are made of steel, and they have propellers that turn like screws.

"They're safer and more comfortable, steamships with emergency sales. There is one leaving with morning tide on April 4th. It is called 'Leonardo da Vinci'"

Grinning, he said, "That is the ship that God would send the nuns on. They say there are three private cabins in immigrant class, a little more expensive and small, but the five of you would not have to go into the dormitories."

"Then that is the ship I will take, Leonardo da Vinci!" Rosa said, "we must arrange for our tickets soon."

Father Michael continued, "I didn't have time to find a buyer for the Rosa I."

"That's all right, Father, I already sold it to Guido."

"Guido? He had money?"

"Yes, Father," she smiled, "it surprised me too." Rosa sat back in her chair and told the priest about Guido and Victor and Dino.

"Guido saved all that money!"

"Father Michael," Rosa said, "you must consider this as you would a confession, you are sworn to secrecy. Guido wants no one to know he bought the boat. He would even be more angry with me if he knew I told you!"

"Alright, alright, I will never speak of it, but Rosa, tell me you are not going without Victor and Dino."

"They asked for one year, only one year. I could not deny this to them," Rosa answered. "If in a year things do not go well for them, they have promised to come to America."

"Rosa, this is foolish." He walked slowly to the table and folded the map. "At least if Victor and Dino went with you they would be some help. If you ran out of money, they could get jobs. What are you to do if you all get seasick?"

"We will take care of each other. What else would we do?" Rosa gently took the map from his hands, "Victor and Dino must have this chance, the twins and I will have our chance in America."

"Oh, Rosa, Rosa, you always were different, never content like the other village women."

"Father you said you would help me, are you changing your mind now?"

Rosa felt her body stiffen.

"No, no, but Rosa, I cannot help but worry what will happen to a woman alone with two small children, going halfway around the world!"

"Instead of worrying about us Father, would you give me your blessings?"

"Yes, yes my child," he made the sign of the cross above her bowed head, "may God go with you and with your children."

Spring came early and with its fresh new growth a deep carpet of green stretch toward the mountains. The villages rejoice in celebration of Easter, but for Rosa, it meant a time for goodbyes. One week and she would leave Italy, perhaps never to see it again.

They had just finished their Easter meal, Maria was putting dishes in the wash pan, humming and Guido sat at the table drinking wine and telling stories to the young fishermen and the twins.

"Maria, I have something to tell you," Rosa had practiced her speech many times, and now standing close to her old friend she spoke softly, "in one week, I will- the twins and I- we will- we are going to America."

Maria's mouth flew open, the pasta dish crashed to the floor and spinning, Spinning itself to a silent stop.

"What?" She screamed, "you are going where?"

Dear God, that is not how I practiced it!

Guido got up and, pulling his cap down to his ears, left the house.

"America," Rosa repeated, searching Maria's face for any small trace of understanding.

"America?" Maria shouted, "why in God's name?"

"There is nothing left for me here." Rosa's voice was gentle.

"Nothing left? Your home is here, I am here." Maria looked over at the twins, "Dear God, are you going to take my babies?"

She rushed to the table and grabbing Angelina held her so tight the child almost disappeared in the fullness of her body.

"You are crazy, Rosa. Crazy! You are mad. The smoke from the fire must have burned your brain."

Squirming to free herself, Angelina's cries were muffled in Maria's breasts.

"Turn her loose, Maria. You are hurting her." Rosa reached for Angelina, but holding her tight, Maria swung the child away from her mother.

"Hurt her? You are going to kill her taking her on a boat across the world! They will catch diseases and die of dysentery, and you are afraid of me hurting her with my love? You are insane, Rosa. Just like that fancy aunt of yours in America, married to that son of a bitch Tony Orso."

Maria lifted her hand to her mouth, "My dear God in heaven… That is what you are going to do! Go to your aunt, you think her husband will welcome you? Not on your life! He did not want you when you were five and he sure doesn't want you now with four children."

"Maria, please, try to understand, please, Maria. I must do this."

"You go if you want to be a tramp and a strega. But you leave the twins with me! You cannot take them from me.

"I saw them before you did when they were born. If I had not been there little Angelina would have died. I kept her in my arms, warm, rocking her, I sat with her, walked with her, kept her from crying to save her energy. And when Eduardo died, I took care of you. He was a saint! You did not deserve him. This is how you repay me! You are a bitch, a spoiled bitch. That is what I think of you!"

155

Freeing Angelina, Maria sprinted across the room and snatched up her sewing basket. She pulled out a little cloth sack and threw it on the table.

"There- miss high and mighty- take that money! I will buy the children! You do not need them. You will only kill them on the ocean. Here, they are at least safe and well."

She pushed the white cloth bag closer to Rosa, "Here, count the money, I know how much there is. I can't read but I sure can count." Maria looked up at Rosa, her eyes blazing in anger, tears pouring down her cheeks.

The twins were both crying, Angelina holding onto her mother, and Gio in Dino's lap. Victor, standing by the fireplace, his eyes fiercely protective, watched Maria's every move.

"Going to America?" Maria said, "you don't even have any way to get to the boat!"

"Father Michael is going to take us there."

"Oh, I should've known Father Michael's in on this too! And this is why you have been teaching the children all those fancy words. You have been teaching them American so they can talk to the Indians before they get scalped. You are a crazy woman, Rosa."

Maria sat down in her chair and buried her head in her hands. She sobbed.

Rosa put her arms across the soft shoulder. Maria drew away.

"Go, you will be sorry. Go to your fancy Nina. Hell waits for you when you get there – if you make it at all.

"You will surely die on the way. I will pray for the twins and Victor and Dino, but you, you can go to hell, and be fish food for all I care.

I will not waste my prayers on you. If I pray for you God will never listen to me again."

Maria stood up and looked over at Victor and Dino, "You talk some sense into her head." She ran into her room and slammed the door.

"I never got the chance to tell her that you boys are staying."

Trying to comfort the frightened Gio, Dino said, "None of those bad things are going to happen," and to his mother, said, "Maria did not mean all those terrible things. You know she loves you. She is just hurt, tomorrow she will forget."

"I don't think so, Dino, she is very angry. She cannot understand that there is more in this world than our small village. This is her world, it is good enough for her, and she thinks I should feel the same way."

"Mama", Victor said, "we will look after Maria when you leave, don't worry about her. And Guido will be coming up here every evening for supper, we'll keep her happy."

The next morning Maria was swollen and quiet, never looking at Rosa. She hovered over the twins, granting their every wish, cooing, and clucking.

"Maria, sit down, I want to talk to you."

"You can talk until hell freezes over, but I still think you are a testa dura. You are brain fried. I have lost my love for you…"

"Maria," Rosa broken, her voice firm, "I am trying to tell you that Victor and Dino will be here, they are not going with us."

"What?" Maria said, sitting heavily down onto the chair.

"They do not want to go to America, they are going to stay here and fish with Guido. Maria, they will be your family."

"Humph!" Maria spoke, the expression on her face changing rapidly between anger and disbelief, joy and anger again. "Now, you are even deserting your sons? Going off without them?"

"Maria, stop that! They are young men, they have chosen to stay, and because I love them, I must let them be free. But I would like to think that you would watch out for them."

Rosa went outside to the garden, and out of the range of accusations. Looking at the wasteland that had once been her home, she was overwhelmed with a sense of aloneness. Would there ever be anyone who understands?

Maria came out of the house, tying her scarf under her chin, "Have you told anyone about this Rosa?"

"No, you are the first to know."

A slight smile worked its way across Maria's tear-stained face. Picking up the empty water jug she said, "I am going to the well, but you should go to church and ask for God's forgiveness for this terrible thing you are doing."

She hoisted the jug onto her shoulder and walked briskly down the path. Rosa watched the old woman, in her long dark clothes gather around the well. Soon Maria was surrounded by the others – the center of attention.

Her hands flying dramatically through the air, she pointed to her house, shook her head, and raised her hands in supplication to the heavens. The news was out, Maria was in her glory, perhaps now she would be able to forgive.

"This is our last night," Rosa said studying each member of her family gathered around the table, "tomorrow we leave. Tonight, I must say my goodbyes to my grown-up sons."

The twins kissed their brothers and made their way to play, and Maria said, "Guido, come here, let them talk. I want to show you what we are going to do so the boys will have a place to sleep. It is too cramped on that boat.

"I would have done this for Rosa if she stayed, but now we do it for the boys". Maria went over to the small corner by the window and moved her sewing table.

"See here Guido", she stepped off the square corner.

"It is up to us now to make a home for the boys, so we will make a small room here, not very big, just enough for two cots, maybe one more for you when you want to stay. I already got some old boards, we will fix it up nice, yes Guido?"

Guido said nothing, but as he paced off the corner, a guttural sound escaped from his throat. Rosa laid her tin box on the table. "There is so little left to show for my life." She picked up her slender gold ring, and taking Victor's hand, said, "This was the wedding band your father gave me. Wear it, my firstborn, and remember your mother who loves you."

From the box, she took a small St. Christopher medal and hung it around Dino's neck, "I wore this in the convent, and gave it to your papa when we married."

Pulling two pieces of paper from her apron pocket, she said, "I have just one more treasure left, I always imagined myself giving this to your wives. I never dreamed I would pass it onto my sons. But since you do not have wives yet, I want you to take it." She handed each a piece of paper.

"What is it?" Victor asked unfolding it carefully.

"Mama! It's written in English!" Dino flattened the paper out on the table and leaned over to study it.

"The bread!" Victor said instinctively lowering his voice and looking over at Maria still busy talking to Guido.

"It is the secret of your bread, is that right, mama?" Dino asked.

"It is our family treasure."

"But why is it written in English?"

"Our secret must be guarded, and also, it will help you remember the English words I taught you. Now, find a safe place, and share our secret only when you marry, that way your wife can make the bread you like so well."

"The secret of your sourdough bread is the seawater we brought you in that little bottle. Oh mama, this is a treasure!" Dino whispered.

From her tin box, empty now except for the bundle of Nina's letters, Rosa picked up the little piece of dark cloth with a red stripe in it.

"This and my wedding ring is all that is left of my life with Eduardo. This little scrap of his kerchief will remind me of the dreams we shared, and someday, somehow, there will be a Rosa II."

Rosa stood up and hugged each of them, "Go now, tomorrow when you return from fishing we will be gone. I will write as soon as we arrive in New York. Never doubt how much I love you both, and may God keep you safe."

She shook hands with Guido and watched him and her two sons walk away. A great knot formed in the pit of her stomach, and her whole body felt like ice. Maria's hand was on her shoulder, "I will watch over them Rosa, you have good boys."

Maria held out a small package wrapped in cloth. "Here, Rosa, so that you do not forget us."

Rosa took the package and hugged her old friend.

"Well, aren't you going to open it?" Maria said.

Carefully removing the wrapping, Rosa saw a small, round, red candle. For a moment, she could not speak.

"Candela dell' amicizia," she said, her voice quavering.

"And you know the legend tells us! When the candle burns away, you must return and get another candle."

"Oh, my dear friend," Rosa reached for Maria's hand.

"But you'll be back home here where you belong long before the candle burns away, you mark my word!" Maria turned away, dabbing at her eyes with the corners of her apron.

The horse-drawn wagon clattered to a stop alongside the dock. Tying the rains, Father Michael said, "There is your home for the next few weeks, Rosa."

"Heavenly Father!" She said hurrying down the dock looking up at the large ship casting a gray shadow on the waiting crowd. "I have never imagined a ship so big."

"Grab hold of my cassock Gio!" Father Michael ordered. "And Angelina, you hold your mother's skirt. Don't let go of your bundles, we'll have to make a run for it as soon as the gangplank is lowered."

Father Michael checked the children again and Gio grabbed a large wad of the black cloth. "All these people will be rushing to get on board, too. Rosa, stay close behind me, and when I say go, move fast or you'll have to wait for the next ship."

A sudden screech of metal – the clinging clatter of the gangplank thrusting into place. A surge of movement, the crash of bodies pushing. The pull of Angelina's hand. A tinge of terror. Hold

Father Michael's coat, walk in his footsteps. A surge of human bodies propelled upward.

At the top of the gangplank, a young sailor stopped them, "Tickets, Signora?" When he saw that the priest had no ticket, he nodded apologetically, "I am sorry Father, only passengers may board."

Father Michael pulled a bottle of amber liquid from one of the three string sacks he was carrying and handed it to the sailor. "I must help this family get settled, she is a widow, traveling alone with two small children."

"Peppino."

"Bless you," he said. Gio ran ahead of Rosa and Angelina, and Father Michael, his robes billowing in the breeze, hurried to catch up. With breaths coming in short gasps, he said, "Even God needs a little help once in a while."

"What do you mean, Father?"

"That bottle I gave to young Peppino, was rum. For a sailor at sea, rum is worth more than a king's ransom."

Rosa held tightly to Angelina as they climbed down to the decks. At the bottom, they stopped in a world of darkness, huddled together until their eyes were able to see,

"Here's a cabin, Rosa," the priest looked into an open door. "No one has claimed it yet, and it's close to the stairs, close to the air."

The only light was that from the open door. The walls of the windowless cabin were the color of mustard, the floor bare, wood planks, the air, heavy, the cabin smelled dank and moldy.

In the tiny space for two beds, one suspended above the other seeming to grow as a tree limb from the rough planks of the bunk bed. Under the lower bunk, a chamber pot, and on top carelessly thrown tin dishes, cups, silverware, and four yellow paper tags. Rosa tossed her belongings onto the lower bunk, "this will be fine, Father."

Frowning, the priest scolded, "I wish you had let me get you a room on the top deck, instead of down here in the steerage."

"We will be fine, Father, this is all the room we need. I plan to spend most of the time on deck, teaching the children English. Look...", she held up a small stool, its wooden legs fold in upon themselves, "Guido made us three of these to have at sea because, he said, there were no chairs on the deck in immigrant class."

Father Michael picked up three yellow tags and handed them to Rosa to write their names, ages, and the cabin number.

"Don't take these off," she said, slipping them over the children's heads. "You must wear them at all times. If you get lost, people will help you find your cabin." She slipped her own yellow tag over her head.

"Now, Rosa, stop a moment," Father Michael's forehead wrinkled, "do you have everything? The fruit? The bread? Did we forget anything?"

"No, Father, I know we didn't forget anything. I feel like a food peddler: I have oranges, apples, bread, and cheese. I have coffee and essence of peppermint. But I don't have any chickens!" Gesturing broadly as if in despair, she chided, "How will we manage without fresh eggs or chicken soup?"

"Now, Rosa be serious, all these things are important."

"Father, if I get too serious, I might run down the gangplank and all the way back to Viareggio. Let me have my little joke, perhaps it will make leaving easier."

Angelina and Gio were bouncing on the top bed, "Mama, the mattress is hard and it sticks me," Angelina rubbed the underside of her leg.

"Get down off of there," Rosa ordered and pulled the gunny sack stuffed with loose straw from the bed. "I have brought blankets to sleep on. The lord only knows when clean straw was last put in here."

Rosa folded and refolded the blankets. The time for the ship to sail was nearing and unable to keep still, she shoved their bundles, first here, then there. There was but one more goodbye to be said, and it brought back to her heart the sorrow of the bittersweet parting from her two sons.

"Rosa, my dear, please stop for a moment. There will be time enough to get settled, you will have eighteen days or more to do all of this, and there are things I must tell you. Where is your American money?"

"It is tied around my middle," she patted the slight bulge on her waist, "if someone wants my money, they must take all of me."

"Guard that well, without it you won't be allowed to enter America. And here, Rosa…" he handed her an envelope, "this is a letter of introduction to Father O' Malley, in New York. I wrote him to expect you, he has your money and will make arrangements for you to get on the train. He will recognize you, for I sent a very good description of you and the children."

"And another," he pulled two more bottles of rum from his sack, "now keep these hidden until you find Peppino, he already helped us find this cabin, but Rosa, be careful who you decide to trust."

"Please, Father, don't burden me with a lot of decisions to make! All I want to do is relax, I have had already too many big decisions to make in the last few months."

"Well, just be careful what you do with that rum. It's a real treasure to sailors, but, it's even better for seasickness."

"Father, if I take everything that is good for seasickness, I will get sick from remedies. Everyone has given me suggestions: don't eat- drink plenty of water- don't drink water- drink chicken soup- never drink chicken soup- get fresh air- don't get fresh air- look at the sea- never look at the sea- eat potatoes- don't eat potatoes. Do! Don't!"

"The only thing everyone agrees on is essence of peppermint and Guido said if that doesn't help me... god help me!"

A deafening blast of the ship's horn stopped the conversation, and before anyone could speak it blew two more times.

"I must go. You will sail soon."

"We will walk up with you, father."

"No, stay with your cabin. Remember what Peppino said."

He turned to the twins busily making their nests in the clean blankets Rosa had spread out for them, "come, kneel down, children. I will give you my blessing and lead you in one last prayer."

Rosa knelt beside her two young children, and bowed her head. "Let us pray together. Hail Mary, full of grace, the Lord..." Rosa looked up and watched a tear slide down the priest's cheek.

"Dear Rosa," he said as he helped her up, "stay well, you have a long voyage ahead, I will pray for all of you, and for a safe journey. Buona fortuna."

Weeping unashamedly, woman and priest embraced. He hugged the twins and left the cabin without looking back. Arms around her children, she watched the black-cloaked figure hurry away down the hall.

The horn blasted again and the floor shivered beneath her feet. "Come, children, let's go on deck and watch us sail out of port. I must see Italy one last time."

Perhaps it would be the last time.

The children behind her, Rosa made her way across the deck. She threaded a path around in between the passengers crowded together until she found a space at the rail and pushed the twins in front of her so they could look out through the wires.

Tearful passengers huddled together, women in kerchiefs, men in coarse ill-fitting garments waved at those on the deck dressed as they were. Well-dressed gentlemen and ladies reached up to wave goodbye to all the passengers out of sight on the decks high above Rosa and her children.

Gang planks lowering, hatches slamming shut, the howling of the horn, and slowly, almost imperceptibly, the dock moving back away from the ship. Rosa swallowed hard, her fingers crossed the rail, oh holy Mary, mother of God, what am I doing here?

Pressed against the railing, people crowded- leaning out as if to pull back the land. Men's eyes held tightly to their homeland, and women sobbed. Rosa stared at Genova rising up out of the edge of the sea from its bed of stone-pink buildings, and as if in supplication to the Lord, stretching its fingers up the mountains towards heaven.

The shoreline of Italy moved slowly back, shrinking away as the Leonardo headed toward the straights of Gibraltar. Rosa starred eastward, was that Viareggio tucked in below the mountain? Desperately she tried to hold onto the image of a world she knew, to carve into her memory every minute detail of the land she might never see again.

The sounds of the ship, now full sail, consumed the air. Left behind, behind the frothing white wake door a dim reminder of the only world she had ever known, and ahead, the sun glistening on the blue water, sending back a blinding spotlight. The fear which gripped her lay in her stomach like a stone.

Wondering why she had disobeyed Father Michael's advice to stay with her cabin, Rosa called, "Hurry, children, come." Would the cabin still be there??

Panic drove her on through the narrow quarters crowded with people, confused and anxious, hurrying to find their way in an unfamiliar world.

Bewildered, red-eyed women clutched infants and herded children with sharp lashes of their tongues.

She opened the door slowly, and when she saw the tiny space just as she had left it, she silently offered a word of thanks to the Madonna and promised her a rosary.

The children, hardly able to contain the excitement, and their eagerness to explore the ship, ask dozens of questions while Rosa put their meager belongings away as best she could in the tiny space they would call home for the next several weeks.

"Are you settled, Signora?" The young sailor poked his head in through the open doorway. "I am Peppino," he reminded her with a white boy-man grin.

"This is a good cabin, fresh air can reach you. You're close to the toilets, so you'll welcome the air. The smell gets pretty bad around there," he pointed down the corridor to the dormitory.

"You're lucky, even if you pay extra for a cabin, it doesn't always mean you get one. We have three cabins, and I think the steamship line sells 10 of them on each voyage." He laughed, "They figure if you don't get a cabin you'll still sail."

Peppino turned away from the cabin long enough to direct a passenger to the toilets, "It is good you had the priest to help you."

He pulled a small medal from his tight-fitting pants, "He asked me to give this to you. It's the patron saint of Italy and San Francisco. It will protect you, he said."

"He has been a good friend," Rosa kissed the medal, and making the sign of the cross, hung it around her neck.

"Look out the door here, the dining hall, if you want to call it that, is down one deck."

Gio hopped off the top bed where he had been playing, "Where do those stairs go, Peppino?" He pointed to the steps behind a pair of louvered swing doors secured together with chain and lock.

"To heaven, young man, to heaven," Peppino said.

"To heaven, really?"

Angelina said, "That's where my daddy is."

"Oh, I am sorry. I was only joking." Peppino looked apologetically at Rosa. "Sailors call it heaven because when people go down there seasick, they pray to die and go to heaven, but before they go they want to stop and see what first-class looks like."

His eyes squeezed into a slant, he smiled at Angelina and ruffled Gio's hair.

"Where do we get drinking water, Peppino?" Rosa asked.

"There are freshwater barrels in the bathrooms and on deck, but don't use that."

And his voice lowered to a whisper, "at the stern of the deck, there's a barrel for the sailors, good water, it's behind stuff like this," he nodded towards the doors Gio had asked about.

"The children can crawl under and if you have your own bottle they can fill it. But do this late at night, so no one will see you. People sometimes get desperate down here." As an afterthought, he added, "the way they're packed in, like a bunch of cattle."

"Did you bring any food, Signora?"

"Yes," Rosa pointed to the string sacks under her bunk.

"You better hang the food from that hook on the ceiling beam or the rats will eat it before we get out to the open sea."

"My dear God in heaven!" Rosa shuttered, prickly nerve endings crippling down the backs of her upper arms. "Rats?" She repeated.

"We have big ones," Peppino bragged and lifting the bag of food, "we have rats that take this voyage back-and-forth with us, back-and-forth. They are relatives of the rats that sailed from Genova with Columbus. And they can spot fresh food as quick as a sailor can smell a bottle of rum," he hoisted the heavy sack up and hung it from the ceiling hook.

A sudden clang of a metallic bell made Rosa jump. "That's only the dinner bell," Peppino explained, "first nights are best, so go along, I have to go up to heaven to work," he left laughing.

Gathering tin plates and cups, the three started toward the dining hall. The corridor was already filled with waiting people, "stay close to me children," she scolded, "don't you wander off." The air soon became warm and close, smelling of human bodies, of fish, and of grease.

169

The people move slowly in front of a line of sailors serving from huge steaming pots. "Hold up your plates, dammit lady, or you'll get nothing!"

A large bellied sailor spoke from behind a deep pot of water soup, his once white shirt stained with grease, a drop of perspiration hung from the tip of his nose.

"You better eat up so when we get to open see you'll have something to puke." He leered at her, and holding the ladle in a two-fingered hand, plopped the soup onto her bowl.

Rosa hurried the children deeper into the long narrow room. Ceilings were low and what little light there was came from a few small portholes.

The muffled sound of quiet conversation we're punctuated by the clutter of spoons against thin metal plates and an occasional cry of a baby. People set up rough plank tables on benches bolted to the floor. Faces did not look up from their food as Rosa and her children sat down.

In Rosa's soup, a single chunk of fish floated to the top and reminded her of Mama Nina's long-ago description of shipboard food. Pigs on the farm, she wrote, eat better than we did on the boats.

Rosa drank the soup her stomach would accept, and when the children finished, she started out of the room. The sailor from the food line blocked her way.

"You got to wash your plates in those buckets there," he said. With his two-fingered hand in her face, he pointed and jeered, "you don't like my hand, little lady? Drunk at sea one night..." He bent down and whispered in her ear, "rats chewed off my fingers!"

Scared, Rosa turned her back to him and edged closer to the line of people, "hurry, children, we must wash our plates." They waited their turn at the water tubs. The sailor followed. "Where is your husband, Signora, already seasick?"

"Our Papa is in heaven," Angelina answered innocently.

"Oh, a pretty widow eh? I take care of lonely ladies on the long nights at sea." He rubbed Rosa's hip and pressed his two-finger hand into the fold of her skirt. "It's going to be a long trip, and if you're nice to Jocko, we can have a good time." he walked away leering.

Rosa shattered. The line moved up and she found herself in front of a large garbage can full of gray water. Chunks of food floated to the top on a sheet of grease. She drew back, and grabbing the children, said, "Don't put your dishes in there! We will find somewhere else to wash."

Rosa could not get the sailor out of her mind; in every dark crevice she imagined him jumping out at her, everywhere she went he was going to appear.

She walked on deck with the children and watched the early sunset turn into night. Rosa put the children safely to bed and was cautiously making her way to the washroom through the dim corridors when suddenly her way was blocked.

With his arms outstretched, Jocko's huge frame filled the entire passageway. "Going to bed, so early, pretty Signora? That is good, put your little bastards to bed and I will come take care of you."

Leaning down closer to her, his stale breath hot in her face, "It's probably been a long time since you had a good Italian man, eh? You haven't known nothing until you feel a Sicilian sailor."

Blood rushed to her face, her heart pounded faster with each word the sailor uttered. "Please sir, let me pass," Rosa pleaded.

He let one arm fall to his side, and as she tried to go by, he grabbed her yellow name tag, "Rosa Dante," he read. "I will see you again." He cupped his two-fingered hand around her breast. "See, I can do good with only two fingers, I show you later."

Rosa ran back down the dark corridor, past the cabin, and into the dormitory. "Go find some other place, all the beds are taken here," a dark-skinned woman sitting on a bunk nursing an infant, stared menacingly.

"I'm sorry Signora I took a wrong turn," Rosa said watching over her shoulder, "may I just stand here a moment?"

"Stand anywhere you like," another voice from deep in the long narrow darkness of the room spoke more kindly.

Rosa looked down the rows of beds stacked three high, lined up like chicken hutches. At the far end of the room, from under the only source of light, a single oil lamp, she saw the outline of another figure.

Rosa stepped cautiously out into the hallway. Looking back over her shoulder and into every turn, she darted down the narrow corridor and through the open door into the cabin. Gio was already in the upper bunk, and Angelina, huddled in a blanket, sat on the edge of her mother's bed, waiting.

"Where were you, mama?" Angelina asked when Rosa slammed the door and leaned heavily against it.

"Mama, leave the door open," Gio said, " it's dark in here."

"No, the door stays shut." Rosa's voice was sharp.

"But I can't see," Angelina complained.

"A candle. Find me a candle in that sack."

"Here mama, here is one," Angelina held out the small red candle still wrapped and its pieces of silk. "Here is Maria's candle."

"No, no, not that." Rosa snatched it from her hand. "That is only for special occasions, for happy times! That is la Candela dell' amicizia."

Rosa crushed the small package to her breast, and with feelings of anger arising within her, said, "No, we cannot light this now. No, dear Lord, not like this." Rosa listened intently for any sound in the quarter, and in the darkness of that tiny cabin, she was afraid.

Her eyes filled with tears of frustration. Angelina pulled another candle from the satchel, and handing it to her mother, said, "I'm sorry, mama."

Rosa hugged Angelina to her, and with words short and clipped, said, "It is all right. Hurry now, get into bed and go to sleep."

"Why didn't you want to burn the little fat candle, mama?" Gio asked from the upper bunk.

Trying to hide her impatience, Rosa answered, "I told you it's only to be burned on special times, times of celebration with family and friends. And when the candle burns all the way down, we're supposed to return to where we got it, and ask for another."

"Will we do that, mama? Will we go back and get another candle from Maria?"

"I don't know," Rosa answered, "only the Almighty knows what is going to happen to us. Now, settle down, and go to sleep you two, it is late."

"Mama, I'm thirsty," Angelina said over the bed rail.

"We have no water tonight, you will have to wait for morning. Here, we will all share an orange."

Rosa unfolded a canvas tool against the cabin door and sat down with her back pushed straight up against the unpainted wood. Her heart still pounding. Soon the twins were asleep. The peaceful sounds of their breathing and the rocking of the ship began to calm Rosa. She pulled the pins from her hair and closed her eyes.

A strong knock on the door. Her body stiffened. She did not answer.

"Signora, it is me, Peppino, are you in there?"

"Come in, come in," she opened the door cautiously, "I am glad it is you, I was afraid it was Jocko."

"He's been giving you trouble?"

"In the dining room... He threatened terrible things."

"I'm sorry, he always looks for the widows, the pretty ones, the women alone. He is a vulture."

"I will tell the captain," Rosa said.

"That will do you no good, it will only make matters worse. Jocko is the captain's cousin, and the captain doesn't worry much about steerage passengers. He's only concerned with the first-class, where he can get tips from."

"Then I won't go to the dining hall. I'd rather starve than face that man again."

"Now now Signora don't talk that way. I am not as big as Jocko and if I get at him that could make matters worse for both of us, but let me see what I can do."

"I'm frightened, Peppino, afraid to leave the cabin. I didn't even get water."

"I'll get you some now." He took the bottle and was back with the first supply.

"Sit down, Peppino, if you have time," she unfolded a canvas tool for him, "tell me about yourself."

Studying his smooth youthful face in the flickering light of the single candle, her thoughts were on the sons she had left behind. "How old are you?"

"Nineteen," he said proudly. "I come from the little town of Chiavari, near Genova, do you know it?"

"Yes, we passed through it on our way from Viareggio. What made you leave your home and take the sea Peppino?"

"When I was 12, my father died and my mother remarried. My stepfather was mean to me and my brother. We ran away, my brother was 11. For a while we did odd jobs in Genova until we got tall enough to sign on a ship." Leaning toward her, he whispered, "really, I'm only 17. I lied about my age to get on. My brothers on another ship. He sails around the Horn."

"Do you miss your home?"

"Yes, and I miss seeing my mama. But I'm afraid to go back because it would only cause her harm. My stepfather would yell and hit her. I couldn't watch that. She won't leave him, she says she can't, where would she go, she asked me. I wish my mother had left Italy when my father died, like you Signora."

"She had a sister in America, I wish she had gone to her when we were small. The man she's remarried to, he's real mean. I can't even write to her, she doesn't even know how to read, so I just pray for her and pray to help others whenever I can. Every time I make this trip, I put money away, and someday I will stay in America."

"What is your job on the boat, Peppino?"

"I have done everything, anything that no one else wants to do. But mostly I'm a cabin boy in first-class. Because I know a little English, they put me up top. But at night I come down here. Some nights when the weather is clear, there's music and dancing on deck, we all join in, I play the harmonica."

"Signora, I must go topside, but if you want to wash, I will wait here with the children, it is late, not too many people will be in the toilets."

Jocko approached silently, "What are you doing here, little squirt?" He asked trying to see into the cabin. "Where is the little widow? I came here to make friends with her," smirking, he elbowed Peppino.

His body slumping, Peppino edge closer to Jocko, and confided, "You don't want that one."

"What do you mean, kid?"

"I learned from you, Jocko, like you always say to do, I burst into her cabin, and sure enough, she was almost naked. Even in the candle light I saw she had horrible sores all over her body."

Peppino spat on the ground, "Good thing I noticed that Jocko, eh? You like to take them in the dark, and maybe you wouldn't have noticed."

"Jesus Christ!" Jocko said, "That's all I need, a case of mallatia venerea. Now I know how her husband died, poor bastard. Thanks for the warning, kid."

Jocko left in the direction of the dormitory. "Guess I'll have to look someplace else."

"Don't leave that door open, Peppino," Rosa scolded when she returned.

"Don't worry Signora, I think I have just taken care of your problem."

"What happened?"

"Jocko came to your cabin."

"How did he find it?"

"Probably saw the number on your tag."

"Stupida! Stupida!" She cried. "I didn't think of that. I was trying to be so careful and all that time I was wearing my number around my neck."

She stuffed the yellow paper tag into her blouse. "How did you get rid of him?"

"Well… ah… I told him… ah… well, Signora, I just took care of everything." Peppino did not look her in the eyes.

"What exactly did you tell him?" Rosa demanded.

"You do not have to know Signora."

Rosa stared at him.

"I, well, I just, I told him you were…"

"I was what?"

"Well, I told him, now promise you won't get angry? I had to handle this so Jocko would understand."

"Tell me Peppino, I will not get angry."

The young sailor blurted out, "I told you bad malattia venerea."

"Oh my god, Peppino, he will tell everyone on board, even the captain."

"I don't think so. But he might tell some of the sailors that I was dumb enough to pick a woman with sores."

Peppino laughed at the thought of it.

"It's not funny, Peppino! What if he tells the captain? When we land in New York they might try to ship me back to Italy."

"Don't worry Signora, they have doctors in New York at the dock. If there's any question they'll examine you, you are safe. You can even go to bed with that door wide open for fresh air.

"Jocko will not try to get into your cabin, he may still harass you, but I can't do anything about that."

He patted Rosa's hand, "Thank you, Peppino, but I hope others don't find out about this and decide that I am now a street woman."

"Now, don't worry, good night, Signora."

"Please, my young friend, call me Rosa."

"Good night, Rosa," he said, "I will see you tomorrow."

Slipping out of her dress, she lay on top of the bed and felt the gentle rolling rhythm of the sea. She clasped the metal around her neck, and running her thumb over the raised figure, said aloud, "Well Saint Francis, I think I am already in your debt, now, please, just get us across this ocean and safely to your city."

Rosa and the children spent the day on deck. They watched the Mediterranean become as fast as an ocean and then, nearing Gibraltar, narrow into a turbulent straight and pass beneath the overpowering rock.

The weather was warm, and Rosa read and studied English with the children. She did not see Jocko and almost forgot about him. Gio and Angelina made up many games to play on deck. Angelina never tired of watching the first-class ladies in their fine gowns. In the evenings Peppino played his harmonica for them, and in English told stories of the sea and of the ports he had seen.

A week out the ship ran into a storm. Rosa lay flat on her back, holding tightly onto the sides of the bed. Eyes clenched shut, she braced her body.

The ship lurched from side to side, pitched forward, and fell back, each time with a tremendous thud. Her arms tight holding on. The dinner bell sounded. The very thought of food made her gag. "Go children to dinner, I don't feel well, I don't want to eat."

Turning away from them she held her stomach. "Dear God, now it starts."

She reached for her bottle of peppermint. A few drops on her tongue, she carefully lay back down on the bed. The room was so dark she could not be sure whether her eyes were open or shut. She tried to draw up into her mind the memory of the hills around Viareggio, and of the sunshine. She hugged the chamber pot close to her.

CHAPTER THIRTEEN

The storm lasted three long days and nights. On the fourth day the waters became calm, Rosa's stomach did not.

Sectioning off a piece of dry orange she left it to rest on her tongue. The taste freshened her mouth. She lay back on the bed, the gentle rock of the boat provided little comfort.

When the children returned from their meal in the dining hall, Rosa gratefully gave them permission to go on deck.

Untouched by the mysteries of seasickness, the twins used their time well exploring the ship. Every nook and cranny was their domain.

Exhilarated by the unfamiliar experience of being on their own, they roamed at will around the strange floating world.

"Come on, Angelina, let's go see what, 'heaven' looks like," Gio said, studying the locked gates.

Angelina shook her head, "No, Gio, Mama said to be good. We'll get into trouble."

"They won't do anything to little children," Gio explained, "that's why they leave that space, so we can crawl under it and the grown-ups can't."

Gio squeezed his body under the gate. "We'll just look, we'll be good," he said reaching his hand out from the other side to help Angelina through. They climbed up the ladder, their short legs stretching from step to step.

They scurried through more pairs of locked doors and when they arrived on the top deck, Angelina said, "I'm scared, let's hide here and watch."

"Look at the ladies over there," Angelina whispered, "look at those beautiful bird feathers on their hats."

"They better not come to our village," Gio giggled, "someone will shoot their hats for dinner."

"I wonder what they're drinking out of those cups?" Angelina said, watching the ladies in the deck chairs, their legs covered with blankets.

Gio whispered back, "They're real quiet when they drink, they don't slurp like Maria does."

The twins, intent upon the scene they were watching, did not notice the tall man's shadow as it covered them.

"My, my, what do we have here?" A deep voice said, "I think you are somewhere you do not belong."

Angelina jumped her feet and ran, but the man had a firm hold on Gio's shoulder. "Now, now, not so fast," he said.

"Sir, we, we, we, we were doing no harm," Gio stammered. "We were just up here watching." The man released him but blocked the way when he tried to run.

181

Angelina turned back toward her captive brother. "Sir, we were just up here looking," she said. "We only wanted to see what heaven looks like. Our friend, Peppino, told us it was like heaven up here."

"Oh, is that all?" The man said smiling. "I thought maybe you were pirates, here to take over the ship." He crouched down, and he wasn't as big as a shadow.

"Are you two friends?" The tall man asked.

"No," Gio replied in a businesslike manner, "we are not friends, we are twins. We do not look alike because I am a boy and she is a girl. But we are still twins because there are two of us." A nervous smile stretched tight across his mouth.

"And I see you each have one dimple." Angelina smiled, "Mama has two dimples, so she could just give us each one."

"And where is your mother, young lady?"

"She is sick," Angelina put her hand on her belly and rubbed it.

"She has been very sick," Gio repeated.

"Didn't you get seasick?" He asked.

"No, sir, we are fine," Angelina said.

"Mama's been throwing up ever since the boat started bouncing around in the storm."

"She has only gone to the dining hall once, but she has told us she was better," Angelina contributed.

"I am glad she's better today". The tall man's grin showed straight white teeth.

"And what is your name young man?"

"Giovanni Eduardo Dante, sir."

"And how old are you, my young travelers?"

"We are six, both of us are six."

"You are going to America, do you know how to state your name in English?" He asked.

Gio shook his head. "Your name in English would be John Edward." Reaching into his vest pocket he brought out a black fountain pen. Both children stared. He unscrewed the top of the pen and handed it to Angelina who kept it in her hands and gently traced its gold band with her index finger.

"That's how you write your name in English, John Edward. And what is your name young lady?"

"Angelina Maria Dante," she replied.

"Well, Angelina, your name will be the same in English. But sometimes you may be called Angela which means Angel."

"I am Signor Martinelli," he put the pen back into his vest pocket and standing up extended his hands to the children, "would you like to join me in a cup of hot chicken broth?"

He walked them across the wide deck to a long table under the protective overhang of the bridge. Delicate porcelain cups were set out on a white tablecloth.

Giovanni saw Peppino wearing a clean white jacket, carrying a tray full of cups and saucers to the ladies and gentlemen in the wooden deck chairs. Pulling away, Gio tried to hide his body behind Signor Martinelli.

Peppino served the last cup from his tray and came over to them. "I know these children, sir, are they bothering you? I will take them below, if you like."

183

"Absolutely not, Peppino, they are my guests. They have been invited up here by me." Signor Martinelli winked.

"And I hear that you are the one who told them this was heaven up here?"

"Yes sir, I guess I did. Now, children be good," Peppino assumed a stern look, "or you will have to answer to me, do you hear?"

"Please, Peppino, we are good, do not tell our mama that we are bad," Angelina said.

"Yes, they have been good, and all good souls deserve a chance to see heaven, Peppino."

Signor Martinelli sat down on the seat of a wooden lounge, his legs to one side. "You both can sit here with me on the deck chair," he said patting the wood beside his leg. "Peppino will bring us some soup. And if you like, you can take some to your mother. It is good for her to have liquids."

The children sat very straight. Gio tried not to make noise drinking the soup, and Angelina imitated the manners of the beautiful ladies.

"That was very good, Signor Martinelli," she said placing her empty cup on the table.

"Now, both of you go and take your mother the soup, and be sure to bring the cup back to me," he said watching Gio swallow the last of the broth.

"How will we find you?" Asked Angelina.

"I will look behind the water barrels in about an hour."

They thanked the tall man politely and walked very carefully with the hot soup. When they came to the locked doors, Gio crawled under first and held the soup while Angelina followed. Quietly entering the dark cabin, they whispered, "Mama, we have some hot broth for you."

Rosa raised her head from the pillow and lit a candle. "Where did you get soup?" She asked, "and such a fine China cup, too?" She brought the warm broth to her mouth.

"We met a nice old man who lives on the top deck. When we told him you were sick he gave it to us for you."

"How very nice of him."

"Peppino was there too," Gio added.

"I hope you're not going places you shouldn't," Rosa cautioned.

"Oh no, mama", Gio said, "we are being very good, and Signor Martinelli told Peppino we were his guests. We have to take the cup back in one hour. Mama, how long is one hour?"

"I will let you know," she said drinking the broth and listening to all the wonderful things they had seen. Cautioning them to be careful, she sent them off to wash the delicate cup and saucer.

"I think your hour is up, she said, and be sure to thank your old man for me."

Gio and Angelina reached the top deck but did not see their friend anywhere. They crouched down behind the barrel and waited until they saw him walking down the deck toward them.

"Well, did that soup help your mother?" He asked.

"Yes, she feels lots better."

"I am glad it helped her. Would you like to take a walk with me and see this part of the ship?"

185

"Oh yes," they spoke in whispers hoping not to appear as eager as they felt. He held each child by the hand and showed them a world of people they had never seen before.

The ladies were dressed in fine colors and beautiful long silk dresses with bustles. The men wore top hats and long gray morning jackets. A little girl, not much taller than Angelina, walked toward them pushing a wicker doll buggy.

She was wearing a white linen dress with a yellow sash around her waist and in her hair a matching yellow ribbon. The girl stopped a few feet ahead of them, picked up the doll, and held it close to her. Without looking at Angelina, she placed the doll in the buggy and moved on. Angelina had never seen anything as beautiful as that doll. No one spoke a word.

Men and women drove past, the women nodded at Signor Martinelli and the men tipped their hats.

Geo pointed to a young boy throwing an iron ring over a peg, and asked, "What is he doing?"

"He's playing quoits," Signor Martinelli explained. The group of small boys dressed in short pants with belts that matched their black shoes took turns tossing the heavy iron rings.

"It looks like horseshoes," Gio said, "my papa played horseshoes, and added, "probably, with shoes from our own horse too!"

They passed by women in deck chairs talking quietly, and small groups of men standing around smoking. The men's voices were loud and sometimes fingers were pointed at each other. The little girl with the buggy came by again and Angelina stopped to watch her. Signor Martinelli paused and tipping his hat, spoke to the blonde child, "What is your name, young lady?"

"Maria, sir," her voice was quiet and polite.

"Oh," Angelina explained, "my name is Angelina Maria. We almost have the same name." Looking down into the buggy, Angelina said, "she is very beautiful." Maria picked the doll up and hugged it close to her.

"And where did you find such a lovely doll, Maria?" Signor Martinelli asked.

"My papa gave it to me," Maria spoke without relaxing her hold on the doll.

"I have never seen such a beautiful face," Angelina said.

"Maybe someday your papa will bring you a beautiful one like that," Signor Martinelli said.

"My papa died in the fire."

"Oh, I am sorry to hear that," Signor Martinelli said.

"But mama says he is in heaven with God," Gio added.

Maria held out her arms and asked, "Would you like to hold my doll?"

"Oh, yes," Angelina said, folding her arms to make a cradle. "She is beautiful, Maria, and her hair is soft, like my mother's."

Cupping one hand over the doll's head, Angelina touched the tiny taffeta dress and glided her fingertips lovingly over the delicate porcelain face.

Angelina placed the doll reluctantly down into the buggy. "That must be the beautifulest doll in the whole world," she said.

"But she doesn't have a pretty dimple like you," Signor Martinelli remarked as they continued their walk.

The three walked on soon becoming fast friends. The tall man patiently answered all of their questions and explained the strange new world to them. "Would you like to have lunch with me tomorrow?" He asked as their stroll around the deck brought them back to the water barrels.

"Oh, yes, yes," they both said, "could we?"

"Yes, you will be my guests, the weather is clearing, and we will have our lunch and even play a game here on deck.

"Tomorrow when you hear the lunch bell, come up. I will order something special and we will have our own party.

"Now, run along, your mother will worry about you, and come tomorrow when the bell rings."

Their route now memorized, the twins squeezed expertly under the locked gate and with the confidence of world travelers, scampered through the dark corridors.

"Mama, mama, Signor Martinelli invited us for lunch tomorrow," they shouted, throwing open the door.

"Who?" Asked Rosa.

"The old man who sent you the soup," Gio explained.

"I hope you are not being a bother," she scolded, "can we go, can we go, mama?" They spoke in unison.

"He invited you to eat lunch with him?"

"Yes, mama, he really likes us, and he is going to order something special for us, and he said he would play a game too."

"Can I wear my new dress, the one Maria made for me?"

"We are saving that for when we reach San Francisco and meet Mama Nina."

"But tomorrow is special! All the people upstairs dress very pretty. Mama please."

" Well, all right, if this is really special, you may wear your new clothes, if," Rosa added, "you promise not to get them dirty."

"I promise, mama, I promise."

"All right, then. Now tell me about this old friend of yours."

The children sat at the foot of Rosa's bunk. "He speaks English and tells us all kinds of new words." Gio held up his identification tag. "See, my name is John Edward in English." With a touch of pity in his voice, he added, "but Angelina's name is still Angelina."

"He had a gray suit on and a vest too, just like the bank man in Genova who gave us the American money. And he had a pen, he called it a fountain pen. It had real gold around the top, and he let me hold it."

Angelina's eyes filled with wonderment.

"My name is John Edward now," Gio repeated.

"All right, John Edward Dante, but now it's time for us to go to the dining hall for lunch." She kissed them both and sank down back into her bed.

Flat on her back in the dark cabin, her fingers holding the Saint Francis metal, Rosa said a prayer of thanks that the storm was over and with it, she hoped, the worst of her seasickness.

A quiet knock on the door, "Rosa, it's me, Peppino, I have a little present for you."

He brought in a heavy bucket. "Fresh rainwater," he said, "the ladies in first-class love the soft water for the hair." He put the bucket in the corner. "Save it, and when you are better, you will enjoy it. How are you feeling?"

"Better, Peppino. Are other people sick too?"

"Yes, it was a bad storm, especially for ones in the dormitory. The children do fine, but the grown-ups were sick. The dining hall has been nearly empty. But now we are past the storm and the weather is warming up."

"Have you eaten anything, Rosa?"

"I have some bread, and the children brought me broth this morning."

"Yes," he laughed, "they found out how to get up to first-class, and Signor Martinelli seems to have adopted them."

"They're not getting into trouble, are they?"

"No, I think Signor Martinelli enjoyed their company. He used to look so lonely before. Don't worry," he said putting a comforting hand on Rosa's shoulder, "they are very well behaved."

"I'll be going now, but you better get some fresh air, you look pale. Right now the sun is as warm as it's going to get." Peppino said and went out the door.

Rosa set up, her arms limp in her lap. "All right, Rosa," she said aloud to the empty room. "Some fresh air, that will be good for you."

She remembered Guido saying the best thing for seasickness was not to be onboard a ship and the second best thing was fresh air.

She bathed the best she could, dipping saltwater from the huge wooden barrels into a crude stone sink in the tiny washroom. But she could not towel away the roughness made of her skin by the saltwater. She used the soft rainwater to rinse her hair, and as she combed the long wet strands, a new energy seeped back into her body. She pinned her hair up loosely and covered it with her scarf.

With Guido's folding stool tucked under one arm, her English book under the other, Rosa went on deck. She saw only a few people. Those over their seasickness were in the dining hall, those still suffering were no doubt lying on their beds below.

Rosa picked her way across the deck through the piles of belongings of who would soon return, but for the moment, she had the deck almost to herself. The water was quiet, the sky pure blue, and in the distance, the last of the gray clouds were drifting further out to sea.

On all sides of the ship, in every direction, all Rosa could see was water. The vastness of the ocean made her feel small, like a child in the palm of God's hand.

The water which touched the sides of the Leonardo, she knew, would someday reach the shores of her homeland.

She could see Victor and Dino standing there at the rail beside her. Not yet grown, but so eager to become men, Rosa felt pride in her two young sons, in the way they reached out to life. She had not been able to deny them this, nor have they tried to deny her, her dream.

Holding tightly onto the railing she looked down into the water, into the white frothing furrow cut by the ship, and as the rays of the sun warmed her body, her spirit flew free.

Cleansed by the freshness of the sea air, held tight by the sounds of the ocean, she felt the excitement of her voyage. She untied her scarf, and removing the pins from her hair, raised her face to the sky.

She held her scarf out over the railing and watched the thin fabric whip in the breeze, dance about wildly, and she dared the wind to seize it.

"The sea breeze feels good this afternoon doesn't it?" A strong voice called to her.

The words pierced the stillness of her mood, and forgotten, her scarf was captured by the wind. Helpless, she watched the white foam engulf the fragile cloth.

"I did not mean to frighten you, Signora, I beg your forgiveness."

She looked around to see who spoke to her. She was alone on the deck.

"Here, Signora, up here."

She stepped back, and trying to see through the strands of hair blowing in her face, looked up at a man smiling at her from the upper deck.

He tipped his hat, and unlike the dark Italian men of her province, his skin was ruddy, his hair Amber Brown.

Tall and lithe, his well-tailored suit subtly revealed the power of his body.

"I am sorry for your lost scarf," he said, "it was my fault."

"No, it was silly of me to jump like that. I guess I was in deep thought."

"With hair as pretty as yours you should never cover it with a scarf," he replied, "you should let your hair blow free."

Her cheeks grew warm, but she did not control her hair nor turn her face away from the voice.

"Were you thinking of your destination or what you have left behind, Signora?"

"A little of both, I guess. But what I have left behind, it's behind." She spoke sadly, realizing for the first time the truth of these words.

"Are you homesick already?"

"Maybe I am, a little. I was thinking about what they would be doing right now, the people I left behind. It's a silly game I sometimes play, a 'what if' game."

As soon as the words left her mouth, Rosa was embarrassed to talk about her private game to a stranger.

"I see you are reading a book," he said.

"I am studying in English, I have forgotten much that I learned as a child. There has been no one to talk to and now I must study hard to regain my knowledge."

"Then, I must not take up anymore of your time. I shall go and let you get on with your English," he tipped his hat again.

Rosa watched him walk away, then placed her stool up against the wall under the overhang. She stretched her feet out in front of her to be warmed by the sun.

Knotting her hair on top of her head, she thought of him calling it too pretty to cover, and felt a sudden sense of excitement. She opened her English book, and stared at the page, but her mind did not register the words.

She listened to the sounds of people walking above her. She wished she had set her stool in the open where perhaps she might see him again, the man she had just spoken to, the man on the upper deck. The twins woke early the next morning and 1000 times asked their mother how soon the lunch bell would ring.

"Standstill while I button you up," Rosa said, "you look very pretty in your new dress."

"And you look handsome, Gio," she added.

"Mama, now that we are going to America, I want you to call me John Edward."

"I will try, Gio, I mean John. It will be hard for me to remember, but I will try."

When finally the bell for lunch rang, Rosa said, "Now, be good, be on your best behavior..." But they were already out the door, headed for heaven.

Stepping out into the corridor Rosa watched her two youngest disappear under the chained doors.

Rosa ate a small bit of bread with some cheese from her barely touched supply food, and putting her hair up as tightly as she could, went on deck.

The narrow space was crowded with people hungry for fresh air and peaceful seas. The storm clouds gone, the sun sparkled on the quiet blue water.

Rosa set up her stool in the forward section of the deck and opened her English book. But she could not keep her mind from running ahead, wondering what America was going to be like, nor could she keep her eyes from skimming the upper railing. The gentleman did not appear again.

Peppino, handsome in his white waiter's jacket, came by and stopped. "The children are having a great time with Signor Martinelli, you would be proud of them, Rosa. Gio is the perfect gentleman, and Angelina the little lady."

"I am glad they are behaving Peppino, and I'm sure I'll hear all about it when they return."

"Yes, you probably will," Peppino agreed.

The children ate many lunches with Signor Martinelli, while Rosa stayed away from the dining hall.

Her encounter with Jocko and the stories the children told of pickled herring and watery soup intensified her resolve to stay away. In the mornings the twins brought her a piece of bread from the dining room and often hot broth from the old man.

In the mornings Rosa drilled the twins in English, in the evenings they walked the deck for exercise. The children had many visits with Signor Martinelli while Rosa wrote long letters home. She dreamed of a better life in America. The days passed pleasantly.

"Tomorrow our voyage will be over," Peppino said to her. Tonight you must come to the dining hall, it is the best night on the ship. We have crossed the ocean safely, and it is time to celebrate. There will be music and dancing. You and I must have a dance."

"I will be there," Rosa said watching him walk away and wondering how she would have gotten away from Jocko without his help, or how she would have survived with seasickness.

The sure self-confident way he walked the deck reminded her of Victor, a little older perhaps but the same energy, the same sense of self. His tall thin frame, not yet filled out, his beard thin, in so many ways, he was more man than boy.

When Rosa arrived, the dining hall was already crowded. The row of serving tables with their huge iron pots were gone, and the floors cleared for dancing. Jocko was nowhere to be seen.

At the far edge of the clearing, Peppino and two sailors were on top of the table playing harmonicas. In front of them had gathered a group of people, clapping their hands and tapping their feet in rhythm with the music.

Peppino waved to Rosa, put his harmonica in his pocket, and hopped down off the table. "Shall we dance?" He reached his hand out to her.

Faces which Rosa had never seen before smiled at her. The furtiveness was gone, lost in the anticipation of a happy tomorrow.

People, crowded into the tiny space, danced their own dances, to their own remembered music. Peppino was more enthusiastic than graceful, but with him Rosa felt alive and happy. For a moment, she existed in a world free of care.

Even Angelina and John Edward danced, moving together with the awkward grace of beginners.

"May I have this dance, young lady?" Peppino said, extending his hand to Angelina. Rosa stood by the open door, watching as the young sailor bent down to dance with her daughter.

"Don't party too long," Rosa knew that voice!

"Tomorrow you will be sailing back to Genova, you whore."

His face close to hers, the sickening sour smell of stale rum, Jocko snarled, "They don't let women like you into America. You have nothing to celebrate." She wrenched backward, he grabbed her arm. "Don't run away from me... You bitch!

The room suddenly suffocating, the smell sickening. She pulled free and ran out of the room, footsteps behind her? Running blindly through the passageways, up the ladder, afraid to look back. Into the blackness of the cabin, she slammed the door shut.

Her body pressed against the door, palms wet with terror, heart pounding on her ears, running footsteps, don't breathe, then a knock.

"It's me Peppino, what happened?" Her hand over her mouth to stop the tears, her legs buckled under her.

Peppino closed the door swiftly behind him. "What happened?" Groping his way in the blackness of the tiny room, he found a candle and lit it.

"He says they won't let me in America!"

"Who said that?" Peppino put his arm around her.

"Jocko, he called me a whore and said I'd be going back to Italy with him," Rosa started shaking, "they don't let women like me into the country, he said." Shaking violently, she held tightly onto Peppino.

Easing her down onto the bed, he knelt in front of her, and holding both her hands said, "That bastard he is of the devil, that one!"

He pulled a blanket around her and for a long time stared silently into the flame.

"Tomorrow morning," he said, a new note of authority in his voice, "as soon as the sun rises, go on deck, to the starboard rail, to the spot where you boarded in Genova, and stand there. Get there first. Have the children with you."

"I will, first thing."

"You'll have to stand there for a long time, but don't move away, don't give up your place for anything, do you understand?"

"Yes, yes, I understand."

"Now listen to me the ship docks at Castle Garden on the tip of Manhattan Island. The first-class passengers disembark first, there's no inspection for them. The steerage passengers get off.

"You go into a big brown building at the side of the dock, that's for a health check, and when you're done, you come back out on the dock from the other side of the building. I'll be there to help you if I don't have to be in first-class.

"Keep the children close, and don't let anyone crowd in front of you. If anyone tries, stick them with one of your hat pins, anything, but keep your wits about you. When you go through that big building, the authorities only want to know if you have enough money, speak English, and are healthy.

"Is anyone meeting you?"

"Yes, Father O'Malley, is to meet us," Rosa said.

"Good, a priest won't be hard to spot."

"Thank you Peppino, I would not have survived without your help."

Rosa went to her satchel, "Here, I want to give you my aunt's address in San Francisco. When you decide to stay in America, maybe you will come to California. You will always have a friend there, eager to repay your kindnesses." Carefully folding the piece of paper and pushing it far down into the small front pocket in his pants, he said, "Now get some rest, tomorrow will be a long day. Maybe Jocko was just making idle threats, but still, it's best to be prepared. We'll get you out before he can raise a fuss. Goodbye, my friend," he kissed her lightly on the cheek.

Rosa held him very close for a moment, "Arrivederci, my friend, arrivederci."

"I will send the children down to you," he said as he left.

Rosa slept fretfully. When she dozed, she woke in panic, and ran to the door to check for the first light of dawn.

198

Finally knowing she could sleep no more, she lit a candle and dressed. When the first warning light was just beginning to make its way down into the darkness, she woke the children. While they dressed, she collected all their possessions. They finished the last of the oranges and bread and got to the deck before anyone else.

"Mama we promised we would say goodbye to our friend, the old man. Can we just run up top and tell him goodbye mama?" Angelina pleaded.

Rosa shook her head no.

"But, mama, we promised," Gio added his eyes pleading.

"Do not leave my side! You will just have to forget about saying goodbye to your friend. Do not move, do you understand?"

The children hung their heads and muttered, "Yes".

The sharpness of her voice surprised her. "It won't be too long," she said patting Gio's shoulder and running her hand gently over Angelina's black curls.

Time passed slowly. The sun rose and people lined up behind them as the boat inched closer to this giant new land. The early morning dim outlines of land gradually developed and buildings, topped with chimneys breathing smoke out into the air. The shore was lined with buildings fit together in accidental sizes and shapes and in back of them rose a spire as tall as the Apuane Alps of home.

Ships of all sizes passed them as they sailed a narrow course between pieces of land reaching out to them on either side. To the east, a river guarded by the single tower of a bridge, to the west the mouth of the Hudson river welcomed them.

Tugboat on each side guided the Leonardo past tiny Lowes Island and steered it toward the huge round Castle Garden building where she would find out if this was her new home or not.

The ship collided close to the dark, then shuddered and stopped as sailors scurry to secure the lines. A gangplank was lifted into position above them for the first-class passengers.

"Watch, Gio, I mean John Edward," Angelina instructed, "maybe we will see Signor Martinelli, and we can wave to him from here."

The first-class passengers dressed in their best, walked slowly off the ship, but among them the twins saw no Signor Martinelli. On the dock the first-class passengers roamed around freely, waiting for their luggage, or greeting friends who have come to meet them.

Rosa studied the faces in the crowd hoping to find the white clerical collar of a Father O'Malley. Instead, she saw Jocko standing near the big brown building talking to a man in a black uniform.

A sailor edged Rosa aside and slid the rail open, he hoisted the gangplank up from below and secured it into place.

Below, men in black uniforms were pulling sections of fence in toward the end of the gangplank, and soon they had outlined a narrow pathway to the big building on the far side of the dock where Jocko had been talking to the uniformed man.

The people behind them were pushing Rosa into the chain stretched in front of her across the railing. She braced herself and grabbed Angelina's hand, "Hold onto my skirt, John Edward," she ordered.

When the sailor unlocked the chains she and the children were pushed along, and moving so fast down the unsure steps of the gangplank, she had to fight to keep her balance.

On solid ground for the first time in 18 days, her legs unsteady, her head spun as if the ship were rocking beneath her. At the head of the column of anxious passengers, Rosa and the children were swept along toward the big building.

She was stretching up on tiptoes searching for Father O'Malley, when she felt a hand grab her arm. "Come with me, girly", a heavy voice ordered, "and hurry up about it."

Rosa tried to pull free. A sharp pain shot through her upper arm. She screamed. "Come along, girly, don't give me no trouble," the voice said. She looked up at the face. It was the man in the black uniform Jocko had been talking to.

He yanked at her roughly, she pulled back. "I'm not too happy about touching you, either, girlie." She heard her blouse ripping. Behind her, the children stood motionless in the midst of their belongings scattered on the ground. Their faces were covered with terror. She screamed back at them, "get help, find Peppino! Hurry, hurry!" Oh god! Fear burned in the pit of her stomach as she strained to watch the children. They scurried under the fences, past the guards.

The man tightened his grip. Again, she screamed. People watched, their faces expressionless. "Shut up, and come with me," his fingers digging deeper into her arm, he dragged her into the building.

John Edward and Angelina pushed their way through the crowd calling Peppino. In the distance, John Edward saw Signor Martinelli getting into a buggy. "Signor Martinelli, Signoa Martinelli," he yelled running as fast as he could.

"Help! Signor, help! Please help us!" Panting for breath, he shouted, "a man took my mama! Come, please hurry!"

Reaching up for his hand, Angelina fought back tears, "Please, Signor Martinelli," she cried, "he took mama, he wouldn't let go of her."

Signor Martinelli pulled his valises out of the buggy and motioned to the driver to go on with the other passengers. "Show me where they took her," he said.

CHAPTER FOURTEEN

"Quickly now, show me where they took your mother!" Signor Martinelli called to John Edward already yards ahead.

"There, in that big building," Angelina pointed as she hurried to catch up. The building was dark inside and crowded with black-garbed immigrants. Everywhere, tight-packed clusters of people waited anxiously for the uniformed men to tell them whether or not they could enter this new country. Rosa was nowhere in sight.

"There he is, that's the man, there he is!" John screamed.

"That's the man!" Angelina chimed in pointing across the room to a man standing in front of a glass pane door that had gold printing on it.

Signor Martinelli quickly covered the distance and towering over the uniformed man, confronted him, "Sir that lady..." And he realized he did not even know what she looked like, "that lady you pulled from the dock, what have you done with her?"

"In there," he tilted his head to indicate the room behind him.

"Medical examiners?" Martinelli read from the door. "Why was she detained?"

"We had a report she was diseased."

"Diseased? We'll just see about this!" Ordering the children to stay where they were, he pushed his way past the guard into the room.

"I am Signor Martinelli," he informed the tired little man sitting behind a cluttered desk. "I am here about the woman just brought in. I demand to know why she is being treated in this manner!"

"The woman? Which woman? We have lots of women here." Looking up from his desk, and taking off his round wireframe glasses, he studied the tall man standing before him.

"Signora Dante, the woman from the Leonardo, the one you just dragged in here."

With effort, the little man got up from his chair and came around to the front of his desk. There was a great weariness in his eyes. "We had a report that she was sick- you know, sick- he shrugged his shoulders, we can't let that kind in."

"Where did you get such a report?" Martinelli demanded.

"I don't know, I suppose it was one of the sailors, they're supposed to watch for that sort of thing."

"Well, I'm here to tell you there is nothing wrong with that young woman, I know the family, and I demand her immediate release."

"You do? You know the family?" Appraising Martinelli from head to toe he said, "Well, all right, wait right here, I will check." He disappeared behind the screen blocking the doorway to the adjoining room.

Martinelli looked around the bare room, the floor, worn gray linoleum, the furniture, two straight back chairs, and one cluttered desk. He looked out a tiny window, through glass roughed with salt spray, to the dock below where every day thousands of immigrants flocked to America.

The man returned and signaled Martinelli to the chair in front of his desk, "If you'll vouch for her you can have her."

He extended some papers, and pushing the glass inkwell across the desk, said, "Sign these forms, and you can take the woman with you." There was an odd smile on his face.

A woman in a wrinkled white uniform came out from behind the screen pulling Rosa beside her. "Go ahead, get out of here," she pushed Rosa forward into the room.

"There's no call for that!" Martinelli said, jumping up from his chair and taking Rosa's arm. "Let's get out of here."

Guiding Rosa to walk close behind him, Martinelli threaded his way around tight clusters of waiting people, and in and out of mounds of rope-tied bags and paper suitcases.

"Mama, mama," the children called out as they approached.

"Hurry up! Follow me," Signor Martinelli ordered, and hardly slowing down pace he swept up their belongings and propelled them away from the building.

Not until they reached the far side of the pier, did he permit them to stop.

Gasping for breath, Rosa leaned against a post. She studied the string sacks in her hands and somehow unknowingly picked up. She saw the two frightened children, and as if recognizing them for the first time, pulled them to her.

"It's all right, it's all right now," she comforted them. When reassured, she looked up at the man standing in front of them silently watching her awakening. "Signor", she said, "how can I thank you...?"

"Are you all right Signora Dante?"

"Mama, mama, this is Signor Martinelli..." John Edward said, and when Rosa did not react, Angelina added, "Mama, this is the man from the boat, he asked us to lunch."

"This is your old man?" Rosa asked, and repeated, "your old man from the boat?" Quickly bringing her hand to her mouth she tried too late to stop the words.

"So I am old, am I?" He scolded the children trying unsuccessfully to conceal his smile.

"This is our mama," Angelina blurted out, "she is not seasick anymore. See, she is better."

"I can see that she is," he said removing his hat. "Signora Dante, may I introduce myself, Signor Martinelli."

Studying her face, he added, "I believe we have already met. I am the one who made you lose your beautiful scarf. Signora, my apologies."

"Mama, don't you remember, Signor Martinelli sent you the soup?" Angelina said.

As she spoke, a weakness traveled down her body and into her legs, she felt herself sinking to the ground.

"Here, here," Signor Martinelli held her elbow to support her, "come, you must rest for a moment." He guided her to a wooden bench. "You have had a bad scare."

Rosa sat quietly trying to comprehend all that happened in the last few minutes. Her breathing was beginning to calm down when suddenly, in back of her, she heard the angry sound of a man's voice.

"Oh God! No!" She screamed, jumping up trying to run.

Martinelli caught her and demanded, "What is it, what is wrong?" He held her still.

"Jocko! Oh God! Not again..." when finally she made herself turn to look, the voice was not that of the two-finger sailor. Leaning on Martinelli's steadying hand, she sat down on the bench and little by little told him about Jocko.

"Unfortunate experience. You are a brave lady to travel alone with two small children, and I thank God for putting me there where I could be of some help to you."

Rosa smiled and silently promised the Madonna another rosary.

"Right now, I am going to take you and the children across to that little café to get us all some refreshment."

"No, thank you Signor, I am afraid I will miss Father O'Malley. He was going to be here and take us to the train station, but I don't see him. Have you seen any priests?"

"No, but in all the confusion, we may have missed him. Come, you have had a shock, and we all need something cool."

When Rosa hesitated he helped her up and said, "We will sit at the front where you can see everyone who walks by."

Martinelli guided them to a table near the large glass window, "What is your final destination, Signora?" He asked pulling out the round basket chair for her.

"California, San Francisco."

"I am also going to San Francisco."

Busy watching the window, Rosa said, "where could he be, is he to get us on our train."

"Now now, don't worry, we will find him, when does your train leave?"

"We left all those arrangements up to Father O'Malley," she said, and her heart sank as she realized for the first time that they could be stranded in this strange city in the strange country.

"We will find your priest," he said, "just as soon as you have something to drink. You won't miss him, he has to pass by here to get to the dock."

Martinelli spoke to the waiter who soon returned and placed four small glass dishes on the table in front of them. "On shipboard," he said, "John and Angelina told me they had never tasted ice cream, and I want to be the one to give them their first taste of ice cream in America."

"Thank you," she said, her eyes never leaving the outside scene. She tasted the sweet white cold, "this is nice."

"They're spoiled for life now," he said watching the children eat, "no other food to ever be as good as their first taste of ice cream."

"But I see how worried you are, stay here, John, and I will go and find your lost priest."

Rosa watched him walk out the door and take John's hand so he could keep up. There was something different about him, about the way he moved. He was not like the men she knew in Viareggio, there was a sense of authority about him, and also one of compassion. She knew why the children spent so much time with him on the boat.

Angelina had a white cream mustache on her upper lip, was busy scraping the inside of her dish for any last drops of sweetness when she said, "here he is, mama", and climbing up onto her chair, "he has a priest with him!"

Still holding John's hand, Martinelli walked briskly toward them followed by a balding respectable pear-shaped priest. Black cassock billowing behind him, the red face cleric tried to keep up.

"Oh, Signora Dante! Praise God! I looked all over for you. I arrived late and couldn't get through the crowd. I am so sorry, Signora to hear of the trouble you had. Those immigration men can be tough. Praise be that Signor Martinelli was here to help you!

"Oh, I hope you weren't hurt, were you?"

" Nothing a needle and thread can't fix," she said. "Father O'Malley, may I present my children, Angelina and G... I mean John Edward."

"Oh yes, Father Michael wrote that you had a handsome pair with you, and he was right," he shook hands with each child.

"I have a carriage waiting. You and the children will stay at the church house tonight and in the morning I will put you on your train to California."

He turned to Signor Martinelli, "Sir, may I be of help to you? Are you traveling on further?"

"I am also going to California. I'll spend the night at a hotel and leave in the morning also."

"Then you must come with us and stay at Saint Patrick's church house, New York's newest and finest. You must let me repay you for your kindness to Signora Dante and the children. And in the morning, I will take you all to the train station."

"That is most kind of you, Father, that would be far nicer than a lonely hotel."

"Good! Then that is settled. Let us go then, and tonight you will have the special meal we prepare travelers coming from Europe."

His eyes twinkle and he smiled, "We will have a delicacy of the sea, pickled herring with boiled potatoes." His hands resting on his belly he laughed and added, "and fish soup!"

"Oh Father, how could you be so cruel?" Rosa looked up at Martinelli who smiled back at her.

"No, no, I am only teasing," Father O'Malley said, "I know what they feed you on those ships. I have made the voyage myself, I know about the food."

"I am disappointed Father, Signor Martinelli said, I was looking forward to fish soup, weren't you, Signora?"

"No, I'm afraid not, Signor. On shipboard, I was spoiled by delicious chicken soup sent to me by a gentleman."

Taking Rosa's arm, Father O'Malley helped her up into the open buggy. "That boat ride is why there are so many people in America, no one wants to take that voyage again back across the ocean! Do not fear, Signora, you should have a good, substantial meal, and if you like, freshwater for a bath."

A warm bath and a clean bed to sleep in! Rosa looked down at herself. Her sleeve torn, her dress wrinkled, suddenly self-conscious in front of Signor Martinelli, she wondered, would she ever look pretty again?

Father O'Malley snapped the rains to wake up the old black gelding, and said, "Now I shall show you the sights of New York City…"

New York? New York is halfway around the world! A lightning bolt of excitement passed through her veins.

209

Am I really here? She squeezed the leather wall of the carriage. Tears of gratitude welled in her eyes. Yes, I am truly here, I am truly in America!

She became aware that Father O'Malley was speaking to her, "… Jenny Lind, you have heard of her, surely, The Swedish Nightingale? Well, yes, she sang in that very building they now use for the immigration service."

Rescuing her again, Signor Martinelli said, "Yes, of course, my father heard her sing once in Florence. He never forgot her. He told us about her 1000 times."

The open buggy took them through the busy streets, and Father O'Malley had something to say about each building. Not even the noise from the horse's hooves or the iron wheels of passing wagons could drown him out.

They traveled down Broadway and into Fifth Avenue, passing horse-drawn jitneys and streetcars pulled by long-tracked horses. Men in suits and top hats walked briskly about.

There were more people on this one street than in the whole village. All of the sudden thrill filled her as she looked at the twins. One seated on each side of Signor Martinelli, their eyes wide.

She knew that with the taste of ice cream still in their mouths, they would never forget this day. Yes, they were truly in America.

"Let me know," Signor Martinelli was saying, "when we can see Wall Street. It is famous all over the world."

"Right here, here is the stock exchange, and there is the treasury building," Father O'Malley pulled the horses to a slow walk. "Do you see that spire at the end of the street there? That is Trinity Church. Flashy, but adequate, I suppose for a protestant church, but wait until you see St. Patrick's! Now there is a church."

"I have heard it proclaimed in Europe," Martinelli said, "that as long as you can see the Trinity steeple, you can't get lost in New York. Is that right Father?"

Suddenly becoming very busy guiding the horse around a parked handsome cab, Father O'Malley grunted. Martinelli grinned at Rosa then went on, "but I have also heard that for sheer magnificence, Saint Patrick's cathedral rivals any we have in Europe."

Deciding that the horse could guide himself after all, Father O'Malley turned his attention to Signor Martinelli, "Oh, sir, you just wait and see, and when we get the two spires in the front finished, it will be unbelievable."

The children twisted and turned in their seats, trying to see everything at once. "Look, mama, a castle right in the middle of the city!" John Edward pointed to a huge gray granite wall as tall as three houses and stretching as far as the next street.

Father O'Malley laughed, "That's not a fort, my little man, those ivy-covered walls hold all of New York's water, and on Sunday afternoons ladies and gentlemen stroll around up there on the top."

The buggy made its way through the traffic up Fifth Avenue. "And there," he pointed to many windows in a long gray wooden building on his right, "that is Grand Central Station where you shall get your train in the morning."

"So many people", Angelina said, and John Edward added, "and so many horses! Paisano would…" And then remembering, he glanced quickly up at his mother and fell silent.

"It's all right, Rosa patted his head, we all remember Paisano, but that was the past, we must think of this now, of the future."

211

Father O'Malley slowed the horse, "there it is," he said reverently, ahead was a massive granite cathedral filling an entire block and drawing all around it.

Not since Saint Martin's in Lucca had Rosa seen anything so grand, so impressive.

Father O'Malley steered the buggy slowly past the broad front steps and rounded the corner. Walking the horse to the far end of the block, he stopped at the rectory. "Before we go in the house, we must take you inside our beautiful Cathedral. If you like, you may say a prayer of thanks for your safe journey to America."

Rosa stepped back to the edge of the street to look up at the gigantic rose window below the steep central cable. At either side of the granite facade towers topped by wooden scaffolding reached up toward heaven.

Martinelli said, "The hotel business has taken me all over Europe, and I have seen most of the great cathedrals. And this is a beautiful example of the Gothic revival. It's not unlike the cathedrals of Rheims and Cologne."

Struggling to open the heavy car doors, the priest said, "Like the other new arrivals in the country, you expected teepees and Cowboys?"

"Father, forgive me. I am afraid you are right. This is certainly magnificent."

Inside, Rosa was overwhelmed with the cathedrals power and beauty. The sounds of her own footsteps moving slowly down the marble made her feel small and safe in the arms of a mighty deity.

Kneeling at the altar rail, she felt a sense of peace and yet of excitement. Thank you, dear God, and my beloved Madonna, for bringing us safely across the ocean. She lit a candle. Please, God, watch over those I left behind. Take care of Victor and Dino, and protect them from the sea.

Leaving the church, Signor Martinelli asked, "Will we be able to attend mass here in the morning before we leave?"

"Oh, yes," Rosa added, "and could we receive holy communion here at the Cathedral too?"

"Of course. I'll be saying the 6 o'clock mass, and confessions are heard before that. Afterward, we will have a light breakfast and I'll see you arrive on time at Grand Central."

He walked them out the side entrance to the church house and into a small parlor. "Would you like some coffee or wine before you go up?" He asked.

"That would be fine," Signor Martinelli replied.

"If I would not be considered rude, Father," Rosa interrupted, "you mentioned bath. I would gladly eat the pickled herring and greasy soup if the children and I could go to our room and have a bath and a rest."

"Yes, of course, but now remember, you promised you would eat the herring if you could have your bath." He turned to the children, "and do your children think this is a good bargain?" Angelina giggled.

" Well," John Edward said, "I'd skip the bath if mama would let me, but I know she won't."

"They'll be no skipping of baths, young man," Rosa said.

A woman in a long black dress and white stretched apron, her hair graying slightly, came into the room.

"Ahh, and here's our Molly O'Brien. She runs St. Patrick's Cathedral, and without her, there'd be no one around to say mass. You can see that she feeds us well," Father O'Malley patted his round belly. "She sees that we get up on time, she's our nursemaid, our cook, our doctor, our everything. Molly can do anything."

Her large blue eyes smiled and her ruddy Irish cheeks turned more red. "Now Father, you make me blush with your blarney", she folded her hands in front of her and looked down to study the tips of her shoes.

"It is rumored in New York," he continued, his head cocked to one side looking at her, "that we will not allow her to travel alone away from St. Patrick's because other parish priests look around corners waiting to steal her from us. If the truth be known, Molly is St. Patrick's. We love our beautiful cathedral, but if Molly would leave us, we would follow her."

"Oh, Father, such stories you tell," Molly brushed a lot of her graying auburn hair from her face and tried not to smile.

"If you need anything, Signora, Molly will see that you get it." Gathering children and parcels, the two women left the room.

Rosa followed Molly down a long narrow hallway of shiny hardwood floors and walnut wainscoting. "Dinner will be at 7 o'clock," she said, "and I promise, no pickled herring. I know Father's jokes. He is a saint among men, but he will have his jokes."

She opened the door into a large sunny room, "You can have your bath, and I'll bring cookies and milk and you can have a nice rest until dinner." Molly took them across the hall to the white tile bathroom. Hot water ran into the tub until ribbons of steam floated up from the water. "And here", Molly said, "some sweet-smelling soap, it will help get the salt out of your skin."

"If you give me that torn blouse, I'll see to it it gets mended." Not waiting for an answer, she helped Rosa slip it off. "You are very kind," Rosa said.

"Mama, look," John shouted, as he pulled the brass chain releasing a flash of water to the ball below. And Angelina, head bowed low, watched the water disappear.

"There are many miracles in America. Now you don't have to go out on a frosty night to relieve yourself, young man."

"I will call you when dinner is ready. Enjoy your bath," Molly said, wiping off the sink with the hem of her apron, as she left the room.

Rosa washed the twins, and in the soapstone, basin scrubbed their hair,

"Mama, one more washing, I will not have a curl left," Angelina complained. Washed and scrubbed, the children sat on their beds and drank the milk and cookies that awaited their return.

Their eyes soon grew heavy. "Have a little nap," she said, kneeling down to kiss them and tucked them in. When she stood, her head swayed to the lingering role of the ocean, and her sea legs tossed her about.

Steadying herself by the iron bedstead, she studied the reproduction of a large oil painting of Saint Patrick chasing snakes out of Ireland. Above each of the four tidy little white beds, hung a crucifix. Why was Christ always portrayed as dead or suffering? She turned away, toward the two narrow windows looking out on New York's Fifth Avenue.

215

CHAPTER FIFTEEN

"Quite a woman, isn't she?" Father O'Malley refilled Martinelli's wine glass and helped himself to another of Molly's cakes. "Yes sir, she's brave to take two little children all by herself across the ocean, and then to have all that ruckus this morning! Darn shame, but praise be to the Lord you were there to help her."

"Yes, my carriage was just about to pull away when the little boy ran at me yelling for help. I couldn't imagine what had happened."

"And now she still has to cross this huge country of ours, and by herself, too!"

"Well, Father, I intend to see that she is not entirely alone. I will look out for them. I think too much of those two little ones to let anything happen to them."

"And Signora Dante?" Father O'Malley watched the young man's face. "Do you know much about her or her family?"

"Nothing, really. I only met her this morning on the dock. But I knew the children, of course. When they sneaked up to get a glimpse of 'heaven', I liked them immediately.

"They came every day, and I helped them with English. They learned quickly, and their mother had already taught them quite a bit."

"Very polite youngsters, too," Father O'Malley agreed while signaling Molly for another bottle of wine.

"They don't know much about age. From what they told her about me, she seemed to think I'd have a long white beard and hobble around on a cane."

"I looked forward to seeing them each day, they helped fill the time on a lonely voyage. They were so eager to learn, and their enthusiasm was catching.

"It's great to look through a child I, it makes life seem simple again."

"You are a man for whom life is no longer simple?"

"Yes, I'm afraid so, Father. I have taken time off from the family's hotel business to go to San Francisco to help my brother who is ill."

Martinelli walked to the window, and after a long silence, he went on, "Yes, for a long time I have been feeling torn in two by the obligations I feel to my family."

"Would you like to tell me about it, my son?"

"Yes, Father, I think that might help." Martinelli took out a cigar and offered one to Father O'Malley. When he had lighted them, he sat down again in the leather chair facing the priest.

"Well, you see, Father, my family owns a beautiful hotel in Torino. Actually, my grandfather gave it to my father to get him out of town, because he had married an Austrian girl, my mother."

"Your grandfather did not accept your mother?"

"No, well, actually the story goes back a ways. You see, my father joined a group of scholars to fight for the rebirth of Italy. He was a young free spirit, and they all wanted to restore Italy to the splendor of Dante, and the Renaissance. And of course, they hated the Austrians."

"Yes, in youth we all tend to be idealists, even priests, I was going to wipe out sin…yes we all have dreams."

"I'm afraid my grandfather did not consider Papa's dreams at all. Papa fell in love with an Austrian girl, and when he married her, grandfather was furious, so were the fighting scholars, they asked him to leave, no one wanted anything to do with Papa after that."

"A sad thing for a family to be torn apart," Father O'Malley said offering more wine.

"My mother was beautiful, small, gentle, poetic. She was fair, with blonde hair and blue eyes. I can easily understand why he married her.

"She was a woman of spirit. But she died when I was twelve, and papa never got over her.

"In many ways Rosa, I mean Signora Dante, has her same qualities. I think my mother would have liked her. In fact, I think my grandfather would have liked her too. But he was furious with Papa for marrying an Austrian.

"Being a wealthy landowner with property in Torino and the Piemont areas, he had vineyards and hotels, he was used to having his own way. After the marriage, it got so he couldn't stand to have Papa around him. So he gave him the hotel and a large block of land in Torino, sent him and my mother on their way."

"Great wealth bestows many options on one, doesn't it?"

"Yes, but when they moved to Torino, it wasn't that much. Papa and mama worked very hard for many years, and they always worked together. My mother supervised the kitchen, and with a blend of Austrian and Italian cooking, she made it famous.

"Papa died when I was 15 and now my oldest brother, Dominic, and I run the hotel. Enrico, the brother I am coming to see, had a falling out with our brother Giuseppe, and then on top of that he was involved in a tragic secret love affair, he sailed for America. He said there was nothing left for him in Italy.

"Enrico is a handsome man, the ladies were always chasing him, and still, to this day he is a bachelor. He is a talented artist, a painter. But he also knows he would starve on art alone, so he bought a hotel in Berkeley. I understand it's a little town not far from San Francisco.

"However, his real love is painting, he is really very good."

Martinelli's expression turned grim and he looked out the window. "He has been very ill, I am afraid it is consumption, and he has no one to help him. I had to come, his letter sounded so desperate. It is hard, sometimes, for a man to know where his responsibilities lie."

"But enough of that, tell me, Father, what is your connection to Signora Dante?"

"A fellow priest in Viareggio took a special interest in her. He asked me to take care of her and see that she gets on the train. He tells me she's had tragedy enough in her life to defeat a lesser soul."

Speaking quietly, his voice steady, Martinelli said, "God works in mysterious ways, doesn't he, Father?"

"Yes, my son and all he asked of us is faith."

Molly came in and bustled about, checking to see if there were enough cookies and adjusting the window shades.

"Thank you, thank you, Molly," Father O'Malley tried to hurry her along.

"We are fine, we have everything we need."

"Well praise be, Father, it's for sure that poor woman up there and those two lovely children have hardly had a decent meal since they left home. I'm looking to pack them a nice basket for the train, providing, of course, that's all right with you."

"Now now, Molly, don't have your feelings hurt, of course, pack her a nice basket, put in plenty, they will have many days on the train."

"Were you able to purchase tickets in the Pullman car for them, so that they will be able to rest at night?"

"No, I'm afraid not. There was just enough money to put them in coach. At least they won't be in the immigrant car and have to sleep on board stretched across seats at night. Do you know that those awful boards cost $.50 extra? At least, and coach they get more comfortable seats with cushions."

"Sounds almost like sleeping on a table, that's a great way to travel, especially with children."

"If Signora was in Pullman, they would have a more pleasant journey."

He finished his wine and took three pieces of folded money from his wallet, "Here, Father, I want their tickets changed so they'll have sleeping accommodations."

"That is very generous of you sir, but I don't know..."

"Nonsense, take it, it is a little money to me. And be sure that she does not know of this. She is very proud and would not accept it."

"You are a kind man, Signore, I will see what I can do, and I promise not to tell her. I will send someone down there right now, this afternoon, so that all will be arranged when we get to the station in the morning."

"Wait a moment," Martinelli said taking his tickets from his inside breast pocket. "Tell your messenger to get them a car near mine. That way I'll be able to look in on them from time to time."

Signor Martinelli stuffed his cigar out, and said, "Thank you, Father, now neither of us has to worry about Signora or the children."

The two men shook hands. "I am growing weary and would like to rest in bed before dinner."

CHAPTER SIXTEEN

Her naked body slid into the warm soothing water. With the sweet-scented soap Molly had given her, Rosa caressed her body, caressed the womanly body so neglected.

Sinking into the warm water, Rosa touched the skin of her face and her throat. Her hands fell across her breast and came to rest at the nipple.

Clean, and warm, and feeling like a woman, she breathed deeply and stretched out until her toes and fingertips tingled. Reluctantly she climbed from the tub.

The stark white tile stung her bare feet with its cold, and through her body sent a wave of excitement, a feeling of being alive.

Naked before the mirror, she admired the slender lines of the woman who looked back at her. Her skin tight, her body firm, "Yes, Rosa," she whispered to the naked image, "out of all the pain in the tears, out of the tragic ashes of your life, there survives a woman anxious to live!"

Running her hands down the length of her body, and turning to the side, she admired her youthfulness. She sprinkled lilac powder onto her shoulders and gently spread the smoothing balm over the softness of her skin. Sitting on the edge of the tub, bending down to reach her toes, she languorously spread the sweet scent over her legs. Turning from the mirror, and covering her nakedness with a robe, she crossed the hall to the bedroom.

The twins were sleeping soundly. When she had brushed her hair she lay down on the bed, pulled the cloud-soft sheets up close around her face, and feasted on their clean, sun-dried sent. Her head sinking into the soft down pillow, she felt safe and warm. Her eyes closed, she gave herself to the gentle rolling of the ocean.

Her hands resting in the crevice of her breasts, she held the St. Francis metal, until the thought of the crucifix above her bed invaded her thoughts. She drew her hands back into the prayer position and studied the image of Christ on the cross. God is always watching. Closing her eyes she started to recite the rosary she had promised, but in a short while, sleep overcame her.

"Rosa, Rosa. Molly was shaking her, it's six-thirty, supper is at 7 o'clock." Rousing the children, she said, "We don't like to let Father get hungry. It's the only time he loses his sense of humor."

She raised the paper shades from the windows and let in the last of the spring daylight. "I found a blouse for you to wear to dinner. See if it fits." Rosa held the white blouse up in front of her, "Oh Molly, it's perfect, it's lovely. You are very kind."

Looking embarrassed, Molly answered gruffly, "I'm working on yours, but it's a nasty tear, I'm not sure what I can do with it."

Rosa brushed Angelina's hair and winding long strands around her fingers formed drop curls to bounce on the child's shoulder. She helped John Edward with the collar button of the shirt. "You both look handsome in your new clothes," she said and wondered what Eduardo would think if he could see them now.

Rosa slipped into the delicate blouse, long full sleeves tapered to narrow cups of eyelet lace that matched the high neck and yoke.

223

She twisted her hair up the back of her neck to form a crown of curls. At last glance in the mirror, she pinched her cheeks.

"Oh how beautiful you look, mama," Angelina said and John Edward nodded in agreement. "Thank you, my admirers. Are we ready," she asked, "to go to our first meal in America?"

Rosa could hear the men talking as she and the children approached the parlor. When she entered, they stopped their conversation mid sentence and stood in silence.

"Oh, our lady approaches," Signor Martinelli said, bowing low.

"Good evening," she managed, hoping they would not see how surprised and flustered she was.

"Is this the same lady I met this morning? No, it cannot be," Martinelli said, winking at Angelina, "maybe we left her on the dock."

"No, no, Signor Martinelli, this is mama, really," John Edward insisted.

"Are you sure?" Martinelli asked the children, and to Rosa said, "and you do look lovely."

"Ah, good," Father O'Malley stood up and rubbed his hands together, "now we can go into dinner." Crooking one arm out for Angelina and the other for John Edward, he led the way into the dining room, a smiling child at each side. Rosa followed, holding Signor Martinelli's arm.

"The other priests are all out doing church work this evening, so tonight we can eat in the little dining room," Father O'Malley said.

"Actually I prefer a small room, it makes for a better conversation."

He directed the children to their seats at the round table. In the center of a white cloth, three slender candles burn, their golden flames dancing on the dark wood-paneled walls.

Father O'Malley bowed his head, "Let us pray: dear father in heaven, grant us this night our salvation. Please guide these children safely on their journey and stand by them that they may follow in your footsteps. Bless the food we eat. In the name of the Father, and of the Son, and of the Holy Ghost. Amen."

Molly brought in covered dishes of tender meat, fresh vegetables, and potatoes, fruits, and cheese. In front of Rosa, she set a large bowl of tossed Green salad. "Here, my dear, I know this is a dish you got none of on that boat, right?"

"See, I told you Molly was a wonder," Father O'Malley said pouring the wine. "Let us toast America with American wine, and may God bless us all."

Signor Martinelli reached his glass out. "Let us also drink to these to fine young people, and to you, Signora Dante." Their eyes met and for a moment Rosa was aware of the stirring deep within herself. Studying the red liquid in her class, she said, "Thank you, Signor Martinelli."

"Signora, I would be pleased if you would call me Aldo, Signor Martinelli is so formal."

"If you will call me Rosa."

"There now," Father O'Malley said, "that's settled as it should be, we are all the children of God. Now tomorrow, Rosa, your train is due to leave at 11:00 AM. But you can never be sure. Train schedules are erratic. The trains seem to operate on their own divine time schedules."

He looked at Angelina and John, "When the train stops at the station, you must pay attention not to wander away too far or you may be left out in the wilderness."

"Yes, the timetables, the subject of many jokes in New York. One such story going around is about a man traveling on the train to Albany. The train was due there at 4:00 AM. And knowing that his watch would be of no value to him, he told the porter to be sure to put him off the train at Albany. He insisted the porter put him off even if he was still in his nightshirt.

"The next morning they were well past Albany," Father O'Malley continued, "when the man woke up, he jumped down out of his berth and started screaming at the porter for letting him miss his stop. When he finally stopped screaming, one of the passengers said to the porter, 'that man is certainly upset' and the porter replied 'not half as upset as a man I put off in Albany'."

They all laughed except John who looked quizzically at Father O'Malley, "Out in the middle of the road with his nightshirt on?" Finally realizing it was a joke, he hit his face and giggled.

Warming up to his audience, Father O'Malley entertained them through the rest of the meal with tales of travelers. Rosa tried to be attentive, to listen to the advice she knew was cloaked in his story, but her thoughts kept drifting. She sipped her wine, and over the edge of the glass glanced at the man sitting across from her. What kind of man was he? Why had he come into her life?

"I am looking forward to our train ride, tomorrow," Aldo said as Father O'Malley paused to eat, "we will see mountains and rivers and valleys of this giant country, and we will travel many times the length of Italy."

You will also see some of the city of Chicago when you change trains. It should be your only change, but then you can never

226

know. It's a good idea to make friends with your porter," he looked directly at John Edward, "then at least, if they put you off in the middle of the road in your nightshirt, you'll have someone to wave goodbye to," he reached over and patted John on the head.

When their laughter died down, Rosa said, "I would like to have some fresh fruit to take with us. This afternoon there was a fruit wagon at the corner, will he be there tomorrow before we leave?"

"Yes, my dear, he is there every day. But there is no need to worry about food for the trip. The train stops many times a day, and quite often you can buy food at the station from townspeople. Box lunches, I have heard, sell for about .40 cents, .50 cents for dinner."

"Yes, and the dining car is said to serve excellent meals," Aldo said. "Yes, excellent, they say, but…"

Father O'Malley rubbed his thumb and index finger together as a feeling a dollar bill, and said, "Very expensive, too."

"One of my priests just returned, and he reported that now there are also a few stops patterned after the 'Harvey houses' on the southern route."

"What is a Harvey house?" John asked.

"It's a restaurant at the station that knows when trains are due so they prepare the meals ahead of time. He said that in no more than twenty-five minutes they had served a whole train full of people. They all eat the same food, of course, but he thought it tasty enough, and not too expensive."

"Oh, mama, can we eat in a Harvey house?" Angelina asked.

"I want to eat in the dining car," John announced.

"We'll see," Rosa answered.

Father O'Malley smiled at the children, and continued, "Molly will fix you a big bag with fruit and bread and cheese for your lunches. Don't worry, she'll see there's enough to last."

"Thank you Father, I don't know how I can ever thank you for taking such good care of us," and, to Martinelli, she said, "without your help, I would not be here, Signore, I mean, Aldo. But now the hour is late and the children are restless, and we must prepare for the long journey that lies ahead of us," she folded her napkin on her lap. "May I please excuse myself?"

Both men stood and Father O'Malley said, "Aldo and I will also retire soon, but I promised him a taste of authentic Irish whiskey."

"And," Aldo said, "I promise to fill him in on the current politics of Italy."

"If you get started on the papal argument between the Irish and the Italians, you'll end up to the wee hours of the morning," Rosa teased.

"I promise to stop talking when it is time to say my 6 o'clock mass."

Aldo stepped forward and kissed her hand. She blushed, no one had ever done that before. He did not see her reddened cheeks, for that moment, he bent down and kissed Angelina's hand. "Sweet dreams, little princess," he said and shook John's hand.

Molly knocked on the door and peeked into the room. "It's time to get up, Rosa." She said quietly.

"Come in, Molly, we are up." She set down two net sacks on Rosa's bed, "I fixed some food for your trip, fresh fruit and bread and a few little treats for the children. Father told me that you lost everything in the fire, she said taking a bundle from under her arm. We always keep a bit of spare clothing in the church cupboards, and I found a few things for the children."

"Here's a nice linen dress for Angelina, and look, it's got smocking across the front, and here's a pair of long white socks to go with it."

Angelina rushed over to examine her new clothes.

"I think it will fit, Molly said, but, if not, you're probably good with a needle. And for John Edward, I found this pair of short-walk blue pants and a jacket that matches." John Edward glanced casually at the clothes and then turned his attention back to the scene outside the window.

"And you, Rosa, you must keep the white blouse. You looked beautiful in it last night. It should be yours, no one else would look so lovely in it. And here's a bit of Irish lace to wear on your head when you go to holy mass."

"Oh Molly, I shall treasure this always, my scarf blew overboard." Rosa kissed Molly lightly on the cheek. "You have been more than kind to me. When we arrive in California, I'll send you a letter to let you know about the trip."

"I hear it's a hard journey. My two sons went a few years ago in immigrant class. Their letters didn't say much, and you know they never tell their mamas the worst. From what they didn't say, I'm afraid it must've been a hard trip."

"You know that San Francisco is not yet as civilized as New York," Father O'Malley said trying to maneuver the buggy through Fifth Avenues morning congestion. He pointed northward for them to admire the Vanderbilt houses in back of them as they passed, he identified the palatial homes of the Astor's and the Stewart's.

Unconcealed pride, he spoke in a spirit of sharing the goodness of his country with the newcomers. When they reached Grand Central Station, Father O'Malley lifted down the two string sacks his housekeeper had prepared. "You must have made an impression on Molly, that is a good supply of food in there. But then you Italians always make our Irish hearts melt."

"She is very kind, I can see why St. Patrick's loves her," Rosa followed the priest through the crowd. "Here's your train my friends, I have enjoyed our visit, short as it was. Godspeed to you all."

"Thank you for your kindness, Father, Rosa," said stepping back while each of the children came forward to say goodbye to the priest.

"Here is something from Father Michael to you," she handed him a bottle of rum, "and he said to tell you that you do not have to share it with God."

"Ah, such a great delight," he held the bottle out at arm's length to admire it. "Father Michael resembles my weakness. And it is well known my God doesn't like to drink, he's not an Irishman!"

"Father," Rosa said, "I have written two letters, and could you post them for me? I think I have enough money here for stamps, one is to Italy, telling them I arrived safely, and the other is to my aunt in California to tell her when to expect us."

"Would you do the same for me?" Aldo reached into his pocket, "it's a short note to my wife telling her I arrived safely."

Wife? Rosa felt a smile leave her face, she was deaf and with the pounding in her ears, and for a moment, her heart seemed to stop. Forcing the smile back on her lips, she tried to compose herself.

"What is the matter, Rosa?" Father O'Malley asked. "Suddenly you are pale, are you worried about the train trip?"

"Perhaps a little, a little anxious, perhaps," she prayed her eyes did not betray her true feelings.

Busy looking at the train tickets, Aldo said, "Don't be frightened, I will be two cars down from you, I will find you after we get settled, or better yet, Angelina and John, you find me. I bet it will be easier than on the ship."

The black-skinned porter carried their parcels on board, and when Aldo handed him a piece of folded money, he smiled broadly and helped Rosa and the children to their seats.

Out the window, Rosa saw the plump little priest waiting on the platform, while ribbons of steam escaping from the engine coiled around his feet.

His lips moved but the noises from the train were too loud for her to hear. Finally, he held up his bottle of rum and patted it, Rosa knew what he was saying.

The children pressed their noses up against the windows and watched as the engine pulled them slowly out of Grand Central. When the last of the huge glass ceiling station was left behind them, they jumped down out of their seats inside, "Now can we go find Mr. Martinelli, mama?"

"No, let him get settled. But you may look around our car if you like. We will see Signor Martinelli later."

Yes, we will see him later, and now that you know he has a wife, Rosa, you must rid yourself of foolish thoughts of him.

She turned her attention to the city buildings of New York speeding past her, and the noise and the bouncing of the train locked her into herself. Storybook images read about at the convent came alive.

Lost in the spell of realizing her lifelong dream, she was really here, here in the once far away land of America. And every turn of the

231

wheel, she reminded herself, was taking her closer to her mama Nina.

"Mama, we found the washrooms," Angelina said jolting Rosa from her thoughts. "Down here, at this end, it's the ladies, and that's for us, mama." She giggled. "And at the other end of the car is men. That's for Gio, I mean John." She looked at her brother, "I'm glad I don't have to change my name. It's such a bother."

"And, mama, the car in front of us has bare wooden seats, those poor people don't have nice red cushions like we have," John bounced up and down on the cushion seat. "And Signor Martinelli is two cars behind us. We didn't bother him, really, mama. The door was open and we just sort of stood in the doorway, and Signor Martinelli was visiting with the Porter," John explained, "and he invited us in. The Porter was real nice to us, too, he gave us each a piece of candy. Signor Martinelli took us in to see his seat. Mama, he has a little room that's all his own."

"The Porter said Signor Martinelli was in a compartment, that's what it's called, a compartment," Rosa explained. "But I am displeased that you left this car when I told you not to."

"Yes, mama, we are sorry, really we are."

That evening Rosa took bread and cheese from her string sack and laid it out on her lap. "When the train stops, we will get a cool drink," she told the children. A voice behind her said, "Would sharing a bottle of wine, be enticement enough to get an old man invited to your picnic?"

Aldo held a bottle high in the air.

"Just what's needed to make our picnic perfect," Rosa cleared a space for him to sit down.

The children told, in great detail, all their explorations, until finally John said, "I met a boy, his name is Joseph, in the best car, he has a sister too- can we go play with them, mama?"

Permission given to the children to leave, Aldo moved to the seat facing Rosa. Lacing his fingers behind his head, he said smiling, "You have raised two fine children. Tell me Rosa, what is it that brings you to America?"

Rosa sipped her wine and leaned back in her seat. "Coming to America has been my dream since I was five years old."

"Father O'Malley told me your mother died and you were raised in a convent in Lucca, is that correct? How was it at the convent?"

"My most vivid recollection is being cold, and always hungry, and I remember the scratchy wool jumpers we wore. The nuns were very strict, the only time you dare smile was when they weren't looking."

"I remember once – I must've been eight or nine," Rosa's eyes sparkled, "we were in chapel for evening prayers when two tiny little mice ran across the altar. They stopped smack in front of the tabernacle, stood up on their hind legs, and looked right straight out at us."

"Francesca was sitting next to me and she whispered that they looked like they were getting ready to give a sermon! Well, that got me started, and I couldn't stop laughing.

"The nuns didn't see the mice, of course, because their heads were bowed, and Francesca and I couldn't stop giggling. No matter how hard I tried, I even pinched myself, but I couldn't stop laughing.

"At first Sister Lucia gave us stern looks, but that only made us laugh more. Finally, she got up and dragged us out of the chapel by our hair! And for the next week, we had to eat our meals kneeling.

Sometimes, even now, when I look at an altar, I still see those mice and laugh. I think I envied their freedom.

"Since I was left at the convent I dreamed of coming to America, but never imagined it would take me this long to get here."

"Your father was dead, too, Rosa?"

"No, but after my mother died, he was so grief stricken that he went off to fight against the Austrians. He never returned."

"Fought the Austrians, eh? So did my father, and he did return. He returned with an Austrian wife, my mother, but that is a different story. Please go on, Rosa."

"I don't think I ever really got over knowing that my father went away and never came back again to see me." Rosa was surprised at her own words.

And as if someone else were doing the speaking, she heard herself telling Aldo about her life even the things she had tried so long to forget.

She told him about Father Joseph, about mama Dante and her bread, and about Giovanni and their two sons, and she told him about Eduardo, and the fire, and how her two sons would not leave Italy, and how it broke her heart to leave them.

Afraid she had been talking too long, Rosa became quiet. When Aldo encouraged her to continue, she said, "And now, at last, I am going to see my mama Nina! I just hope I have not made a terrible mistake in leaving Italy."

"You did the right thing," he said, "one must be able to recognize when the world has dried up. But I know how difficult it must have been for you to leave," With his arms resting on his knees, hands folded together, he leaned close to her and said, "you are brave,

I admire that in you. You have made the right choice. Here, in America, there are many opportunities."

Without warning, tears poured down Rosa's face. "What is wrong, have I said something to hurt you?"

"No, no, you haven't. It's just that you are the first person who ever told me I made the right decision. All I heard before was that a woman with two little children couldn't pack up and go to America. They said I shouldn't leave, that I was crazy, on and on the village people went. My friend Maria, the priest, everyone, thought I was wrong."

"Aldo you are the first person to say that what I did was brave, or even that it was right, you have given me strength and hope. I thank you."

Her eyes still misty from her tears, she folded her hands on her lap, "I have said enough, it is your turn now."

"I promise, but only if you and the children will have dinner with me tomorrow night in the dining chair. I will reserve a table for you, say about 6 o'clock, and we can eat while we talk and watch the prairie flowers go past and the children can watch for those Indians everyone talks about."

"I know the children would enjoy that, and I would too of course."

The Porter who had helped Aldo carry their luggage aboard came to make up their beds, and the children watched every skillful motion he used in transforming train seats into berths. A heavyset man, black skin lined with wrinkles and hair long ago turned gray, when he was not answering questions for master John and mistress Angelina, he hummed. He had no sooner arranged their berth when the children climbed in and fell under the spell of the secret childhood magic of twins.

When finally that night, the children's excitement quieted, when their questions were answered, and they're giggling stilled, Rosa heard only the monotonous rhythm of the train's wheels turning on the rails.

She looked around the tiny space which now confined her and snuggled down into the softness. Rosa knew she was going to like America.

Rosa did not tell the twins of all those dinner invitations until late in the afternoon. They had made friends with other children, and for them the days were busy. But for Rosa, time passed slowly. She opened her book and told herself she should be studying English, but her mind kept hopping off the page.

She watched the countryside, and a tree or a building would remind her of Viareggio, and she would think of her sons, and Maria, and Guido.

A fleeting odor of damp hey rotting in a shallow ditch triggered an image in her mind of Jocko's two-finger hand, and when the smells of the countryside became sweet again, her thoughts drifted to the soft fresh rainwater from Peppino, into the hot chicken soup in the delicate china cup.

Her thoughts were too active, too alive for her spirit to be tethered to the printed page. She closed her book, and while the countryside passed before her, thoughts raced ahead to the future. The dining car was set with clean white cloths, a single flower on each table." Let the children sit by the window," Aldo said, "they can watch for Indians. If they don't see any, I'm afraid this whole trip will be wasted."

A meal of roast chicken was served on white gold-trimmed China plates and dark burgundy wine in tall stemmed crystal glasses. Aldo held up his glass to Rosa, this afternoon, I went to the baggage car, and found the boxes of wine I am taking to my brother. I'm sure he would not begrudge us a little.

They drank their wine and Aldo said, "You look lovely tonight, Rosa. I have admired your beautiful hair ever since I first saw you, that day on the deck, when your hair was blowing so free in the ocean breeze."

"Yes, and every turn of the wheel that carries us further away from the winds of that ocean takes us closer to the other."

Angelina took the last bite from her plate and wiping her mouth carefully with the corner of the white linen napkin, asked, "May we go back to our car, now please?"

"We want to get in our berth and watch out the window," John explained.

"Yes, both of you may go, what do you say to Signor Martinelli?"

"Thank you, signor Martinelli," Angelina stood on tiptoes and threw her arms around his neck, and kissed him on the cheek. "Thank you, oh thank you, it was so lovely eating here."

John stood up, his shoulders back and chin pulled tight, he extended his hand, "Thank you, sir."

When they left, Aldo said, "They are good children. You have done a fine job with them, Rosa."

"Thank you, Aldo."

"They are polite and have lovely table manners."

"Thank you, sir, I think that for peasant children they are quite mannerly."

"Oh, Rosa, I did not mean…"

237

Rosa put her hand on his, "That's all right, Aldo, they are the children of a fisherman, but they were raised by a mother educated in a convent who remembers having her knuckles wrapped whenever she did not behave properly. That mother wants more from life for her children."

"You have already done so much for them."

"And there is much that lies ahead."

"Does the future frighten you? Do you worry, wondering what lies ahead?"

"Yes, at times I am terrified, but there is no turning back. There was nothing left for me, or the children, in Italy, in our tiny fishing village. There was no hope there for us. Now when we get frightened, I try to remember that I had no other choice."

"All I want is to see my twins educated so they will have a decent chance. That is my main goal. I want to support the children and myself, to have my bakery…"

"A bakery, Rosa?"

"Yes, oh perhaps I am being foolish, but I had a good business going back home, supplying bread for the inns…"

"Bread? What else did you make?"

"Just bread. Mama Dante was known all over for her delicious sourdough bread, until she took the secret recipe to the grave with her, but finally, I discovered her secret!"

"And what was this secret?"

Rosa wagged her finger at him, "A secret, that's what it was, and that's what it remains. I am the only one who knows it."

"Well, since my brother is in the hotel business, I thought… But never mind, just keep your secret that my poor brother will have to do without."

Rosa laughed. "Well, perhaps in the future, I might someday let you have a tiny taste of it."

He poured them each another glass of wine, "I love to hear you laugh, Rosa. Tell me more about this bakery you plan to open."

"If the Italians in San Francisco love mama Dantes bread as much as they did in Italy, I will have no trouble finding customers," she said and told him all the ideas she had for getting started.

You have a good business head, and if your bread is as good as you say, you will fare well."

"Thank you," she said standing up, "I do have good feelings about coming to America. I think the children and I are going to be able to make a good life here."

Aldo escorted her to her car, and as she watched him walk away, she wondered about his wife. Was she pretty? What kind of woman was she? Who was this Signora Martinelli?

CHAPTER SEVENTEEN

For the children, the days that followed were filled with adventure, picnic lunches in their seats, hours spent listening to the porter tell stories of his boyhood in the south, games with newfound playmates from other European countries, English lessons with Aldo, and, as always, those special games shared only by twins.

Leaving a trail of heavy smoke the train plodded relentlessly across the plains, across the last open land where often there was nothing but railroad tracks ahead and telegraph poles to the side.

The children practiced their English counting farmhouses and cows and horses, and once, after the train left Nebraska, they passed a covered wagon and a herd of buffalo.

In the Wyoming territory, they saw cattle herds and men on horseback, and always, they cherished a secret hope of seeing Indians. There were dozens of stops every day, and at each new town or waystation, they struggled to pronounce names uncomfortable on young Italian tongues, such as, Ogallala, and Cheyenne.

Wherever the train stopped, Aldo seemed always to attract the local people eager to talk about their work or their towns. In the Chicago yard, he made friends with an old railroad man eager to show the children how engines work and took the trouble to explain why the Erie and Pennsylvania engine went back to New York leaving the car for the Union Pacific to carry on.

"When later, Central Pacific engines took over..." Aldo smiled as he listened to John explaining this transfer to other younger children.

Many times Aldo joined Rosa and the children for lunch or went with them to the station to buy bread or fruit and cheese from the townspeople. Rosa watched with growing admiration the quiet easy ways of this man so gentle with children and yet so manly, and was so keenly interested in everything about him.

One evening after a lingering meal in the dining car, Aldo said, "Since we may never come this way again across this giant new country, let us go to the open-air car, and take a good look at this place they called the Wyoming territory."

Alone in the car except for a solitary figure smoking his evening pipe, Rosa and Aldo stood on the rear platform, watching the railroad ties shoot out from darkness, like these pleasant hours that are slipping away, she thought.

Together they stayed up at the star dotted sky, and watched silently as the full moon dabbed its quick shadow on the swiftly passing land, Rosa shivered, and Aldo quickly wrapped his coat around her.

Relaxing down into its warmth, she breathed in the lingering scent of his presence and felt the sudden touch of his arms around her shoulders.

That evening he told her about his family. "All four of us brothers are very different", he said, "and sometimes we fight. Dominic is the eldest, and he is stubborn, and a difficult man to get along with. He's a radical, and as hardheaded as a rock. I'm afraid the Austrian and Italian blood in him did not mix well. He has a hot temper and he swears he does not care anymore what happens to Enrico."

"Enrico is gentle, and he has the soul of an artist, he finds beauty in everything. Giuseppe is the warrior. It is easy to understand why Enrico left.."

"Where do you fit into that trio, Aldo?"

"I am not sure, somewhere in the middle, I hope. That is something I have often tried to understand. I have thought a great deal about."

When he turned back toward her, there was pain in his eyes.

"I do not mean to make Giuseppe sound like a tyrant, he is a good man in many ways."

"Is he married?"

"Yes, he has a sweet wife, but we don't see much of her. My wife and his have little in common. I guess you could say that they do not get along very well. We do not see much of them except at work."

"When families don't get along it makes it difficult for everyone."

Aldo said nothing for what seemed a long time, and then explained, "If my wife- Isabella- had been willing to come to America with me, I might have sold my business interests and let Giuseppe have my share of the hotel, and stayed here with Enrico."

"But enough of talk of the past now…" His words trailed off as a heavy metal door opened and familiar voices shouted, "There she is!"

The twins ran toward her, "Mama, mama," John said, "we couldn't find you!"

"We were afraid you were lost," Angelina grabbed her mother.

"Oh, my goodness," Rosa hugged them both, "I thought you were in the berth looking out the window."

When the children were reassured and had seen all they had wanted to see, John declared, "It's too cold out here," and together, they left.

"They just needed to know where their mama was," Aldo said gently, and in his eyes, there was a yearning.

"You have an understanding of children," Rosa said.

"I am fond of children, I enjoy having them around. I have four nephews, Giuseppe's four sons, all strong, good-looking boys. Of course, Enrico is not married and I…" sadness crept into his face, "I have none."

"Oh, I am sorry, I should not have…"

No, no, it is quite all right. People always wonder, and it is true I am very fond of children, but my wife is not strong, she spent a great deal of her time in Como, at her family's villa there. She is very close to her mother…" for many minutes he said no more.

"Rosa, I am afraid that I have been going on too long, some things I should not say. But it is so good to have someone to talk to."

"Perhaps tomorrow I should speak only in English, that way I could not be so free with my words."

"That sounds like a good idea," Rosa said, "but I did not mean that you were too…"

When she saw the understanding smile on his face, she went on, "what I mean, is we should all do that. We should all speak English only, for the children too. Yes, tomorrow will be our English day."

That night Rosa lay on her back in the darkness listening to the rhythmic clatter of the wheels. She was strangely excited and happy, never before had she felt so close to another person as she felt to this man who had come into her life, this man she had told her life story to, and even her dreams for her future.

She has lived with two husbands, and yet, never before had she shared in this way, not even with Maria.

Dear Maria, good friend that she was, could understand only her own world, and could not imagine a future outside the boundaries of that tiny little fishing village.

Never before had anyone, especially not a man, shared feelings with her the way Aldo had done tonight. She wondered about him, a gentleman at ease with all kinds of people and rich enough to travel first class, who chose to spend much of the ocean voyage with her children, and who was not now seeking out her company, a man whom she first thought unhappy and lonely.

What kind of man was he? Her mind's eyes conjured up a portrait of him, and she wondered if what she saw in those quiet amber eyes was more than friendship?

She stretched out full length and ran her hands over her body, overwhelmed with a hunger, a longing, her flesh cried out in deep loneliness. There was the vision of her naked body in the mirror at Saint Patrick's church house. She prayed, dear God, it is the devil putting these feelings into me.

Turn into her side, Rosa hugged the pillow close to her breast, "Good night, dear Aldo," she whispered.

The English day began with enthusiasm, even the children were at first eager to participate in the new game. But soon they discovered that speaking English without an occasional assist from their native tongue could be bothersome. For Rosa, the inconvenience of having to stop and consult the dictionary was often hopelessly complicated by the bewildering ways of English pronunciation.

When the conductor walked through the car, Rosa smiled up at him and said, "Good morning, conductorre."

"Good morning, Madame," the conductor touched his finger to the bill of his hat.

Aldo laughed at her, "Rosa," he said, "English does not have a vowel at the end of every word. It is 'conductor', not conductorre."

"Well," Rosa retaliated, "he knew what I meant." She slumped down into her seat, "thank goodness I can at least laugh in Italian."

Angelina, who had sought to escape the constraints of English day by playing with children in the next car, came back looking very dejected.

Struggling with the words, she said that a little blonde girl had called her a 'spaghetti eater' and a 'wop'. Crying, Angelina asked, "Mama, why did she call me those names? Why doesn't she like me?"

"You mustn't pay attention to what others have to say, you have only yourself to answer to, to what you know is right."

Aldo bent down and kissed the top of her head, "You must always be proud," he said, "of being Italian. You are of a noble race."

They had been traveling close to a week when the train emerged from the hot Nevada desert and began its slow climb into the Sierra.

On either side of the tracks, an ever-thickening cover of green, and above the mountain peaks topped with snow. The smell of the green pines reminded Rosa of that day so many years ago when first she crossed mountains into Viareggio. A sudden lurch and the screaming of metal on metal brought Rosa roughly back to the present.

The train stopped, and soon there were coverall clad men walking up and down along the tracks peeking in under the cars, waving lanterns and shouting orders back-and-forth to each other.

They finally got the train started, and laboring painfully along, it passed a sign that said Boca, California. Aldo came back inside and explained they were 8 miles east of Truckee, and if they could make it that far, there was a railroad yard there where they'd get fixed up.

When Rosa asked what had happened, Aldo shrugged his shoulders and pursed his lips in imitation of the reaction he had received from the railroad men when he asked the same question.

"Truckee is a gold mining town," Aldo said once they finally pulled into the roundhouse, "millions of dollars of gold was shipped out of here during the gold rush of 1849. They say we will be here for at least two hours, so may I take the children to see it, to see what a real western mining town looks like?"

"Yes, of course," she replied.

"And would you come with us, Rosa?"

"No, you and the children go," she said, "let this be their adventure, I have letters to write, letters I can write only when the train is still, otherwise they look like chickens have danced on the paper."

Putting on his hat and coat, Aldo said, "If we're not back by train time, don't worry, it means we hit a vein of gold!"

In the near deserted train car, Rosa watched him and the children hurry towards town. Feeling at peace within herself, she breathed deeply of the scent of pine and grateful to God for such blessings, said a rosary. Nothing wrong, she thought, with being one rosary ahead, one set aside for emergencies.

Taking out the last sheet of writing paper, she started, "My dear sons... we are almost there."

"Mama, look at what we have, look!" John bounded up the steps into the car.

Following closely behind her brother, and trying to squeeze past the rapidly closing heavy train door, Angelina was rescued at the last moment by Aldo. "Mama, we're back!" She said undaunted by her narrow escape.

Rosa slipped her unfinished letter into her book. "Did you find gold, John?"

"No, mama, we didn't have time to do any panning," John explained as he carefully unwrapped a flat black stone.

"Look mama," Angelina said, "I have one too." Each child held a stone, black and shiny.

Looking up to Aldo for explanation, she smiled at the delight she saw on his face as he watched the children re-examine their treasures.

He sat next to Rosa, "Hold out your hand," he said, "I brought you a treasure, too." He placed another flat shiny stone in her palm, "I brought you a touchstone. It is what the miners used to tell the difference between fool's gold and real gold."

Covering her hand with his, he closed hers around the stone, "so that you always know the true from the false, the genuine from the pretender", tenderly he squeezed her hand.

The stone, hard and smooth, was real in her hand.

"Tonight is our last night," Aldo said, "it is almost time for dinner. Would you like to eat in the dining car again?"

The children shouted in delight.

"Shall we take your mother too?" He winked.

"I don't know," John said, looking stern, "do you think she would behave herself?"

"Oh yes," Angelina answered, "I know she will be good." and patted Rosa reassuringly on the arm.

"Thank you, Aldo, but we have already accepted so much from you," Rosa said.

"But in return, think of the pleasure you and the children have given me."

"Please, mama, please."

"Happily unable to resist such an entreaty," Rosa accepted.

While waiting for their dinner, Aldo explained how the touchstone was used to tell if the gold they dug out of the earth was good quality or not. He took out his fountain pen and rubbed his gold band across the stone leaving a yellow mark. "Now," he said, patting at the pockets in his vest, "we need something else to compare this with."

"Would my ring do?" Rosa asked, extending her hand toward him.

"Splendid, and you do not even have to take it off your finger."

Holding her hand, he rubbed the stone across the underside of her ring leaving a slim gold line on the stone. "There we are, can you see the difference?" He held up the stone for the children to see the two different lines. "Because you know you're ring is pure gold, anything else that leaves a lighter line, you can be sure is not pure."

"When we get to California, can I pan for gold, mama can I, can I?" John asked.

"We are already in California, John," Aldo explained, "we were in California when the engineers put on the other engine to help us get up these mountains. But when you get to San Francisco, perhaps your mama will let you ask your Uncle Anthony to take you gold mining."

"Me too," Angelina asserted. "I want to go too."

"Of course."

The waiter brought their meal, and when the twins finished, they were excused to play with the children in the next car.

"This is a pretty ring," Aldo said. "It is not an ordinary wedding band. Those cherubs touching hands are in the style of Luca Della Robbia."

Rosa told him the story of the ring, and he said, "Della Robbia did make some jewelry early in his career but only for his family. Your husband and his mother might well be descendants of the Della Robbia family."

"Well, maybe my children have some artistic blood in them. Perhaps they will be artists like your brother."

"But didn't you hear John Edward say he is going to be a gold miner? Do you think your uncle Anthony would take them gold mining?"

"It would be hard for me to say. I was only five when I saw him, and I didn't like him very much for taking my mama Nina away from me."

"I'm not sure he even likes children. They've never had any, although I remember him saying they couldn't take me with them because they would be having children of their own."

"Do you hear from them very often?"

"Oh yes, Nina writes frequently, she talks a lot about the important things Anthony is doing."

"Is he a fisherman?"

"Among other things, I guess. When they moved from New York he bought a boat, and then a boarding house and opened the diner for the fisherman. Now she says he has his own fleet of fishing boats and owns an apartment house."

Rosa stared at the fragile wisps of steam escaping from her newly filled coffee cup.

"A penny for your thoughts, Rosa," Aldo spoke gently.

Realizing that she had been twisting her wedding band around her finger, Rosa thrust both hands into her lap. "I guess I was thinking about how sad some of Nina's letters sounded. Oh, she never complained, but there were little things, here and there."

"Once, she said she had to stop writing and wash her dress for work the next day. If Anthony was doing so well, why did his wife have only one dress?" Rosa watched the scenery speed past, taking her every minute closer to Nina. What would she find in San Francisco?

"Do you worry about her?" Aldo read her thoughts.

"Well, there are some things I don't really understand, but I guess I will have to wait and see. Her last letter sounded so happy that we were coming. I can hardly wait to see her," Rosa sipped her coffee, "and I imagine Anthony will be just fine. Perhaps the years have mellowed him." The waiter added water to their already full glasses and hovered about. Rosa said, "Oh, Aldo, we are the last ones in here!"

"No wonder we are getting such attention." The waiter smiled as they stood up, and when Aldo thrust paper money into his hand, he rushed ahead to open the door for them.

They walked back to Rosa's car for her shawl and found the children watching intently out the window.

"What are you looking for?" They asked.

"Indians. This is our last chance to see them," John said, his voice heavy with disappointment.

On their way to the observation car, Aldo said, "I don't think you have to worry about that one, if he doesn't find gold, he can always be an Indian scout."

"I just want him to grow up to be a decent man, whatever happens in the future."

Rosa pulled her shawl tighter around her shoulders as they went out into the observation car.

"Tell me, Aldo," she asked, "do you worry about the future?"

Lighting a cigar, he said, "Yes and no. My future depends a great deal on Enrico, on how sick he is. When I left Italy, I planned to stay only a year at the most, but the more I see of this country, the more I can see a great future here."

"Rosa, will you promise me something?"

"If I can."

"Promise me that if I can ever help you in any way- any way at all- you will call on me?

"I think a great deal of you, and the children too, of course, in fact, I almost wish this bumpy old train would go on further and our journey would not end tomorrow."

He took a piece of paper from his billfold, "This is Enrico's address. Please, call on me if you need me."

"You have already saved my life twice," she said. Then seeing that serious look on his face she added, "Yes, you are very kind, of course, I promise to contact you if I have trouble."

"And this is where we will be," with Aldo's pen, she wrote Nina's address on a small card and smiled as he slipped it into his vest pocket and patted it tenderly.

The evening air was cold. "It is good we are warm from our dinner wine."

Rosa studied the sky, a rich dark blue in back of thousands of clear bright stars. "It looks like you could touch a star," she said, standing on her toes, reaching up toward the heavens.

The train lurched around the curve, and Rosa fell against him. Catching her, he wrapped his arms around her and did not let her go. As she looked into his eyes, she felt a warm rush of excitement.

His heart pounded against her as he drew her up against his body. His arms strong and comforting around her, she trembled. He lifted her chin and kissed her. He kissed her in a way that she had never done before. She held him tight, afraid he would slip away from her. Breathing in unison, their bodies as one, their arms remained locked together.

Refusing to let go of her, he said, "I tried to tell myself it was only admiration for you, but it is more, it is…"

Rosa put her hand up to his mouth, "Do not say more. We can be friends, good friends, but that is all there can be between us. Let us not spoil that."

She turned to leave, but he held onto her arm, "Do not go Rosa, stay, I have so much to tell you," his voice pleaded.

"There is nothing more to be said, your life is in Italy." She started to leave, then turned back, "Dear Aldo, she took the hand he held up to her, "I shall never look at a star again and not think of you, my dear friend."

"Oh Rosa, oh my dear Rosa…" he cupped his hand around her face and kissed her on the forehead. "God forgive me, I cannot help how I feel."

CHAPTER EIGHTEEN

Shivering, Rosa pulled up the covers around her. She could not get warm. You cannot be in love. It is too late. He is married, and you are not a silly child. You must banish these feelings from your soul, from your mind, and from your flesh.

The rhythmic beat of train wheels roaring in her head, she pushed open the heavy green curtains. The snow is almost gone, but the stars were still shining down upon her. She yanked the curtains close, in the morning he would be gone from her life. Dear God, she prayed, protect me from this temptation.

Early the next morning, Angelina was ready in her new yellow dress, John Edward in the new pants and jacket Molly gave him, and Rosa in the white blouse Aldo had admired. She dreaded seeing him this morning, yet in truth, part of her could hardly wait for him to come through the train door, while another part feared that he might.

After a breakfast of bread and the remains of the fruit, the children asked permission to go visit Signor Martinelli.

"No, do not bother him now, he will be getting off the train before us, and it's probably too busy right now to visit."

"Why can't we see him, mama? We have to say goodbye to him."

"Why doesn't he get off with us?" Angelina asked.

"You know why," Rosa scolded, "he is going to Berkeley, and we are going across the bay to San Francisco."

Seeing the disappointment on her daughter's face, Rosa regretted the harshness of her tone, and as compensation, added, "When we get to Oakland, we will ride across the bay on a ferry boat, don't you want to ride the ferry?"

Unimpressed, Angelina slumped back down into her seat.

John Edward was asking, "Is San Francisco an island?"

"No," replied Rosa. "Do you remember the map I showed you, where we saw the big bay, just like Genova's? When we get off the train, there will be one side of the bay, and we have to take a ferry boat across to get to San Francisco."

Both children quickly lost interest in their mother's geography lesson and turned their attention to watching for Signor Martinelli.

The train was traveling through city buildings and streets and had begun to slow down when the children saw Aldo approaching. Before he had a chance to push open the door, they rushed toward him and threw their arms around him. "Mama would not let us come and say goodbye to you," they protested in unison.

"Well, I imagine she was afraid that you'd get these pretty clothes of yours dirty."

"But we worried we would not get to see you again."

"I would never, never go without saying goodbye to my two little traveling companions, now you know that, don't you?"

The conductor came through the car, scanning passenger's faces, this is Oakland, sir, next stop is 16th Street, Mister Martinelli, sir.

"Thank you, George. How soon?"

"Five minutes sir, and we just stop long enough to let passengers off."

The children turned their attention to the passing scene, and Aldo said, "May I sit with you until we reach my stop?"

Rosa nodded, trying not to look at him.

"Rosa, please, I could not stand it if I thought you were angry at me."

She said nothing, still afraid to look at him.

"Quietly, gently, he raised her face up to his, "Your eyes tell me everything I want to know, Rosa."

Tears welled up, and she turned quickly away from him.

The train slowed to a stop. Aldo hugged each of the children, and reached for Rosa's hands, and looked at her.

"You are a very special woman. Don't let what happened last night drive you away. We can be friends." He kissed her gently on the cheek.

Rosa could not permit herself to speak. He turned away, walked down the aisle, and out of her life.

Two blasts of the engine's whistle, the train shuddered, pulling Rosa away from the only man in her life who made her come alive. His kiss was friendship. Admiration. Passion. He had stirred feelings in her that she long buried deep within her.

The children crowded in front of her at the window to wave goodbye to the old man standing on the platform, alone, a crate of wine and a suitcase beside him.

Desperately needing to put aside her feeling of loss, Rosa scolded herself. After all these years, here I am finally in America, soon to see my mama Nina, and all I can feel is a longing for a man who can never be mine.

The children were off looking for their friends and the porter to say their goodbyes and the train traveling along the shoreline sometimes looked like it might fall into the water. Slowing down, it started out on a long skinny bridge built low over the water curving along, like a long lazy snake.

"End of the line, end of the line, everybody off," the conductor called as he walked the length of the train, dislodged passenger and baggage alike. Rosa ordered the children to stay close and hold tight as the mass of bodies swept along the pier and fumbled onto a fat sprawling boat, which for her conjured up frightening visions of seasickness. "Don't worry, you won't get seasick on that old crate," Aldo had assured her when she confided her fear to him. "This is a bay, not an ocean, and the boat is so fat, nothing can rock it," he had said.

As the boat made its way across the quiet waters of the bay, Rosa studied the shoreline, wondering where Berkeley was and what it was like. When they neared the San Francisco side, people once again pushed and crowded. At the other end of the high narrow passageway, inside a high ceilinged building, the crowd thinned out, and Rosa and the two children stood alone searching to find a familiar face.

"Nina?" Rosa called, her throat tightening around the sound.

"Rosa, Rosa, my Rosa." A slight woman in a black dress, shawl across her shoulders, suddenly broke away and ran toward them.

They kissed and hugged and cried and laughed.

When finally the two pulled apart, the older woman turned her tear-stained face to the children, "What bella!" she cried, throwing her hands up into the air. "What pretty faces." She crouched down to hug their heads. "Oh Rosa, at last. I have you here with me!" And again, Rosa was wrapped in her arms.

"Anthony, my husband, this is Rosa," she reached out for his arm to pull him closer.

"Rosa, you remember Anthony?"

A thin man wearing a black pinstripe suit, slightly taller than his wife, snapped shut the cover of his gold watch and putting it back into his vest pocket, kissed Rosa on the cheek and, without expression, nodded at the children.

"Come, come now, we have already wasted enough time waiting here for you. Damn trains, never on time. Talk later, plenty of time to talk later. There is work to be done."

They followed Anthony out of the building. Clean-shaven, with a pencil-thin mustache, his face pale, he was not like the fisherman back home.

"Come, come," he said, looking back, "we must hurry, we have to get to the diner." He crossed the busy street so quickly they had trouble keeping up and, when the driver of a hansom cab was forced to pull his horse up sharply in order not to hit them, Anthony appeared not to notice.

He swung himself into the driver seat of a large two-seated wagon, in which the smell of fish was strong, and, the rains poised in his hands, "Jump in!" He shouted.

The horse pulled them over the cobblestone streets along the edge of the bay, past peers that reached finger-like out into the waters to welcome ocean-going ships. A beautiful day, the sky a cloudless blue, the sun shining, people were strolling, enjoying the spring warmth. Rosa felt San Francisco was saying welcome, Rosa. We're glad you're here.

The large ocean ships were gradually replaced with smaller vessels and soon the buggy took them past an inlet filled with small fishing boats, boats like those Rosa had grown up with. The street was narrowed with drays loading and unloading their wares, fishing nets hung out to dry, and hovering above it all, seagulls screeching for food, so much like Viareggio.

Rosa looked at Nina, the black dress, the shawl over her shoulders, her hair in a tight bun. Her skin was smooth and fresh, but with her brown eyes that set deep in their sockets, she looked older than her years. This is not the Nina Rosa had seen in her dreams.

Here we are, said Anthony stopping in front of a square two-story building. There was a white plate glass window on the ground floor with 'Nina's', written up across it. As if he knew her thoughts, Anthony explained, "When the fishermen see a woman's name on the door they think the food will taste like their mother's cooking, that's a salesmanship!"

Nina was pulling on the tail of his coat, "But Anthony, Rosa, and the children are tired, we should take them home so they can rest."

"Nonsense! Rosa, you and the children don't look tired at all. All you have been doing is sitting on the train for eight days. You might as well get to work right away. Tomorrow is Sunday, you can rest then, after mass."

CHAPTER NINETEEN

Tying the buggy to the hitching post in front of the diner, Anthony watched the women and children get down.

"Maybe we should change the name to 'the pretty Rosa'," he said. "You are young and pretty, you could attract many customers." He patted her on the bottom.

"You can have the best product in the world," he went on, "but if you don't sell it right, if you don't display it, you make no money."

"I am the salesman. They come from all over San Francisco to buy my fish. They come even from across the bay."

Rosa saw Nina disappear into the diner, and she paused on the doorstep to look out over the water. Everything reminded her of Italy. There was that same brisk saltiness in the air, the bobbing fishing boats with their lateen sails the same azul blue as those in Genova.

The fishnets, hanging to dry or coiled in huge rolls, were the same, she could have been looking at the sea from the shores of Viareggio.

Hungry still for the beauty of San Francisco Bay, she walked across the road at the water's edge and reached down to touch the water. She let her fingers linger in its coolness.

Tasting the moisture from her fingertips, she wondered, will my bread taste the same? Anthony was still talking, "over here," he indicated the fish stand a few yards further down the wharf, "we sell to people to buy just for their evening meals."

"We have shrimp, we have crab, we have deepwater fish, just like in Italy, and some days we even have lobster! See, just like home!"

"The sea is wild here, the fish are many, you will not go homesick for the fish, or for the fishermen." Annoyed at Anthony's intrusion into her mood, she said, "I had better get back."

He walked alongside, and when they reached the diner, he pushed the door open for her, "I have an office upstairs, but they come here, sit at my tables, drink my wine, and then they are happy and buy big orders of fish for the restaurants and hotels."

The door opened into a large, dimly lit hole with three long tables of well-worn boards and benches. At the back of the room, opposite the staircase going up, double swinging doors opened into the kitchen were two great pots of water boiled on a black iron stove. Nina was standing in front of the floor-to-ceiling four-door wooden icebox, pouring two glasses of milk.

Anthony's voice, no longer personal and insinuating, became crisp and businesslike, "You will work here for your board and room," he said to Rosa.

"The children must work too. They are big enough to hold down full-time jobs," taking hold of John's arm and squeezing his muscle, he said, "see how strong he is."

Rosa could see the pain on her son's face, but John Edward said nothing.

"And you, my little lady," he patted Angelina on the bottom, "you will soon be old enough to sell the fish out in the open market. You'll soon be pretty enough to attract all kinds of customers. That is salesmanship!"

He laughed and tickled Angelina under the chin. "Then I can get rid of that old widow lady who sells the fish now. She scares customers away, I only keep her so Nina has a friend."

"The children will be going to school," Rosa said, "if they can help out in the afternoons."

Staring silently at her, "We'll see," he finally said. "And that is enough talk for now. Come, come now, the tables have to be set, the dinner cooked. There is a lot to be done."

Apologetically, Nina handed Rosa an apron. Wrapping the long belt twice around her waist, "Don't worry about us, we will be fine," Rosa said, "it will be fun working together."

Anthony's voice calling Nina came from the dining room. She immediately sat down the long-handled stirring spoon and hurried to him.

"Here, show these children what to do so they don't have to stand around looking stupid," he snapped.

Nina showed John Edward where the glasses were kept and where to put them on the table, she showed Angelina the dishes and laying out one place setting, showed her how to arrange the silverware.

"And here are the napkins," Nina opened a deep drawer in a long wooden chest. She picked up one rolled napkin inside, "and they all have rings on them, and each ring has a name on it."

"See, this one belongs to Alfredo, and this one to Paulo, and here's Mario's. The men keep the same seat as a napkin. I will put them out now, so you have time to learn where everybody sits."

She bent down and kept her hands around Angelina's face and kissed her and reached for John Edward and kissed him a loving wet kiss.

"I am so happy you have come into my life. I hope you will be happy here. Your mama was like my very own little girl, and I have loved you since you were born, even though I have never seen you. Do you believe that, my children?"

"Yes, aunt Nina," they both said shyly.

"Call me Nona, please call me Nona. You are my only family. I will be your grandmother," and she hugged them until they could hardly breathe.

She went back into the kitchen. "They are so beautiful, Angelina has eyes like you, Rosa, when I left you, when you were hardly more than a baby, I will never forget your eyes, your curls, everything."

"Gio looks like your papa, Rosa, I know you cannot remember him, but he was a handsome man."

"John, John Edward," Rosa corrected. "Now that we are in America, he wants to be called by his English name."

"Oh, Rosa, I will try, but there have been so many changes, sometimes it is very difficult…" her voice trailed away.

Putting her arm around the only mother she had ever known, "We are all so happy to be here with you," Rosa said, surprised at how frail she seemed.

"Where is Anthony?" She asked.

"Oh, he is upstairs in his office. We will not see him again til the men come to eat, then we will have his dinner. Today is payday, he pays them on Saturday night, and has a lot to deduct room and board, laundry, and wine from their paycheck.

"Anthony is very careful- he keeps good records. He won't even let anyone do the books or even look at them."

The men started coming into the large dining room at 6 o'clock, and Rosa picked up one of the large bowls of pasta and went into the dining room.

"Oh, we have a new girl to look at, eh, Anthony?" A short fat man sitting near the door spoke.

"The food is first, you feed us well, and then you feast our eyes. Eh, Paisano? You are something! Where did you find this pretty one?"

Every mouth opened and every eye in the dining room turned to Rosa.

"I brought her all the way from Italy, just for you," Anthony said reaching out to pat her bottom.

Everywhere wine glasses raised in view of endless love to her, and offers of marriage came along with promises of gifts and merriment.

Laughing at their good nature gibes, Rosa retreated to the kitchen where she could watch in safety. Their love calls died down with her disappearance, and like pigs lined up at the trough, the men dug in.

They emptied the platters of fish, ate the pasta, and broke off huge hunks of bread to dunk in the sauce. And washed it all down with dark red wine.

"Never do they change," Rosa said, "Italian men feel unmanly unless they talk like big lovers. I guess it is the same all over."

"It is one of their few pleasures," Nina said, "they work really hard, and sometimes they don't seem to get very far."

As the wine in the bottles went down, the boarders' voices became stronger and their laughter louder. When the meal was over they leaned back in their chairs, belched, and lit up their cigars.

"Nina, are you going to retire now that Anthony has brought us a pretty new face from Italy?" A ruddy-faced fisherman seated next to Anthony asked as she came into the room.

Right beside her, Rosa returned his mischievous smile and said, "Of course she is. We are both going to retire and live on the love you paisanos are always offering."

Nina knew what the men had been saying and what they'd been thinking. "Now listen to me, you buffone, listen to me!"

There was a sweetness to Nina's voice, but not one man in the room doubted the strictness of her message. "Rosa is my niece, she is not a peasant girl. She has come to live with us. She is part of my family. You will watch those rough tongues of yours in front of Rosa and her children."

There was not a sound while Nina picked up a stack of dishes, and looking up at the remorseful faces watching her, she said, "Her children call me, Nona," she smiled and flung her head backward with a "so there!" message which immediately released the worried men from their prison of guilt.

"Now, now, Nina, we mean no disrespect," Mario said, "we were just having some fun, no harm in a little fun. It is Saturday night. Tonight is fun night," and he patted her bottom as she walked by. "We work all week- tonight we have fun, no?"

"Not in my kitchen," she said, leaving the dining room.

"Sometimes I think they are little boys who never grew up."

"Oh, I am used to it, they are no different than Eduardo's paisanos."

"They never felt more like real men than when they were bragging in front of others."

John Edward and Angelina ate dinner at the small table Nina had fixed for them in the corner of the kitchen, and were fast asleep, their heads on the table.

Rosa was gathering up the last of the dishes when she passed Anthony and felt his hand on her. She flashed him a warning look.

"Don't be so high and mighty with me, girly, or you and those children of yours will find yourselves without a home," he spoke to her under his breath, then looking around at the listening fishermen, he winked and said, "that is a woman, good and firm!"

Nina looked inquisitively as she returned to the kitchen, and pointing to the sleeping children Rosa whispered, "This is the last of the dishes."

Nina propped open one of the doors into the dining room, and, washing the dishes quietly, they could hear the men talking.

Rosa recognized Anthony's voice speaking to each man as he gave them his money: "So, Maris, not much left for you. This will only buy you one or two girls this week. Here, Luigi, you owe me, so you get $12.00 this time."

At first, each of Anthony's remarks followed gales of laughter, but at the end, there were many voices raised in anger. Rosa could not make out what they were saying.

The dining room became quiet and soon Anthony came into the kitchen and walked around inspecting. He said, "If you are done, I will drive you to the apartment. I have business tonight. Hurry."

Anthony waited for them at the curb but this time he had a closed carriage with a driver instead of the vegetable wagon he used to pick them up.

The woman helped the sleepy children into the carriage and Anthony ordered the driver up the hill to the apartment.

"Can't you stay with us tonight, Anthony? This is Rosa's first night with us. Stay home tonight, Anthony. Please," Nina pleaded.

"Now, now, you know that Saturday nights I have business. You know I have to get everything ready for Monday morning."

The driver helped the children down out of the buggy and carried Rosa's luggage to the front door while Anthony looked on disapprovingly. Before Nina had the door unlocked, his buggy had disappeared around the corner.

"Business," Nina shook her head, "monkey business," and unlocked the door at the top of a half flight of steps leading into a long hall carpeted with a handsome Chinese rug. To the left, French doors opened into a small room with bay windows which looked out onto the street.

"Let us settle the children down first, then I will show you the flat, and we can talk," Nina said.

She led them to a pleasant room with two beds.

"This bed is for you and Angelina, and this little one is for Gio- I mean John Edward."

Turning down the coverlet on the big bed, Nina fingered a white and blue quilt, "This quilt is yours, Rosa, I've been working on it ever since the very first- since we first left you in Italy. And now it is finished. It is yours."

Rosa picked up the corner of the delicately stitched quilt, "Oh, Nina," she said, "that is the nicest thing anyone has ever did for me." She hugged Nina.

"And I have made the children nightshirts. And a nightgown for you, Rosa." She spread the delicately embroidered clothes out on the bed. And when she filled the bathtub, she said, "I put rose water in here for you, Rosa."

When the children were bathed and in their new nightshirts, Rosa said, "Run and thank your Nona and then to bed."

Nina had hot milk waiting for the children.

"Somehow," Rosa said, "I don't think they will have any trouble sleeping tonight."

The children in bed, Rosa sat down with Nina at the kitchen table. In the middle, were two glasses and a tall bottle of deep red wine.

"I know I am too excited to sleep. I am so happy to have you here with me." Nina filled their glasses. "We must celebrate your first day in San Francisco with a toast."

"Everything looks very beautiful, so much like home, I know I am going to love San Francisco."

The wine was rich and warming, and in the quiet comfort of their love for one another, years faded from Nina's face. Rosa looked into the fired eyes, "Tell me about you, your life here," Rosa said.

"When Anthony and I arrived in America, I was full of hope. In just a few years I would be able to send for you. We worked like slaves. From sun up to sunset. Catch fish, clean the fish, sell the fish.

"But we worked together and it did not seem very hard because he was with me, we were always together.

"The sea had every type of fish imaginable and our day's catch was always sold long before nightfall. Then we bought a boat and we worked twice as hard.

"We didn't have babies because I wouldn't be able to work. 'Later', he would always tell me, 'when we had more money'.

"Then we got another boat, and it was the same story, 'later, when we have more money'. When he made more money, he bought this flat.

"Then I thought, at last, the time had come, we would have children, but oh no! Oh, he would make love to me but he would always pull out and let his seed fall on the bed. I would cry, 'Anthony, do not do this, I want children', he would get mad and sometimes slap me.

"'you want, you want' he would say, 'do you not think of what I want?' And he would storm out of the house. Every time I said anything about babies, he would storm out of the house. Finally, I said nothing and just hoped some night he would forget, but he never did. That is why I have no babies."

Nina poured the last of the wine, "I will get more," she said.

"No," Rosa stayed her hand, "get us some coffee instead."

Nina moved methodically about the kitchen preparing the coffee, and setting two cups on the table, she continued:

"I thought maybe I am not pretty enough, so one day I went down to the foot of Telegraph hill. That is where all the fine ladies shop and buy their gowns and their hats. Anything you wanted you can buy. I took some of the fish money and went, all by myself, to shop.

"I felt out of place. I stood outside for a long time just watching the ladies go in and out. I didn't feel pretty, not even as pretty as the salesladies. But finally, I got enough courage and went inside. I wanted my Anthony to be proud of me.

"I would look so beautiful, he would not be able to resist and then we would have babies.

"The saleslady was very kind, she showed me everything in the store and suggested that first I should have what she called a 'walking dress'" Nina jumped. "Wait, I will go get it and show you."

She returned, her arms full and carrying a large hatbox. A pair of chocolate brown doeskin gloves slipped from her hold. They were softer and richer than anything Rosa had ever felt before.

"Look, Rosa," Nina held up a striking canary yellow long-sleeved jacket trimmed around the front and collar in chocolate brown velvet.

The long sleeve cuffs also finished off in the brown velvet, the jacket's front and back were pleated in long up and down rows of delicate hand stitching.

A wide brown belt of velvet cinched the waist, tight. The long full skirt made of the same yellow challis had hand-sewn pleats in the back and just a hint of a bustle.

"Isn't it beautiful?" Nina asked. Not waiting for an answer, she laid the dress across Rosa's lap and bent down to open the hatbox. She held up a narrow brimmed hat of crisp golden straw.

A brown satin ribbon around the crown, tied in a bow, held a small delicate bunch of lavender, "forget me nots." Nina put the hat on and lovingly held up the oyster white, lace-trimmed cotton blouse in front of herself.

Her eyes were dancing, "This is my beautiful walking dress," Looking at the reflection of herself in the window, the excitement fell from her face, "it probably doesn't fit me anymore."

"It is truly beautiful. What did Anthony say when he say you?"

"I had planned to surprise him on Saturday night. I got all dressed up, put on my new dress, and waited for him to come home. He didn't come. I waited and waited and finally put my dress away and decided I would wear it to church on Sunday, that would be just as good, I thought.

"It was late when he came in and he was very drunk. He fell into bed, almost pushing me out. When I tried to move close to him, he pushed me away. He smelled of whiskey and there was perfume on him too. I turned over and cried myself to sleep. Maybe I was too late with my new clothes.

"But the next morning I tried again. I got up early, dressed up in my new outfit, and fixed him a nice breakfast. When Anthony came into the kitchen I was all ready.

"Well, he took one look at me, and the blood drained from his face. 'Jesus Christ' he said, 'what have you done? You are not going to church in that outfit, take those damn clothes off! If my fishermen see you', he said, 'dressed that way they will want a raise. Good god woman, take that junk off your body', he was screaming at me."

Rosa took the coffee pot from the stove, and with her hand resting reassuringly on Nina's shoulder, she refilled both their cups.

Nina fingered her saucer, "I stood up to him, though! I told him, no, we had enough money, and that I wanted to look nice too. I said I wanted to be pretty like American women instead of looking like a peasant woman from Lucca. It was time, I told him, that I had some new clothes."

271

"That must've taken a lot of courage?" Rosa said.

"Yes, it did, but then his face turned purple and all hell broke loose. I have never seen him so angry. He grabbed me and hit me across the face."

Nina's voice faltered.

"That's all right, Nina don't say any more," Rosa tried to comfort her.

"No, no, it feels good to have someone to tell this to, I want to get this off my chest."

She blew her nose and went on:

"I must have lost consciousness for a minute because suddenly there I was on the floor and he was gone. I didn't see him until the next morning at the diner.

"I was fixing breakfast for the fishermen and the bruise on my face was so bad I couldn't go to mass. When the fishermen asked me what happened, Anthony told them I clumsily had fallen down the stairs."

Nina took the hat from her head. And fluffing up the petals of the forget me nots said, "So I stay in my black dress and scarf. I have never worn the dress or the hat."

She picked the jacket up and said, "Here, Rosa, you take it, you need a nice dress."

Making Rosa stand, she held the dress up to her. "It may be a little short, but other than that I think it will fit. I will let the ham down while we talk. Yellow is your color, you'll look beautiful."

"No, no, Nina, I cannot take your lovely dress, save it, someday you will wear it."

"No, I gave up those silly ideas long ago. I wanted to change, to become part of this country, but he doesn't want me to, and I don't have the strength to stand up to him."

Nina's back was to Rosa, "After all, wearing the shawl and scarf is better than having him beat me."

She turned back, and with despair in her eyes pleaded, "Can you understand that? I don't want to be buried in that dress, and if he sees me in it, then you will see me in the casket next. Will you try on the dress, Rosa, I would like you to wear it."

"No, Nina, not the dress", she tried that hat on and satisfied that it was becoming to her, said, "May I wear this to church tomorrow? It will go nicely with my skirt and jacket and with my white blouse. But the dress, that is for you."

Rosa folded the jacket, "Did things get any better for you with Anthony after that?"

"Well, he never hit me again, in fact, he apologized. He said he was sorry that he had lost his temper, said he had business problems, and was worried. But he also said for me to never wear those clothes again. He couldn't afford, he said, to give the fishermen a raise. He didn't want to look rich!"

"Nina folded the skirt and wrapped it up, life went on pretty much the same after that," Nina said. "He was gone at night most of the time. He likes to gamble with the Chinese. He goes to Chinatown, I think. He drinks and gambles and usually comes home so drunk I have to undress him and put him to bed. He never remembers that I do this."

Suddenly straightening up, Nina said, "Come with me, Rosa, I want to show you something."

Nina's bedroom was large, with two windows, hardwood floors darted the oriental scattered rugs, and a white four post bed facing a card mahogany armoire.

Above the bed hung a crucifix, and next to it, a small dresser with a picture of the Virgin Mary and the infant child above it. Nina took a package from the bottom drawer, and starting out of the room, said, "Hurry, come with me, I will show you."

CHAPTER TWENTY

Nina placed the tightly tied box in the center of the kitchen table. Never taking her eyes off the package, she stepped back and asked,

"Should we have another glass of wine?"

"Nina!" Rosa said, her patience tested to its limit, "what is in there?"

Nina's cheeks were flushed. "I will show you," she spoke slowly, prolonging the moment.

The size of a fat shoebox, the package was tightly guarded and layers of newspaper and secured with bits of string tied together. Nina undid every knot slowly and precisely, and when the last bit of string finally fell away, she began peeling back each separate thickness of newspaper.

Rosa's patience was about exhausted when, at last, through the wrappings, Nina, her eyes watching for Rosa's reaction, removed the lid of the box.

"Holy Mary, mother of God!" Rosa cried collapsing into a chair.

In the box, in front of her unbelieving eyes, stood three stacks of neatly packed paper money.

"Where did you get all that money? Does Anthony know you have it?"

Rosa picked up one pile and glancing apprehensively toward the door, put it quickly back into the box and reached for the cover.

"Don't worry, Rosa, Anthony never gets home before 3 o'clock Sunday mornings. We have time."

She handed the money back to Rosa to hold. "And no", she said, "he has no idea that I have it."

"How in the world?"

Nina settled herself down at the table opposite Rosa, an expression of satisfaction creeping over her face.

"When Anthony started gambling and coming home drunk – so drunk I had to undress him and put him to bed – there were always lots of money loose in his pockets. At first, I folded it neatly and put it back. Then I thought, I will borrow a little and save it, and maybe Anthony and I would go for a vacation down to Monterey, or across the bay to Marin. But he never did any of these things with me, so then I decided to save it for you, so you could come to America."

"But, by the time I had enough, you were married to Giovanni, and then you had a baby, and then another one. That meant that more money would be needed to pay for all of you to come." Nina leaned across the table and patted Rosa's hand, "You see, all these years you have been constantly in my thoughts.

"When I had almost enough saved, I began to worry that maybe you should not come. I worried that Anthony would not be good to you, that he would somehow hold onto you like he does his fishermen. You heard today in the diner how he is to the men, and you saw how he treated you. I didn't want that for you, and so I gave up hoping you would come."

"But I didn't stop helping myself to the coins and a few extra bills whenever Anthony came home drunk. He never missed it."

Rosa smiled, she felt better about Nina.

"When I got your letter I was so happy. It was a selfish happiness, and I couldn't bring myself to tell you not to come. I know it was selfish of me, but now that you are here, I hope I have not done an evil thing by not telling you the truth."

Rosa reassured her that she understood, and would have come anyway because there was nothing left for her in Viareggio.

Nina put the money back in the box and lovingly replaced each layer of newspaper and retied every knot just as it had been.

Watching Nina's ritual, Rosa said, "It doesn't matter about Anthony, because I said I'll be out on my own just as soon as I can. I did not come here to work as a maid for him."

"You didn't tell him of my plan to open a bakery, did you? I don't want him to know about it, at least not until everything is settled."

Nina put the box carefully back into the drawer in the bedroom and covered it with neatly folded undergarments. "Anthony never showed much interest in anything I said, and so a long time ago, I stopped telling him things. No, I didn't even tell him you were coming until after your boat left Italy."

"Good! Tomorrow, after church I want to walk around and see the city and look for a good building for my bakery. It will take time to find the right location and to find out how much things cost. I still have money, I hope enough to put in the ovens and get started."

Nina washed out the cups and the two empty wine glasses and looking around to be sure nothing had been left out, she put them back into the cupboard.

"It is time for bed, Anthony will be getting home soon."

"Now that you are here with your beautiful children, Rosa, a new light is shining in my life." The two women hugged, their eyes wet with tears of joy.

The small rumpled cot was empty, but the two children were together in the big bed. The twins often got lonesome for the other's company, and tonight, in this unfamiliar room, they comforted each other. Rosa looked at them with envy, each had the other. How safe they must feel.

Lying alone in that small bed her mind raced through all the things that happened to her that day since she woke up in her tiny berth in the train that had carried her all the way across this giant country. She thought of Aldo. Where was he, had he thought of her at all that day?

Raising up on one arm, Rosa looked out at the street, out at a whole new, unknown world. A bright clear night, she looked across the bay to where she imagined Berkeley must be.

Street noises interrupted her reflections about Aldo and bringing her thoughts back to Anthony's house, she thanked the Madonna that she was finally reunited with her Mama Nina.

She pulled the handsewn quilt closer up around her face and smiled about the secret cache, Nina has found a way to take care of herself.

With the clutter of metal wheels on the cobblestone street, a carriage stopped in front of the flat. Anthony's voice ordered, "Be back here at nine-thirty for church."

Rosa went to the window. The driver, a young boy who reminded her of Peppino, was trying to help Anthony down out of the carriage.

Anthony pushed him away roughly, and then the front door slammed and she heard him stumble up the stairs into the front hall. She could hear his body rubbing up against the wall as he got it himself down the long hall.

The bedroom door closed and Rosa heard a heavy thud. There was silence, then the guarded sounds of someone rustling about. Rosa lay back and smiled, another few dollars for Nina's paying money.

The next morning Nina came into the room.

"It is almost 9 o'clock, time to get ready for church. The children are having hot milk and bread, I let you sleep as long as I could."

Rosa dressed and, with her hair combed, she reached for the lace Molly had given her at Saint Patrick's. Then she set it aside and placed Nina's straw hat on her head, wondering if Anthony would recognize it.

John Edward and Angelina were at the kitchen table eating their breakfast as Nina hovered over them.

Anthony came out of the bedroom fixing his tie and brushed past without a word. Consulting the gold watch in his vest pocket, he announced, "Alright, alright, it is time to leave. Hurry now, the buggy will be waiting."

His hair was just beginning to gray at the temples, Anthony was handsome in his dark suit and vest, and showed no ill effects from his late and unsteady return last night. He led the way.

Rosa walked behind Nina who was wearing a somber brown skirt and a matching jacket which fell loosely from her shoulders covered by a black knit shawl. On her head, she wore a black scarf.

The sky was clear in the morning air perfect with its warm taste of spring. The top of the carriage was open, folded back behind the seats like an unused fan. The carpet was a rich burgundy and the leather seats tufted and soft. Polished black, the outside was trimmed in bright shining brass.

The same young man Rosa had seen last night, sat straight and stiff at the front of the carriage, reins in his hands.

John Edward was next to her, Rosa held Angelina on her lap.

"You better not have more babies, Rosa, there isn't enough room in the buggy," Anthony said, laughing and patting her knee. Rosa thought his hand had lingered a bit too long.

Tapping his hat to a passersby, Anthony smiled pleasantly at the buggy ride with all. Anxious to learn their routes, Rosa read street names allowed, "Dupont, Greenwich, and Vallejo." Anthony laughed at her pronunciation, telling her she sounded like she just got off the boat. Hiding her resentment at his ridicule. She made him repeat each name until she could say it the way he did.

Pulling the horse to a stop, the driver sneaked a quick look at Rosa and smiled. The church was a large brown wooden framed building.

"Saint Francis of Assisi and sisters of the holy family."

Anthony hopped agilely out of the carriage, lifted Angelina to the ground, and assisted Nina as she stepped down.

Before he could reach out a hand to John Edward, the boy jumped out of the carriage, and giving him a fatherly pat on the head, Anthony turned two help Rosa.

Anthony smiled broadly and nodded at those already seated, as he escorted the two women down the center aisle to the front pew, the children following closely behind.

Genuflecting with a deep bow, he stood aside and guided first Rosa, then the twins, then Nina into their seats. Entering last, he sat next to the aisle.

Rosa had trouble concentrating on her prayers. So intrigued was she by Anthony's sudden charm and solicitous behavior.

She heard the gospel and an endless string of notices about fundraising events and meetings. After a handful of announcements read from the floor by parishioners, the priest opened a notepad, and enthusiastically began his sermon, a thinly disguised appeal for contributions to the building fund.

"I call upon your Christian generosity…" Rosa was fascinated with the way the priest's cheeks bounced each time he thrust his head back and then downward to emphasize a point. "…And I ask you all to reach far down into your pockets…"

His arm raised, as it might be were he carrying a sword, Rosa noted the fleshiness of his upper arm and shoulder, "… To support our building fund…" She thought he must be well past 30, almost 50, sometimes it was hard to judge a priest's age. "… Chairman of the building fund -our own Mr. Anthony Orso- will pass among you with the collection basket."

The choir rose to sing, and the priest took a seat between two small well-scrubbed, and white cloaked altar boys.

Genuflecting once again deeply, Anthony walked importantly along the altar rail to the statue of Saint Francis. Reaching behind he drew out a velvet-lined wicker basket on a long handle.

He returned to his front pew and resting the basket on his empty seat, removed a coin purse from his pocket. Full face to the congregation, he held the purse above his head and directly over the collection basket.

Undoing the clasp, he tipped the purse until the coins fell like drops of water into a waterfall. A hushed gasp traveled through the congregation.

Rosa wanted to laugh, but with effort, managed to retain a respectful demeanor. She admired the way Nina had left coins enough in his purse to make a proper demonstration of Christian generosity.

She watched while Anthony, the great benevolence, passed the collection basket from pew to pew, down one aisle, and then the other.

Mass over, Anthony acted with the same solicitous attention. He helped everyone out of the pew and directed them down the aisle. Outside, he introduced Rosa and the children to Father Paul.

"This is Rosa Dante, my niece and her two lovely children, John Edward and Angelina Dante. They are twins. Aren't they about the most beautiful children you have ever seen?" He patted them both on the head. "Rosa, dear, this is Father Paul, he runs St. Francis."

"Sent for them when I heard of their terrible feet. Today, I will take them for a ride in the park, and if we have time we will go to the beach and show the children the Pacific ocean."

Nina's eyes sparkled and she smiled at her husband's words. The priest said, "You are fortunate to have such an uncle as Anthony. He is an important member of our church and community. He has been a big help collecting money for the building of our new church."

Anthony wandered off to chat with others, and he called, "Rosa, my dear, would you please come here a moment when you are through talking with Father Paul? I would like you to meet some of our other friends."

Rosa excused herself and went toward Anthony standing with a group of well-dressed men and women. He introduced her first to Mr. and Mrs. Pardini, "They own one of San Francisco's finest grocery stores."

She also met Mr. Page, a counselor at law, and his wife, Anna, and Mr. and Mrs. Fugazi, who were in the travel business.

Everyone shook hands, and Anthony continued to parade Rosa and the children around, explaining repeatedly how he had brought her from Italy.

Introductions over, Anthony assisted them into the buggy with continuing gallantry. Nina, who was still smiling, said, "If I had known you were going to take us for a ride in the park I would have packed a picnic basket for lunch."

"There is not time to ride in the park today. I invited the Pages and the Fugazi's for dinner at 3 o'clock."

He explained to Rosa, "They are important business friends, and they love her cioppino."

"It's what we used to have in the old country, but we called it cacciucco."

Rosa nodded her head and preoccupied with the disappointment on Nina's face, wondered how Anthony could not notice.

When the buggy stopped in front of the diner, Anthony said, "I will get what you need for supper and be right back," he indicated that they were all to remain seated.

Nina watched him disappear through the doorway.

"I am sorry, Rosa, it would have been nice to take a ride in the park. It's such a beautiful day, and there is not even a hint of fog yet. It's the kind of day Sunday should be so people can ride in the park."

283

Nina smiled at the children, "But next Sunday I promise you, even if we have to take the horse trolley, we will go for a picnic in the Golden Gate Park."

Leaning close to Rosa, Nina whispered, "The hat looks nice on you. Anthony didn't recognize it. I told you he wouldn't remember."

She smiled a mischievous smile like she had indeed put something over on him. "I'm surprised he didn't tell you he liked it, Sunday is his day for compliments."

Anthony reappeared, his arms filled with food and supplies.

Setting it all down into the carriage, he said, "There, with fresh fish like this, the cioppino can't help but be good."

"I can help you, Nina, with the cioppino."

"She doesn't need your help," Anthony said, "you come with me, I will show you what your duties are going to be, so that in the morning when I am busy, you won't have to bother me."

The children started to climb out of the carriage after their mother, "No, go home with your aunt Nina, she will take care of you. "

Looking to their mother for instructions, the children reluctantly sat back down. Nina put her arms around them, and the carriage moved away.

CHAPTER TWENTY-ONE

The other carpeted stairway from the dining room to the second floor where the borders lived opened into a straight narrow hallway line with a dozen doors staring dumbly across at each other.

Rosa's footsteps echoed hollowly on the wooden floor, and the sickening yellow-brown hue of the wood-slatted walls did little to reflect the matter like entering through the single window at each end of the lonely Corridor.

In front of the door nearest the landing, Anthony said:

"This is my office," he selected from a bunch of keys tethered to his belt a long metal chain, " no one enters this room without me. No one. Do you understand?"

He undid the oversized padlock, "You do not even clean this room unless I am right here."

Signaling her to enter the room before him, Anthony stepped inside, and when he did, his body rubbed up against hers.

Rosa searched the face of this man, this man- this husband of her Nina- had it been deliberate?

The room was small and cluttered and was dominated by a massive rolltop desk.

In the middle was a table strewn with papers and ledgers.

A square black safe sat in the far corner.

The single window was nailed shut, and the air was heavy with the smell of dust and smoke from long-dead cigars.

Anthony moved up behind her, his body brushing lightly against hers.

She moved toward the window feigning interest in the elaborate scrollwork which glided in front of the safe.

He followed, "I keep all my valuables in here," he said, "and no one touches it but me."

Edging away from him, Rosa moved closer to the desk, and Anthony reached quickly to shut an open ledger.

"I used to have a cleaning girl in here who got nosy," he sneered, "I sent her away to work in another business of mine."

Rosa cringed at the expression on his face, so unlike the pleasant smile, he used at church. There was an arrogance about him now, his satisfaction with his own cleverness. He thinks he's king, Rosa thought, the king of his own empire.

He moved closer backing her up against the rolltop desk until she had to reach behind to brace herself.

His face close to hers, tiny beads of sweat dripping from his mustache, he traced a circle around her face, "You be nice to me, Rosa, and we will get along fine."

He pushed his body tight against hers and said, "Just so you understand your position here!"

Rosa broke away and ran out the door toward the stairs. If she could just get down to the wharf, to the fishermen tending their nets, but Anthony grabbed a hold of her.

"Where do you think you're going?"

"I haven't finished with you yet, I haven't showed you your work."

Letting go of her arm, he blocked her retreat with his body and herded her along the hallway.

Halfway down he opened a door, "This is where we keep the sheets, and the brushes and rags. You will change the beds every Saturday and scrub the floors, on your knees, none of this mop business. And I inspect to make sure it is done right."

His voice had become louder and anger raging from his eyes, he added, "And don't wear that damn hat! Why can't you just wear a scarf like the other peasant women?"

Snatching the yellow straw hat from her head, he ripped her hat pin loose dislodging a clump of hair. Rosa caught the long pointed pin.

Anthony threw the hat and it sailed crazily down the hall like a spinning top and came to rest on the edge of its brim, up against the furthermost door. Grabbing at her loosened hair, she tried to tie it back into a bun.

"Leave your hair," he said facing her, "I like long black hair."

He ran his hands over her head. She could feel his heart beating as he pressed against her. Drawing back, she took a deep breath to compose herself, "Anthony," she said struggling to hold her voice steady, "I must hurry back to help Nina, Nina, your wife, with supper."

He grunted and pulled her further down the corridor to the window looking out over the water.

287

"Look down here at my wharf. Look at what I own, see the power I have." His arm around her waist, he fingered the buttons on her skirt.

"I own most of those boats you see down there. I am a very powerful man. I can help you if you just cooperate." His voice slimy, he pulled her up against him.

"You're not bad looking, and I bet without all those clothes you look even better."

He had backed her up against the wall, "Do you want to be nice and show Anthony?"

His face wet with perspiration, he rubbed his body back and forth against her, she could feel the hardness of his penis. "If you're nice to me, I could find you a better job, no scrubbing floors."

He pressed his mouth up against hers, she tried to push him away.

He buried his face in her neck. Frantic, she struggled and then – a thought! With strength born of terror, she pulled back from him and drove the long sharp hatpin into his buttocks.

He screamed in pain. She broke free and ran to the stairs.

He ran after her yelling, "I will get you... You bitch... You'll be sorry, you damn peasant... Damn peasant."

When she reached the bottom of the steps she had to stop to get her bearings. On an otherwise peaceful Sunday afternoon, Rosa raced across the crude wooden planks to the wharf with such speed that seagulls napping in the warm sun were awakened, with shrill cries, flew off in rightful indignation.

Rosa ran until out of breath. He was not following her, not yet.

The streets were all uphill and she forced herself onward stopping only to rest. Poor Nina, does she know what kind of man she is married to?

She must not know, how else could she have put up with him for all these years?

Within sight of the flat Rosa stopped, she could not tell Nina what had happened. She tucked her hair up into a knot at the back of her neck as best she could and straightened her clothes, and wondered what she could say to Nina.

Angelina opened the door, "Oh, mama, we are having fun. Me and Nona set the table, come look."

"Not right now Angelina," Rosa pushed past her, "I have to go to the bathroom."

Nina stuck her head out of the kitchen. "Is Anthony with…?" When she saw Rosa pass her, Nina did not finish her sentence.

Rosa locked the bathroom door, and shuddering at the thought of Anthony's wet mouth against hers, washed her face and scrubbed her lips.

She took off her clothes and bathed and dried her body until her skin was red from the towel and then moistened herself with sweet-smelling rosewater.

Naked, she stood before the open window to let the cool air cleanse her body. She shook her dress out in the fresh air, combed and brushed her hair, and when finally she felt clean again, she dressed and went into the kitchen.

"What is wrong, Rosa, are you sick?" Nina asked.

"No, no it was just nature's call," Rosa tried to smile.

Nina was still staring when Angelina pulled at her mother's dress,

"Mama, come see the table." After looking for her aunt's approval the little girl pulled Rosa to the two carved wooden doors that separated the kitchen from the dining room.

The table, covered with a white lace cloth, and set for nine, was surrounded by high back chairs with cushions in dark green.

At each place, between heavy silver spoons and forks was a large white china bowl soon to be filled with Nina's cioppino.

In the center of the table, a silver bowl generously filled with fresh fruit set between two silver candlesticks. Above the hand-carved buffet at the far wall, hung a boldly colored oil painting of ripe grapes, apples, and oranges in a harvest yellow straw basket.

"A lovely room," Rosa said and then becoming aware that her child was waiting for her approval, smiled down at the beaming young face, "And who set the table so beautifully?" She asked.

Still shaking inside, Rosa did not care about the table or the room or the furniture, all she wanted was to get away, to be somewhere else, somewhere alone. But she said, "This furniture is like that in a museum, I have never seen anything like it."

"It is beautiful, isn't it? But we so seldom use it, only when Anthony invites his friends in for an early Sunday dinner. Where is Anthony? Didn't he come back with you?"

"No, no, he stayed at the wharf."

"What happened to your hat? You didn't have it on when you came in."

Damn! She had forgotten all about the hat.

"Oh, Nina, it blew off and into the street. A horse and buggy ran over it before I could get to it." Caught off guard, Rosa felt a rush of blood to her face, she should not have lied.

"That's too bad, Rosa, but do not worry about the hat, the wind can come up so quickly in this town, and when it does, you have to hold onto everything."

Nina walked around the dining table to the far side of the room, and first wiping her hand on the long white apron covering her Sunday dress, she pushed open another pair of carved sliding doors.

"Come, Rosa, I want to show you the parlor. This is Anthony's room, sometimes he comes in here to read his paper and smoke his pipe, but I only sit in here if we have company."

"Sit down here, Rosa, try this nice soft chair, I am going to get us each a glass of wine."

"No…" Rosa started to protest but Nina was already gone.

"There," Nina said when she returned, "I think a little glass of wine is just the thing."

Rosa sipped her sweet red liquid, grateful for Nina's silence.

The room was a dark room. On one wall a fireplace with a gray hearth was framed in dark carved wood that reached the ceiling. On its heavy mantle, a vase of paper Chinese flowers stood opposite a silver-framed picture of Anthony.

On one side of the fireplace was a broad chesterfield and on the other, red velvet chairs flanked a heavy leg table on which Anthony's pipes were displayed.

Nina pushed back heavy dark green drapes from a bay window which jutted over the street.

"Oh dear," She said, "the fog is coming in already. We will not have the sun for long today."

She straightened up a crocheted antimacassar, "Anthony does not like the drapes open. He's afraid that the sun will fade the furniture and craze the shellac."

There was a depressing heaviness about this room. Nowhere could Rosa find a touch of Nina and the darkness weighed down upon her mood.

"Shall I close the drapes?" She asked as they got up to leave the room.

"No, let them stay open while he's out. What Anthony doesn't know won't hurt him. See! I am already braver because you were here." Nina turned to hug Rosa, "Now that you and your babies are here, there is already more love and sunshine in this whole house."

The two women went back to the kitchen.

This room was Nina's, while the dining room and the parlor were a man's room, everything in the kitchen was painted white, large shiny pots on the stove, and the small table covered with cheerful wax cloth, this was a happy room.

And the pretty yellow dress, that is Nina's too. Someday I will see her wear that pretty dress.

Angelina was arranging white china cups on their saucers, "Look, mama," she said, "these are just like the cups Signor Martinelli sent your chicken soup in, right mama?"

"And who is Signor Martinelli?" Nina asked, a little spark of excitement in her eye.

"He is the nice man who took us to lunch up in the fancy first-class dining hall."

Looking toward Rosa with increasing interest, Nina asked, "and what is this about chicken soup?"

Between mother and daughter, Nina heard the whole story of Signor Martinelli.

"He sounds like a fine gentleman, I am sorry I did not get to meet him."

Angelina had tired of arranging China cups, and now hopping about on one foot, answered, "He said he would see us again, and I will introduce you to him, Nona, can I mama, can I?"

At that very moment, Rosa and Nina both heard the sound of a key turning in the downstairs door, and as is by previous arrangement, the three fell silent.

With customary lightness of step and as usual attitude of assured ownership, Anthony entered the room.

The sight of him made Rosa shudder, he was carrying the straw hat.

Flinging it on the table, he said, "You left this at the boarding house."

Rosa grabbed for the hat.

Nina looked at Rosa and said nothing. She looked to the hat, then to Anthony, then back to Rosa. She remained silent.

Rosa sat motionless in her chair. Taking the hat from her, Nina brushed its brim with the sleeve of her dress and said, "it's good it was not lost."

Anthony did not look directly at Rosa. She was glad for that, the sight of him was almost making her sick. Had Nina not been there, she would have run from the room.

Anthony went to the stove and lifted up the lids, "Did you put all the crab I bought you in the cioppino or were you stingy again?"

293

Nina nodded. He walked into the dining room and counted the chairs.

"It's not necessary for the children to sit at the table with us. Let them eat in the kitchen."

Nina stood up, "No! They're well behaved and they are my family- at last, I have a family, and they will sit at the table!"

Nina's voice was stronger than Rosa had ever heard it, as she stood, hands on her hips, staring at her husband.

Anthony glared at her and then turned away, "Well they better behave, or to the kitchen they go. I won't have any kids spoiling my Sunday supper. Rosa, you better make sure of that, these are important people coming tonight."

For the first time Anthony looked right at her, and the anger Rosa saw in his eyes frightened her.

CHAPTER TWENTY-TWO

Anthony greeted Mr. and Mrs. Fugazi at the front door, and when he had seated them in the parlor, called for Nina and Rosa to bring in the antipasti.

A short stout matron, Mrs. fugazi was wearing the exquisitely tailored suit she wore to church and added a blue fox fur across her shoulders.

Her dark complexion suggested she came from southern Italy, but her accent, whether real or put on, was that spoken only in the most learned circles of Rome.

The Fugazi's owned a travel business, and she lost no time in mentioning that there were few parts of the world she was not familiar with.

Mrs. Fugazi kissed first Nina and then Rosa, and exuded tremendous joy at being in such lovely company. When the children came in, she smothered them in similar affection.

With only slightly less exuberance than his wife, Mr. Fugazi shook hands with Anthony and kissed the women. The plumpness of his figure threatened the expensive cut of his suit and severely taxed the bottom holes of his vest. He had just accepted a tumbler of straight whiskey from Anthony when the Page's arrived.

As Mr. Page was tall to Mr. Fugazi's short stature, Mrs. Page was shy to the loquacious Mrs. Fugazi. Mrs. Page, Anna as she immediately asked to be called, was pale-skinned and slight in stature. She moved with an air of uncertainty about her and seldom spoke without first glancing at her husband. Mr. Page was handsome to the point of looking almost unreal.

His features were fine and sharp and his gracefully waved hair grew from his high forehead in a widow's peak.

His manner was regal, toward his wife he was gentle and protective.

Much of the dinner conversation was among the three men, they talked of business and City Hall and about the law. They dwelt on finances and investments and many times the expression 'smart money' was used. The woman ate quietly and murmured complementary compliments about the children's lovely manners and about the delicious food.

When the dessert cakes were eaten, Anthony refilled the wine glasses and stood up. Clinking his spoon against the glass as if to address a large hall of listeners, he waited until he had everyone's attention.

"I would like to propose a toast to our newest arrivals, my dear niece, and her two adorable children I brought from Italy," he lifted his chin and drained the glass.

Suddenly strangled by a swallow of air she could force neither up nor down, Rosa looked to her aunt, but Nina stared into her glass.

Everyone at the table stood up, and with wine glasses raised, saluted her. Head pounding, Rosa managed a weak smile.

Mrs. Fugazi asked about their boat ride over, and Rosa had barely given an answer when she deftly manipulated the conversation and was soon recounting her own last trip across the Atlantic.

Rosa was grateful to escape the need to talk, her throat was still tight and her head ached. And barely aware of what was being said, she sipped her wine.

Mr. Fugazi tried to interrupt the tail he had heard too many times before but unsuccessfully resigned himself to listening.

When she stopped to take a breath Anthony stood up and suggested the men go into the parlor for their Brandy.

Nina went off to get glasses for the men and Mrs. Fugazi moved into the vacant chair between Rosa and Anna Page.

To her captive audience, she recounted in great detail how on her last trip to Italy she had to speak harshly to the steward for neglecting to clean the cabin.

Rosa's already throbbing head worsened when she heard this woman's silly complaints and thought of her own dark and tiny cabin in the bowels of the Leonardo.

As soon as Nina returned Rosa excused herself. Wanting to get away from this woman's endless chatter, and desperate to have a moment to herself, she explained that she had to put the children to bed.

The twins were already in their nightshirts and while Rosa folded the clothes they had worn to dinner, Mrs. Fugazi sat on the edge of the bed and kept up a constant barrage of questions about Nina and Anthony, all personal and all offensive to Rosa.

"Tell me, how did you find Nina when you arrived? I hope she is well, she works too hard, never has time to buy things for herself.

"I worry about her. I know Anthony must make enough money, doesn't he?" Never waiting for an answer she rattled on.

"Look at this beautiful house he has given Nina, but still Nina stays the same. I wonder if she misses Italy and that's why she clings to the old ways. Anthony certainly has modernized but poor Nina, she is still the poor peasant lady who got off the boat."

Rosa tucked the children in and kissed them good night.

Signaling to Mrs. Fugazi, she watched her paddle down the hall, still talking, apparently unaware that she had received not one word of response to her questions.

No longer an irritant to Rosa, this stout little woman had become a source of amusement, and Rosa's head no longer ached.

Nina and Anna were still sitting at the table smiling and talking quietly. A roar of laughter came from the parlor and the women looked at each other knowingly, the men were telling their risque stories.

"Rosa, come and sit with us. I was just telling Anna about how much English you know and how you already taught the children so much."

Unhappy at not being in charge of the conversation, Mrs. Fugazi asked, "Tell me about what your plans are. Are you going to work for Anthony?"

"I'll work with Nina for a while, but first I want to get the children in school and then see where I can learn more English and study for citizenship."

"Why that's just wonderful, Rosa", the usually quiet Anna spoke with interest, "most people wait to see if they like America and then, later on, think about becoming citizens."

"Before I left Italy, I knew America was to be my home. I made that decision a long time ago". As if in all of roses self-sufficiency, the women looked to Nina, who was nodding approval.

"All right," Mrs. Fugazi said, "then you get right over to the sisters of the holy family, they have good classes for the little ones in Italian, and they also teach them English too."

"They teach in Italian? But why when we are in America?" Rosa interrupted.

"Well, Rosa, when you've been here longer you will learn that San Francisco is just like Europe," Mrs. Fugazi spoke with authority.

"Each nationality end up living in its own little section of the city. The Germans have settled down on Montgomery and Bush Street near Pine. The Chinese around Sacramento below Broadway, and the Russians on Russian Hill.

"The French are mostly over at Lafayette Park near Octavia. So you see we are all in our own little communities!"

"But all the more reason to learn English. How can we communicate if we don't speak the same language? How could your husband do business with all the different people if he didn't know how to talk to them?"

"My husband speaks English perfectly." Mrs. Fugazi replied a hint of erring in her voice. "He was born right here in North Beach."

"Is Anthony a citizen Nina?" Anna asked.

"No, he said it wasn't important for his business, and he thinks it would just be a waste of time."

"I am a citizen," Anna said apologetically, "because I married an American citizen. I didn't get to go to any of the classes. I really know so little…"

"You don't really have to know anything, Anna, as an attorney Tom knows everything that is necessary. You don't have to worry about those things," clearly Mrs. Fugazi was tired of this subject.

"Well I have no husband," Rosa said, "my children's father is dead, and for myself, I know I want to learn to really speak the language."

"But Anthony will take care of you. You really have no need to go to all that work."

Rosa shuddered at the thought of how Anthony would take care of her.

Anna, said, "I have books I will give you. One time I started a citizenship class and bought the books, but Tom didn't like me going to school with- those- those people. I tried to read the books on my own, but I didn't understand enough. I guess I'm just too dumb to learn."

"I'll bring the books to you, they would be good for the children too."

Just then the men returned and announced it was time to go. Anthony put his arm around Rosa's shoulder, "and this little lady has to get up very early in the morning."

Reflexly, Rosa drew back. His arm left hanging in mid-air, Anthony glared at her.

Mr. and Mrs. Fugazi kissed everyone good night, and Anna left silently holding her husband's arm.

Anthony went to the wharf, and Rosa and Nina went into the kitchen to do the dishes.

The following morning Nina finished with breakfast for the fisherman, the children were sweeping out the dining room, and Rosa was finishing cleaning the upstairs when Anna Page walked through the door, her arms loaded with books. Nina brought three cups of coffee and two glasses of milk, and they all sat down in the deserted dining room.

Anna looked prettier than she had last night, there was a certain animation, a spark in her eyes that had not been there before.

"When we got home last night, Thomas had some business to attend to down at City Hall, and I took these books out – I haven't looked at them in months – and you know, I did manage to get through some of them."

"And, Rosa, I remembered about a public school for children that's only a little away from you and they teach in English. They don't teach religion at all, and I heard it is a very good school. It's on Washington, near Mason. I'm sorry, but I don't remember the name."

Nina had stepped into the kitchen and Anna started talking in English. "You see, I know a little English, my sister and I immigrated from Italy, and I met Thomas here, in this country."

Nina came back, and when she heard the English, her face sagged.

"Oh my," she said, "I wish I wasn't so dumb and knew more English."

"Yes, and I wish I knew more about American history, and that I could have gone to the citizenship class," Anna added.

"So do I!" Nina said slapping her hand against the table and startled at the intensity of her gesture, all of them began laughing.

"We should all go to the Americanization school together!" Rosa said, noticing that Nina's English was coming easier for her.

"Well, I don't think Thomas would like that," Anna said.

"And Anthony would be furious – he would say I was wasting my time when I should be working."

"If we all did it together, how could they complain?" Rosa asked.

301

"I will find out about the school."

"If we all went," Anna said, "we could help each other, and if there was something I didn't understand, you could tell me."

Nina said, "I have secretly always wanted to do this but I was afraid to do it all alone," her happiness reflected the understanding she saw in their faces.

When Anna went home she left behind her two happy conspirators.

The sun, full in the sky, Rosa could see the boats coming in. Escorted by winged beggars hovering over ahead and heavy with fish, they rode low in the water.

Careful to stay out of Anthony's sight, Rosa walked along the water's edge. Her attention consumed with lists of things she must attend to, and her spirit filled with plans for the future, her feet carried her far.

When she returned, the boats were emptied and the fishermen had to turn their attention to selling their catch.

Brokers walked up and down the dock comparing baskets of squirming fish, signaling for those they wanted, and walking past those that did not measure up. Rosa saw Anthony and stepping behind some large crates, stopped to watch.

He was weighing the first fish and separating the best. "Take these, they are small but I am being good to you today."

Throwing others into a basket on his feet, he said, "I don't want these, sell them to the chinamen."

Rosa watched this process for a long time before she noticed that when the fishermen placed fish on the scale and bent down to get more, Anthony would ever so slightly lift up on the hanging scale and write down the lighter weight. He did this so quickly that it took several repetitions for Rosa to convince herself that she saw what she saw.

Staying behind the line of crates where Anthony could not see her, Rosa moved further down the wharf where other brokers were working.

She did not recognize any of the fishermen and realized that she had seen Anthony deal only with men from the boarding house.

She had not gone far when she heard angry voices behind her and turning back saw Anthony and Mario facing each other, waving their arms and shouting.

"The price you pay for fish is robbery!" Mario yelled, "you pay less than any other broker, you charge me an arm and a leg for dock space, and by the end of the month, I owe you money!"

"Just remember, who picked you up off your face when you first got here, if it wasn't for me helping you out, you'd be at the bottom of the bay now instead of fishing in it."

"And by heaven, sometimes I think I'd be better off not having you help me!" He picked up his basket of fish.

"Go on, get out of here, you sound like an old woman, whining and crying."

Mario turned on Anthony, his fists clenched, and Rosa thought he was going to strike him. But instead, Mario remained silent and Rosa watched as the anger in his sturdy fishermen's body turned to resignation and defeat. He walked away, an old man.

Rosa continued toward the end of the wharf where a group of Chinamen stood waiting and watching what the caucasian brokers were buying.

They were very little people, sallow-skinned, with their black hair and long cues down their back's, dressed in dull blue jackets and sandals on their feet.

The fishermen who had sold what they could to the caucasian brokers brought the rest of their catch to the Chinese. Although neither the Chinese buyer nor the Italian fisherman understood the other's language, by making faces and using gestures, they somehow arrived at an agreement.

Well, the fisherman counted on their fingers, the Chinese used colored beads hanging inside a wooden frame, which they slid back and forth faster than the eyes could follow. When the deal was made the Chinese packed the fish into baskets at either end of a long slender bamboo pole, and shuffled off with the pole across their shoulders.

As Rosa headed back toward the diner, she stopped to exchanged greetings with the old woman stocking up Anthony's booth to sell the housewives for their evening meal.

Rosa saw Mario walking toward them and felt a sudden stab of pity at the sagging shoulders and downcast case. His face brightened when he saw them.

He smiled and said, "Oh, two lovely ladies, what more can a poor fisherman ask of life?" In an often-repeated game, he reached for the old woman's hand pretending to kiss it, while she, a toothless mouth stretched into a wide grin, pretended to beat him off.

Just then Anthony walked up and without warning berated the two women for wasting time. His voice becoming louder he told them he was not paying them to spend their time visiting.

When he ordered Rosa to go inside and get to work, she felt Mario tense up. She placed herself between the two men and with her hand, edged Mario away.

Inside the building, Mario said, "Thank you, Rosa, I am afraid that someday I will do something to that man that I will regret."

CHAPTER TWENTY-THREE

Rosa enrolled the twins in the school Anna Page told her about, and Angelina was excited, but John was more interested in the fishing boats, and many times wished aloud that he had been permitted to stay behind in Italy and fish with his two older brothers.

After the supper, dishes were done and the kitchen clean, Rosa and the twins sat down at one of the long dining tables to look at the new school books the teacher had given her. Nina sat down beside them, "I will learn along with the children," she whispered.

Mario and some of the men had been huddled in the corner of the room talking, and when he noticed Rosa, went to her table. "Good evening," he spoke respectfully, "what are you girls so busy doing?"

"We are studying our English," Angelina said, "next week we get to go to school."

"Good for you young lady. I wish I had time for that. Maybe when you get real smart, Angelina, you will teach me?"

"Yes, sir, I will be glad to."

Mario put his cap on, and then embarrassed at his lack of good manners, took it off, and bowing to the ladies, sort of backed out of the room.

"Mario seems especially fond of you, Rosa," Nina said.

"He is a kind man," Rosa answered, "a good man at heart."

"Did something happen today between him and Anthony?" Nina asked.

Rosa shook her head that it had, but couldn't say more in front of the children.

Sensing a good chance for escape, John asked if they could go outside and play. When the door closed behind the children, Nina said, "I know something is eating at Anthony. I've seen this many times. He gets something caught in his craw and it eats away at him until he blows up, and when he does, no one is safe. I try to stay out of his way when he's like this."

Just then Anthony came in, and the tension in his walk, the anger on his face- everything about him- bore out Nina's supposition that danger was building inside of him.

"What in hell are you doing now, Nina?"

He strode across the dining room toward them, and glaring at their books, said, "Rosa are you putting silly ideas into her head, trying to teach her English?" Not waiting for any kind of answer, he went on, "I knew you were going to be nothing but trouble if we let you come here."

He snatched a book from the table, "I'll show you how to learn English," and spreading the book open by the covers he tore it to pieces, page by page.

"No, no, don't do that!" Rosa screamed, "they don't belong to me. They're borrowed!" She tried to grab the book from him.

Anthony pushed her away, and losing her balance, she fell.

"Dear God in heaven!" Nina screamed and rushed to Rosa who lay still on the floor. Nina glanced up at Anthony who was staring at the figure on the floor, his face drained of color.

"You've killed her!" Nina screamed at her husband, "you've killed her!" Sobbing, she buried her head in Rosa's breast.

Rosa moved.

"Oh thank God!" Nina said, weak with relief. Her fear for Rosa turned into anger, she looked up at Anthony, but all she saw was the door closing behind him.

A cold cloth and a glass of wine revived Rosa's body, but the torn pages on the floor cast her spirit downward, and she started to cry.

Mario, who had seen Anthony storm out of the diner, came back in to see if everything was all right.

When he heard what had happened, he put his hand on Rosa's shoulder, and said, "Don't cry Rosa, it is good for you to study your English, and you too, Nina."

There was pain in his voice as he said, "To have no schooling is to be a prisoner. You learn, Rosa, don't let anybody make you give it up."

Mario was halfway to the door when he stopped and came back, "if it would not hurt, you teach me English, then I can become a citizen?"

Rosa shook her head, and encouraged, he added, "maybe it would not hurt if all of us," he pointed out to the dock, "got a little smarter."

He walked out the door, with his shoulder's straighter, his step a bit lighter.

"Oh, Rosa," Nina said as she and Rosa walked behind the children back to the flat. "I was afraid something like this would happen. You had better stay as far away from Anthony as possible. Something has been bothering him, it's been building up since Sunday."

Pain stabbed at Rosa: how much did she need to know? What did she suspect?

They started up the hill, "Anthony is a smart man, and I don't always understand him," Nina said. "It is like he wants to keep everyone else dumb, so he can be like…" Unable to find the right word, her voice trailed off.

"King?" Rosa suggested, instantly regretting her choice.

"Yes, king," Nina said, "a king like those foreign rulers- like the ones who have a room full of wives."

Rosa studied Nina's face for any clue to her thoughts.

They arrived home. "Anthony always gets what he wants," Nina said without explanation.

The children went without protest to catch up on the sleep their early schedule deprived them of, and the two women sat in the seldom used parlor.

"Rosa," Nina said, her face more troubled than before, "I may not always understand Anthony, but I do know what he's like, I know that something happened Sunday."

Rosa caught her breath, a sudden rush of heat poured over her body like a shade pulling down over a window.

"I saw your face when he came in- and the hat."

Rosa's heart sank. She didn't want to lie but didn't know how she could tell Nina the way Anthony acted, and yet if she remained silent, Nina might think it worse than it was.

"Nina, I am so sorry…" Rosa said beginning to cry.

"Sh-h-h, it's not your fault, it's all right."

Then a look of terror clouded Nina's face as she lifted Rosa's head and looking deep into her eyes said, "as long as you were not hurt. You weren't hurt, were you?"

"No, I am all right, oh Nina, I am so sorry…"

"There there, it's all right, Rosa, my child, it's not your fault. I know him. He chases all the nice girls who come here to work."

Nina held Rosa. "Sylvia- the last girl- a pretty little thing-disappeared suddenly. Anthony said she had another job, but I know she wouldn't just leave without a word, she had no one, no place to go. I still worry about her."

Little by little Rosa told Nina what had happened Sunday at the boarding house. Nina listened silently, and when Rosa was done, she said, "No one says no to Anthony". She went to the window and pulled the drapes away, and for a long time stared out across the water.

"Wait here, I will be right back."

Nina, her face alive and resolute, returned carrying her box of money. Setting it down on the chesterfield between them.

"This is something I have been thinking about for a long time," she was untying the string and unwrapping the paper, "I want you to take this money…"

"No, no! I wouldn't hear of it," Rosa protested.

"Wait, now hear me out. I have a plan. You are not safe here with Anthony – you and the children must get away from him – and as for me, there is no way to tell what might happen.

"I want you to take this money and use it to buy a flat for us, a place where you and the children will be safe away from where. Where you can start your bakery. And where I can come if I ever need another home.

"Look for a building with a store where you could put ovens, a flat for you and the children, and maybe an upstairs you could rent out. It would be perfect."

"But Nina, that's everything- I'd be taking everything you've saved for so long."

"Rosa please you must do this. It wouldn't be taking. You must find a place where you are safe and where I can come if I need to."

"Rosa take this, do it for the both of us. I must know there will be someplace for me to go too, if…"

"But I worry about leaving you alone with Anthony."

"Do not worry Rosa, I have learned how to survive all these years. Don't you worry."

You must do all of this in your name. Anthony must not know that any of this is mine, if he found out, he could get it away from me. Start looking right away, I will cover for you at the diner. And Rosa, stay out of Anthony's sight."

In the following weeks Nina and Rosa had little cause to worry about Anthony, he seemed to be as intent on avoiding them as they were anxious to avoid him.

Rosa cleaned the boarders' rooms and helped Nina in the diner. Almost every morning Anna Page came with some excuse or other, and always stayed for coffee.

Although she seldom spoke of herself, her loneliness cried out to Rosa and Nina for comfort she spoke of her husband with reverence, how the son of immigrant parents had worked his way through college to become an important lawyer, and how he had even changed his name from Pagenelli to Page to be more part of America.

"Thomas is an important man, and always very busy." In all of Rosa and of her plans to go into business for herself, Anna often prefaced her own remarks with, "I would be afraid," or "I wouldn't know how…"

When Rosa told her about the Americanization class that was going to be taught at a public school, she was too timid to go along to inquire about it, but she asked Rosa to find out if she could come to the classes even though she was already a citizen.

Rosa went to the school and found out that although they were having trouble finding teachers for all the citizenship classes, everyone was welcome.

"The more people we can teach about America, the better, bring all you want," the teacher said.

Rosa asked how soon she could start classes and how long it would take her to learn enough to pass the citizenship test.

"I don't think that it will take you very long," she said, "you already seem to have a good understanding of English, and of course you'll know everything you have to know long before your two years are up."

"My two years?" Rosa asked.

"Yes, you have to live here two years before you can take the test."

"I can't do anything for two years?" She asked.

Smiling at Rosa's disappointment, the teacher encouraged her to start her classes right away, to bring her friends, and to come.

"There is no limit to how many classes you can take, and I think you'll be a good student and can help me with the others."

Whenever there was a spare hour, Rosa trudged around the streets looking at buildings for sale. She had no luck, when, one day toward the end of the week after the children had started school, she returned home to Nina handing her a letter, asking, "Who is it from?"

Rosa's fingers trembled as she ripped open the envelope. It's Signor Martinelli, she answered, sitting down to savor the moment:

Why dear Rosa:

I hope your homecoming with your aunt and uncle was everything you wish for and that you are now comfortably settled.

Please do not think it's presumptuous of me to write, but I missed the conversations we had on the train, and want very much to see you and the children. I have many things to tell you.

As I feared, my brother is very ill. On Saturday next I am bringing him into San Francisco to be admitted to French hospital, where they have a new machine. It is called an x-ray machine. It can look into Enrico's lungs. Modern medicine is wonderful.

I should have Enrico settled by noon and would like to call on you and the children. I hope that you will be able to see me. If I hear nothing to the contrary, I will arrive at your aunt's home at about 12:30 Saturday.

Affectionately,

Aldo

PS. Am I to be permitted to taste your bread?

Rosa's face flushed and she felt her heartbeat deep within her. She had just settled back into the chair to re-read every word when Nina broke in wanting to know everything.

Rosa told about Aldo, about his life, why he had come to America. She told Nina almost everything but did not mention his wife.

Nina laughed at the story of the chicken soup and said how smart the children were to have met him.

"No you go with him on Saturday," Nina said, never mind Anthony. I will make an excuse for you. On Saturday's he is busy and comes to the diner just long enough to pay the men, the twins will stay with me, you go and have a good time."

"No, no, he is coming to see the children too. It is best if I take them with me." She did not tell Nina that she didn't trust herself to be alone with him.

The days that followed alternately dragged and sped by for Rosa. Happy anticipation made the menial tasks seem like nothing at all, and yet when she thought of waiting until Saturday, the hands of the clock moved slowly.

The days fell into a routine, before she could go out and hunt for a place for her bakery, she got the children ready for school, helped Nina in the diner, and cleaned the boarders' rooms.

She liked the simple little rooms the fishermen had, and always took special pains with them. Each had a narrow metal framed bed, a dresser with a picture of St. Francis above it, a straight back wood chair, and a hook to hang a Sunday suit on.

In every room, on top of the unpainted wooden dresser were pictures of families left behind in Italy, and somewhere in each room, a crucifix hung on the wall.

It was still two days before Rosa would see Aldo, and her mind was more on the forthcoming visit than on what she was doing when she noticed some important looking papers lying open on the dresser she was dusting. She recognized the names Joseph Paluchie and Anthony Orso.

It appeared to be a legal paper, a contract for the sale of a boat. It was written in English and had a lot of big words she had never seen before.

Looking out into the hall to be sure Anthony had not come up to his office, she sat down to read the papers. It appeared that Joseph bought a boat from Anthony and agreed to sell him all his fish, and there was something in there about 12 months, but Rosa did not know what it meant. Wishing she could keep the document to study, she put it back on the dresser and went to finish her work.

That afternoon when the two women started for home, Rosa suggested to Nina they walk along the wharf. She asked where Anthony got the boats the fishermen used.

"In that building over there, the one with the ramp going down into the water. They build them in there, then Anthony sells them to the fishermen. He keeps a few both of his own that he rents to the men looking for work. They usually either buy them or buy a new one from him."

When Rosa said she wanted to see the boathouse, they turned and went back to the street and followed along the edge of the water to a tall wooden building. The unpainted wood had turned a gray-green from the sea air and was liberally streaked with white from pigeons perched on the roof beams.

Nina slid open a tall door on iron runners and they walked into the space big enough for a boat to go through. Inside, three men were working on boats mounted on wooden cradles with large iron wheels rusting on railroad tracks.

Nina spoke to them all by name and introduced Rosa. "Tell the boss this one is almost finished," one man said, "she'll be ready next week, just like he ordered."

"Those men work for Anthony?" Rosa asked as they left.

"Oh, yes," Nina said, "he has a lot of people working for him. I think that is why he gets so crazy sometimes. He tries to do too much."

"Where does Anthony find the men to buy his boats?"

"He goes right to the dock and meets them getting off the boat from Italy, and at the train station. He always seems to know when Italians arrive hungry and broke and looking for work.

"He brings them to the boarding house, feeds them, gives them a room, and gives them a job. If they have nowhere to go, he lets them stay here free for a few days. He especially likes to meet the ships that come around the horn.

"These poor men, after that trip, they are almost dead. They're sick, they're homesick, and starved for good food. They're so thankful for any little comfort or kindness that they usually end up working for Anthony.

"Then, when they get a few dollars ahead, he sells them a boat. It's as simple as that. Oh yes, he is very good to them when they first arrive."

As Nina talked, the words Rosa had seen on the contract in Joseph's room were beginning to make more sense. The more she understood, the more she worried – except when her thoughts leapt ahead to Aldo's visit.

CHAPTER TWENTY-FOUR

When Saturday finally came, Rosa was up early baking bread. Mario had brought her seawater from far out in the bay and when he asked why she smiled mysteriously and told him it was for a secret potion.

But she was not completely happy with the way the bread turned out. The taste was right, so it wasn't the seawater, but there was something not quite perfect, she thought, about the texture.

It must be the ovens, they are not hot enough, they are not stone ovens.

The children were dressed and waiting long before they heard the knock on the door and collided headlong with each other trying to be first to open it.

"Oh, Mr. Martinelli, we missed you. We are so glad to see you," the children's arms were locked around his neck, and when he straightened up they hung there like human necklaces.

Laughing at the sight of him with the two children dangling from his neck, Rosa tried to pry them loose, but he took her hand and kissed it. Giving her a small bouquet of deep lavender forget me nots, he said, "My dear Rosa, you look beautiful. San Francisco agrees with you."

The children were pulling at his coattails both trying to talk at once. "Quiet, now," Rosa said, "you will get your turn."

"How would you like to go on a picnic?" Aldo asked of everyone.

"My buggy is waiting, and I had the hotel pack us four lunches."

He smiled that same wonderful smile Rosa thought of so often.

"We will find a park to eat our lunch in and then take a ride to see the city. Would you like to do that, children?"

They agreed with delight and waited at the door while their mother put on her hat. "That is lovely, Rosa, you have already been shopping," Aldo spoke to her reflection in the mirror.

"Oh wait", she said, "I almost forgot the loaf of bread I baked for you this morning."

When she came back from the kitchen she apologized, "I am not too happy with it. It's not my best. The ovens were not hot enough."

Aldo helped them into the buggy, and the driver turned the horse and started up Telegraph Hill where they would be able to see most of the city.

At the foot of the hill, they passed the women's shops where Nina bought her fine dress and further up saw stores filled with many different kinds of merchandise: foods, sausages, and spaghetti hanging on lines to dry.

Then the stores were replaced by flats and houses.

"Look," Rosa said, "at those little houses, clinging to the side of the hill, afraid they might fall off, and see, they built little fences around the backyard to keep the children from falling down on the neighbor's roofs."

319

"Really mama?" John asked. Rosa squeezed him affectionately and they all laughed.

The horse was lathered by the time the driver pulled him to a stop at the top of the hill. The children hopped right out of the buggy but were more interested in rolling in the nearby patch of grass than looking at the view.

"Look Rosa," Aldo pointed at the bay far below them, "if the little boats are like the ones in Genova, even the sales are shaped the same, like the ears of a horse with the wind in them."

Silently, each in their own thoughts, their eyes moved like slow motion cameras from the golden gateway far down to the southern end of the bay.

Rosa turned to Aldo and said, "I am glad that you are here to see this with me. I look out there around this beautiful land, and think how near I am to home, and yet how far away home is from me."

"You are homesick?" Aldo asked.

"For Victor and Dino, I miss them. That is what I miss most, everything else is the same here. The other night during supper, when we were eating shrimp, John said it tasted the same as it did home. We have traveled all this way and the fish still tastes the same."

Aldo laughed, "The mind of a child somehow makes everything very simple."

"How about you, Aldo, are you lonesome for Italy?"

"Oh, of course, there are some things and some people– I miss, but I really do love it here."

The children had been running around busy as two puppies just released from their holding pen, and Angelina brought a handful of wildflowers, "Here, mama, now you have two bouquets."

"Come children, I think it is time to eat our lunch and taste your mother's bread."

They all watched his face as he chewed and waited anxiously for his verdict. His expression changed from playful to serious, and he said, "Rosa, you are right, this is the best bread I have ever tasted. Even my mother's was not like this."

Savoring the look of admiration on his face, Rosa said, "This is not quite what it should be, but when I get the right ovens, you will see, it will be even better."

"Now I know why you were able to sell to the inns at home, this is really excellent. When you get your bakery started, you will have no shortage of customers, that I am sure of. I know Enrico will want some of this for his dining room."

"Have you been able to make a start yet?"

Rosa told him her plans and found out that he knew about starting businesses and would be happy to help her whenever she needed him.

The children finished eating and told Aldo all the things that had happened to them, how they worked in the diner and about the fishermen who ate there and about school, and how they couldn't study because uncle Anthony tore up their book.

Rosa interrupted the children, "You have told enough stories, go play."

As they ran off Aldo asked, "What is this about the book, Rosa?"

"It is nothing, and I am anxious to hear about your brother. Please, tell me from the very beginning how you found him."

"Unfortunately, it is as I feared, consumption or tuberculosis, as they call it now. This morning we had him admitted to French Hospital. I mentioned in my letter the new x-ray machine they have, it can take a picture of his lungs and tell them what to do for him. Sometimes they collapse one lung, but it's risky and I'm afraid Enrico is too weak."

All he is is skin and bones held together with a cough, but at least he's not spitting up any blood. Right now what he needs is rest, no worry, good food, and plenty of that. They hope that with proper rest maybe in three months he'll be well enough to come home."

"Oh, it is so sad to see someone you love, struck down like that."

"It started simply. He thought he had bronchitis, but the cough never left."

"The only way I got him to agree to go inside the hospital was by telling him that if the word got out that he had tuberculosis, people would stop coming to the hotel. He agreed only if I would stay."

"He has a good man managing the hotel, but he doesn't know much about the financial end of it and that worries Enrico, but now that I am here I will be able to take over that part of the management."

"I am glad I made the trip, he already seems happier. We told everyone at the hotel that he was tired and going on a long holiday while I take over for him. That seemed to satisfy them."

"Do you think you'll get good care at the hospital, what did you call it?"

"The French hospital, and I know he'll get good care there because it used to be the Italian hospital."

"You can joke about it?"

"Yes, I can joke because although I worry about him, I also feel optimistic now that he has gone into the hospital."

"He has a private room all to himself, but unfortunately it is rather drab, all white and sterile."

"Do you think that it would be all right for me to go visit him sometime?" Rosa asked.

The gratitude and Aldos eyes belied in his previous joking.

"That would be marvelous. Oh Rosa, would you really? They say it is very important to keep his spirits up, he would love to meet you. I am afraid that he knows a great deal about you. I told him almost everything about you and the children."

"There would be no danger to you to visit him, they give you a mask to put on, and I have already told him that he could not kiss you, because I was applying for the job."

Surprised by the switch in the conversation, Rosa lowered her head and blushed.

"I am sorry, Rosa I did not mean to tease you. Someday my teasing will get me into trouble."

She agreed with him and laughed.

Aldo stood and reached his hand out to help her up. "We should take our ride to see the city before it gets too late."

She was halfway up when he playfully slacked his arm as if to let go of her, and then quickly pulled her to her feet and close to him. Holding onto her he asked, "Friends?"

"Friends indeed! Friends don't let ladies fall to the ground."

"But I did not let you fall to the ground. I see you don't trust me yet, so that will have to be my project for the rest of the day- trust among friends."

She knew he was talking about more than a little playfulness in the park.

Walking toward the buggy together, Aldo stopped to look out across the bay: "Rosa when I feel lonely, I go to my favorite hill and look across the water to where I know you are. And oh, so many times I have wanted to jump on the ferry and come to you."

He turned toward her, "Do you know that you are very special to me?" He gently touched her face.

"And I too cherish…" She chose her words carefully, "your friendship", she looked up at him, sad to see the disappointment her words had caused him.

She called the children from their game of hide and seek among the trees, and they started down the hill.

Aldo took a folded piece of drawing paper from his breast pocket. "I almost forgot to give you this, Rosa. Enrico sent it, it is a pencil sketch of his hotel."

It was a carefully drawn picture of a sprawling two-story wooden building, a wide Victorian veranda of carved posts and railings around it started with deep cushion wicker chairs and lounges.

"It is painted a pretty light blue-gray", Aldo said, "bland, you can sit on that porch in the morning sun and look out across the bay while you drink your coffee, it is a marvelous spot."

"What is the name of the hotel?"

"'Torino by the Sea hotel'. There is a big sign in the front, but he left it out of the sketch. Isn't that a wonderful name?"

The children wanted to see the picture, and Aldo added, "It is a very light and happy looking place, and reflects Enrico's usual mood. He has the entry carpeted with rich oriental rugs he brought with him, but the furniture is Italy! It is a touch of Torino in America. You must see it, Rosa, you will love it."

It was getting chilly, the fog was almost about to pull its thick carpet over the bay, and the children, snuggled down into the blanket, were asleep. The driver put the top of the buggy up and turned them away from the water end up Jones Street.

"Now," Aldo said, "I want to hear about you. Did Anthony really tear up that book? You know I worry."

"I don't want to burden you with my little troubles, you have enough problems, you don't need to listen to mine. I just wish the twins hadn't said so much."

"My dear, that is what friends are for."

Taken by the sincerity in his face, Rosa told Aldo everything that happened. She told him how one minute Anthony was a tyrant at home and the next minute a perfect citizen and gentleman at church.

And she told him about the fishermen, and how they had to sell to Anthony and how sometimes they ended up owing him money, and she told him of the contracts she had seen.

"You still didn't say what happened to the book," he said when she paused.

She explained what had happened and told her Nina gave her the money to buy a flat because she thought she was not safe there.

After a thoughtful pause, he said, "Anthony sounds like a man not to be trusted". And searching for the right words, he asked, "Rosa, has he… has he ever… bothered you?"

325

She lowered her head, so as to not have to look him in the eye. "Oh, Aldo, I am so ashamed."

He insisted.

"He tried to… to get romantic with me, but I got away from him."

"Did he hurt you, Rosa?"

"No, no, really Aldo."

"Please tell me."

Rosa lowered her head, and feeling again the tear of Anthony's attack, told him as much as she could, and added:

"I am afraid of the anger I see now in his eyes. That's why Nina gave me the money so the children and I can get away from him."

"I would like to meet this Anthony." Aldo said, almost more to himself than to her.

"Stop the buggy!" Rosa sat up bolt upright.

"What is wrong?" Aldo ordered the driver to a stop.

"I think that's Anthony's," she pointed to the carriage turning the street in front of them and spoke quietly as if Anthony might overhear her.

They followed up Jones street for several blocks but could tell no more that there were two people in the carriage.

"Maybe that is Anthony and Nina." He suggested.

"No, Nina is at the boarding house getting dinner ready."

They watched as the buggy pulled up in front of a small two-story Victorian house with white trimmed windows, and an ornate wrought iron railing at the side of the steps.

Rosa recognized Anthony as he got out of the buggy and went around the sidewalk side and opened the door.

A blonde, amply built woman and a red dress trimmed in short black fur, got out carrying a black fur muff.

As she passed under the streetlight, Rosa saw very red lips on a lily-white face.

The woman held Anthony's arm and at the top of the stairs, stepped aside and waited while he took a key from his pocket and opened the door. They both went in and he closed the door behind them.

CHAPTER TWENTY-FIVE

Rosa, Aldo, and the children arrived at the boarding house as the fishermen were coming in for supper. Nina, obviously delighted to meet Rosa's visitor, asked him to stay to eat with them.

"I don't know where Anthony is, he never misses Saturday night dinner, that's when he pays his men," she rattled on and on, "well he'll be along, I know he'll want to meet you."

All during the meal Nina hovered over Aldo, who ate as if he enjoyed the food and didn't seem to mind that the fishermen kept looking him over. After dinner, when Anthony had not yet arrived, the men became restless, wanting to know where their paychecks were.

"If we have to wait," Mario said, "let us have music."

Men hurried up the steps to their sleeping rooms while others went out the front door toward the boats. Soon they reappeared with accordions and harmonicas, and Nina put extra bottles of wine on the table.

The room came alive with enthusiastic, if not perfect, renditions of Italy's best-known operatic love songs. Alfredo and Mario sang a duet of folk songs and then someone started playing the tarantella.

The tables were moved back and Aldo let Rosa out onto the floor to dance. They were soon joined by Mario pulling the reluctant Nina, then the children came and before long the fishermen were bobbing about and si-eighths time with each other.

The music and the noise of stamping feet became so loud, no one noticed Anthony come in.

As they noticed him making his way across the floor, a wave of frightening silence spread over the room. He stopped at the bottom of the stairway, turned and stared at the revelers, then silently disappeared.

Wordlessly the tables were put back in order, the wine bottles corked and returned to the cupboard, the harmonica and accordions removed from site. The fishermen waited stiffly at the tables.

Anthony reappeared with the ledger and cash box. Nina ran to him and motioning Rosa to follow, introduced the two men.

They shook hands, and also civil, Anthony was far from cordial.

Aldo complimented the supper he had eaten and said it was time for him to leave. While he helped Rosa gather the children, Anthony studied the stranger. Not until the tall visitor left the room was the cashbox opened.

Nina went back to the flat with them. Why don't you two go on out, have some fun? There are many little coffee houses open on Saturday night.

"Go, I will put the twins to bed,"

She sounded like she couldn't get rid of them fast enough. Rosa laughed at Nina playing Cupid, but she herself had no desire for the day to end.

329

In a narrow dark café with violin music, they ordered coffee and sipped brandy at a small table in the light of one candle.

"You are beautiful in the candlelight," Aldo told Rosa.

Afraid of the weakness she felt to resist Aldo, Rosa smiled, then asked, "Now that you've seen Anthony, what do you think of him?"

"Well, that two-minute conversation was hardly enough for me to size up any man," he said, reluctant to change the conversation.

"Please Aldo, tell me. You know first impressions are usually right."

He patted her hand, well, after seeing the way he is, "I think his fisherman's contract might not be completely fair to the fishermen."

"For your own safety, you must leave Anthony's affairs alone, he could be dangerous. You must get out of there. But I know you won't listen. So may I give you some advice?"

"Yes, please do," she replied, wondering how he knew this about her when she herself was just now realizing it.

"The first thing we must do is see the contract, find out what it says. The fishermen seem to like you, is there one you think would feel safe giving you a copy?"

"Yes, I think so," Rosa replied not quite sure.

"Then we need to have someone read it, could you ask your citizenship teacher to translate it? Or maybe your friend Mrs. Page could ask her lawyer husband to look at it for you?"

"Don't take any chances with Anthony finding out what you're doing."

"I'll get the contract."

"In the meantime, just keep your eye on what Anthony is doing, but say nothing. Don't even tell Nina what you're doing. She probably has her suspicions and might forget and confront him."

When Rosa shook her head that she did not agree, he hurried to add, "You said yourself she is getting braver now that you were here."

"Just watch yourself and the children, and if anything happens, get out! He could be dangerous, and I don't want you to get hurt."

"With Enrico in the hospital, I won't be able to get away from the hotel for a while, but I will write to you."

As if thinking aloud, he said, "I wonder if Anthony would open your letters if he thought you were wise to him? He might do that."

"I'll be writing to Enrico every day, and so I could send you a letter to him at the hospital and you can pick them up when you visit him."

"Do you really think Anthony would open someone else's mail?" Rosa asked.

"I don't know, Rosa, but there is no sense taking chances. If the things you suspect about him are true, he could do almost anything."

The waiter replaced their burned down candle, and Aldo said, "Another thing, Rosa when you find a building to buy, let me help you. If a woman goes in with a lot of cash, the word would soon be all over North Beach and Anthony would hear about it."

"When you are ready to buy, let me go with you, it will be less noticeable if a man makes the purchase."

Finishing the last of her Brandy, Rosa agreed to let him help.

"Another thing, please, try never to be alone with him. I don't like what he tried to do to you, he is dangerous."

"Be careful, too, with your studies. Don't let him see you studying."

Rosa laughed and he said, "Yes I know, I am acting like a mother hen, but Anthony reminds me of the feudal lords in Europe. 'keep the peasant dumb and uneducated then you will always have someone to do your work for you'. That is what he has done with his band of fishermen, what he has done to Nina, and what he would like to do to you and the children."

"But now we must go", he looked at his watch, "If I miss the last ferry, I will have to sleep curled up in the buggy all night."

Aldo covered her with the lap robe and pulling her close, wrapped his arm around her. She snuggled down beside him, happy and safe.

The buggy pulled up in front of the flat, Rosa started to speak, but he silenced her with a tender gentle kiss on her lips. He kissed her again, and for one moment she returned this case, then she pushed away from him.

"That was not the kiss of friends, you know that, and I know that", he released her. "I know I do not have the right, but I cannot help it, Rosa, I love you."

He turned away from her in despair, "I have never loved anyone like this before."

The beating of her heart told her to rush into his arms, to hold onto him and never let him go. Then the thought of his wife broke the spell and brought her to her senses.

"My dear Aldo, you have a wife in Italy, we can never be more than friends. That is all we'll ever be to each other, and unless you can promise me that we will just be friends, then I'm afraid I cannot see you anymore."

After a long pause, he replied: "I promise. I could not go on knowing that I would never see you again."

"Then let us be good friends while you are here in America. You will go back to Italy, and your memories will soon fade and I will become the lady you met on the pier in New York, nothing more."

He kissed her hand, "You will never become a memory to me. You will always be a part of my life. I could never go back to what my life was in Italy, for a long time it has been hell."

"But for now, we will just be friends."

Rosa kissed him on the cheek and went into the house.

She leaned up against the closed door and listened to his footsteps taking him down the steps. Sliding lace curtain back from the windowpane in the door, she watched the buggy drive away.

Oh my dear Madonna, please do not let me love him. Tears rolled down her face. Dear God help me.

She hugged her pillow, and Aldo's face etched deep in her mind, she tried to fall asleep. A buggy came back up the street, it's Aldo, she sat up in bed. He missed the ferry, he had to come back. At that moment she knew she would go with him anywhere.

But it was not Aldo. The buggy rolled on past the house, never knowing how deeply its sound had touched her life.

Moisture filled her eyes and she was crying inconsolably.

My dear Aldo, I do love you. I love your understanding and your warmth, I love your every thought. I long to be with you every minute, but you are a married man. Your wife is waiting for you in Italy.

You say little about her, and I am afraid to ask. If only somehow we could continue the way we were, just friends. But down deep in my soul, I know that it is not possible.

I want you as my husband, I want you here with me, in my bed. Maybe I should be like Anthony's lady on the hill? Oh no, dear God, I could not do that.

Rosa turned her face to the wall. He will go back to Italy, and I will stay here, alone again.

The next morning, Rosa and the children left for church before Anthony stirred, and in the days that followed she stayed out of his way. Her eyes open, she watched everything that went on on the wharf.

Her morning visits with Anna continued, and over cups of Nina's coffee, they read Anna's books about America.

In the evenings after supper, the children did their lessons in the dining room, and when Rosa and Nina were finished with the dishes, they practiced English.

One evening Mario and Vito came back into the dining room and said, "Rosa, can we talk to you for a minute? We have been talking – me and the men – and we want to learn more, better, English. And some of us- me too – want to be United States citizens. But we got a little time. What can we do, Rosa? Will you help us?"

"You can sit here with us after supper when we study our English." Rosa looked to Nina to see if she agreed, and added, "Do you want to do that?"

The men all agreed, and Vito said, "I will help you clean up after the meal. I am a good sweeper, I will sweep out the dining room, we can all help."

"That would be good, thank you, Vito," she watched the little man, cap in hand, leave the dining room.

"This is my book," Mario said, bringing a small thin volume from his pocket, "the priest give it to me when I leave Livorno."

Nina and the children had gone to the kitchen, and looking at Mario's book, Rosa said:

"We will use this for our practice. Put it away now, we must not let Anthony know what we are doing."

She remembered what Aldo had said about the feudal lords of Europe.

"We must be very careful not to let him know that we might be getting a little education. We will watch for him, don't you worry. I watch for you. I saw you run out of the boarding house that Sunday, and since then I keep my eye on you, and if he tries anything...!"

"Oh Mario, you are a good man. Sometimes I am afraid of Anthony – there is a look in his eyes that scares me."

"He is not a man to be crossed. I know."

"Why do you stay with him?"

"I have no choice- not now, at least."

Mario told her how Anthony met him at the boat. "We came across the horn, through storms no ship has a right to live through. Everybody was sick. And my wife... She died. I never should have brought her with me, she was with child."

Rosa reached for his hand to comfort him.

"The first one I saw when I got off the ship was Anthony, he brought me here, fed me, gave me a bed to sleep in. Then when

335

I was well, he gave me a job. The same story for Vito and all the other men."

"Why do you say, why do you tailor to him? The fishermen who sell to other brokers don't grumble and holler like you all do."

"We have to sell to him. We signed a contract with him when we bought the boat. He said he gave a special... we didn't know."

"He had been so nice to us, gave us a job, a place to stay, we trusted him. We signed the contracts."

"Didn't you read the contracts?" Rosa asked but she knew the answer.

"Many of the men can read only a little, and anyhow, the contract is in English. Anthony said that to be legal it had to be in English because we were in America. So we signed it. As long as we owe him money for the boat or anything else, he gets the first pick of our catch. We can't sell to any other broker until he takes what he wants. What's leftover, we sell to the chinamen."

Mario paced back-and-forth, the pain in his face deepened and the pitch of his voice rose.

"He changed the time on me. At first, he told me I had 24 months to pay off the boat, then all of a sudden it was 12 months! With everything else he charged me for, I can't get money ahead to pay off the boat. I don't even have enough to go party, but he owes the girls too."

A shocked look on Rosa's face stopped Mario's pacing, and apologizing for mentioning such a subject to a lady, he sank down onto the bench and buried his face in his hands.

"That is all right Mario. Tell me what more you know about that."

"No Rosa," he said avoiding her eyes, "that embarrasses me, you are a lady. I cannot tell you."

"All right, Mario." Rosa remained silent and then said, "I would like to read that contract. Do you still have yours, Mario?"

"Yes, I do."

"I would like to see it."

"Sure, but it'll do you no good. It is all full of long words and little tiny letters. I can hardly even see them. I get it for you."

When he returned, he said, "Don't let Anthony see you with it."

Nina and the children have left to go for the night, and Mario walked along with Rosa.

"Isn't there someone who can help you and the rest of the fisherman?"

"No, even our union says I signed the contract, so there's nothing I can do about it."

"What's the name of your union, Mario?"

"The Fisherman's Protective and Benevolent Association. Its headquarters are down there," and he pointed in the direction of Vallejo Street.

"Who runs the union, who told you there was nothing you could do about it?"

"Mr. Page is the attorney who helps the fisherman and he read it and said the contract was legal."

"Mr. page?" Rosa questioned, "the friend of Anthony's? I met him last Sunday when they were over for dinner at Anthony's and Nina's. Is that the same man?"

"I don't know," Mario said, "I think his first name is Thomas."

CHAPTER TWENTY-SIX

From the little tin box saved by the ashes of her home in
Viareggio, Rosa took out her last letter from Victor and Dino
and re-read it.

Dear mama,

Your letter took a long time to get here but you must not worry
about us, mama. I go to mass every Sunday and holy day, and Dino
goes every day, and he's always making a novena for something,
and we are careful not to break the commandments.

Every day we say a prayer for our mama and our little brother and
sister in America.

We are working hard to try and build up our business, Guido tends
the boat. Dino goes to Lucca at least two times a week. I have
another cart and horses so I can sell the fish in the small villages. It
is very late by the time we come in to eat.

Maria cooks for us so that we do not have to eat on the boat. She
still grumbles to the Virgin Mary for not keeping you here, but
even if she does not know it, she is happy.

Guido and Maria are even getting along, and she sits on the dock
and helps Guido sew the nets.

They argue all the time, but you know them, they would not be happy if they do not argue. I am beginning to think they really like each other.

Your loving sons,

Victor and Dino.

(I write for us both because Dino is in church.)

Rosa answered her son's letter, then leaning back in her chair, she settled down to reread Aldo's letter she had picked up at the hospital on her first visit with Enrico. The pages were worn from the many times it had been taken from its envelope.

My dear Rosa:

If you are reading this letter I know you saw Enrico. How did you find him? I am sure that your visit cheered him.

I caught the ferry boat on Saturday night. I had to make a run for it and leave from the dock to the moving boat, but I made it without taking a salt water bath.

Oh, Rosa, I sat outside on the ferry boat in the foggy night trying to see San Francisco, and all I could see was your face before me.

Even when I sit at my desk and try to do the hotel accounts, there you are before me and I want to catch a ferry boat and run to you. But I promised you that we would just be friends, and I am trying to keep my word.

Have you any information from the fishermen about the contract? Please be careful. I am praying that you will be safe.

On the next clear day, climb to the top of our hill and throw me a kiss, do not let my kiss get lost in the fog.

Your friend,

Aldo

She wrote:

My dear Aldo:

How nice to have a letter waiting for me when I reached the hospital. Everyone seemed to expect me, and they were all very kind. I had trouble understanding the little French nurse, but then we made up our own sign language and got along fine. She showed me how to put on the gown and mask, but it was uncomfortable and kept slipping off my nails. I always thought a good Italian those would easily hold up such a flimsy piece of gauze.

I was rather timid about going to see someone I haven't met, but Enrico made me feel at ease. He's everything you said he was. He said for me to tell you he had gained 4 pounds from the French cooking. He thinks the Italians must have taught the French at the hospital how to cook because it was so delicious. I brought him a loaf of my bread and a jar of jam that Nina had made last summer.

He was so full of compliments for my bread, you would've thought I gave him the crown jewels. He kissed his fingertips to his lips and said the bread was a beautiful crusty brown, like the loaf of bread in a picture by Vermeer, I think he called it "maidservant pouring milk." He told me I was as great an artist as Vermeer! I do not know of Vermeer, but I do know that Enrico will never be without bread in the future.

His room is drab as you said, and asked the nurse if next time I could bring him a plant. She said yes, and so I have started a small jade plant for him. His spirits seem good and he didn't complain, but I rather doubt that he would complain to me.

I am going to come again next week, for I do think he's getting lonely, and perhaps there will be another letter there for me. As for the matter we talked about earlier, I have a copy of the contract. Do not worry about me, I am very careful.

Affectionately,

Rosa.

She had just started to address the envelope when she heard Anthony coming up the stairs to the flat. Scooping up her letters, she ran to the bedroom. She stood motionless behind her closed door until he stumbled past and down the hall. There was the familiar thought of him falling into bed, followed later by whispering sounds of Nina rustling around.

Good for you Nina, help yourself. Remembering Mario's words, and what Anthony had said to her in the boarding house that terrible Sunday morning after church, and about Sylvia's disappearance that Nina talked about, the pieces of the puzzle were beginning to fit together. Perhaps the money was not from gambling after all.

After many days of walking around the city searching, Rosa found what she was looking for: two flats and a small nearby building just right for her bakery. The lower flat had three bedrooms, plenty of room for her and the twins, while the other flat was smaller, with two bedrooms.

The store, originally built for horses, had been remodeled and was just the right size for her bakery. Both buildings on Vallejo St., the bakery would be handy for the people riding the trolley car to and from North Beach. Rosa knew she had found the perfect place.

Before she even mentioned her find to Nina, Rosa paced off the size of the store and planned exactly where her ovens would fit, and the work tables, and the storage areas.

Then, the following day she took Nina to see it, Nina wanted to go write that very minute and give the real estate man the money.

No, Rosa told her, she wanted to wait until Aldo could see it, and explained what he had said about going with them to make the final purchase.

When they arrived home that evening, Rosa had no sooner taken her hat off than Nina handed her the writing paper with instructions to tell Aldo to come as soon as possible.

Rosa's head bursting with thoughts of her bakery, and Nina, beside herself, the two women shared their excitement and their plans in whispers for fear Anthony might find out too soon.

Nina wanted Anna to see the building, and when they showed it to her, she was too drawn into the excitement.

Their days were busy. In the mornings, during Anna's visit, the three women read aloud and talked together in English.

In the evenings, Rosa supervised the children's homework, and once a week the three went to the Americanization class. Whenever the fishermen could get away, they went with the women to "learn to be Americans."

Rosa had seen Aldo only once in the last several weeks. On business for the hotel, he had stopped at the diner to see her but stayed only a short time.

They walked on the wharf until he had to leave, and when he had gone, she knew her love for him had grown even stronger.

She yearned to be near him, but she feared it and reminded herself again and again that they could never be more than friends. She needed him, she wanted him, and she could not in God's eyes have him.

On Wednesdays, she went to the hospital to visit Enrico. She was becoming very fond of him, and almost always there was a letter waiting for her, from Aldo.

The children sent pictures they made for him and the walls of his hospital room were soon covered with their happy, brightly colored artwork. Although they had never been allowed to visit him, they liked him because he was Aldo's brother and knew he must be nice like him.

The jade plant Rosa had started was thriving on his windowsill, and every morning he tended it.

Enrico was doing very well, and his strength was improving. In the hospital bed, he appeared frail and seemed not to be as large a man as Aldo.

But he had about him the same strong features and the same eyes, tender and understanding. like Aldo, he had a marvelous sense of fun, he too loved to laugh.

As he felt better, he became more eager to help Rosa with her English. She told him what she learned in school about American history, and he always asked her dozens of questions.

He wanted to borrow her books but the hospital said she would not be able to take them home again, because they may be contaminated.

Rosa always saw that she had freshly baked bread to take to him, enough for him to share with the nurses.

The staff all loved him, and even the ladies who did the cleaning found excuses several times a day to poke their heads into his room and pass the time of day with him.

As Rosa made her morning preparations to visit Enrico, she felt very excited, there was something special about this time. She did not know why, but her spirit was charged with excitement.

The horse-trolley ride down Geary Boulevard, sometimes long and tiresome, today took on a tone of pleasure, and when she arrived at the hospital, a letter from Aldo was waiting for her. Putting it safely away in her purse, she would wait until after her visit and read it on her way home.

Enrico was propped up in bed waiting for her, and with the sun shining in on him through the open window, he almost looked well.

"My dear Rosa, how glad I am to see you. Look at me, today they weighed me and I have gained another 5 pounds. As long as I keep getting better like this, they won't have to collapse my lung. I feel very lucky today. Oh, Rosa how I wish I could come close so I could give you a great big hug! But now you must tell me all the news."

Rosa sat down by his bed and told him about the children, and about finding a flat and a store for her bakery. She told him that Aldo had offered to negotiate the sale for her, and how even now she was waiting to hear from him.

"Aldo is a good businessman, he will see that they do not take advantage of you because you are a woman. Even though he is my favorite brother, he is a good man."

Rosa felt Enrico watching her, and the skin on her cheeks grew warm.

"I think that you are fond of my brother?" He asked. "Yes, I am," and she hastened to add, "and of course the children are very fond of him too."

"Aldo has always loved children. Rosa," He continued, "can I talk freely to you?"

"Yes." She said, and immediately worried about what she was going to hear.

"When I left Italy several years ago, I wanted Aldo to come with me, to come into business with me here, but his wife would not come with him. I still remember the look in his eyes the day I left to come to America. We had both been working for our older brother, and I can no longer tolerate his temper. And finally, one day, when I'd had enough, I said, 'this is it' and I made him buy me out. Aldo and I could have a great business together but his wife would not budge. She is another story! But anyway, Aldo wouldn't leave her. Do you know something, my dear Rosa?" He waited for a reply.

She shook her head no, not knowing if she knew or not.

"The best thing that has ever happened for my brother Aldo, is that I got so sick."

"How can you say such a thing?" She asked.

"Because it gave him the excuse to come here. And now he sees for himself why I love America. Without my sickness, he would still be in Italy. Now he loves it here, he loves my hotel…"

Enrico's voice softened, and watching her closely, he added, "and I think also, that he loves you."

Taken off guard, Rosa's mind went blank. She went to the window, and with her back to him said, "you mustn't talk like that Enrico."

"Perhaps not, but I know my brother, and I have never seen him so happy, and yet, in such great pain."

"Pain?"

"He is in a loveless marriage."

"Enrico! You must not say such things!" He remained silent.

"How do you know that? Has he told you?" Rosa asked, turning towards him.

"Oh, he never said anything to me, in fact, he always made excuses for her. But I have eyes, I see his pain. Has he told you anything about her?"

"Very little," Rosa replied, "and I don't really want to…"

"Well, maybe you should. Will you listen to me for a minute?" Enrico asked.

When Rosa did not protest, he went on: "Isabella is a very pretty woman from a wealthy family, her father is a land baron. Perhaps I'm speaking out of turn, but so that you know what kind of woman he is married to, I tell you this incident I saw myself. At her parent's home, one time, long before she even knew Aldo, she became very angry at a servant for bringing the wrong bottle of wine to the table.

"She was very rude to him, and when he spoke up saying it was what she asked for, she insisted her father fire him. I think she had given him the wrong name, but in any event, I never saw that man around anymore, so I guess he was fired. They have a huge estate with a beautiful Villa surrounded by acres of land and trees. The place is full of servants, and both her parents dote on her.

"She's a vain woman, and whenever she does not want to do something, she feigns illness. I know Aldo wants children, and I heard her tell him that she is afraid it would ruin her figure. She is an unhappy woman and she has made Aldo unhappy too.

"But when he talks of you, this old sparkle comes back into his eyes, and he is happy."

Rosa put her hand up, and he said, "Alright, Rosa, enough for now. But there are other stories and sometime you will hear them all. But for now, just remember that God invented love for men and women to be happy together. He did not put us here for love to make us unhappy."

346

"But," Rosa said, "through the church, he gives us rules we must live by." Hurrying to change the subject, she unrolled the pictures the twins had sent. One, a crayon drawing of San Francisco Bay, showed a bridge that went all over the water and landed nowhere. While they were laughing about the bridge with no end, and trying to decide where to hang it, the nurse came in, "another visitor for you Enrico."

Aldo appeared.

Even covered with a gown and a mask across his mouth, his presence made Rosa catch her breath.

"Look at John's artwork- a bridge to nowhere." Rosa held up the picture for him to see.

"I guess you will have to swim the rest of the way home, Aldo," Enrico added.

The brothers shook hands and Aldo said, "You look especially pretty today Rosa. I stopped by the boarding house to drive you to the hospital, but I was too late. Did you get my letter?"

She nodded, yes.

"Well, then you expected me?"

"I have not read it yet. I came in here to see Enrico first," she answered him.

"Oh, you came here first? Well, that is the way it always is when your brother is a lady's man." Aldo said with pretended insult.

"Enrico and I must take care of a bit of business here, and when we are done I was hoping you would show me the flats and the building you found for your bakery."

Rosa watched the two brothers, so much alike, spoke of business matters, and was warned by the respect they showed for each other.

Both handsome men, Aldo was more serious and deep while Enrico, the younger brother had an engaging charm, she wondered why Enrico had never married. Business done, they said their goodbyes, and Enrico answered, "Now Rosa, you remember what I told you!"

"What's this, secrets already?" Aldo asked as they left the hospital.

Aldo helped Rosa down the hospital steps and into the waiting buggy. "Enrico looks better every day, your visits to him are good, Rosa. He is not as depressed, even his letters to me are cheery. You are very dear to come here and I love you for that," he leaned over and kissed her lightly on the cheek.

"Now tell me where this new bakery of yours is so I can direct the driver."

"Vallejo St. near Powell, but I almost wish it was someplace else, I have such trouble saying 'Vall- a- ho'."

"This language is very strange, words look one way and sound another. I am happy with words like 'generate' 'possible' 'compliments' and 'spaghetti' words that sound the same in English as an Italian."

Aldo smiled in agreement, and she went on, "Just when you think you understand you get the 'except words'! That's what the teacher called them, 'except words', like Vallejo. I don't think I'll ever learn," she said.

He hugged her close. "You will learn, Rosa. You will learn."

"And the spelling," she continued, "if you sound out an Italian word, you can usually spell it, but in English, oh, dear God, for every case there's a different spelling rule!" She threw up her hands in disgust.

"You will learn Rosa, of that I am sure. You already speak English very well, and that will be a big help to you and your bakery business. Tell me about the store you found for your bakery, and about the flats, too. Who owns these buildings?"

Rosa took a card from her purse, a 'Mr. Angelo' owns both the flat and the store.

"All the information is here on this card."

"Did he say why he wanted to sell?"

" The store has been empty for a long time, and he has built a new house on Pacific Avenue, and his wife is very anxious to move."

"I see he's is asking $1,500.00. Do you and Nina have that much money?"

"Yes, I have almost that much myself, and with Nina's money, there will be plenty to turn the store into a bakery. Oh, Aldo, sometimes just the thought of going into business scares the daylights out of me, and then other times I get so excited about it that my feet will hardly come back down to reality."

The driver stopped in front of an empty store with boarded nails over the front window.

"Come around here," Rosa led the way along the sides of the building, standing up on a cement block and an uncovered window. "You can almost see all of it from here."

Her words, high-pitched with excitement, tumbled out one upon the other so fast as she told Aldo her plans, that he had to ask her to slow down. Aldo walked fully around the building,

"It seems to be sound," he said, paying particular attention to what he could see of the foundation.

349

" I know an engineer who will take a look at the building for you, if you'd like, Rosa. That way, you'll be sure what you're buying."

Rosa agreed but did not hide the fact that she was quite sure already that the store was exactly what she wanted and quite perfect in every way.

"Hurry and now you must see my new home," Rosa headed up the block pulling Aldo by the arm.

They stopped past three side-by-side buildings, and then, stepping out toward the street, Rosa stopped to look up at her flat. No one, not even Charles Crocker, Collins Huntington, Mark Hopkins, or Leland Stanford ever looked upon his mansion as lovingly as Rosa gazed upon this two-story, Italian baroque building.

"I love its color green, it reminds me of the field in Italy covered with spring grass, and I love the way the windows reach out to grab the sun from all the sides. I will put my chair in the middle and get the sea breeze in the sun from all three sides."

Aldo looked more at her than at the roll of white on a brace holding up the roof she pointed to.

"Look at those little accents of green on the trim, they're like kelly green gumdrops on white frosting, and aren't the carvings beautiful?"

Without taking a breath, she pointed out the two carved wood doors and the shiny snow-white railing up each side of the granite steps. "The children will have fun sliding down this railing."

"I'm sure the children will love all of this, Aldo said, has Nina seen it yet?"

"Oh yes, I couldn't wait to show it to her. She liked it and liked the idea there were three bedrooms so she could come visit."

"Well she likes it, and you certainly like it, and the price seems right, so let's go get Nina and pay Mr. Angelo a visit."

Nina was so excited about going she almost forgot to take off her apron, "But wait, I will go get some money, she said excitedly."

" No need for that now, Aldo reassured her, we're just going to talk to Mr. Angelo at his office."

They directed the driver to Montgomery and Sutter Street and went into a large stone building decorated with elaborate millwork and stone carvings. In the front window of the real estate office, a pretty young brunette sat there in front of a large square machine. Fancy gold letters on the face of it said 'Alexander's typewriter'.

When she saw them looking at her, she smiled and began moving her fingers over the black keys. A single sheet of white paper sticking out of the top jumped as she worked. Mr. Angelo came forward to greet them. Shaking hands, Aldo said, "May I present my mother, Mrs. Dante, and my sister, Miss Dante. I am Aldo Dante."

Mr. Angelo explained all the details of the property to Aldo and Rosa, but Nina was more interested in the contraption in the window. As the girl hit the keys with her fingers, the machine made a loud click-clacking noise that resounded in the high ceilinged room. As the paper moved out of the top of the machine, Nina could see letters on its white surface.

Aldo and Mr. Angelo made arrangements for them to look at the buildings and for his engineer to make his inspection. If they were satisfied, Mr. Angelo said he will draw up the sale papers. The realtor said, "After the papers are signed it will take us about a week to move out. If you need any furniture, talk to my wife. She wants to sell a lot of what's there. She has already bought new things, so go see her."

"I hope you will be very happy in that house, you'll be getting a very good buy, Mr. Dante."

"I must remind you, Mr. Angelo, it is my sister who is getting the house, not I."

Tugging at Nina's arm to get her attention away from the noisy machine in the window, Rosa followed Aldo from the building.

"Can you stay for dinner," Nina asked as the carriage pulled away from the curb, "tonight we have minestrone and Rosa's bread."

"It breaks my heart to refuse such an invitation and a cup of your soup, but I must get back to the hotel," Aldo said.

"But early tomorrow morning I will talk to the engineer and we will check on the building and, if he says they are sound, I will be back in a few days to help you finish out the deal on the house."

"In the meantime, I want you both to promise me that you will be careful not to do anything to make Anthony suspicious. If he finds out you are using Nina's money, he could take it all away from you, so be very careful."

Just as Nina stepped out of the buggy in front of the diner, Anthony walked up. "Where have you been? There is work to be done!" He demanded and then noticing Aldo walking around the buggy, changed his tone. He took off his hat and said, "Please dear, we have hungry fishermen to take care of."

Smiling cordially at Aldo, he said "I am lost around here without my dear wife." He took Nina's arm and, holding the door open for her, they disappeared into the diner.

"I think you surprised my uncle, notice how sweet he became when he saw that Nina was not alone."

"Yes, and a man like that is a man to be wary of." Kissing her on the cheek, Aldo issued another cautioning word about arousing suspicion and drove off.

That night the kitchen was warm with the smell of freshly made coffee as Nina poured two glasses of Brandy, threw in a twist of lemon, and poured the rich black liquid over it. She said, "Aldo is such a fine man. You could never, in your wildest dreams, have asked for anyone more perfect for you."

Perfect? How can he be perfect for me when he already belongs to another woman?" Rosa buried her head in her hands.

Gently stroking Rosa's black hair, Nina spoke in a quiet, almost timid voice, "I know he loves you too, I see it in the way he looks at you. Maybe – with his wife thousands of miles away…"

"Nina, I know what you are thinking, but you know I couldn't! The church would never forgive me, and he too is bound by the rules of the church. No, Nina, there is no solution, you know that. No matter how great our love is, nothing can ever come out of it."

Burdened by the desperation of her own words, Rosa finished her brandy and kissed Nina good night. On her back in the darkened room, she listened to the steady peaceful breathing of her children.

Reliving each scene of her day, she saw her new home, and her bakery, and Aldo. Her eyes closed and she was transported to an ethereal setting in a mythical park high above a city of lights.

His arm around her, he drew her close and held her tight. "My love, you are so special." He kissed her and she clung to him. He caressed her and pulled her ever closer. She felt their hearts beating in unison.

Her head told her to pull away, but her heart screamed, "No." Her body rejoiced in his caresses.

"I love you, my dear Rosa, I shall love you through eternity. No power on earth can change that," he said and kissing her ear and neck, sent shivers down her spine.

The trees closed in around them, swaying and nodding and whispering, they told her to go to him. Suddenly the trees became straight and still, and a cold mist descended upon the park.

Aldo stood before her, desperately reaching out, while every second he was being pulled further and further away from her. Rosa woke up with a chill. Her hand reached out, but there was no one. There were tears on her pillow, she was alone.

The following week Aldo sent word that the engineer had found the buildings "sound as a dollar."

In order not to arouse suspicion, he said, he would not pick them up at the diner, but would instead meet them the following day in Washington Park.

Riding downtown in Aldo's buggy like three conspirators, they decided to make the purchase and Rosa's name because if Anthony found out, he would have legal claim to anything in his wife's name. And, in order for her not to be conspicuous, Nina gave Aldo the money to hold.

Mr. Angelo greeted them with enthusiasm, "The papers are all ready. Go right into my office and I'll get them for you."

Trying to understand the papers, Rosa stopped frequently to ask Aldo about unfamiliar words, while Nina was again more interested in the girl in front of the big black machine. She wanted to know if the contract papers were made on the machine, when Mr. Angelo assured her they were, she took more of an interest.

355

When they indicated that everything was in order, Mr. Angelo held out a pen for Aldo to sign with, "You sign here Mr. Dante, and Miss Dante, you sign below."

"This will be my sister's home, she is buying it. My signature is not necessary, I will not own any part of the house."

"That is highly irregular. All our papers require a man's signature, Mr. Dante."

And why is that? There is no mortgage on it. I see no reason for me to sign, Aldo said.

"Oh, well well well, this is highly irregular!"

Nina spoke out, her voice strong and confident, "If it is too irregular, perhaps we should buy elsewhere. There are plenty of homes to buy in San Francisco."

Surprised, Aldo and Rosa stared at Nina, whom they thought had been paying no attention.

Mr. Angelo edged toward the door, and making a sort of half-bow, backed out saying, "Please excuse me for a moment. I will see, this is most irregular."

They watched him talking to a man across the room seated behind a very large desk with a Tiffany lamp on one side. He waved the contract papers through the air and from time to time they both looked back at them.

When he returned, Mr. Angelo was smiling and said it was alright, one signature would do.

Business concluded, and they stepped outside, and Aldo said, "I think we should have a little celebration, may I buy my mother and sister lunch at a nice quiet restaurant?"

Aldo would not hear of Nina treating them. When their meal was ordered, Rosa said, "Thank you Aldo for helping us. If Nina and I had done that alone Mr. Angelo really would have thought of us 'irregular'!"

Nina touched Aldo's arm in a maternal gesture, "Going in there alone, I would have been frightened. Anthony does everything with the business, I know nothing of it. He would never teach me, but now that Rosa and I own our own property, I think it is time for me to learn."

The waiter brought a bottle of red wine and for each of a heaping platter of ravioli. Although they cleaned their plates, each said that the sauce did not quite match the perfection of the sauce they had known in their childhood.

Aldo wiped his mouth, "Nina, did you notice the bank we passed on Montgomery Street?"

Nina nodded and he went on, "It would be a good idea for you to put your money in the bank, and the deeds to your properties in their vault, where they will be safe."

"Can we trust them? They will not take my money will they?"

Nina tightened her grip on the purse containing her newspaper-wrapped money. "It would be much safer than having it at home, and no one will use it. They will put it in a metal box and only you will have a key. No one else. Everything will be safe, much safer than if Anthony should find it."

"We have time to stop now if you wish," Aldo looked at Nina for an answer.

"Yes that would be good," Nina said, "I think we should find a nice bank and see if we want to do business with them."

Rosa looked at Aldo and they both smiled at Nina enjoying her first trip into the world of business.

"I will let you girls go in and make the arrangements. But be sure to put everything in Rosa's name, some banker in there might know Anthony."

Nina handed Rosa her package of money and settling back in her seat, said, "You go in and take care of everything, Rosa, you be my agent." Nina's voice was sure and confident.

When Rosa came out of the bank, she handed a shiny silver key to Nina, "Here is the key to your money, all safe and sound."

Nina studied the thin flat key, Anthony has a key just like that on his key ring. I wonder what he has in his bank vault?" There was a look of sudden enlightenment on her face.

When they arrived at the wharf, Nina thanked Aldo again and hurried into the dinner.

"She is proud of herself isn't she?" Rosa said.

"It makes me very happy, for the first time she is showing some independence. She is not relying on Anthony. Do you think she would ever leave him?" Aldo asked Rosa.

"She is bound by her vows, I don't think she would leave him. The teachings of the church are strong, you do not shed them easily."

"Do you think it is ever right to shed one's vows, Rosa?"

"Oh, Aldo, do not ask such a question. All my life I have tried to never offend my God."

"But sometimes, Rosa, the rules of the church do not work. Sometimes, we have to look beyond the church rules, and ask what it is he wants for us."

"We have to face the fact that sometimes the rules of the church are not God's will. Like for me, although in the eyes of the church I am bound to Isabella until I die, I can never return to Italy and live as her husband."

"Sh- sh- sh Aldo, I do not want to hear that kind of talk."

"Well, perhaps it is about time you did hear. She has not been a wife to me in years. She refuses my touch. She bolts the door and feigns illness. There is no sweetness- no softness to her. Inside of her, there is a kind of hatred eating away at her. Isabella is not a loving woman, she is a woman filled with anger and hatred," his voice became intense.

He tied the buggy up to the hitching post, and they walked along the water. "Rosa, I should not have burdened you like this, but sometimes I am desperate."

"Today is a happy day for you, and I should have said nothing to upset you. But sometimes I feel like John Edwards yo-yo. One minute I am up and happy, one minute I am depressed. I cannot go on like this. All I really know is that I want to be with you." He turned to her and held her by the shoulders.

She had a moment of panic and she knew if, at this moment, they were anywhere other than walking along the wharf, she would've given her body to him.

He broke from her, kissed her lightly, and was gone. She walked slowly toward the diner, tears welling up in her eyes. If only she had never met him.

Her hand on the doorknob, Rosa heard Anthony inside barking orders at Nina and the children. When he saw her, he turned his side toward her and unleashed a battery of complaints against her and her children.

His anger grew worse with each passing day. The children, afraid to leave their tasks, set dishes out on the table and watched their mother furtively.

She did not listen to Anthony's words, she knew what he was going to say. Tying the long white apron around her middle, Rosa wondered if there was a tender side to this man.

What was he like in the early years, with Nina? Could he be gentle and loving? How was it with him and the lady on the hill? Was he ever kind and thoughtful?

Was Anthony's mistress just a trophy to show that he had arrived at a certain wealth, or did he really love her? Did she love him? Could I be that sort of woman? Could I live like that? Could I be some man's mistress?

Aldo's wife is 3000 miles away in Italy, while only a short few blocks separate Nina from the lady on the hill. And Nina, a good, God-fearing woman, never hurt anyone, while Isabella is a selfish headstrong woman.

Anthony's voice rose and jarred her from her thoughts.

"For God's sake woman, what are you dreaming about now? About that fancy pants boyfriend of yours? Don't expect anything from him, I have seen his type- the walking stick crowd, lunch at the palace with their high falutin ladies."

He finds a nice little peasant girl like you, filled her head with all kinds of silly ideas, and then, poof – he's gone!

"That type of man wants a real lady, Rosa, face it, you are not good enough for him."

Anthony stood very close to her, "Face it Rosa, you are nothing but a peasant woman from the old country, and that's all you'll ever be!"

Anthony crossed the dining room in quick angry strides and slammed the door behind him. Nina came from the kitchen, she had heard. She put her arm around her niece.

Rosa said, "Sometimes, I think he is right."

"Oh, Rosa, do not let Anthony's angry words bother you. Aldo is not like that. Today in the buggy he watched you walk into the bank, and without taking his eyes off you said, 'isn't she beautiful?' All the time he's talking to me he watches the door of the bank for you to come out."

He admires you, he told me he's never known anyone like you before in his whole life. Rosa, I think he is in love with you. Now don't lose him, a man can just be so patient."

"Nina, you say that so easily, but you know he has a wife!"

"Not much of a wife, who would let her man go off alone to a new country by himself!"

"But, still, in the eyes of God, his wife."

Nina grunted her disagreement.

"And you know I cannot turn my back on the church, and God and all of the things I believe in."

Just then John Edward burst into the room, and his most grown voice announced that the men were here for their supper. Nina put her hand gently on Rosa's shoulder, "God will find a way, you will just wait and see, he will find a way!"

Rosa loved Nina for wanting to comfort her, but she also knew that sometimes, unwilling to face the truth, it was easier for her to hide her fears behind a wall of faith in God.

CHAPTER TWENTY-SEVEN

Arriving at the hospital with a large gray metal box under his arm, Aldo wondered what was so urgent that Enrico had to have this box today. He had not seen Rosa since they bought the flat, and now he was going to have to wait until next week.

The twins' birthday was on the feast of Santa Croce, and he promised to take them on a big outing in the park.

Enrico looked tired, "I hope you're not overdoing," Aldo said.

"No, just a few things on my mind, I guess. Sit down, let me have the box."

Aldo watched Enrico unlock the box and saw that the expression on his brother's face was more worried than fatigue.

Enrico took out a letter, and, propping his pillows up against the white metal headrest of his bed, asked, "Aldo, do you remember how you met Isabella?"

Aldo's neck and shoulder muscles tightened up at the sound of his wife's name, and he said, "Enrico if you're going to give me a lecture about my duty as a husband, I won't…"

Enrico interrupted, "Aldo, will you just listen? This is very difficult for me. Hear me out."

There was a desperation in the younger man's voice, and Aldo sat down, holding his silence.

"I should've done this a long time ago," Enrico continued. "Do you remember how you met Isabella?"

" Of course I do, you introduced us. She was related to Renata, a second cousin I think."

"Yes for years I had run into her at all the family gatherings, and you met her at the Christmas party the night Renata and I announced our engagement. We were to be married the next spring and then…"

Aldo felt a twinge of pain as he saw sorrow deepen the lines on his brother's face. "Don't go over all that Enrico. That is too painful for you and what is the point?"

"It is very important that you hear all of this. Please, Aldo, let me talk."

Enrico drank from the water glass at his brother's table:

"You remember how sick Renata was, and Isabella stayed and helped me take care of her? She was very kind all through those terrible months.

"We talked for hours at Renata's bedside, particularly toward the end, and when the end came, Isabella comforted me.

"After her funeral, I prayed to God to take me too, to let me be with Renata. Then Isabella took me to her parents' villa in Como to rest and recover. Do you remember that?"

Aldo shook his head yes.

"I was there for weeks... she was very kind, we took long walks around the estate, and around the countryside. Isabella could be very entertaining. I could not forget Renata but the pain in her death was becoming less of an ache in my heart.

"Then, sometime, I can't remember just when it was, she started waking me up in the mornings. Instead of the servants, she brought me coffee and bread. She opened the curtains to the morning sun and told me she would be my sunshine now.

"And when it was time for me to leave, she begged me to stay longer. But I felt if only I could get back to my painting- that was the only thing that would save me."

Again, Enrico drank from the bedside pitcher.

"That evening before I left, she had a magnificent banquet prepared, the best wine, everything. She was particularly charming that night, though I didn't think much about it then."

"When I got into bed, with all the heavy food and the good wine, I fell right into a deep sleep. Sometime later, I woke up with a start..." Enrico's voice trailed off.

Aldo went to the window, his back to his brother he squared his shoulders and said, "Go ahead, tell me what you have to."

"Isabella was standing at my bed. Her hair hung loose on her shoulders. All she was wearing was a flimsy lace gown.

"Her body silhouetted in the light behind her, she was like a beautiful dream. Then she came at me and pulled the blankets away. I felt nothing. I was as cold as a marble statue. She lay down beside me and whispered in my ear that Renata had died because we were meant to be together.

"When I finally got my wits about me, I told her I could not love again, I felt only friendship for her, that was a mistake. She went into a tantrum…"

Aldo watched Enrico struggle with the words.

"She scratched my face. I pleaded with her, but she was like an animal. She didn't hear me. I tried to reason with her, and finally, I picked her up and put her out of my room. She screamed at me through the closed door that I would be sorry, that she would never forgive me. She banged on the door and screamed that I would live to regret it. Everyone in the house must have heard her. I left the house immediately. I didn't see her again."

The nurse came into the room. She stopped and looked from one man to the other.

"Is everything alright? Now we are not getting ourselves worked up are we?" She said, fussing over Enrico's blankets.

Swallowing his medicine, Enrico tried to reassure her. When the swishing of her rubber-soled shoes on the polished floor could no longer be heard, he went on.

"Now that I look back on those days I see how blind and stupid I was the whole time but I was too lost in my own grief to see anything clearly. I never saw Isabella again."

"That next year had to be the worst year of my life, I went home, and I tried to paint, but nothing would come. Then Dominic and I had that big argument and like a hothead, I packed up my bag, and my broken heart, and sailed for America. I begged you to come with me. If only you had. The next thing I heard was that you and Isabella were married!"

The room was silent. Each man struggled with his own inner turmoil. Sitting down heavily, Aldo said, "Yes, it all happened so fast. I never quite knew what happened."

"I assumed- I prayed that you were happy, and then, this came…" Enrico held up the letter.

Aldo moved toward the bed. Putting the palm of his hand up, Enrico said, "First, there is something I must know, Aldo."

Aldo waited.

"Do you love Rosa?"

"What does that have to do with…" Aldo's voice was angry.

"Please, just answer me, do you love Rosa or not?"

"Yes, you know that! I have told you that many times."

"Would you marry her if you were free?"

"At this very moment, if she would have me."

"Would you take her for your mistress?"

"I would take her any way I could. But Rosa would never consent. That I am sure of. But what has this got to do with all that you are telling me? I do not understand."

"I had to be sure. Here, now you must read this."

With a feeling of dread, Aldo accepted the letter. Recognizing Isabella's handwriting, the color drained from his face.

"It is dated Florence, November 12, 1875. That is 3 days after we were married, we were on our honeymoon." Aldo looked at his brother for explanation.

"Read it, Aldo."

November 12, 1875

Florence, Italy

Dear brother-in-law, Enrico,

Yes, my high and mighty, Enrico, I am married to your dear brother, Aldo, it was so easy to make him want to marry me, you know what a sentimental soul he is.

I told you that you would regret your stupidity and now you will! You should not have turned your back on me, no one says no to Isabella! I know you love your brother Aldo more than anyone else in this world, next only to Renata, and now, because of you, he will soon be living in hell.

All those weeks I helped you nurse Renata, you thought I was her devoted friend, but I couldn't wait for her to die, that's what a good actress I am.

Right now my dear husband thinks our marriage is perfect, but soon, he will hate the thought of our marriage bed, I will see to that.

He thinks we will have many children, but he does not know that in France I got a "gold button", and no child will ever come from this marriage.

And remember, dear Enrico, that your brother's misery is all your fault. Every pain he feels and every disappointment he suffers will be because of you.

Your devoted sister-in-law,

Isabella

Aldo let the letter drop to the floor. He said nothing and Enrico studied his face for some type of emotion. He could only see a look of disbelief.

"Gold button!" Aldo said.

"I had never heard of such a thing, but one of the old doctors here at the hospital explained to me how it kept a woman from having babies."

"Why didn't you send this to me the minute you got it?"

"The evil of her deed was so tremendous that for a long time I don't think I really believed what she said- I thought Isabella would change, that she would learn to love you and would become a good wife."

"In your letters, you never complained, I thought you were happy I couldn't take a chance with your happiness."

"My wife had married me to spite you? Dear god!"

"Not until you came here and I saw the unhappiness in your eyes did I realize that she meant those threats. She went to your marriage bed as a fraud."

"My dear god, she never intended to be a wife, much less a mother!" Aldo paced back and forth. "She planned to rob me of the one thing I have wanted all my life, children. And I never even suspected.

"At first she was so full of passion, on our honeymoon she was so- so, well so eager. Then after we returned to Torino she changed immediately. I could not count on my fingers the number of times she allowed me into her bed. Finally, I moved out of her bedroom and sought release elsewhere and in hard work.

"But why, Enrico, do you tell me this now? If you didn't tell me when you got her letter, why do you tell me now? What good is it for me to know now?"

"When you got here, and I saw you, I knew immediately that she had meant every word she wrote in that letter. And then I met Rosa…"

"But telling me this now just makes everything more unbearable. What good is it now?"

Waving the letter victoriously in the air, Enrico said, "Don't you see, this might be the answer to your problem?"

"An answer to my problem? There is no answer as long as she is alive."

"Let me explain, please Aldo, you know I would never do anything to hurt you. About a week ago," he began. "A young Jesuit, from St. Ignatius came to see me. He says Sunday mass here sometimes."

"He studied theology in Rome and is somewhat of an expert on Canon Law."

"I asked him about your problem, without mentioning any names, of course. If only you could know how guilty I feel being the cause of your unhappiness."

"Well, Father Nagle– that's his name – said he would take a look at this letter. But of course, I did not get any further with the matter, it is up to you."

"But I still do not see the point of this Enrico, why would a priest…?"

The point is, my dear brother, that this letter may be grounds for an annulment!"

"Annulment?" Aldo spoke as he would mouth an unfamiliar word of a foreign language.

"An annulment? You must be mad! What makes you think the church would grant me an annulment when even king Henry VIIII was turned down by the pope."

"Unfortunately I do not have Henry's power, I cannot create my own church, no, Enrico perhaps your sickness has weakened your eyesight."

"The church does not advertise this, but Father Nagle says these things can sometimes be worked out."

"Go, brother, what can it hurt? Take this letter, go see him, go as soon as possible. Take the letter and go to him."

Enrico watched the expression on his brother's face change from disbelief to understanding. For a tiny moment, there was a sparkle of hope in his eyes, his face darkened and he said, "No! It would be no use, and I could not bear to put my heart on the line only to be disappointed again, no I will not!"

"Go, my dear brother, do not be afraid, go see Father Nagle."

Enrico wrote an address on a slip of paper, and getting out of bed, slipped it into his brother's breast pocket. "Put your faith in God."

Aldo plucked at his coat pocket as if the contents scorched the skin of his chest, and taking up his hat and coat, said, "I know you think you are helping." He walked heavily out of the room.

Alone, Enrico slumped deep down into his bed. His eyes closed, a single tear ran down his face. "Dear God," he sighed, "take my brother to Father Nagle!"

CHAPTER TWENTY-EIGHT

Nina and the fisherman were finishing their lessons, and the twins were fast asleep in the kitchen. Rosa looked in on the children and stopped to pour herself a cup of coffee from the huge urn in the corner.

As she raised her hand to open the swinging door, she heard Anthony come into the room. A stab of fear pierced her insides, and settling in the cup down, she listened at the door.

Enraged at catching them at their studies, Anthony immediately started berating Nina!

Opening the door a crack, Rosa saw him take Nina's arm and hurry her toward the street. The fisherman followed them as far as the door, then huddling up close to the window, they waited.

Anthony was shaking his finger at Nina, then he grabbed roughly both her arms and started shaking and scolding her. Seeing the terror and Nina's face, Rosa started after her. Mario put his hand out and said, "Let me go, if he sees you he'll be madder than ever, do not get into it."

Rosa stepped back out of his way, and then the men fell in behind Mario.

Rosa stood back and listened through the open doorway. Mario was saying, "Anthony, there's no use yelling at Nina, we decided on our own to take the classes and become citizens. Nina has nothing to do with it."

Anthony turned to Mario with rage in his eyes. "You stupid peasant, you don't have brains enough to become a citizen! If it wasn't for me, you'd be lying dead on the wharf."

Anthony grabbed at Mario, and snarled, "And what I do with my wife it's none of your damn business!" Vito and Luigi struggle to pull Anthony off Mario. Anthony's face was crimson, the veins in his neck throbbed. "You stupid jackass, this is the thanks I get?"

They held him firm. "You can say what you want to, Anthony, but the men, all of us, are signing up to become citizens," Mario said.

"You are not the boss of our lives. We do what we want- this is America! What we do with our free time is our own business." He looked Anthony right in the face, "And if you ever strike your wife again..."

The threat left unspoken, they released Anthony and herded together into a tight warrior band, the fishermen moved toward the water.

Anthony stared at the departing band of tormentors, and the hatred in his eyes sent fear through Rosa's spine. For the first time, the fishermen had stood up to him. He couldn't stop them, they had beaten him. Anthony did not tolerate humiliation well.

Free of her husband's grip, Nina hurried back across the street.

Rosa stepped out to bring her in, and Anthony turned toward the building. Knowing that Rosa had witnessed his humiliation, his fury raged upward, he strode toward the two women shouting,

"You, you damn bitch. You get the hell out of here! Take your worthless children and find someone else to live off of."

He followed them into the diner, "Since you arrived you've been nothing but trouble. You're just like all of them! You come over from Italy and expect the relatives to support you. Go find yourself a job. See how easy that is. You'll soon find out the streets aren't paved with gold. You'll end up with your face in the gutter, whoring on the waterfront."

Rosa could feel Nina trembling as they hurried across the deserted dining room trying to get away from him.

When they reached the kitchen, Anthony stopped. Turning to go, he shot back over his shoulder, "I'll give you one week to get out of my house."

Rosa watched him walk away, brushing off his trousers, trying to straighten up his suit and his tie.

CHAPTER TWENTY-NINE

Sleeves rolled up above her elbows, Rosa scrubbed the kitchen cupboards while Nina unwrapped a set of dishes she was giving her.

"I will miss you, Rosa. Having you and the children living with me has brought me such happiness that…" Nina's voice faltered.

Rosa brushed her forehead with her arm, and looking at the older woman, felt for her a surge of all the years of their separated love.

"I know Nina, but I am so grateful to finally be here in the same country with you at last, and in the same city. We will be but a few blocks apart."

"I was hoping we could live together as a family. I am sorry that it could not be."

"We are not far from each other and when you feel alone, you come here. We are your family. You heed never be lonely again." The two women embraced. A few tears fell down Nina's cheeks.

"Come, Nina," Rosa said hoping to turn the conversation to a more happy note, "Come see the box of clothes Mrs. Angelo left. She asked me if I would keep them here and give them to some of the new people who don't have enough."

Nina looked briefly at the collection of men's and women's clothing, then, looking around Rosa's new home so fairly, sparsely furnished with the Angelos' discards, asked, "Can you manage here, Rosa, by yourself?"

"Now do not worry, of course I will manage. This way is better for all of us. At least now with Anthony not having to see me, he will not get so angry. But still, I do worry about you, Nina, do you think Anthony might...?"

She could not force herself to speak the word.

"Do I think he might beat me? Is that what worries you? No, I know how to handle him. I stay out of his way when he's angry. I do not cross him − there is no use. He doesn't listen to the words I say, and yet he gets mad if I talk. That is funny, isn't it Rosa? He doesn't listen to what I'm saying, and yet he knows he doesn't want me to say anything! Men!"

"It is so good to hear you laugh," Rosa said, "even if it is about something like that."

She filled her bucket with hot water from the kettle heating on the stove. "I am not sure that I remember hearing Anthony laugh?"

"The only time he laughs is when he makes the jokes. He does not like much of anything. He has lost touch with the simplest pleasures of life."

Rosa and Nina sat at the rickety little table for a lunch of bread and cheese. Looking around the kitchen, her nostrils assaulted by the odor of strong Lysol soap, Rosa said, "As soon as we get this kitchen scrubbed, it will be time to start baking for the twins' birthday and for the festival."

She looked around the kitchen sizing up the work areas she would need.

Nina cut a wedge of cheese for each, and said, "The children are surely blessed. First, they are born in Italy on the Feast of Volto Santo, and then, their very first birthday here in America falls right on the Feast of Santa Croce. Yes, they are twice blessed."

"Twice blessed," Rosa said, "yes that is perhaps why God saw fit to send me two babies instead of one."

"Eight years," Rosa put the cheese into the cooler built in the outside wall of the kitchen. "It is hard to believe that it was eight years ago that my two babies were born. We almost lost them, did you know that?"

Rosa told Nina of that night when Father Michael was snatched out of the procession to baptize the two tiny infants less they be taken to God before receiving the sacrament.

Nina scrubbed and polished the heavy black cooking stove, and while the two women worked, they talked nostalgically of the feast days of their childhood.

"That is one thing that does not change," Nina said, "you can move an Italian halfway across the world, make him talk English, and put him in different clothes, but you will never get the church out from inside him. You can never take away his feast days."

When Rosa and Nina left the kitchen, their muscles ached with fatigue, but it was a good kind of tiredness. The cupboards and floors were spotless, and the air was filled with a delicious scent of anise and peppermint cakes.

All week Rosa watched the twins' excitement building up for their birthday- for their very special day. Her own excitement was a little less than theirs. In America at last with her Mama Nina, and in her own new home, with her bakery taking shape a few doors down, and soon it would be the day of the festival and the twin's first birthday in America, how could she not be excited? And best of all, Aldo would be there to share her joy. Rosa decided to buy a new hat.

Her mind full of images of herself looking beautiful in a new hat and graciously accepting compliments from Aldo, she walked with a light and youthful step, holding tightly onto her money from the tin box.

She was surprised when she found herself near the bottom of Telegraph Hill, standing squarely in front of a dress store window. A beautiful empire gown of blue and white taffeta called out Rosa's name. She could not look away. The high tiny waist, the soft curving line of the décolleté bodice, the gentle flow of the neck into the tiny capped sleeves... it held her firm.

"Madam, may I show you...?" It took rosa minutes to realize the young sales lady had stepped out of the store to speak to her.

"Oh, no thank you, no. I am just looking for a hat."

While the saleslady brought one hat after another for Rosa's trial, her thoughts were unable to break away from the spell of that dress.

"That is just your color. You could try it on if you like." The saleslady watched Rosa's eyes for signs of weakening.

Finally deciding on a broad-brimmed straw hat that would go with her "best dress," the one she wore that morning the train delivered them to Oakland, Rosa waited next to the beautiful blue taffeta dress while the saleslady put her new hat in a box.

Walking back up the hill to her flat, Rosa was giddy with excitement. It was all she could do to keep a firm grip on her two packages.

When the Sunday morning finally came, the children could hardly contain their excitement. Up early, they were scrubbed and dressed. Tingling with excitement, Angelina could barely stand still while her mother arranged her hair.

"Mama," she said, "when I grow up, will I be as beautiful as you are?"

Just then there was a knock at the door. John Edward, who had been lying on his bed looking at a magazine, jumped up and darted down the hall.

When Aldo had worked his way through the hugs and excited questions of the birthday twins, he smiled at Rosa and said, "You look like a spring day. No one will ever bother to look at the procession. All eyes will be on you and no one else." He kissed her on the cheek.

"We want to get to the procession in plenty of time," he hurried them along. There was a look of mischievous excitement in his eyes as he held the door open for them.

When they reached the sidewalk, Aldo signaled the driver who climbed down from his perch, and holding a large wicker basket in front of him, stood facing them. His lips were stretched into a large smile.

Inside, curled up in a ball, was a tiny white and black shorthaired puppy. His paws, too big for his body, were matched only by his wide, liquid brown eyes. He looked up at them with instant love, and trying to scramble out of the basket became hopelessly and tangled in his blanket. As if imprisoned by some giant malevolent animal, he whimpered to be rescued.

Aldo put him down on the ground in front of the twins, "Happy birthday, Angelina and John Edward."

The puppy ran frantically back-and-forth trying to smell everything at once. His tail wagged so hard it threw his body from side to side as he moved.

"I hope it is alright, Rosa?"

"Of course," she said, "we have our own home now, we can keep a little dog. Besides, I don't know who's happier, the children or the dog. They'd be wagging their tails too if they had one. It's a perfect present for their birthday."

"It's a living gift," Aldo said, a sadness creeping into his eyes, "so that you will not forget me."

Worry grabbed at Rosa, but Aldo had turned his face away from her and became busy giving instructions to the driver.

The twins put the puppy on their laps as the buggy made its way down the hill to where they could watch the parade. The procession passed within inches of them, but Angelina and John Edwards were only interested in their new little four-legged friend.

The parade started off with a marching band in blue and gold braided uniforms and highest of hats, followed by Father Paul from St. Francis and the procession of the holy statues.

A band of children was followed by the Honorable Isaac Kalloch, San Francisco's mayor. He rode in a two-wheel buggy pulled by a jet black stallion. Behind him carrying the banner of the church, and turning his head from side to side smiling at the crowd, marched Anthony Orso.

"Look at him," Rosa said to Aldo. "The crowd is cheering the mayor and he thinks they're cheering him."

When she turned to speak to Aldo she saw that he had been watching her. He said, "I would rather look at you. I want to fill my mind with your picture. You are radiant today."

"Aldo, is something wrong? What is it?"

"No, no, nothing is wrong. I just want to get my fill of you, that's all."

Again, Rosa worried and again he turned away, this time toward the children. "What are you going to name your new friend?" Aldo asked.

"Paisano," John Edward announced.

"Because he is our friend," Angelina explained.

Outside the church after mass, Aldo invited Nina and Anthony to have breakfast with them. Anthony declined, for as he said, the men would play bocce and have an early lunch. Nina added that it was the time for the men to drink wine and talk politics.

Although he was wearing his Sunday manners and said nothing, it was clear Anthony did not approve when Nina agreed to go with them. In his most gracious manner, he helped his wife into the buggy, and bid them goodbye.

Nina sat between the twins, and soon the puppy was sound asleep in her lap. Twitching and squirming in his dreams, Angelina asked, "What do you think he's dreaming of?"

"About the wonderful life he is going to have living with you and the fun he will have running and playing in the park today."

As they approached the cliff house, Nina studied the massive building perched on the edge of the cliff, and said, "This looks like a castle. No, it is more like a gingerbread tower seven stories high, and all white so it can be seen far out at sea."

"But it's not a castle guarded village," Rosa added, "it's perched up on the side of the hill to welcome people from all over the world. But what will keep it from falling into the ocean?" She asked.

Aldo smiled, and said, "God does, I think he was the architect."

They left Paisano in the care of the driver and walked toward the restaurant, stopping for a moment at the sea wall to look at the sea lions barking and running themselves on seal rock.

In the quiet, elegant restaurant, three walls looked out on the Pacific Ocean. Rosa looked straight down at the waves crashing into the jagged rocks below, and when the water flowed back out to sea, she felt herself being pulled out with it.

The motion of the moving water made her feel light-headed and her stomach churned as it did during those stormy days on the Leonardo. Fearful her seasickness would come back to her, she raised her eyes to the horizon where the bright September sun, still not high in the sky, reflected on the water like dancing diamonds.

Aldo ordered a bottle of champagne and, pouring a tiny bit for the children, proposed a toast. The twins ate quickly and thinking no one saw him, John Edwards slipped a piece of ham into his coat pocket. He asked if they could go out and wait at the buggy with the dog. When they were gone, Rosa proposed a toast to Aldo for giving her children the best birthday they had ever had, one they would always remember.

"I am glad," he said and again Rosa saw the sadness in his eyes, "that is what I want, for them to remember me."

After breakfast, they drove along the water's edge and turned into the road of Golden Gate Park. An elegant open carriage came toward them. It was carrying four people and was pulled by a team of graceful white horses.

Alongside the horses, under the watchful eye of the footman, a large white and black spotted dog, head as high as the tail arched over his back, trotted along in step with the horses.

"Look at that dog," Aldo called excitedly, "John Edward and Angelina, look at that dog! It's the same kind as yours. Someday Paisano will be that big."

"That big?" Rosa asked, having considered the puppy's present size permanent, "I wonder if our flat will be big enough?"

After a long slow drive past the young groves of new plantings in the park, they stopped at a beautiful meadow beside a lake where a group of children sailed toy boats.

Aldo spread the lap robes on the ground and brought a basket from the luggage compartment of the buggy.

"Now everyone sit down, I have a few more surprises for you. Today is everyone's birthday. This is our first celebration of all of us together in America."

Rosa thought she saw a shadow of unhappiness cross his face. He handed Angelina a package wrapped in sheer tissue paper.

She tore open the paper and found a doll, like the one the little girl on the boat had in her buggy. She had long black drop curls, a beautiful porcelain face, with big brown eyes that opened and shut and looked almost real.

"Thank you, thank you," Angelina hugged Aldo so hard he almost fell over from his kneeling position. "It is the most beautiful doll I have ever seen. I will love her forever. I will call her Sophie, just like the little girl on the boat."

John Edward, who was waiting as patiently as an eight-year-old boy could grabbed eagerly at the package Aldo offered him. Holding up a metal steam engine and a passenger car, he said, "This is just like the engine we had! Look, Nona, this is just like our train. Oh, thank you sir, thank you sir."

First holding himself back shyly, John Edward suddenly flung his arms around Aldo and hugged him. "Now for the ladies in my life." Aldo handed each a carefully wrapped package tied with pink satin ribbon.

"But why? It's not my birthday," Nina said while she removed the paper wrappings.

"Because dear Nina, this will be our universal day. Yours, Rosa's, the twin's, and mine."

Nina held up a black silk handbag. It was fastened with a gold metal clasp, and black jet beads formed designs on each side.

"I have never had anything so beautiful in all my life." There were tears in Nina's eyes. "Thank you, you are so kind."

Rosa opened her gift. She found two combs of jet beads and gold.

"They are beautiful," she said trying to put them into her hair. Then overcome with sadness, she blurted out, "but I have nothing for you."

"Don't cry, those were given to make you happy, not to make you sad."

Rosa held the combs out to show her aunt, but Nina was walking out toward the grass, to the children playing with Paisano.

"Let me help," Aldo slipped the combs into her chignon, and, turning her around, put his arms around her waist, and kissed her. For a brief moment, she permitted herself to hold him close, only to feel him pulling away.

"I want you to promise me, Rosa, that you will always remember this day, and that you will know that I love you."

"Aldo something is wrong! What is it? Tell me!"

"No, it's just that I never want to lose you. You and the children mean everything to me. Never forget that. That is what you can give me today, your promise of trust."

Just then, the ball the children were throwing for Paisano to fetch, rolled onto Aldo's toes. In his attempt to return it to them he was soon in the middle of the game, and the puppy was always underfoot.

Trying not to step on him, Aldo lost his balance and landed on his back with the puppy climbing all over him trying to lick his face. The children tried to help him up, but they soon were pulled down on top of him wrestling and giggling. Laughter, puppy barks, and squeals poured from the massive body stumbling on the grass.

"Look at that," Nina said, "have you seen such a sight, I don't know who is the bigger child out there. The puppy's the smartest one, here he comes to get a rest." Paisano landed on Nina's lap and after circling several times to make his nest, took a deep breath and fell asleep.

"You are a lucky woman, Rosa, to have a good man like Aldo who cares for you."

"Yes, I know he cares for me, and I care for him, but the cruel joke is that he already has a wife."

"Yes, but his wife is thousands of miles away. Be wise, Rosa, do not lose him. He loves you yes, but he is only a mortal man, made of flesh and blood, he is not God."

Rosa patted Nina's hand to thank her for her caring, and asked, "Does he seem different to you, today?"

"Different how?"

"I'm not sure. I find him looking at me..."

"Because you are beautiful."

"No, it is different, sometimes his eyes seem to be telling me goodbye, and the next time they are filled with confidence, and even excitement. Something is troubling him. He will not tell me what it is, but I sense it."

On the way home the twins and Paisano fell asleep, they did not even wake up to say goodnight to their Nona when they stopped at her house.

Aldo made two trips to carry the children into their beds. "They will have no trouble sleeping tonight," Rosa said, pulling their nightshirts down over their heads as they stood up, eyes closed tight.

Quietly closing the bedroom door behind him, Aldo said, "I am afraid that I must leave, or I will have to swim across the bay."

Disappointed that he could not stay, she was also relieved that she would not have to fight against the terrible yearning building up inside of her. She thanked him again for "the happiest day of my life."

He took her hand, and twisting her ring in a gesture he seemed unaware of, leaned down and touched the side of her face with his fingertips. Tracing a circle around her lips, he kissed her gently and tenderly and looked deep into her eyes as if to paint her picture forever in his mind.

"I must leave, Rosa," he kissed her fingertips and turned and walked away. A chill traveled the length of her spine. She would never see him again! She fought an impulse to run after him.

Rosa watched him leave. It was not fair, why does God make rules that hurt only the faithful and good? She remembered what Nina said, "... He's only a mortal man." They could not go on this way.

She undressed and, naked, she fell into bed. She prayed to the Madonna to let her see him just one more time.

She knew now, she would surrender her body to him. She loved him too much to lose him, and now she was afraid, like she had never been afraid before, that he would turn away from her as he had tonight.

She buried her head in the covers and tried to think only of the fun they had all day as a family. The children loved him, Nina loved him, she could not take that away from them.

She could not separate the children from someone they had grown to love as they had loved Eduardo. She slid out of bed, and from her trunk, took her nightgown, the only thing she had left to remind her of her life with two different men, two husbands.

She had not worn it since the night of the terrible fire. She held it close to her face, and, slipping it over her naked body, folded her arms close around her, hugging the material to her breasts. She thought of Eduardo making love to her, and wondered what he would tell her to do if he knew.

She closed her eyes and through her tired mind ran jumbled images of nuns, of Jesus and his cross. She saw the faces of Mama Dante and Father Joseph- of Giovanni and Eduardo– and of Aldo. Their silent, empty faces stared at her, vacant empty faces with no words.

CHAPTER THIRTY

Sitting by the open window, warmed by the afternoon sun, Enrico breathed deeply in the fresh air. His artist – soul studied the subtle way of the sunset, while his brother – soul wondered if Aldo's code of honor had permitted him to go to Father Nagle.

Familiar footsteps sounded in the long hospital Corredor. Enrico turned to face the door.

Through the hospital gown covering him from head to toe, Enrico could find no clue as to what Aldo had done. "Well? What happened? Did you go see him?" He tried to break into his brother's silence.

Without a word, Aldo tossed the box of chocolate onto Enrico's bed. "To fatten you up," he said.

"So you did go see him!"

"Yes, I saw Father Nagle. He says there may be a chance for an annulment!"

"Well, go on. Don't make me drag every word out of your mouth. What do you have to do?"

"It is not so easy. First of all, it could take over two years."

"That long?" Enrico said, disappointment clear in his voice. "Is there no way to get it done faster?"

"If I went to Italy..."

"Yes, Father Nagle thinks that if I could speak directly to the bishop, show him Isabella's letter and a letter from Father Nagle..." Aldo paused, the hope in his eyes darkened, "and if she would agree to an annulment- do you think Isabella's family would agree?"

"Ah, her father! The power of that man! He is not the type to take such an affront sitting down. You would have to deal with him very carefully. He could keep you chained to his daughter for life."

Aldo sank down into his chair, "I do not want this to get nasty, Enrico, I don't want anyone to get hurt."

"Perhaps a not too small donation?"

"Yes, of course a donation. But even if I put my entire estate on the line, I could not compete with the wealth and the power of her father!"

"That is a tragedy. The church is, unfortunately, more flesh and blood men than saintly spirits disinterested in everyday riches."

Aldo paced back and forth in short clipped steps, "But when the bishop hears of the golden button, perhaps Isabella and her father would have no choice?"

Enrico watched his brother. "Every good catholic knows it is the duty of a Catholic marriage to bring forth children to populate the earth!"

"Yes, you must go. This is not something that can be properly dealt with through letters. It would take forever that way. You must go right away, do not waste a day."

Aldo stopped pacing, and wrapping his fingers around the white metal hospital bed, faced Enrico. "But I cannot leave you, at least not until you are well."

"I am quite well enough. The doctor says before long I will not need to be in a hospital, I can go to a sanatorium. That is how well I am getting."

"What wonderful news, why didn't you tell me?"

"Enrico shrugged his shoulders good-naturedly, and said, "So you see, you are free to leave. I am all right."

"But there is the hotel- so much to take care of."

"Jenson can manage. You told me yourself, just the other day, how well he handles the accounts now. I trust him, he's a good man. So you can leave any time now."

Aldo did not speak. "And it's not like you'd be away that long."

"But that's just it. Once I leave, there will be no way to know what will happen, or if I will ever be able to return."

Watching the conflicting emotions fight their battle on his brothers face, Enrico said, "My dear Aldo, if you do not go and set yourself free from this woman, don't you see that I can never be free from the terrible haunting guilt I feel for being the cause of all your unhappiness? In the name of God, do not sentence me to a lifetime of watching your unhappiness and knowing that I caused it."

"You must go, it is the only way you can ever hope to have Rosa. You must go, and now!" Enrico's eyes filled with tears as he watched the pain lift from Aldo's face.

"You are more than a brother to me, you are a true friend. When you put it that way, I cannot argue. I will go."

Enrico reached for a card in his nightstand by his bed, "Here, I already have a travel agency for you, Agenzia Fugazi, is the name. They fix it so the Italian immigration can join their families.

They'll get you to New York and get you on the ship too, they handle both railroads and steamships. The owner is John Fugazi and he has his office right here in San Francisco. If you get busy you can be in Italy in six weeks!"

Opening his gift box of candy, Enrico deliberated long before biting into a dark chocolate candy filled with cherry red cream. He held the box up for Aldo. "Have you told Rosa yet?"

"No, I cannot tell her. What if for some reason I don't get the annulment, or what if something happens to me, and I never return to her? I must not give her any false hopes. She's had too many tragedies in her life already. I love her too much to let her expect something from me which may never happen."

"You are a foolish man, my big brother. Any woman in a hopeless love would be glad for even the slimmest bit of hope, no matter how quickly it might turn to gall. Rosa loves you too much for you to shut her out like this."

"It is not fair to keep this ray of hope from her."

"No!" Aldo shouted. "I do not want her to know, I will not let her be hurt again!"

"But you can't just disappear with no explanation, that is not fair, if…"

"No, Enrico! I will not have her told! I will tell her something, but I will not tell her the real reason, and you must not either! On our mother's grave, I am swearing you to secrecy, Enrico. You must promise me that. Will you promise?"

"What will you tell her?"

"I don't know yet, but I will think of something."

"I don't like it, but I will keep your secret. I promise. How soon will you leave?"

"I shall see, give me Fugazi's card."

CHAPTER THIRTY-ONE

"Here, Rosa, Anna sent these flowers to you. They're from her garden. She said they would help christen your new home. She misses you at our morning study sessions," Nina took off her hat and coat, "I tell her it's just until you get your flat fixed up."

"Tell her to come to see me, I miss our time together, too."

"I did, but you know how shy she is. You are going to have to invite her yourself."

Rosa arranged the flowers in a tall glass bottle, and set them in the middle of her little kitchen table, "Yes, I must. Anna is such a dear person, I would not want her to be hurt."

Nina pulled a long slender package from her purse, "For your table for tonight." Rosa unwrapped two red tapered candles.

"And did you remember to tell the twins to come to the diner after school this afternoon, so you and Aldo can be alone tonight?"

"Yes," Rosa said, smiling at her aunt's lack of subtlety. "Yes, they are looking forward to spending the night with their Nona."

Rosa considered the mischievous gleam in Nina's eye. "I don't even know for sure if he is coming tonight. He has not answered my letter yet."

"Oh, of course he'll come," Nina spoke with confidence.

"There hasn't been enough time for his answer to get here yet. He'll come. Don't worry about that."

"I'm not sure I want him to come. Most of the time lately I'm not sure I even know what is right and what is wrong."

To Nina, she said, "Will I burn in hell for loving him?"

Nina put her arm on her shoulder, "God understands, he knows you are a good woman, Rosa. And I think…" She turned away, and speaking thoughtfully said, "he also knows that not all marriages are made in heaven. Women have to see beyond man-made rules."

When Nina left, Rosa turned her attention to dinner. It was a long time since she had cooked for a man.

With a long wooden spoon, she stirred her sauce that had been simmering since early morning. From the cooler, she took a package of veal hand-selected yesterday at the market.

The house will soon be filled with the tempting scent of tender veal cooking and delicate wine sauce, and the aroma of freshly baked bread.

Measuring out the pasta, she imagined herself that evening sitting across the table from Aldo. Did the lady on the hill ever cook a romantic candlelight dinner for Anthony?

Her skin tingling from the hot bath, she dripped rosewater on her shoulders and neck. From the bottom drawer in her dresser, Rosa unwrapped a new satin corset. The laces looped around the bedpost, she tugged until her waist was almost as slim as it had been at 15.

As if removing the host from the sepulcher, Rosa took the blue and white taffeta dress from its bed of tissue paper and slipped it down over her head.

Her flawless white skin curved sensuously down from her delicate throat and across her breasts held high and firm. Under the ample curve of her bosom, the dress hugged her waist to perfection. The sales lady had said the corset would fit her body into the dress.

Pulling her hair close to her head and up into a soft knot, she studied the long curve of her throat and the outlines of her head. She carefully placed her new combs in the soft knot of black hair. From around her face, she pulled free tiny whispers of hair and twisted them into curls.

She studied herself in the mirror and tugged at the neckline and pushed the dress down onto her shoulders. In the sensuousness of her profile, she saw the wisdom of the saleslady's words.

Everything was ready. In the middle of the table, Nina's candles and Anna's flowers waited patiently for the guest to arrive.

In the bay window, the table was set to look out upon the water simmering in the twilight. Rosa smoothed an invisible wrinkle in Nina's embroidered tablecloth. "He will be here soon," she spoke aloud. In the darkening evening light, her image from the window glass faded away and for a fleeting second she saw the silhouette of Sister Lucia and heard her say,

"We must be clean in body and thought. We are temples of God." Fear suddenly chilled her body.

A carriage came up the street and stopped. "Signora Dante?" A young man in a dark delivery uniform handed her a long thin box. He touched his finger to the visor of his cap and disappeared.

On top of the tissue, wrapped long-stemmed American Beauty roses, a plain white envelope bore her name. She lowered herself into a chair, overcome with dread. Her hands trembling, reluctantly, her fingers opened it.

My dearest Rosa,

Please forgive me for not being there with you tonight. An emergency has called me back to Italy, I must leave immediately or miss the ship in New York.

Never forget that I love you and be sure that it is because of my love for you that I must make this trip. Remember that I love your children, as I love their mother. Pray for me, and for a safe journey.

I hope that you can forgive me for tonight, and will write to me at the hotel in Torino.

Your loving Aldo

And unbearable heaviness washed down over Rosa. Her spirit was deadened and her soul sick. This is God's punishment! He knows my intentions.

Suddenly conscious of her blue taffeta dress with its decollete neckline, Rosa covered her bosom. He is punishing me. I am alone again. Abandoned by another I dared to love.

Rosa stood in the window. She looked up into the sky and felt very small, very much alone. Finally, the sheer wake of her sorrow broke through and the tears poured down her cheeks.

When all the tears were spent, Rosa mechanically set about putting away dinner, the celebration dinner that would never happen.

"I have driven him away with my stubbornness, with my purity and self-righteousness. That is why I have lost him."

Talking aloud to the empty room, Rosa's voice rose. She grabbed the carving knife and thrust it with all her force into the loaf of bread, the loaf of bread she had baked specifically for Aldo, Aldo Martinelli, the married man.

What a fool! She was to think God would ever let her be happy!

Pulling her coat close around her, she ran out of the house. Am I never permitted happiness? What does he want of me? Without knowing where they were taking her, her feet hurried, half running half walking through the evening- quiet streets, resting only when they reached the wharf.

She stood for a long time looking out across the water toward Berkeley. I will never see him again, he is on his way back to his wife, back to their marriage bed.

Enrico told me his brother would never return to Italy, then why did he go? What emergency would be so secret that he could not tell me? It could only mean that he is returning to his wife's bed.

Dimly aware of approaching footsteps, Rosa turned just as Anthony thrust his face forward at her and taunted, "Alone? Where is the Signor Martinelli tonight?" The evilness in the word alone cut through Rosa's raw flesh like a razor.

"Oh, Anthony, you startled me," calling on her self-control to avoid a conflict with her uncle, Rosa tried to speak pleasantly.

Holding her by the forearm, with a change in his tone, he asked, "You are expecting someone?"

"No, no, I was, I was just…"

Putting his other arm on her shoulder he pulled her closer, and the sneer on his lips softened into a smile.

Terrified, but finally able to comprehend what he was doing, Rosa raised her foot and drove the heel of her shoe down with a mighty blow squarely onto the top of Anthony's instep. He screamed in pain, and as he released her, she ran across the street toward the diner. She could hear him yelling, "you bitch! I'll get you, I'll get you!"

Closing the diner door safely behind her, she paused to catch her breath. Only then she raised her head and opened her eyes and she realized that Nina and two of the fishermen were there staring at her.

Mario and Vito helped Rosa to the table while Nina brought her a cup of hot coffee.

"You're almost frozen half to death. Where is Aldo? What has happened?" Unable to speak, Rosa handed Aldo's letter to her aunt. Nina signaled the two men to wait outside, and when she finished reading, put her arm tenderly around Rosa's shoulder.

Staring as if in a hypnotic trance, Rosa said dully, "I could've kept him with me."

"If it is God's will he will come back to you. Let us pray now for his safe passage."

The two men brought the wagon around. When they stopped at Nina's house, she insisted on taking the children with her. Rosa did not want to be alone, she invited the men in, "come and see my nice new home," she said.

She closed the door to the parlor and shut off the view of the deserted diner table still waiting in the bay window. She steered them to the kitchen.

397

They spoke admiringly of each feature of her new home that Rosa pointed out, but it was clear there was something else on their minds.

Pouring them each a glass of dark red wine, she asked, "What is it, Mario, what is bothering you?"

"When me and Vito went outside so that you could talk to Nina, we saw Anthony out there. He was in a foul mood. He came over to us and he said, ah, he said..." Mario looked to Vito for help. "You know, Rosa, how he is, the bad words he has to use all the time? Well, he said something not so nice about women."

"Yes, that's it," Mario added, "he said something like- women were no better than dogs, that they would turn and bite you."

As Mario spoke, embarrassment forced his chin deeper down into his chest until Rosa could hardly hear him.

"Yes?" Rosa urged him on, dreading what more she might hear.

" Did you have a run-in with Anthony just before you came into the diner tonight?"

When Rosa had told them what happened, they were immediately up on their feet ready to go after him to teach him a lesson.

"You mustn't do that," she insisted. "If you confront him now, someone will get hurt and it will only make matters worse."

She told him what Aldo had said about Anthony being a dangerous man. Fighting hard to control her thoughts that kept rushing back to Aldo and to why he had left her, she knew she had to think of other things.

She told the two fishermen that she would take the contract to her citizenship teacher and ask if she could get her lawyer friend to look at it for them.

CHAPTER THIRTY-TWO

Rosa did not see the building she passed as the Geary Street railroad bounced along. When they came to the end of the line, she mechanically took her place on the horse trolley for the rest of the long ride to the hospital. Her somber thoughts turned inward, Rosa would have passed her stop, had not the kind driver reminded her.

Enrico was sitting in the chair looking out the window. With the morning sun silhouetting his profile, he looked like Aldo. For one brief moment, Rosa forgot why she had come.

Enrico started to stand. She held her hand up, "Please, no Enrico. Do not trouble yourself." She searched his face for any kind of answer to the terrible question that had brought her there this morning.

He too was studying her. What did he expect? A wailing woman, tears, anger? She smiled at him with what she hoped was reassurance. I will not collapse at your feet, she thought, maybe last night I would have. But now I look for any tiny bit of understanding that will give me peace.

"Enrico," she said in barely more than a whisper, "I drove him away from me, didn't I? Isn't that why he has gone home to her?"

"Oh, my sweet dear Rosa, sit down. You did not drive him from you."

"He has sworn me to secrecy. I can only tell you that he has done what he had to do."

Rosa walked nervously around the room. "What kind of emergency can it be that took him back to Italy? He said he would never return and then poof- like that – he leaves."

Rosa's eyes pleaded with Enrico for answers, but he remained silent. "And that terrible voyage across the ocean again, and soon it is this coming winter."

"Rosa, please, you must have faith. I promised I would not tell you. I must keep that promise, please do not make it more difficult for me."

She did not want to burden Enrico or to appear weak, but the tears came, and she could not make them stop.

"Please Rosa, don't cry. I wish I could hold you and comfort you," he reached out his hand as if to touch her.

"I love you too Rosa, so be brave. We both miss him, but we must try not to worry."

"Let's you and I make a pact. I will do everything possible to get well. I will drink all the milk, eat all the food, breathe all the fresh air, all the things I should do. And you must keep busy, start your bakery, study for your citizenship, take care of those two children I have heard so much about. The time will pass quickly."

"But what about you Enrico? Who will help you now? Who will look after your hotel?"

After Enrico had quieted her fears, he asked her about her bakery, and said, "I think I may have your first customer."

"The bread here is terrible. I told the doctor they should find a better bakery. You know Rosa, these French think they can cook, but it takes a real Italian to show them."

He laughed as if at a private joke, "I wish they'd turn me loose in that kitchen, I'd show them how to cook!"

"When I gave them a taste of your bread they right away wanted the recipe! I told them it was a family secret, then I said that perhaps I might ask you to stop in someday and see them, if, I added, you had the time!"

"You are a clever salesman," Rosa said feeling better, and somehow closer to Aldo.

"Before I make a contract to bake bread for anyone, I must find a way to deliver it. I am looking around for a wagon to buy."

The nurse came in with a tall glass of milk and stood guard over Enrico while he drained every ounce of the creamy white liquid. Then she supervised his return to bed.

"How soon will you be able to start baking, Rosa?" He asked the minute the nurse left.

"In about a week, maybe two at the latest."

"I have a delivery wagon that the hotel doesn't use anymore, and a perfectly good old horse not doing a thing to earn his keep. I tell you what, Rosa if you will supply me with daily bread," Enrico clasped his hands in prayer, "you can use the wagon and the horse for your deliveries. You can bring your bread to the hospital and see me at the same time."

"Oh, no I couldn't…"

"Nonsense! Of course you can! As a matter of fact, Aldo and I discussed this before. So it is not just an offer from me, it is from

401

the two Martinelli brothers. Please do not disappoint me by turning down our little gesture of faith in you."

"It is most generous. And I do gratefully accept."

"Good! I will contact the hotel and have the wagon and the horse delivered to you. Remember now, this means that as soon as 'The Rosa Dante Bakery' is running, I will get my daily portion of that famous mama Dante bread, right?"

Rosa agreed.

"What will you call your bakery?"

"I haven't given it a name yet," Rosa said, her thoughts lingering on Mama Dante and life in Viareggio. "Maybe I should call it 'The Rosa II'", and she told Enrico how Giovanni and Eduardo blindfolded her the day they christened the Rosa I.

"It will not be a boat as they had hoped, but it will be a link to what I left behind."

Rosa looked out onto the city from the top of the hospital steps. Her thoughts, full of the future and its unanswered questions, she walked back towards the flat and what she already knew, but ahead to the unknown.

Aware only of the struggle going on between her heart and her head, she walked a long time. She came to the rise of the land where she could look down and see the Cliff House with the Pacific Ocean stretching out endlessly behind them.

Down past the barking sounds of the sea lions, she walked now briskly, until she reached the beach and stopped to rest at the seawall.

No other human being was visible in this world silent except for the rushing sound of the waves, and the harsh complaints of a hovering band of scraggy seagulls. Rosa drank in hungrily the salty smell of the sea, the smell that took her heart back home to the shores of Italy.

She thought of Giovanni and Eduardo, and of her two sons so far across the water. Would she ever see Victor or Dino again? She climbed down to the broad flat beach and trudged across the sand.

Sitting, she drew her knees up under her chin and looked out across the endless water. Very much alone, she thought of her younger self who, on the beach at Viareggio, made the decision to move her family across the sea to America.

Yes, she had survived the trip, but now, she was thousands of miles from her two sons, and once again abandoned by someone she loved.

"Are you alright ma'am?" A man's voice startled her. Behind her stood a tall, blonde man wearing a dark blue policeman's uniform.

The tall helmet made him appear even taller. A club hung from his belt and a silver bag shined in the sunlight. "I am sorry I startled you," he spoke in English, but in a way Rosa had never heard before.

"I was deep in thought," she replied.

Squatting down beside her, he said, "Do I see tears? Are you troubled, have you a problem?"

"Just doing a lot of thinking, but I am alright."

He said, "You speak English well, but I think you are Italian, am I right?" He spoke with a very thick accent.

"Yes I am still learning English," she said.

Rosa had never seen a man so fair. His white forehead mottled with the tiny blue veins, and the pink skin across his nose and cheeks was dotted with freckles. His pale eyebrows and lashes drew no attention to themselves around his blue eyes. What little blonde hair she could see beneath his helmet blended smoothly into his skin and concealed any grey that might have given a clue to his age.

"I have never heard English sound the way you say it. Do you have an accent?" She asked.

"I am Norwegian," he replied, smiling pleasantly down at her.

Realizing she must be staring, she tried to apologize, but he laughed and said, "You Italian women always look at me that way."

"I am sorry, I just have never seen anyone so blonde."

"God gave me no frame for my face like he did for you. He gave you lovely black hair to outline your face and dark lashes and browse to set off the color of your eyes."

"You are too kind," Rosa said, pleased yet feeling unsure of the stranger.

"But why they call the color of your skin olive, I will never know," he smiled at her as if sensing her residency, "the only olives I ever saw were black or green, and your face is neither black nor green. It is more of the color of priceless ivory."

"I never thought of it that way." She laughed. "Do you see many olive-colored people out here?" She asked.

"A few. Usually women come to the beach. All this is my beach here," he waved his arms to indicate the length of the beach.

"They come for many reasons, and I like to talk to them, to make sure they are all right."

His eyes studied her face intently. Struggling to get up on her feet, she reassured him, "I will be alright. Something just drew me to the ocean, somehow."

When she stood up her head barely came to the top of his shoulder.

Again he knew her thoughts and said, "Although God did not give me dark hair to frame my face he did give me a tall frame to carry it on." He laughed.

"I will drive you home in the police wagon. I am soon off duty and you are a long way from home."

"No, thank you," Rosa said, wondering to herself if the horse trolley would still be running. "I will be fine."

But while she protested he was already leading her to the wagon. He was determined to deliver her to her front door.

While the old black horse plodded leisurely along, he introduced himself, "I am officer Nelson, Hans Nelson." Although his smile was boyish, Rosa decided he must be at least as old as Nina. He asked many questions about her and her life until finally, Rosa knew how worried he had been about her.

When they arrived at her flat, she considered for the first time how it would look to anyone who saw her riding in a police wagon. He helped her down out of the wagon, and when she looked around she was glad that the streets were deserted.

"Would you like to come in for a glass of wine or coffee?" She offered.

"Yes I would like that," he said, "I am off duty now."

Rosa unlocked the front door and Paisano greeted Officer Nelson as only a puppy can do.

Rosa made coffee and when the twins arrived home from school they asked dozens of questions of this tall blonde man who spoke in a strange manner and parked a police wagon outside their house.

Their questions answered, the children left to take the puppy out for a walk. Hans said, "I see that I should not have worried about you. You have a lovely family."

"So you were worried about me!" Rosa said, "I knew it."

"Well, yes my beach is a lonely place, and I see a lot of unhappy people, particularly women. They come and stare at the ocean, and sometimes they just walk out into the water and disappear."

Rosa broke in, "You thought I was one of those women?"

"Well, Mrs. Dante, I thought you might be. You had that far away look and you were alone. I always check."

"I am sorry I caused you all that trouble."

No need to apologize, ma'am, the beach is my beat, but it was my pleasure to drive you home."

"But I have made you late, and your wife will be worried. I am sorry."

"I have no wife. I am my own boss."

Getting up, she said, "If you have no wife to cook for you, then stay and have supper with the children and me. Please let me repay you for your kindness to me today. Please stay and try some Italian home cooking."

"Thank you, Mrs. Dante, I would be happy to stay, I love Italian cooking." Watching her move in the kitchen he said, "I can see now that you were not thinking of suicide, but you do have some trouble. Am I right?"

"Everyone has troubles," she smiled, "but, at the moment, mine is nothing I cannot handle."

She was thinking of Anthony's contract with the fisherman and his other illegal activities and wondered if maybe Officer Nelson would be of some help.

There was urgent knocking at the front door.

Panting for breath Nina said, "Rosa what is wrong? Anthony said- well no matter what he said- why is there a police wagon parked out in front? What is wrong?"

Nina kept trying to look past Rosa. "What is wrong?" She pleaded.

"Nothing, Nina, nothing is wrong. Get a hold of yourself! Come to the kitchen and meet Officer Nelson. I met him at the beach today and he drove me home. He's going to have dinner with us."

"Anthony came into the diner saying that you were already in trouble. Out of our house for one week, he says, and in trouble already. He probably passes by here just to see what is going on."

Officer Nelson stood up as they came into the kitchen, and when Rosa introduced them, he asked, "Are you in any relation to Anthony Orso?"

"Why yes, he is my husband. Do you know him?"

"I have met him," the policeman answered, the inflection of his voice clearly putting an end to this subject.

Rosa wondered how he would have occasion to meet Anthony. His beat is clear across town, nothing to do with the North Beach area. "Nina," she said, "are you through at the diner, can you stay?"

"No, I had better get back. I just left everything. I was sure something was wrong. But I will come back later tonight if Anthony goes out. Is that alright Rosa?"

"Yes, Nina, I will be here," Rosa kissed her and walked with her to the door.

Hans helped her move the table from the bay window back into the kitchen. She served a simple meal to this kindly man and watched him eat four large buttered pieces of her bread all the while keeping her children spellbound with stories of his Norwegian boyhood.

Over coffee, Rosa tried to find out how officer Nelson knew Anthony, but each time she probed, he became ill-at-ease.

Finally, he did say he met Anthony at the police station a while back, over a case that had something to do with a young Italian girl.

"It was really nothing," the uncomfortable officer said.

Obviously anxious to change the subject, "Tell me about your bakery, Mrs. Dante. Are you going to make Etle cake, or perhaps special treats for the holidays?"

He tried to explain the Norwegian apple cake of his childhood, and the Jule cake made only at Christmas time, full of plump raisins with citron and ground Cardamom.

Promising she would try if he gave her a recipe, she said, let us walk over and look at the bakery. I am anxious to see how much the workmen did today.

The stone ovens were almost done, and in about a week, she thought, she could start baking.

Officer Nelson admired her store and told her there were several restaurants in the German-Dutch part of the town that might be interested in her bread.

"If you like," he said, "I'll contact them and let them know."

"Yes, that would be a good help, though at first, I may not be able to take care of too many customers, not until I find someone to make the deliveries for me. "

"Have you decided what to call your bakery?"

"I think I will call it 'Rosa II'," she said without explanation.

"Roz- ha- tu," he said, "very nice," but his face showed a lack of understanding.

"Now I must leave. Thank you, Mrs. Dante, I will let you know what the restaurant men say about ordering bread."

"Good night, and 'Mrs. Dante' sounds so formal, I would like to have you call me Rosa."

"Thank you again, Rosa, I am Hans."

CHAPTER THIRTY-THREE

Rosa rinsed her rag in the bucket of vinegar water and twisted it dry. Busy washing the big square window of her bakery she at first did not hear the wagon approach.

It stopped in front and she read the large gold letters, "S. S. P. D." painted on the black windowless sides. Hans waved at her from the driver's seat and swinging his long legs out, slid easily to the ground. She had not seen him since the day, a week ago, he drove her home from the beach.

His face glowing with a mischievous grin, Hans went silently into the back of the wagon where he pulled out a long slim package wrapped in brown paper.

The smile on his face delighted Rosa as, cap in hand, he came toward her.

"Good morning," he said, "good morning, I have brought you something."

Standing the long skinny parcel on end, Hans pulled the wrapping away from the top while Rosa denuded its lower portions. As they stripped the paper away, there appeared to be nothing more than a long flat piece of wood.

When the last thread of brown wrapping paper was torn away, Hans ceremoniously turned the pine board around to face her. On the front were carved bold deep letters. Puzzled, Rosa read each letter, "R- O- Z- A- H- T- U." Uncomprehending, she sounded them out, "Roz- ah- tu!" Now she understood! She knew that now she had the name for her bakery.

"Now you are officially in business," he said holding the board up at arm's length in front of the sparkling window.

Grinning proudly, he asked, "Did I get everything spelled right?" Without waiting for an answer, he went right on, "I hope you like it," he went after a hammer and nails from the wagon, "It's pretty, isn't it?"

Unwilling to hurt his feelings, Rosa did not know what to do. She watched him racking the sign above the glass window. "What a nice person you are to do this for me. It's beautiful!"

When he was finished she said, "Come in, let me thank you with a nice hot meal."

"I can't stay now, but I could come back later today," and then looking embarrassed as if he had been too forward, he added, "that is, of course, if you really meant it."

Reassured by Rosa's smile, he explained, "I have to go see the Sisters of the Holy Family, while I was in the neighborhood I thought I'd bring you your present." He left with a promise to return that evening to have supper with her and the children.

When she turned back toward the storefront and its newly acquired sign, she laughed out loud. Well, she thought, "ROZ- HA- TU" it is and that is what it shall be. She walked across the street to study the sign. It sounds Italian and looks Italian, and because it was made by a Norwegian, it is truly American. I shall bake my Italian bread in the "ROZHATU" American bakery.

The twins came running around the corner, and without so much as a glance at the new sign, John Edward said, "Mama, did you see the big ship coming into the harbor? Nona says it's from Genova, can we go see it, can we please, mama please?"

Rosa remembered what she heard about Anthony meeting the ships and getting men to come to his boarding house. She agreed, and she and the children walked down the street toward the Filbert Street pier.

A handful of people were already waiting on the dock. Dressed in their best clothes, there were families, men and women alone searching the faces staring down at them from the crowded decks above.

Sailors were helping six passengers down the gangplank. Two sailor's carried a litter off ship followed by several others who needed help walking.

Rosa overheard fragments of conversation about the storms and the rough seas they have been through, and when she looked at the sallow faces on deck, she knew it had been a bad trip.

Finally, a sailor signaled and the people on deck funneled down the gangplank. Rosa saw Anthony step forward, he'd been waiting at the edge of the dock, sizing up the crowd.

She instinctively sunk back out of sight. She watched him approach a small group of men who soon formed a circle around him. Rosa edged as close as she could without him seeing her, but still, she could not hear what he said.

When the circle around Anthony thinned out, he helped one man on the far side of the dock to a wooden bench and had him sit down, and then he went back toward the boat. Rosa felt like running over to warn the waiting man not to sign any contracts, but he would only see her as a foolish woman and would pay no attention to her.

Soon Anthony took another man to the bench and again went back toward the boat, toward the stern where another group of passengers had disembarked.

He stopped and leaned up against the wagon. Lighting a cigar he settled down to wait and to study the new arrivals.

Two pretty young girls, about seventeen or eighteen, moved away from the crowd at the bottom of the gangplank, and Anthony, quickly coming alive, walked directly over to them.

Putting out his cigar and taking off his hat he bought ever so politely. The three appeared to be having a polite conversation when one of the girls shook her head, and they both turned and left.

Watching them walk away from him, Anthony shrugged his shoulders and went back to his post, and continued his vigil.

Another woman, clutching the railing, made her way awkwardly down the gangplank. She was alone, and reaching the dock, stopped, her eyes starting around, searching for something or someone.

A tiny woman, not more than twenty, her classic Roman features were clouded with worry. Holding tightly to the dark scarf which covered her head and shoulders, she swayed from side to side as she moved across the dock.

As she walked she pointed her right toe down in a futile attempt to compensate for the shortness of the leg.

Anthony started toward her. Then, seeing her limp, he stopped, considered, and started again. Tipping his hat to her, they soon engaged in conversation.

Rosa strained to hear, but could not make out any words. Anthony picked up her suitcase and cloth bag and supporting her politely by the arm, led her to the buggy parked in the street.

He drove back to where the two men waited, and after introducing the young woman in his polite Sunday manner, he drove off with the three new arrivals.

Rosa watched Anthony's buggy until it was out of sight, and only then became aware that she did not know where the children had wandered.

She looked around, the doc was pretty much deserted, most of the people were already off the ship. The only activity was around a gangway stretching out from the hold low in the hull of the ship, where a few sailors were coming ashore.

Two young sailors ran down the gangplank and threw themselves flat, kissing the earth beneath them. Rosa smiled at their antics and wondered how many times they made that dreadful trip through the rough waters around the Horn.

Her thoughts turned to Aldo somewhere in the middle of the Atlantic ocean, and she prayed to the Madonna to keep him safe.

The children were calling, "Mama, mama, look who we found!"

They were coming toward her with a sailor between them, each child was holding one of his hands and waving at her with the other. She stared but did not recognize him until they were almost upon her.

"Peppino?" She shouted, "Peppino!"

She reached her arms out to him, and as he reached for her, their bodies collided. They were instantly surrounded by the children's excited embraces and serenaded by their youthful shrieks of happiness.

Loosening their embrace, Rosa and Peppino stood back. Each spoke at the same instant. Indicating for him to go first, Rosa waited.

"San Francisco agrees with you, you look beautiful, Rosa, much better than you did during that storm," and he hugged her again.

"Can you come to the house with us? How long do you have? Are you hungry?" Rosa's questions came swiftly, leaving no time for answers.

Peppino swung his sea bag up over his shoulder, and arms wrapped around each other, the four started off. Stopping suddenly, the young sailor turned back toward the ship and saluted.

"Goodbye to the sea," he said, "and goodbye to the last damn ship I will ever set foot on."

"Do you mean that Peppino, are you really here for good?"

"You told me you would give me a job if I came to San Francisco, so after that last voyage across the Atlantic I signed on to come to California around the Horn.

"I wasn't getting anywhere, just back and forth across the water. I couldn't even get money ahead. Right now I have only a few dollars and the $35 I'll get for this last trip. Yes, that's it! I am officially through with the sea!"

"I think the lord has sent you to us, Peppino," Rosa said, taking a hold of his arm. "I am ready to start up my bakery and need a man to help me, and to make deliveries. Do you know how to drive a wagon, Peppino?"

"Of course I can, did you ever know a little Italian boy who didn't have to take care of the family horse? Do you already have a horse and wagon?"

415

"Yes," Rosa explained about Enrico's horse and wagon that was right now waiting for her a few short blocks away in Luchessi's Livery Stables.

"So you really do have a job for me? The lord must be looking after both of us."

"I won't be able to pay you as much as you earned on the ship, at least at first. But as soon as we get the business built up…"

"That is fine. I don't need much, just a place to sleep and a little food to eat, that is all I need. Give me an hour to get my land legs and time to find a place to stay and I will be ready for work."

"Peppino, you will stay with us! I have bought a building with two flats in it, and a nice Italian couple rents upstairs, and our flat has three bedrooms and you can have the empty room. It is really empty, there is not even a bed in it yet. But for tonight, Angelina can sleep with me, and you can have Angelina's bed. Tomorrow we will see about finding a bed for you."

"How lucky I am! I think I am the one who found heaven!" He squeezed both of the children to him, "I have a job, a place to live, and good friends. But are you sure that it will be no trouble?"

"Peppino, if it were not for you and your kindness to me on the ship, I wouldn't even be in America."

"Do you know what happened at the pier in New York?"

"I saw the commotion, but I couldn't get to you. Jocko saw to that, and then I saw the children come back with Signor… oh what was his name?"

"Martinelli," Rosa replied, then hoped she had not spoken too quickly and revealed her feelings for him.

"Yes, Signor Martinelli, that's right! And then when I saw you leave the dock, I knew everything had been worked out somehow. You remember Jocko, don't you?"

"I don't want to remember him," Rosa said.

"Well, he's still sailing the Leonardo, he was one reason I changed ships. I was glad to get rid of him, he is an evil man, and everywhere he goes he seems to spread meanness. I hope I never see him again."

They rounded the last corner and Rosa pointed, "There it is! My bakery. Isn't it beautiful?"

Peppino agreed to its beauty, and studying the sign, he asked, "ROZ-HA-TU? What kind of name is that?"

"That's an American name. ROZHATU," she laughed and told him about her Norwegian friend making the sign for her.

"Well, I wouldn't change it either," Peppino agreed.

Rosa unlocked the front door and Paisano immediately took over the duties of making Peppino feel welcome.

When finally exhausted by his own efforts, he retreated to his basket for a nap, Rosa started dinner and the children showed Peppino around.

Only with reluctance did the twins permit him out of their sight long enough for a bathe.

Peppino fell asleep and Rosa cooked a feast to celebrate his arrival. She remembered the meal at St. Patrick's Molly made for them that first night ashore. The meal she prepared for Peppino was fishless.

"I am never again going to wear that sailor suit," he said. Rosa introduced him to Hans, and right away a bond formed between them. Peppino had grown since she last saw him. His skin clear and smooth, his black eyes – full of laughter, he looked older than his years.

Hans has been a sailor in his native country, and during dinner, the two men exchanged stories of the sea and Peppino told him of his voyage around the horn.

After dinner, Angelina showed Peppino and Hans the doll Aldo gave her for her birthday, and John Edward brought out his toy engine.

And when Peppino found out that Paisano was also a gift from Aldo, he said, "So, Signor Martinelli did not sail out of your lives after New York, eh?"

Rosa tried to act disinterested, but she knew she had failed when Peppino nudged her and whispered, "Perhaps there is more to this than you are saying, eh, Rosa?"

Although Hans said nothing, she knew he had not missed anything, and she became uncomfortable talking about Aldo.

There was a knock at the door, and grateful for an interruption, she left the room. Nina was peering through the holes in the lace curtain.

The door was barely open when Nina blurted out, "Rosa, Anthony said you were down at the dock kissing sailors. Do you know any sailors?"

"Yes, Nina I know one sailor, come and meet him."

She could well imagine someone reporting to Anthony and how they put it.

After introductions, Nina pulled a bottle of wine from her dishtowel bundle, "This one Anthony did not count, so I thought we could enjoy ourselves."

Nina poured the wine and soon the conversation focused on politics.

They talked of the battles waged in Italy's struggle for unification, and Hans told them of Norway's rule under Sweden.

Rosa went to tuck the twins into bed, but her thoughts were with her two sons left behind in Italy.

She wondered if they wanted to go off to war. When sounds of accordion music floated down from the upstairs flat, the simple Italian folk tunes took her even closer to Victor and Dino.

She had received another letter that week that Guido had been ill with a cough he couldn't shake off. Rosa could see Maria nursing Guido back to health, and although the letter didn't complain, she knew that things were not going as well as they had hoped.

The accordion was still playing when she came back into the kitchen where Nina and the two men were talking.

The sight of the young Peppino sitting there at her kitchen table brought back into her mind all her images of Aldo, that first glance on the ship, the terrible time on the dock, and many hours bouncing along the train.

What if he never came back? What had made him leave? Enrico said his wife was beautiful, and now she knew in her heart that if she had yielded to him that night, he never would have left her.

"Rosa," Nina said, "did you hear me?"

"No, I'm sorry, the music made me think of something else."

"I was just saying, Anthony's brought two men and a poor little lame girl to the boarding house this afternoon. They are all from Genova, the men are fishermen. Anthony is going to have a whole house full before he knows it.

419

"She is a pretty little girl – big brown eyes. She's all alone, she has no one. Poor thing, she has been lame all her life. She's not much more than 19, and such a sweet thing. I feel so sorry for her.

"If Anthony and I had a child she would have been about her age now. She wanted to start right in to help me with the work, but she was so tired and sick that I told her to go to bed and rest until she got her strength back."

Nina stood up to leave, and said, "Mario and Vito told me to tell you they would come to see you on Sunday, after church. They have a surprise for you."

When she had left, Rosa started to explain to Hans and Peppino about Anthony's fleet of boats and the boarding house, but both men already knew of others who, like Anthony, plucked immigrants off the boats and indentured them.

As the three friends finished Nina's bottle of wine, many such tales passed among them.

CHAPTER THIRTY-FOUR

Peppino was as good a worker as he was pleasant company. Rosa explained that she could not afford to give him a salary and he would have to work on commission.

"But," she said, "I know that you will soon be as good a salesman as you were a sailor."

He dogged her footsteps in the bakery, and before the week was up he knew all that Rosa could teach him.

She scooped up a handful of cornmeal, and, throwing it onto the hot oven, explained, "If the flower smokes before you count to 10, the oven is too hot. If it smokes at 10, then the heat is just right to bake bread."

"If I need to check the heat of the oven while the bread is baking, I put in a piece of white paper, and if it turns dark brown, I know the oven is too hot and has to cool off a little.

Then after the bread is baked and I can let the oven cool down a bit, that is when I can bake the sugar cakes and, when it's down a bit further, I do the wine and spice cakes."

Rosa leaned against a barrel of flour, and patting it, said, "You see this barrel? This will make two hundred and sixty pounds of bread."

She smiled at Peppino's eagerness to learn everything all at once, all in one day, and she added, "That is two hundred and sixty pounds of bread for you to deliver and make a commission on!"

It didn't take him long to learn the streets of San Francisco and start making deliveries on his own. The children loved Peppino, and many times rode with him in the afternoons when he visited stores and restaurants to drum up new orders for the Rohzatu Bakery.

Quick to learn and anxious to improve his English, Peppino had written a list of English sentences he would use on his delivery routes, and when the children were with him, they spoke only English.

When he learned of the citizenship classes the three women and the fisherman went to, he went with the men, agreeing that in their new country, they should all talk American.

Rosa continued to visit Enrico on Wednesday afternoons, and with each visit, she became increasingly impatient that a letter from Aldo would be there waiting for her.

She found him sitting by the window drinking a glass of milk and reading a letter when she entered.

"Good afternoon, Rosa." He said with a big smile. Mechanically setting down the basket of bread she brought him, her eyes didn't move from the letter he held.

"No, Rosa, I'm sorry. This letter is not from Aldo, it's just full business. But do not worry, he'll be safe, and we will hear soon. Do not worry."

But she did worry, and it was only when she started telling Enrico about the children and all that Peppino was doing and the orders they had that she was able to think of other things.

Visiting hours were almost over when Enrico pointed to his sketch pad on top of the chest of drawers, and said, "Bring that to me, I have something to show you."

He peeled back the pages of the pad, past sheets filled with sketches of nurses, medicine bottles, of trays of food, and flowers, sketches of thousands of details seen so clearly through his artist-eye.

When he found the page he wanted, he turned the pad toward Rosa, and there, looking out from the page was Aldo. So clear, so like him, Rosa gasped. Reaching for the picture, she could not see through her tears.

Enrico asked, "Do you like it?"

That afternoon she arrived home to the flat just before sunset. She was weary, and the steps were steeper than usual. On the floor just inside the door, there were two envelopes below the mail slot.

She reached down for those white pieces of paper. Afraid of being disappointed again, she tried not to let herself hope it would be from Aldo.

There it was! "Mrs. Rosa Dante" written in Aldo's hand.

She felt such a flush of relief that, for that moment, no matter what the letter contained she would be happy.

My dearest Rosa,

It is reassuring to be able to send mail now to your home where you do not have to worry about someone else opening your letters.

Of course, Rosa thought, I never even thought that he would send the mail here! She went hungrily back to the letter:

I arrived in New York after a very long, boring train ride across America. When I saw the places we had never seen together and remembered how beautiful they were, I was surprised at how uninteresting they had become without you. Even the children on the train were not as bright or beautiful as the twins. The food was bland and the wine even more tasteless. I spent most of my time on the train reading. I stayed overnight at St. Patricks, and Father O'Malley sent his regards. He is still full of jokes and Molly sends her best.

He said he could see I was in love with you, and he told me that he could easily have predicted it that night we had dinner at the church house together. He complimented me on my good taste.

I was impressed with the very large library St. Patrick's has and Father spent a lot of time with me looking things up. He is a very knowledgeable man.

My ship sails early tomorrow morning and I must now say goodnight, my dear Rosa, my love. Give Nina and the children my love.

With great love, until I see you again,

Aldo.

She wondered why he said so much about the church library, and finally decided he wanted to have something to read on the ship.

In the bedroom, she reread the letter then put it away in the black tin box and unrolled Enrico's drawing of his brother.

She imagined Aldo once again on the dock of the ship being tossed mercilessly about by huge waves and storm winds, and she knelt down and prayed to the Madonna to keep him safe.

After mass the following Sunday, the children had finished their breakfast, and Rosa and Peppino were lingering over a second cup of coffee when they heard commotion on Front Street.

Rosa went to the door and saw Mario and Vito and half a dozen other men hovering around a wagon carrying a large object.

She recognized the boat builder she met the day Nina took her to the boat house. "Mario, what have you got there?" She called from the top of the stairs.

"You will see," he said, struggling to lower their heavy burden from the wagon to the ground.

When they got it to the foot of the stairs, they all stopped and faced her. Mario took his hat off, "We knew you didn't have much furniture, so all of us at the boarding house decided to make you a present."

" What is it?" Rosa said, "take off the blanket, I cannot see what it is!"

They laughed, and each in his own words told her she would have to wait until they got it up the stairs.

It took them a long time and many invectives before they got the heavy and awkward object up to the landing.

When, finally, they removed the blanket, Rosa saw a beautiful table with heavy hand–turned legs and a glistening polished top.

"Where shall we put it, ma'am?" Someone asked. Speechless, Rosa pointed to the almost empty dining room.

When the table was in place, she ran her hand over the glass-smooth surface, "It is the most beautiful thing I have ever seen, and I think it's the nicest thing anyone has ever done for me."

"You may as well know, Rosa, we have selfish motives also. If you did not have a table we would not be invited to dinner. So we got Alfredo, the carpenter, and we all helped and made you a table."

"The men all helped sanding the wood, and Vito here stained it," Mario glowed like a proud papa.

Overwhelmed, Rosa walked around and around the table. "Peppino," she said after she had examined every inch of it, "Get the wine, we must drink a toast to this beautiful new table, and to our good friends who made it."

When the gift table had been properly toasted, the conversation drifted back to fishing, into the boarding house, into the two men and the girl Anthony had brought in.

The fishermen were anxious to fill Peppino in, and they told how each of them had fallen into Anthony's trap and we're now so heavily in debt that they didn't know how they would ever get away from him.

When the fishermen left, Rosa washed the wine glasses and Peppino dried them. He told her he had heard many stories from sailors who had run away from men like Anthony and couldn't work on land for fear of being caught.

Rosa told Peppino about the contract and about giving it to her citizenship teacher to get someone to read it for them. She also filled them in about seeing Anthony with his lady on the hill.

Peppino asked, "Does Nina know anything about this?"

"She has her suspicions, but how much she actually knows, I am not sure. I think she knows he likes the women, especially the young ones, but I don't think she suspects any of the other things he has going for him. I'm so afraid she will be hurt."

"I don't know how much feeling she has left for him now, but she is completely dependent on him, and has never given any sign of leaving him. I don't want to do anything to put her in danger.

"Even if she knew all the things we suspect, I'm not sure she could leave him."

"I know my mother wouldn't leave my stepfather," Peppino said. "We were the ones who had to leave, my brother and me. But then her only relative she could turn to was a sister far off in America, while Nina has you right there. Maybe that would make a difference."

"But tell me more about the contract you have. What has your citizenship teacher said about it?"

"She said she would show it to a lawyer friend, but the last time I saw her, she hadn't had time to look at it yet."

"The contracts with the fishermen," Rosa said, "is just one small part of his operations. We won't be sure what all he's involved in until we get a look at his books he keeps locked in his office.

"Is there any way that you can get into the office?"

"No, he keeps the keys with him at all times."

"Even when he sleeps?"

"Even when he sleeps! When he comes home drunk, that would be the only time he'd let loose of them."

"In that case, you may have to tell Nina. Anyhow, I think she has a right to know everything that you know, particularly about the lady on the hill, she should know. Do you think she would help?"

"I don't know Peppino. I know she loves me and would do anything for the children, but Anthony is her husband. At times she defends him, but she's also afraid of him. He has struck her a few times.

427

But again, she tells me that now that I am here, she is braver around him."

"I think that if you want to get the keys, you are going to have to tell her everything. She might get angry, but on the other hand, she may know more than you think."

Rosa went to check on the twins to see if they were sleeping, and from the bedroom, she heard the front doorbell. Peppino's footsteps hurried to the door, and then she heard him say, "Oh my god! What happened?"

CHAPTER THIRTY-FIVE

"Nina, what happened?" Rosa took hold of Nina's arm and helped Peppino get her a chair.

Nina's face drained of color, her cheeks streaked with tears, and her eyes wide but unseeing. Her body collapsed down into the chair as if all will to live were gone.

Rosa held Nina's limp hands and rubbed them while Peppino held a glass of brandy to her lips. Little by little between sobs, Nina told what had happened:

That afternoon after church Anthony left to go downtown on business and Nina went to the boarding house to see the poor little lame girl from the ship.

Sick from her journey and with most of her possessions lost, the girl had nothing, and Nina was taking her some clothes. When she got to the boarding house it was all quiet, but near the end of the hall where the girl's room was, there were muffled sounds, like someone was crying.

"Anthony- my husband- he had that poor little crippled girl- she was pushed up against the wall- he had one hand over her mouth- he was pawing at her. And her young enough to be his daughter!

"She saw me come in, and when he turned to see what she was looking at, he broke away. She was like a hunted animal- she grabbed some clothes or something off the floor to cover herself with, and stumbled out of the room- she almost knocked me down.

"She hurried as fast as she could- the poor little thing- like a wounded doe- in fear of her life- she ran out of the building.

"When I turned back Anthony was glaring at me. 'What are you doing here?' He asked. He was furious, he acted as if I were the one who did something wrong! He swore at me and said terrible things to me. He ran past me, out the door saying that now I had done it!

"I ran here. I didn't know what to do, and that poor girl, where will she go?"

Gently patting Nina's bowed head, Rosa searched desperately for a word of comfort to offer, while inwardly she struggled to temper her fury at Anthony. Nina raised her head, and Rosa saw the pain that was in her eyes- the deep pain of a woman betrayed.

"Yes, Rosa," Nina said, her voice hardly audible, " I know about Anthony."

"You will stay here tonight," Rosa said finally, "and I will send word to Hans about the girl, she will be easy enough to find."

Nina made no objections. She sat on the edge of the bed watching Nina drink a glass of warm wine. The two women talked until the exhausted Nina fell asleep.

Rosa knew that with this incident Anthony had ripped from his wife's eyes the last curtain of ignorance she could use to shield herself from the truth about him. How betrayed she must feel now to see her husband's unfaithfulness in the stark light of reality.

It was time, Rosa knew, to tell Nina more. And soon she would be ready to help.

Rosa wrote a note to Hans and asking Peppino to take it to the police station said, "On the way back, stop by the boarding house and tell Mario what happened, and ask him if he can see if someone can be around there tomorrow to watch out for Nina."

"I will go to the diner tomorrow and watch out for her myself," Peppino said.

"No," she answered, "I have other plans for you." Peppino left and Rosa went into the kitchen and poured herself some brandy.

Early the next morning, Rosa and Peppino were loading their first batch of bread when Nina came to the bakery to apologize for being a nuisance the night before.

When she started to make an excuse for Anthony, Rosa and Peppino both put down their work and turned to face her squarely.

She looked away from them and the sagging of her shoulders clearly showed that she knew it was no use.

"What shall I do?" She asked.

"Are you able to go to the diner, and act as if nothing is wrong?"

Rosa searched her aunt's face to see how deep was the wound of Anthony's betrayal.

"Mario will have someone there to keep an eye on you, so you won't be alone."

"Does he know about what happened?" Nina asked, humiliation darkening in her face. "I don't want everyone to know."

"Nina, the fishermen have eyes. They know. But they love you and they want to help. Go to the diner, do just what you do every day. Try not to have a confrontation with Anthony, not just yet."

"But what is that poor girl, where is she? What will become of her?"

"Do not worry, Nina, Hans will find her. Just try to stay out of Anthony's way, alright?"

"Alright, Rosa. And if I know Anthony, he will make himself scarce around here today. That's what he does whenever anything is wrong," she kissed Rosa and started down the wharf.

Peppino set off on his deliveries, and Rosa went back to the flat to see that the children got off to school on time.

When they left, she made a fresh pot of coffee and sat down at the kitchen table to think things through.

There was a knock at the door.

It was Mr. Rossi. The upstairs tenant who had come to pay rent.

Exchanging small talk with him at the front door, she had to raise her voice over the noisy clattering of the early morning buggy's passing by.

Just as Mr. Rossi handed her the rent money Rosa noticed a carriage going by very slowly. It looked familiar, and she thought it might be Anthony's.

Mr. Rossi gone, she wondered about all the things Anthony's driver must know, the places he drove to and the people and things he must've seen.

They would have to find out more about him.

Later that afternoon, Mario came to report that he himself had stayed ashore to be sure that nothing happened to Nina, "You and Nina," he said, "are like family to me."

He sat down at the kitchen table with Peppino, and Rosa said to them, "We must do something about Anthony. Nina is beginning to see now what kind of man he is, and soon she will be able to help us. But we must be careful not to let him get suspicious, not yet.

"We must start finding out where he spends his time, where he goes. We have to follow him. Will you help me?"

They both agreed, and she asked, "Mario, do you know anything about Anthony's driver?"

"No, he stays to himself, never talks to the fisherman."

"Is he the only driver Anthony uses?"

"Only one I ever saw."

"Would he know you?"

"I think he must know who I am by sight," Mario answered.

"I could get friendly with the driver," Peppino said. "He doesn't know me at all and I will find out Anthony's routine."

Rosa looked at Mario who was shaking his head in support of Peppino's plan, and she said, "Alright, and when I get the chance I'll follow him too."

"No!" Peppino said, "you must not do anything so foolish," he stood up as if by being above her, his words would be more forceful.

Rosa nodded in acceptance of his objection and stood up next to him.

"You are not much bigger than me," she said, "don't throw out your sailor suit, I may be able to put it to good use."

"Rosa, I don't know what you're thinking," Mario said, "but you're going to get into trouble. If Anthony finds you, the way he is now, he just as soon have you killed."

Rosa said no more but listened silently while the two men talked over the best way to get information without being found out.

They heard Nina let herself in- she had her own key now that she kept pinned her chemise where Anthony wouldn't see it. By unspoken agreement, the two men stopped talking.

"I couldn't wait to tell you!" Nina's voice was animated, and her face was not that of the dejected woman Rosa had last seen that morning.

She put her English books down on the table and took off her hat and coat, "The only time all day Anthony showed his face around the diner was when he came in because he thought he had something real terrible about you to tell me. He was all puffed up like he knew a big important thing that would set me straight about you Rosa."

"Well, tell us," they urged, "don't keep us in suspense, what did he say?"

"This is really a good one for you Rosa! It seems Anthony saw you this morning talking to a man on your front step, and he couldn't wait to come and report to me that he saw my niece 'taking money for favors,' as he put it, right in front of our god and everybody!"

"Taking favors?" Rosa laughed.

"Yes. I knew your tenant always comes to pay the rent on Monday, but I didn't tell him that. I told him that just because some people did evil things, it didn't mean everyone was an S.O.B."

"Nina!" Rosa spoke in mock horror, "you swore at home in English? You used those words?"

"Yes," Nina replied, "yes, I was brave. Then I walked out of the kitchen and left him standing there with his mouth open."

The men laughed and Peppino followed Mario into the dining room to study.

"How did things really go today, Nina?" Rosa asked.

"It was not too bad. As expected, Anthony made himself scarce. He probably wouldn't have come around at all except that he thought he had something terrible to tell me about you. You know, Rosa, sometimes I think Anthony is jealous of my love for you and the children."

Rosa poured some wine for Nina.

"Mario hovered around me all day, and I felt that all the men were watching over me."

Rosa knew Nina was right, the fishermen all loved her and resented the way Anthony treated her. "Nina, before the men arrive for their lessons, I want to talk to you."

Instinctively Nina looked away from Rosa and from what she knew was going to be an unpleasant subject. But she nodded her head and waited.

"It is about Anthony," Rosa started, "I think he may be involved in some things that are not legal…"

"Not legal? You mean like the fishing fleet?"

"No, well, that too. But I mean other things that he keeps a secret from us."

"I need to find out more, and I need your help."

Rosa waited for her words to reach Nina, and as they did, her aunt's face clouded over.

"I know he is your husband, but if my suspicions are corrected he's in some really bad things."

Nina looked at her as she might look at a stranger. "I think the answer to a lot of the questions are in his office."

Nina got up, and with busy motions, washed their wine glasses.

"I need you to get the key to his office."

Nina turned to Rosa, now the expression on her face was of horror and disbelief.

Rosa spoke quietly, coaxingly.

"The next time he comes home drunk- so drunk he passes out- I want you to get his keys and give them to me."

"Oh, I couldn't!" Nina said, folding the dish towel into a tight nest rectangle.

"What nights does he usually come home drunk?"

"Saturday nights, sometimes other nights. But Rosa, you couldn't take the chance and go into his office, what if he caught you?"

"How can he catch me if he is in bed passed out drunk?"

Nina had no answer, and for a long time, she seemed to be searching for one. "No, Rosa, I cannot do it. It's too dangerous! And besides, what is it you suspect him or?"

"Nina you must help us, otherwise there is no telling how many people will get hurt."

"Us? Who is us?"

Most of the fishermen know, and well, Mario and Peppino know too."

Surprised and then angry, Nina said, "No, Rosa, I cannot! He is my husband, and it is too dangerous!"

Rosa started to say something but changed her mind when Nina, teeth clenched, jaw firm, picked up her books and went into the other room.

CHAPTER THIRTY-SIX

The Sunday afternoon sky was clear, and in the warm autumn sun, Rosa and Paisano and the twins headed for the green and the bocce games.

As long as the Indian summer evenings lasted, the fishermen and all the Italian men would come to play bocce, smoke their little black cigars, drink some wine, and be with their paisanos.

Rosa was relieved that tonight Anthony would not be there, he had told Nina he had business to attend to.

The children ran ahead and seeing Mario, they hurried toward his court to cheer him on. He winked at them, then turning back toward the game, became deadly serious.

Two steps, he bent down and slid gracefully forward and let the ball glide out of his hand. As if drawn by a magnet, the ball rolled deliberately and quietly down the court toward its target. As gently as a lover's kiss, the wooden ball brushed up against the pallino, and without backing away, it stopped.

Mario sprung up like a jack in the box, and with both hands gesturing victory, he chided his shapeless foe.

Anna and her husband had arrived just in time to observe the victory.

Mr. Page shook hands with Mario and his partner Vito and congratulated them on their victory, then he asked Mario to give him a few pointers on the game.

Taking his suit coat off, he explained, "Anthony signed me up for the church tournament, and I don't want to beat me too bad."

He rolled his sleeves and followed Mario and Vito to the court.

Rosa and Anna strolled across the green and sat down on the grass under a heavy oak tree.

Angelina came running over to them complaining that "they never let her play just because I'm a girl!" She said, "they're mean!" But the indignation vanished from her voice when she noticed Paisano chasing a seagull, and she ran off to aid him on his quest.

Anna was the first close woman friend Rosa had had since she and Angelina had been best friends in the convent. She remembered those lonesome years in Viareggio and the village women who never accepted her as one of them, and she knew they were right, she was never really like them.

Since she met Anna, Rosa had watched her become more open, more willing to share herself with others.

The three women, Anna, and Nina, and Rosa had become good friends and shared many things, and Rosa was grateful. In a small way, it made it easier to bear Aldo being away.

"Where is Anthony today?" Anna asked, "he usually never misses a chance to play bocce."

"Nina said he had some business to attend to, but I thought maybe she would come alone. She usually fixes a big Sunday supper for Anthony and whoever he invited in, so maybe she's home cooking."

"Nina is so good, she works so hard and never complains," Anna said.

Rosa knew that there was something bothering Anna, that she was asking for more of a conversation about Nina but at that moment the men reappeared.

"How did Mr. Page do, Mario?" Anna asked.

"He did okay," Mario said grudgingly. "But too much talk, not enough concentration on the game."

Thomas patted Mario on the back and said, "Sorry I asked too many questions, but I guess lawyers can't help being curious, eh, Mario?"

Mario's face told Rosa he did not think it a laughing matter.

"Well, I will do better next time," he laughed.

Mario grunted, and to Rosa, he whispered, "His questions I'm afraid of- his bocce is nothing."

The fishermen wandered off, and Mr. Page said to Rosa, "The fog is coming in and it's getting cold, I'll give you a ride home if you like."

They rounded up the children and the dog and headed up the hill. "This is a beautiful carriage, Mr. Page," Rosa said.

"You must call me Thomas," he added, "Anna tells me how much your friendship means to her and she says you have started a little bakery of your own?"

The way he watched her answer his questions made Rosa uneasy, and she knew what Mario had meant.

Thomas helped them down out of the carriage, and said casually, "We must have you to the house sometime soon."

Anna seized the thought and said, "Oh yes Rosa, do come tomorrow for lunch, and come early so that I can show you my rose garden."

Rosa thought she saw Thomas send a brief signal of disapproval to his wife, but said, "I'd love to come, that would be fine."

The next day Rosa hurried up Russian hill, and when she reached the top she paused to look out over the bay toward Berkeley, wondering where Aldo was at the moment.

When she found the address Anna had given her, she was surprised to see a big, white two-storied house. Its tall thin windows were framed with intricately carved moldings, and gracefully slender columns reached to the roof.

The upstairs windows were covered with lace curtains and those on the ground floor concealed behind heavy draperies. The house, surrounded by gardens locked behind wrought iron fences, looked imperiously down the city below, and Rosa felt vaguely uncomfortable.

On either side of the broad granite steps which lead up the double door entry, rose bushes blooming in spite of the lateness of the season stood guard.

One perfect red blossom caught her eye, and it reminded her of the bouquet Aldo sent with his note that night- the night he left for Italy.

The doorbell sounded a chord from a church organ. She waited. The heavy wooden doors opened slowly. A slight Chinese man stared out at her. From inside Anna's voice was heard and, bowing deeply he moved aside for Rosa to enter.

"This is Mrs. Dante, Lu Chin," Anna said, "please bring in the tea now." He backed silently from the room.

Anna led Rosa into the parlor.

"Thomas called to say he would join us for lunch, so I thought we would have a cup of tea while we wait for him. Lu Chin will fix it the way Chinese do, they know how to brew and drink tea."

"This is a beautiful home, Anna," Rosa looked around the long and narrow high ceilinged room. The light shining in through four tall windows highlighted the rich oriental rugs and reflected off dark highly polished wood paneled walls. There was a feeling of authority about the room, and as Rosa sat down on the stiffly cushioned sofa, she felt strangely unwelcome.

"Thank you," Anna replied as if she too were a guest. "Thomas has had most of this furniture brought from the orient," Pointing to a large vase standing on the floor near the fireplace, she added, apologetically, "you can see he likes cloisonne."

Lu Chin arrived with a large silver tray. He poured hot water slowly into the large cups with tea leaves floating to the top. He watched the leaves carefully and covered each cup with a matching lid.

Anna explained, "The tea is ready when the leaves settle to the bottom," she offered Rosa a plate of tiny cookies.

When they had finished their tea, Anna took Rosa through the house. They passed the kitchen where another Chinese man was cooking. He bowed as they went by, but Anna offered no introduction.

Passing a closed door, Anna said, "I cannot show you this room, it's Thomas' office and he keeps it locked." In a whisper she added,

"He says he can't trust the Chinese. He never allows anyone in his office."

There was a padlock on the door, very much like the one Anthony kept on his office at the boarding house.

The sudden ringing of a bell caused Anna to jump, and embarrassed, she explained, "The telephone- in Thomas' office- no one else can answer it."

They paused in the doorway of the master bedroom, also oriental. There was a four-post bed of dark wood carved in a delicate lace-like pattern.

Anna opened the door and stepping inside, "This is the nursery," she explained. The room contained everything a baby could need. Rosa looked at Anna for explanation.

"I have already lost two babies." Anna walked across the room to the window, "and I do very much want to have a family. Thomas had Lu Chin giving me some kind of oriental herbs."

"He says it will help, that I will be able to have many babies like Chinese women. It tastes bitter, and he stands over me like a watchdog every night at bedtime to be sure I drink it all. He calls it the magic cure, but I don't think it's doing any good. Although it does help me sleep at night."

"But enough of me, come now, let me show you my rose garden," Anna led Rosa from the room and closed the door behind her.

They walked along a stone path lined on either side with tall tree roses. The path led to a gazebo with wicker chairs and a round table inside.

"I like to sit out here in the afternoon and in the evenings when it is warm. Thomas is so busy, he works so hard, and I am here alone much of the time."

On either side of the garden rose bushes were planted in neat, well-tended patterns. "I take care of all of this myself, I forget everything else when I'm tending my flowers."

They went back into the house through a small basement room filled with garden supplies: bags of roses, dust for the aphids, seeds, and digging tools.

Coming up into the long hall that led to the front entrance, Rosa asked, "Does Thomas garden at all?"

"No, I'm afraid he is much too wrapped up in practicing law to think much about flowers."

"He is a lawyer for the city?" Rosa asked, not knowing how Anna would react to a question about her husband.

"Yes, he is one of their attorneys," she said, "I don't know what all he handles. I know one thing he did about three years ago. We were still living down on Dupont street- he helped close down a lot of the..." Anna's face flushed,... 'houses'. He cleaned up the whole steer, and he even found decent work for some of the girls. Thomas is like that, he loves this city, and he does whatever he can to make it better."

"I'm not sure what else he does, he used to tell me but now he's so tired when he gets home he usually goes in his office and reads. I don't pry."

"Is that where Thomas met Anthony, through his work for the city?"

"No," she answered, her face losing some of its softness, "They became acquainted through the church several years ago. They were on the building fund together. I think Anthony is the treasurer for the fund this year, isn't he?"

Just then Thomas thrust open the front door. He glanced quickly from one to the other, seemingly worried that something might be wrong. Apparently reassured, he kissed Anna on the cheek and spoke cordially to Rosa.

"How nice of you to come. Did Anna show you her gardens? We are very proud of her roses."

Thinking that perhaps she had imagined his concern, Rosa took her place at the table. Lu Chin brought in their meal, Anna sat quietly, and Thomas talked pleasantly about many subjects. Rosa learned that he had grown up in North Beach, that his name was really Pagenelli, and that he had changed it only after his parents died.

"The greatest sorrow of my life," Thomas said speaking with a simple sincerity, "was that they didn't live long enough to see their only son finish college. That was my father's dream."

"Then you didn't know Thomas' parents?" Rosa asked Anna.

Answering for his wife, he said, "No, we didn't meet until after they were dead. Did Anna tell you how we met?"

When Rosa shook her head, he said, "We met by chance. I was on my way down Montgomery Street when a runaway horse came charging around the corner, galloping for all he was worth, and dragging a little two wheeled buggy behind him."

"Anna was coming towards me, crossing the street. She didn't seem to notice the horse and buggy coming right down at her. I yelled at her, and when she saw the horse coming right at her, she froze dead on the spot. Right then I ran at her and tackled her, throwing her out of the path of the buggy."

Thomas smiled paternally at his wife, "She landed hard, I could hear her hit the ground. I guess I scared her half to death."

"She was crying and not until I realized what had happened, did she start to calm down. I took her into a little cafe there across the street and had her drink some brandy."

Thomas sat back in his chair, and ready to accept any praise that might be offered, concluded, "and that is how we met!"

Anna was watching Thomas with worship in her eyes. Rosa smiled, and of Anna asked, "and then?"

Before Anna could answer, Thomas took over, "she was working in a little dress shop with her sister, and before long we started 'keeping company'" he said. "We were married soon after that- it will be ten years in December. Her sister married a farmer and lives in the San Joaquin valley."

Lu Chin cleared away the dishes and brought in a fresh pot of tea.

"That is a very exciting story," Rosa said, looking at them both.

Thomas about forty and Anna maybe not much older than she, in her early thirties. They were a very handsome couple.

Anna sweet and simple in her adoration of her husband, and Thomas- he was more of a puzzle, so much to admire in him, and yet...

CHAPTER THIRTY-SEVEN

The months soon turned into a year, the twins had their second birthday in America, Peppino grew from a young sailor into an astute and hard-working businessman.

The Rozahtu was thriving, and Paisano finally grew into his paws. Hans, who was like a member of the family, cried as he told how he had found the body of the poor little lame girl.

During the week Anna came almost every day to visit and she and Rosa worked with Nina and the fishermen on their citizenship studies. All this time the fishermen were on alert to watch Anthony, and Peppino was often away from the flat on missions he would not discuss.

Nina was becoming ever more aware of her husband's activities, and Rosa could see that there was a life and death struggle going on within her aunt between the faithful wife schooled by hundreds of years of Catholic doctrine and the woman who was beginning to admit all was not as it should be.

Soon everyone's attention focused on the upcoming citizenship test. Nina and the fishermen were working harder than ever, and although Rosa still had not been in the country long enough to take the test, she and Anna, already a citizen because of her marriage, both worked just as hard as the others. The closer the test came, the more excitement there was.

For Rosa, it was a time of mixed feelings. She was both proud and envious of those who were eligible to take the test. For her, all the reading and the studying had been a labor of love, and while she kept telling herself to be patient her turn would come, her heart ached to be able to stand up with the others when they took their test, and said the oath of allegiance.

Rosa desperately wanted to belong to this, her new land.

Two nights before the Friday of the citizenship test, the fishermen showed up at Rosa's. Frightened by the thought of being questioned by a judge, they gathered together for a final study session.

They decided to review their learning- by asking each other questions, but no one wanted to go first.

Mario said, "Alright, Rosa, you are the teacher's pet, you take the first question." Someone said, "Yes, name all the presidents," while the others protested the task too hard.

Having spent some time memorizing the president's names, Rosa smiled inwardly but pretended uncertainty, "Well that's pretty hard, but I guess I could try."

She stood up and inhaled deeply, "Washington, Adam's, Jefferson," and while the men's mouths hung open in awe, she raced through all eighteen presidents' names, and then a victorious wave of her hand, ended with Rutherford B. Hayes- all this within fifteen seconds.

The men cheered Rosa, and with their own confidences now vicariously restored by such stunning success, Mario winked at Rosa and with mischief in his eye asked Vito, "Who is the father of our country?"

The stout little fisherman puffed his chest out and responded, "Amerigo Vespucci."

"No, Vito, he is not the father of our country," Mario teased.

Another explained, "America was named after Amerigo Vespucci but he is not the father of this country."

Vitos face reddened, he proclaimed, "I was named after my father, and I have his name because he is my father!"

Another fisherman jumped into what was obviously not the first time this conversation had been held, "but you are not a country, you are just a little fisherman, it is not the same."

Vito held firm. As far as he was concerned Amerigo Vespucci was the father of America.

Rosa broke in, "I will give you a hint, he was not even Italian!"

Rosa and the others tried to explain to Vito how much had happened between the discovery of America and the creation of this nation. They talked about how the founding fathers had worked so hard to make sure that the rest of us could live free, and never be afraid of the church, the police, or the government.

Nina listened attentively to what the rest said, and finally, she spoke, "Yes, those men who fought the Revolutionary War and flew the first American flag had courage. They fought so we could live without being afraid."

"Nina," Rosa asked, "tell us what the colors of the flag stand for."

"Red, white, and blue," Nina answered. "The red stands for courage, the white for truth, and the blue for justice." Nina looked up and Rosa saw in her face she was thinking about Anthony.

Before they left, Rosa read aloud the oath of allegiance which they would say in court, and then saluting the flag, they said the pledge of allegiance.

Rosa reminded them to be at the courthouse at 1:00 Friday and to wear their best clothes. As they filed out the door she wished each man the best of luck.

Mario assured her, "I will see they all dress nice and wash good."

Nina said she wanted to help wash the coffee cups and wine glasses, but Rosa knew something was bothering her.

"Rosa," she said, "am I doing the right thing, not telling Anthony that I am going to become a citizen? I worry sometimes that..."

"Of course you are Nina, remember when we first started studying English and Anthony tore up my books? Remember how mad it made you and how you decided you wanted to speak the language of your new country and to be a part of it. Remember?"

Nina nodded and putting her hat on, said, "It's funny but sometimes I think he knows and just doesn't want to say anything about it."

"Would that be like him?" Rosa asked.

"Yes," Nina said thinking it over for the first time, "I think that is exactly how he would handle it if he knew he wasn't going to be able to stop me anyhow."

"Yes," she said, "I believe he would." Nina kissed Rosa and left.

Rosa was proud of Nina's growing courage, but she was worried about her own part in her aunts changing her attitudes and prayed that she was not making things worse for her.

Rosa looked around the empty room. She was proud of the simple fishermen who a few minutes earlier had been sitting around her table, learning about America. She was glad for them, but yet she felt a twinge of envy that she could not stand with them to take the oath of allegiance.

On Friday Rosa and the twins were dressed in their best clothes waiting for Peppino to return from his deliveries. For several days Peppino had been keeping strange hours, and whenever she asked where he went, he avoided giving her any information.

She knew he didn't want her to worry, but Anthony could be a dangerous man, and she did worry. They waited as long as they could, and then afraid to be late, Rosa and the twins went to meet Nina and together they drove to the courthouse.

Everyone was already there waiting on the front sidewalk. The men, gathered in a group around their teacher, all shined up and hair was slipped down.

Intimidated by the solemnity of the occasion, they tried to hide their excitement behind a respectful quiet. Rosa and Nina were the last to arrive, and still, there was no sign of Peppino.

"Let's go now, we cannot keep the judge waiting," Mrs. Johnson said, leading the way up the steps and into the courtroom. Nina walked up the front with Mario, while Rosa and the children sat in the back where they could watch the door.

Each time the heavy doors opened, Rosa prayed it would be Peppino. Anna came in, and without a word slipped apologetically down into the seat next to Rosa.

Promptly at one o'clock, the judge, dressed in long black robes, opened the door from his chambers. His face stern, he walked to the bench with resolute steps much like a warrior entering the battlefield.

When he had his robes arranged comfortably under him, he looked up.

451

Every eye in the room was fixed on him. He studied each row's faces, and as his eyes worked their way across the room, his face softened, and a kindly, paternal smile overtook him.

Again the big doors open. Hans looked in. The judge stared at him. Every head in the courtroom turned to see who the judge was looking at. Hans smiled sweetly and tried to disappear down into the nearest seat.

Rosa wondered if he knew anything about Peppino and watched him, hoping for some sort of signal, a reassurance that Peppino was all right.

But Hans was still smarting over the embarrassment- his own late entry, and he smiled innocently back at her.

The judge turned back to the others and explained the procedure. He was going to ask each person a question.

"Do not worry," he said, "take your time, I know you know the answers, Mrs. Johnson said you were her best class."

He called each person by name and having them stand, read his question. They all did well, and then he called on Vito.

"Mr. Lavaggi," he said, "who is the father of our country?"

Muffled gasps could be heard among the stand listeners.

Vito stood. "The father of our country is... " And he hesitated for what seemed like an hour, "Giorgio Washington," he answered. "But..."

"Do you want to say more, Mr. Lavaggi?" The judge asked.

Mario yanked Vito's coattails.

"No, sir," Vito said unwillingly and sat down.

All the fishermen breathed out in relief. Puzzled, the judge looked around for an explanation. But when none was offered, he called on the next person.

"Mrs. Nina Orso."

Nina stood up. He looked at her for a long time and finally asked. "You are Mrs. Anthony Orso?"

"Yes, your honor," Nina answered.

There was a long pause, then he said, tell me, Mrs. Orso, why do you want to become a citizen?

Rosa felt sick inside. Nina knew all the dates and even the state capitals, but they had never even practiced answers to questions like that.

Nina stood with confidence, and started out a strong and sure, "Well, you see, sir, I have been in this country for over twenty years, and then last year my niece Rosa, here, came from Italy."

"She taught me it is important to be a citizen, and…" Nina's voice faltered, "and not to be afraid."

Murmurs of approval rose from those around her, and Nina went on,

"I like it in the Declaration of Independence where it says we are all created equal- no one is better than the others. It means that no one has to be afraid."

Nina looked down at Rosa, and when their eyes met, she silently shook her head yes, and Rosa knew at that moment Nina had made up her mind to help get the keys to Anthony's office.

"That is why I want to be a citizen," Nina said and she sat down.

The room was silent. Someone tentatively started clapping, but when others were afraid to join in, the clapping stopped self-consciously. Then the judge stood up, and clapping his hands together firmly, led the room in applause.

"Bring in the flag!" The bailiff opened the rear doors and stood aside as uniformed soldiers, carrying the American flag and the California state flag, marched into the room.

"The oath of allegiance is a most solemn oath," the judge said.

"With God as your witness, you will promise on your honor to support and defend the Constitution and laws of the United States against all enemies. In taking the oath you obligate yourself to love this country and to defend its flag. Now repeat after me:

I hereby declare, on oath, that I absolutely and entirely renounce and abjure all allegations to any foreign prince, potentate..."

Prayer book in hand, together they repeated the oath, each trying to brush the tears away from their eyes. When they were done, the judge came down from behind his bench holding a small wooden box in front of him. He passed among the new citizens shaking hands, and giving to each a tiny American flag.

"This is the flag of your new country," he said, "guard it well."

The new citizens placed their flags in their prayer books, and with hand over their hearts closed the ceremony with the Pledge of Allegiance to the flag.

Afterward, everyone gathered at Rosa's, everyone except Peppino. Nina and Anna laid out the food they had brought, and Rosa sliced bread and poured wine. Soon there was music and dancing.

Rosa watched the door for Peppino, but still, he did not arrive. When Hans came in, she signaled him, and moving to the deserted corner of the room, told him of her increasing concern for Peppino's safety.

"It is not like him," she said, "to miss the ceremony at the courthouse, he had promised the children to be there. It is not like him."

Hans tried to reassure her, but he did not well conceal his own concern.

"If you are really worried, I will call the sergeant at the station, he said, and see if there has been any trouble. Will that make you feel any better?"

Rosa watched the twins dancing the polka, and smiled at a fisherman who whirled by and said, "It's good there is no carpet, it makes even me a good dancer."

Everyone, Rosa thought, had someone to dance with, even the shy Anna was dancing. Rosa took a glass of wine and went to the bay window to look out across the water. The fog was hanging low in the fleeting light.

She lifted her glass and silently made a toast: dear Aldo, where are you now? Are you safe? Will I ever see you again?

Behind her, an accordion was playing a waltz and she shivered. If Aldo were with her they would be dancing together, he would be holding her close, and Rosa yearned for the feel of his body against hers.

Anna's voice behind her said, "Why are you sad tonight, Rosa?"

"I am just sharing memories with those not here tonight, and with my two sons far away."

"Again, you worry about the ones you left behind," she said, "they are your sons, so I know they are good men. Please do not worry over them."

Rosa turned around and hugged her.

Hans returned, and the look on his face as he walked across the room toward her made it clear that he had learned nothing, "But Rosa, you know if anything had happened to him, we would've heard."

He led her out to dance with him, "So this is really good news," he added.

Hans had the rest of the dances with Nina. This was the first time Rosa saw him in a civilian suit, and he was a handsome man. There was an eagerness in his eyes. She noticed too that there was a lightness in Nina's step as she danced around the room.

When the evening was all but gone, the wine low in the bottles and the plates bare of food, Mario tapped on his wine glass.

"It is getting late, let all of us – all of us new citizens of the US of A stand and sing the Star-Spangled Banner."

Everyone stood at attention. Mario played a few chords and started the song. At first everyone sang, then gradually their voices faded out until only Mario's great baritone was heard.

Playing his accordion, he swayed back-and-forth and poured his heart out in song. When he reached the final verse:

"Oh! Say, does the star spangled banner yet wave? O'er the land of the free and the home of the brave?" A silent hush fell over the crowd. Each brand new citizen silent in his own private dream.

CHAPTER THIRTY-EIGHT

Rosa got up very early the next morning. She knew Peppino wouldn't be much help, he had come home just shortly before dawn, and there was so much to be done! She was going to have to hire someone to help in the bakery waiting on the women who came in all day long wanting bread for their families.

And another driver, yes, she needed another driver to get the orders out. Peppino had turned into such a good salesman, they had orders from big hotels, like the Lock House and the Russ Hotel, and regular orders with several big restaurants. Rosa thought of him much like her own son, and now she thanked god that he was home safe.

The door to the bakery opened and Peppino poked his head in, waiting to see what his reception would be. "Come in, come in," she said, searching his face for answers.

"I am all right," he answered, seeing her anxiety, "I am sorry I worried you. There was no way to let you know."

"Tell me how the ceremony was."

"Not one word until you tell me what happened to you that you missed the ceremonies and the party last night? What time did you finally get in?"

"It was very late. Everyone was asleep and I didn't want to wake you. I am sorry I missed everything but I do have a lot to tell you."

He tied his apron around his middle and began his tale.

"Well, I was finishing up my deliveries, I did them real fast so I'd get back in plenty of time for the ceremony when I passed Anthony's carriage parked at the wharf, and his driver signaled me."

"He signaled you?" Rosa said, "He knows you?"

"Yes, yes," Peppino answered impatiently, "I have been courting him for months."

"Courting him? I thought everyone said he really kept to himself."

"He does, that's why it took me so long to get him to trust me." Rosa did not understand.

"Well, alright, I'll tell you the whole story then. The first time I talked to him was several months ago, I put more spit and polish on Anthony's brass and monkey's…" Remembering his manners, he did not complete his expression.

"But anyhow, it was then I found out that when he wasn't driving, he did repair work and odd jobs for Anthony, and so I planted the seed in his mind that he could hire me to do the dirty work for him. He'd have someone to boss around too because you could tell he didn't like doing that kind of work.

"Well, he must have liked my idea because a few weeks later he had me do some work for him. He was really just checking me out. He gave me every dirty job in the book, including cleaning out a cellar that had flooded and moving heavy boxes of whisky from one place to another.

"After I had them all moved, he came down and ordered me to move them all back, right back to where they had been."

"Did you do it?"

"Damn right, I did, and I did it without a question. I think that was exactly what he was testing me for, he wanted someone who would obey orders and not ask questions, so that's just what I did."

"And then what happened?" Rosa asked checking the heat in her ovens, "did he have you work for him again anymore after that?"

"No, not for a long time, but there was something else about that first job."

Impatient with the slowness of his story, Rosa urged him on.

"When I was kicking out that cellar I heard two men talking out on the street. They didn't know I was working down there, one of them said something about unloading Orso's chests. I didn't know what they meant."

"Well, when I got all done, I thought I'd take the long way home, just in case the driver decided to follow me."

"Well, anyhow he didn't, but I passed a Chinese ship being unloaded, and damned if I didn't hear those same two voices talking again. So I squeezed in behind some crates and listened."

"At first I thought they might be unloading furniture. Then Anthony shows up and goes aboard ship, and then comes back down and talks to these two guys, and it looks like they're having an argument. Then Anthony leaves and I still don't know what the big fuss is all about, so when the wagon drives off, I set out to follow them, and me on foot, too!"

"Did anybody notice you?" Rosa asked, worried.

"No, but it took all my endurance to keep in view. Well, I followed them down Dupont," he continued, "to Broadway where the wagon stopped. Have you seen that part of town, Rosa?"

459

"Yes, only in the daytime, but I know it's not a very nice part." Rosa lifted the finished loaves out of the ovens and poured two cups of coffee. She sat down to listen.

"Well, so you know," he said, "what a neighborhood! I've gone ashore in ports all around the world, but this one! It has most of those other places beat. Gambling houses, dance halls, saloons, dopers walking around like the dead, lying in the gutters."

"I saw a rich old fellow wearing huge diamond stick pins and all that, and this girl comes up to him, and he just took his cane and pushed her away- almost like she was an animal," Peppino grimaced in disgust.

"Women were hanging out of the windows, looked like they had their underwear on. Some of them handed out business cards, I even got one," he grinned self consciously and handed Rosa a card from his shirt.

BIG MATILDA

300 lbs. of passion.

Rates- .50 each; 3 for $1.00

Rosa laughed, "I hope you didn't have .50 cents on you or did you?" She teased.

Trying to appear inscrutable, he said, "But back to the story now."

"Yes," Rosa urged, "I'm still hoping to find out what kept you out all night."

"Then let me tell you. By the time I next caught up with those guys, the wagon was half empty and the men were nowhere in sight."

"By this time I was beginning to get an idea what they were carrying."

"You did? What?"

"Let me tell you the rest of my story."

"They came out and drove to another dump, Clay street, and unloaded some more boxes. That place was almost as bad as the first, and there were an awful lot of Chinese around."

"Then they made another stop on Sacramento street. This place was entirely different. It was like a big mansion, not painted fancy or anything, it's what they call a 'parlor house'."

Peppino got up and helped them both to more coffee, "The two guys went inside and stayed. But this time the tide was coming in and I was beginning to think I'd freeze to death out there."

"Well, when they finally came out, a woman came to the door with them and somebody said something about 'wine', about not forgetting the wine tomorrow."

"And?" Rosa demanded.

"And what?" Peppino asked, innocently sipping his coffee.

"Peppino, don't tease! What do you think was in those boxes?"

He put his cup down, and making the most of her impatience, said, simply:

"Opium."

"Opium! Oh my god! It's worse than I thought."

Peppino finished his coffee and took a stack of the warm bread out to the wagon. When he came back in, Rosa said, "But Peppino, I still don't know about last night."

"Yes, I didn't hear from the driver for a long time, and I began to think maybe I hadn't passed the test, I even worried that someone had seen me following the wagon."

"So what happened last night? I'm beginning to wonder if you are really enjoying this and wanted to make the most of this adventure," but her patience was about gone.

"Then I really got an American education," he laughed. "I was down near the dock and Anthony's driver pulled me over.

"He was all dressed up. He said he had a job for me if I wanted it. I wasn't going to pass this up, it was the chance I'd been waiting for.

"I loaded a wagon full of cases of champagne and he told me to drive carefully, not to hit any bumps. He said it would explode and I would have to pay if any got broken. He said one of those bottles sells for $5.00 in that place.

"He gave me a list of addresses, and the last place on the list turned out to be the same place as before, the parlor house on Sacramento Street. When I got there the madam showed me where to put the champagne. I had a hard time trying to keep my mind on my work. There was lots of pretty girls around, they were wearing real pretty dresses and they all had feathers in their hair."

"Did you notice anything else," Rosa teased.

"Yes," Peppino ignored her jibe, "the house was all reds and yellows, and there were lots of heavy drapes with tassels on them, and the air smelled of perfume.

"But there was another funny smell too, something heavy, first I wasn't sure what it was. Oh yes, and it had real thick carpets, and everything looked sort of oriented, a lot of chairs with those big high backs, carved. I think there was gambling going on upstairs, that's what it sounded like.

"But to get back to what I was saying. I was so busy looking around that I dropped one case of the champagne."

"Did it explode?"

"No, but one bottle broke, and I was in a sweat waiting for the rest of them to explode, but they didn't."

"Sally- she's the madam- must've felt sorry for me, she said to put that case on the bottom and by the time it was used, they wouldn't know who broke it. She said that by that time my youthful clumsiness would be settled down. She told me to come back when I got rich because her establishment was strictly cash."

"Was Anthony there?"

"I didn't see him, but something was going on upstairs, I heard a lot of men's voices like they were playing poker or something, and Sally went up there to get money to pay for the champagne. Anthony could have been there. All the men I saw were dressed up, like the gentlemen from Nob hill. This was a fancy place, not like the one off clay street or the ones on the Barbary Coast. This place was fancy."

"If only I could go there again, this time I'd get upstairs."

Not completely sure how he meant that, Rosa patted him on the arm, and speaking like a mother, warned, "No, Peppino, it would be too dangerous."

CHAPTER THIRTY-NINE

Looking around, Rosa made one final check that all was in order before she closed the bakery and went home to her flat. She heard the front door open, and being completely sold out of bread, she hoped it was not another customer. She hurried to the door, it was Hans.

"I just came from the Sisters of the Holy Family and I thought I would stop by and see you and Nina," he looked around, "she is not here?"

"Yes, she might, she often drops in in the evenings. I think she will come tonight."

"Oh."

"Yes," Rosa smiled, "come sit down!"

"Oh, no," he said, "I wouldn't want to interfere with your meal."

"Please, sit down, there is something I want to talk to you about." She poured Hans a glass of wine and told him what Peppino had found out about the 'chest'.

Hans said nothing.

"That does not surprise you?"

"Nothing surprises me, nothing about a man like Anthony Orso."

"You do know of him, Hans?"

"Yes, I have run into him a few times at the station."

"About opium?"

"No," he said showing surprise that she knew, but added only, "Something else." Hans turned his attention to petting Paisano who had been sticking his nose in under his hand. It was clear he was not ready to say anything more.

"Peppino should be back soon," Rosa said, "unless he's got another job from Anthony's driver."

"Sounds like Peppino's getting to be a regular detective."

"Hans, do you know anything about Thomas Page, he's an attorney at City Hall."

"Yes, he's that fellow who closed down some of those houses off Clay Street a few years back. There was a big lot of talk about it, but they all opened again very soon, just as soon as everything quieted down. That's the way it always works."

"Does a city attorney make very much money, Hans?"

"They make a good living, but not enough to get rich on. Why do you ask?"

Rosa told Hans about her visit to Anna's and how elegant their house was.

"Do you think they could've inherited some money?"

"No, I don't think so, not from what Anna says."

Hans looked at his watch, "It's getting late. I guess Nina won't be here tonight."

"Just be patient, Hans, tell me what brought you to the Sisters of the Holy Family?"

"Oh, I drop in there from time to time, just to check up on, on..."

"On the women you save from suicide?"

"The Sisters take care of them, they help them get back on their feet. Most of them have no family, not anyone."

"Who do you have there now? Tell me about her."

"Her name is Sylvia, and she's been there quite a while, longer than most. It happened just like most of them. It was late at night, and I was making one last sweep down the beach, and when I got down there where the old pier juts out into the water, I thought I saw something move, lots of times hobos or dogs get in there, but this time it looks like a woman.

"She was sort of half-standing, half crawling. There was a full moon but with the shadows from the pier, I couldn't tell for sure what it was. I tied up my horse, and by the time I got to the head of the pier, I couldn't find her."

Gently pushing the dog away, Hans turned to look at Rosa, and the suffering she saw on his face made her want to put her arms around this huge man and comfort him.

"Then I saw her, she was bobbing up and down in the water, the tide must've carried her out, she was way out there. When I got to her she struggled, she didn't want to be saved, I thought she was going to drown us both. Then all life seemed to go out of her, and I brought her in. She was just a mirror whisper of a girl. Her face was... Was..."

Hans stood up, walked around a bit, and with reigned control finished, "She was black and blue, someone had really worked her over."

"The Sisters of the Holy Family, they nursed her back to life. Oh Rosa, it was so awful. No matter how long I'm on the force, I don't think I'll ever get used to seeing a sight like that.

"I found out later that her father died on the boat, and when the boat landed, she was all alone." The sorrow in his eyes turned to anger, "A- a- a man- on the boat promised her a place to live and a job. What else could she do? She didn't want to go back on that ship again, so she went with him."

"Anthony?"

Hans stopped his pacing. He looked into Rosa's eyes then looked away.

"Yes," he said, his voice scarcely more than a whisper. "Anthony," she said aloud to herself. "When was this?"

"Last spring. She's a young pretty girl, about seventeen, I imagine."

"That was just before I arrived in San Francisco. She worked for Anthony?"

"Yes, she said she did."

Rosa told Hans how Anthony had treated her, and how he had threatened her and told her about a girl he had sent out to a better job."

"If only I could get enough proof to nail him."

"When we brought him in to the station house he denied knowing her, said she was an opium-eater, hallucinating."

"But she did identify him, and she was willing to testify. We were ready to close the house down when she changed her mind and said she made a mistake, it wasn't Anthony after all. I know someone got to her, she was as scared as a baby kitten. When we got word from City Hall no less, to back off."

"City Hall?"

"Yes, Rosa, City Hall. That is where the protection for these places comes from, I am sure of it but I have no proof. It's up high in the government. The city figures sometimes intervene with high-minded attempts to close down the brothels, but it's just a smokescreen. They send the girls running into the street but by the next morning they are back in business."

"You're saying it's impossible to clean up the streets?" Rosa asked.

"Well, the way things are now, it's next to impossible. But if we could get proof, I mean real proof, against some of the top men, we could do a lot towards cleaning up the city."

"The worst of it is the whole slavery business, it's getting so strong, so hard for us to crack."

"Is Anthony in deep in- in getting girls- or was this just this one girl? Is that why he picks them up at the boat?"

Hans shrugged his shoulders, "We have no proof. Everyone is afraid to testify. That is what happens, if the girls do not cooperate, they get them hooked on opium and sell them."

"She must've been frightened to death."

"She was. When we went to see her at the Sister's house, she refused to even see me. The Sister's said that some man had come to see her and after that, she would not talk to anyone."

"Do you think it was Anthony?" Rosa asked.

"No, it was someone else. I asked her that."

"How was she when you saw her today?"

"She's better, she helps make vestments for the priests. For that, she gets food and a home where she feels safe. But what she needs is to get out in the world, to get a job, she needs to stop being so afraid. It's taking her too long."

"Hans, is there anything I could do to help Sylvia?"

"Well," Hans thought for a long time, "She has hardly anything at all, clothes or anything. The nuns have given her what they could."

"I have clothes that Mrs. Angelo left here for me to give away. There's a nice warm coat. I'll take it to her."

"I will go see her Monday. Maybe I can talk to her."

Hans stretched his long arms as if he was getting very impatient waiting so long. He leaned up against the wall, "Rosa. You be careful. The men that are behind all this, the slavery, the prostitution, the opium, they are powerful men, and they do not stop at anything. Sylvia is a potential threat to them, and so anyone who befriends her…"

"You are telling me not to go see her?"

"No, I am telling you to be careful. To trust no one. They are not playing a child's game, this is a deadly dangerous business. If you want to go see Sylvia just because you are a compassionate woman and want to help her, fine.

"But if you think you are going to solve these crimes and put the criminals in jail, then forget about it. You are out of your league. We feel sure we know who is involved in all this, but even if you get proof, it is another matter to get a conviction."

Rosa was shocked to hear him say 'convicted'. She had never thought in terms of sending Anthony to jail, but rather just making him stop.

How would Nina react to having a husband in jail? To Hans, she said, "Thank you for your concern, I will be careful. The front door opened and then there was noise, a 'thud, thud, thud'. She smiled, "Peppino is coming."

"How do you know?"

"He never takes one step at a time, he lopes up the stairs. Every third one he jumps. I think he's practicing to take the whole flight of stairs at once."

"Oh! Officer Nelson," Peppino said, saluting him, "we meet so soon again."

"So soon?" Rosa asked.

"Yes, Rosa, did Hans not tell you that he has been teaching me how to be a detective?"

"No, he didn't," Rosa was genuinely surprised.

"I am sorry Rosa, but the information was confidential, Peppino and I decided you would only worry, so the less you knew what he was doing, the better."

"Yes," Peppino said, taking an orange from the cooler and breaking into the peel with his front teeth, but this morning I told her everything, I had to- she knew I was out all night, so I had to tell her."

"So," Rosa glared at Hans, "when I was telling you what Peppino did last night do you already knew?"

"No, no, I really hadn't heard that part of it."

"But did he tell you his crazy idea of dressing up and patronizing in one of those- those houses?"

"Yes, and I'm afraid I agree with him. It's the only way you'll ever find out anything."

Outnumbered, Rosa sat down.

"Peppino, I do not imagine that you have a fancy dress suit, do you?" Asked Hans.

"Once you get in there, you're to gamble- just gamble-nothing else, Peppino!" Hans smiled a fatherly type smile, "and listen to what is going on. Saturday night would be the time to go. With any luck, Anthony will be there."

"Hans, that is too much, I don't want Peppino to get hurt."

"Rosa," Peppino broke in, "remember I was a sailor and lived with the likes of Jocko. Don't you think I can handle a fancy night of gambling? I really am grown-up."

"He is right Rosa. There will be no danger for him, all he needs is a good story, where he's from, what he does for a living, all that stuff. That will not be hard to do. But we do have to get him dressed up."

"I think I know where to get a suit- Aldo's brother."

She looked at Peppino, "Stand up," she said, "I think it might be big, but I can alter it. If Enrico will lend us a suit then we will be all set."

Peppino leaned back in his chair balancing on the two back legs. He was looking very self-satisfied.

"All you need now is a big cigar and a full beard," Rosa laughed and tease him.

Hans stood up, "It is getting late, tomorrow is Sunday, so you can sleep a little later but I had better get going."

At the front door, he said, "I'm not going to stop to see you anymore when I am in the police wagon, or in my uniform. I think it's better if I look like an ordinary friend coming to visit. I'll have to stop dropping by the bakery for my morning coffee and warm bread. I do not want Anthony to see a police wagon parked outside.

Good night, he said, and turning to Peppino, "If you can get into the house, you might find some of the missing pieces that we need to close those places down."

"Does that mean that we won't need to look at Anthony's books?" Rosa asked.

"No, we still need to see them, do you think you can get them?"

"I don't know. Nina is not ready to help us yet. I do not want to push her too hard. He is, after all, her husband."

"Well, right now, we need to find out who all is in this, and that's where Signor Peppino, the gambler, fits in."

"Just as long as he doesn't get himself killed." Rosa leaned over and kissed Peppino on the cheek. "Too busy to shave?"

"No, not too busy. I am letting my beard grow," he said fingering the hairs double on his chin, "that way, I'll look more like a man about time and a big time gambler."

CHAPTER FORTY

Father Paul closed his Bible. His face lined with worry. He looked out upon the faces staring up at him from the crowded pews, "My children," he said, "we are living in a cesspool of sin!"

The eyes of the congregation were suddenly cast downward, bodies moved uncomfortably amidst the sounds of hushed voices. He waited. Then, his voice rising to anger, he went on, "I am talking about the streets of sin! The streets of opium! The streets of gambling.

"This great city, named after the most gentle of men, Saint Francis, has turned into a city of sin. Our women are not safe! Young girls, our daughters, are being sold into slavery.

"As I stand here before you good people and before God, I vow to spend the rest of my life, if necessary, cleaning up those streets of sin. But I cannot do it alone! We must all work at stopping this!"

Rosa could only see the back of Anthony's head. He was not in pious agreement with the priest's words. What could he be thinking right now, she wondered.

Before mass, Rosa and her two children watched Anthony and Nina arrive. Strutting down the aisle like a rooster, he nodded at this one and that, and when they reached the first pew, he, the perfect gentleman, stood ceremoniously aside so his wife could enter first.

If only she could see his face right now, to know what thoughts were going through his mind. Thomas page and Anna were there too, sitting across the center aisle. Anna looked pale, and not at all well, but Thomas sat with his head held high as if reaching upward toward heavenly reward. Rosa remembered Sylvia and then, looking at little Angelina, she shuttered.

Rosa jarred out of her thoughts by Father Paul's words that Mr. Orso would pass the collection basket among them. The priest then read from the building fund report and paused to acknowledge the efforts of Mr. Orso, this year's chairman, and last year's chairman, Mr. Thomas Page.

And, Father Paul announced, he was happy to see that the building fund investments were returning substantial interest for the church. Smiling broadly at the fiscal solidarity of his parish, Father Paul's face bore none of the righteous anger which so recently looked down upon the sinfulness of the city.

From down the center aisle, the collection basket was thrust into Rosa's pew and stopped under her nose. She did not look up, but Anthony's presence was intimidating. She dropped her coins into the green felt.

The basket did not move. It shook as if expecting more. From the corner of her eye, Rosa saw Angelina, without lifting her hand from her lap, wave shyly at her great uncle. Without sign of recognition, he moved onto the next pew.

Out on the front steps of the church, while Thomas and Anthony were accepting handshakes from the priest and the others of the congregation, Nina and Rosa chatted. Nina looked very worried, older, and sad.

"Is everything all right, Nina, you look tired."

"I guess I am, a little," Nina moved them away from the crowd.

"Anthony came in late again last night. I had moved into the other bedroom but he didn't seem to notice that I was not there. I didn't go in, and this morning he was mad at me because he was all wrinkled. He didn't even ask me where I was or why I wasn't in our bed. All he worried about was his suit being wrinkled."

Rosa put her arm around her.

"What are you going to do today, Rosa? I miss the children, can I come over?"

"Yes, come over, Peppino and I have to go see Enrico but that is all I planned."

"I will take care of my babies while you go, that is good."

Anthony stepped up to them. Without looking at Rosa, he said, "I have invited Father Paul to dinner this afternoon, we better get home." His tone was one of command, not question.

"Oh, Anthony", she pleaded, "I have just made other plans."

"Well, then change them!"

Rosas heart ached as Nina looked apologetically at her and said to her husband, "Alright, Anthony if you need me."

Then, as an afterthought, she turned back to Rosa, and her voice more alive, she said, "Rosa, you and the children come too."

Rosa did not want to be anywhere near Anthony, but she could not turn down the pleading in Nina's eyes, "Yes, I would like to. Shall I bring the bread?" She was gratified by the look of relief on Nina's face.

"Then the children can come with me now," Nina called the twins who went lovingly with their Nona.

When she arrived back to the flat, Peppino had the wagon hitched up, and was waiting for her. It was a cold winter day, wet and dreary, and clouds that threatened rain. Peppino wrapped an extra blanket around their legs.

Enrico looked well and when they told him of Peppino's latest exploits, he was full of questions.

"I am glad that you are here to help our Rosa, Peppino. I hate to think that she was trying to do this all by herself. I have tried to stop her and so did Aldo, but she is stubborn."

"After Father Paul's sermon about how sinful the city is and how our young girls aren't safe walking the streets, all I could think about was Angelina. I am now more than ever determined to stop what Anthony is doing," Rosa said.

Peppino told of his plans to enter a parlor house as a customer, and Rosa asked if he had a suit Peppino could borrow.

Enrico laughed. "Now you are going to be a big-time gambler, eh, Peppino?"

"Only for one night, and he had better not lose," Rosa shook her finger playfully at Peppino, "I can't afford that sort of thing."

Enrico pointed to the closet inside, "I have a suit in there, get it, Peppino and try it on."

When he came out of the washroom, Peppino looked just like a boy dressing up in his father's suit.

"Well, Peppino, the sleeves are a little long and the trousers are long, but I can fix that," Rosa said adjusting the suit on his shoulders.

Peppino went out to find a box to put Enrico's suit in, and then Enrico turned to Rosa, "You have not asked me about Aldo today?"

Embarrassed that her thoughts should be so easily read, she said, "I thought you would tell me if you had anything to tell."

"I got a letter from him Friday, and he said he was sending one to you too. The nurse told me there was a letter for you at the desk."

"A letter here? But the last one came to my house, why would he...?"

"I do not know, but you could find out. Why don't you go and ask the nurse?"

Turning to leave, she almost collided with the returning Peppino, "Here, Rosa, the nurse gave this to me for you."

She studied the envelope, "The postmark is Rome. What is he doing in Rome?"

"Go ahead, Rosa, read it. Peppino and I will talk."

"Do you mind?" She stood in the light from the window:

My dear Rosa,

I arrived in Italy safely. The voyage was uneventful and rough at times. I am becoming a good sailor and have learned how to prevent perils of being seasick.

Most of the passengers spent their time in their cabins. It was dull without my little friends sneaking up to first class with sick mothers to entertain me. I spent most of my days reading and my night dreaming of you. I would wake up and be disappointed that it was a dream and you were not really with me.

Rome is beautiful, but I am alone and have no one to share it with me. But I only wish is that you were here with me. My business in

477

Rome is taking longer than expected, I will probably remain here for the next six weeks.

My love is yours and the children's,

Aldo

She folded the letter tenderly and put it back in the envelope and looked out at the gray sky. It had started to rain and the world outside looked very dreary. Tears gathered in her eyes.

"No, do not cry, Rosa." Enrico had been watching her, "You know what he thinks about you. When he writes to me, all he does is ask questions about you and the children and then, he suddenly remembers who he is writing to and adds that he hopes I am feeling fine."

Rosa smiled and wiped her eyes. "What is he doing in Rome?"

"For one thing, he is buying furniture and rugs and having them shipped here for the hotel. Do not worry, Rosa, he will return, the time will pass."

"Yes," Peppino said, "and our time here is passing too," and with Enrico's suit folded and wrapped in paper, they said their goodbyes.

It was a slow and silent ride home behind the plodding horse. Peppino dropped Rosa off a few blocks away from Nina's flat where there would be no chance of meeting with Anthony.

John Edward answered the door, "Nona's in the kitchen, and Angelina went with Anthony."

"Where did he take her, John?" Rosa tried not to give in to the sudden rush of her fear which overtook her.

"I don't know, ask Nona," he said running off to play.

Rushing to the kitchen she asked, "Where is Angelina?"

"She went with Anthony and Father Paul to get some wine at the wharf," and, as if comprehending for the first time the message written on Rosa's face, Nina said, "My God, Rosa! Surely you don't think Anthony would harm Angelina!"

Feeling like a small child caught telling a falsehood, Rosa apologized.

"No, no of course not! I guess I am just a nervous mother, that is all, I am sorry, Nina." But Father Paul's words of the morning were not silenced in her heart.

Angelina, Anthony, and Father Paul returned, and monumentally uncomfortable in the presence of children, the priest struggled to make conversation with the twins.

He asked first Angelina and then John, what grade are you in at school? Receiving the predictable monosyllabic answers, he laughed out again:

"What is your teacher's name?" That information noted, and, as if finally remembering his own cleric's orientation, he added, "and are you a good girl/boy?" Apparently satisfied at having discharged this paternal obligation, he turned the conversation to the morning sermon.

All during dinner Father Paul was filled with energy and excitement which grew out of his righteous commitment to chasing any mortality from his ferric city. While he talked endlessly of his crusade and its noble origins, the gentlemen in him prevented him from offering sordid examples while he was a guest in the presence of ladies and children.

The conversation went next to the church building fund. He was almost at a loss for words to describe the fine job Anthony and Thomas were doing investing the church's money.

"Tell me, Anthony," Rosa asks, "how is the money invested?"

479

Anthony's expression clearly reflecting his annoyance at her importance, he snapped, "Investment properties, with growth potential, rentals, that sort of thing."

Rosa controlled her urge to ask more. The meal done, Rosa went to settle the children down to play in the kitchen, and when she returned, Nina was sitting quietly on the settee in the parlor while the men sipped Brandy.

Oppressed by the tension in the room, Rosa went to the window. In the late afternoon light of the dreary fall day, the sky was dark, the streets wet with the heaviness of the fog.

She shivered with the drabness of the view and turned back to the room. The marble mantle where Nina kept a statue of the Madonna she had brought from Lucca, and next to a daguerreotype portrait of Anthony warned, "Rosa, be careful," and watched her pick up the picture.

"This is a good likeness of you, Anthony", she said ignoring his caution. She held the picture out for the priest to see, and cloaking her real meaning in an innocent tone, asked, "where is the portrait of Nina?"

Father Paul took it from her and commented on the delicacy of the silver filigree frame as he edged closer to the lamp and rotated the picture in his hand. In the brighter light, Rosa noticed a series of numbers handwritten on the brown paper backing.

Anthony got up quickly and took the picture politely but firmly from Father Paul. "This is not a portrait, the newspaper had it taken of me when I won the bocce championship." Anthony placed it back on the mantle, and after carefully arranging the easel-like legs, turned and looked menacingly at Rosa.

When Anthony left to drive Father Paul back to the church house he told Nina he had business to attend to and would not be home until late.

"That means not at all," Nina said, "I don't know how long I can put up with this, but thank God I have you and the children."

They went in to tidy up the parlor, and Nina said, "Anthony is very proud of that picture, he doesn't like anyone to touch it. He said it's very delicate."

Rosa took the picture to the lamp, "the silver work is lovely. But what are these numbers that someone has written on the back for?"

"Anthony told me if he wanted copies, those were the numbers."

Nina fluffed up two little square pillows on the settee and Rosa turned down the lamps.

"I noticed Anthony isn't wearing his diamond stickpin in that portrait. Where did you get that pin?"

Nina shrugged her shoulders, and answered, "he said he won it playing poker."

When Rosa and the children walked home the fog was so heavy they could not see across the street. But still, they were on their way to their own home, and Rosa felt a freshness, a crispness in the air.

CHAPTER FORTY-ONE

It was a two-story building, plainly made a neatly kept. Either side of the front door small crucifixes were carved in stone.

Rosa rang the bell and waited for someone to answer the chimes which sounded inside. A tiny nun, her face a solid network of wrinkles and all but lost under the stiff white wimple, answered the door.

"Good morning, Sister", Rosa said, "I am Rosa Dante."

The little nun's face showed no signs of comprehension. Rosa added, "A friend of Officer Nelson?" Still no sign. Rosa said, "I came to see Sylvia." Then I looked at her intently and silently stepping aside, permitted her to enter.

Rosa followed her into a small sitting room. It was the same as parish houses and church parlors everywhere. Dark, seldom used, and infrequently ventilated. It was sparsely furnished with a simple wooden table and chairs.

On the walls hung pictures of the Virgin Mary and of Jesus Christ hanging heavy on the cross.

Heavy footsteps announced the arrival of another nun, and she was as large as the first one was small and as talkative as the first one was silent. "Yes," she announced in a baritone voice, "I am sister Bathilda, and you are Mrs. Dante? You came to see Sylvia." Her gaze piercing, she looked up and down Rosa, "Is that right?" She demanded.

When Rosa nodded her agreement, the sister stepped forward toward the doorway and signaled, a frightened young woman entered the room, and stood, head bowed, in the protective closeness of the sun.

Rosa got up and approached the girl slowly, offered her hand, "Hello, Sylvia, I am Rosa Dante, a friend of officer Hans Nelson."

Afraid of frightening the girl the way, Rosa spoke quietly and gently.

The girl did not speak. Small framed and thin, she looked at Rosa with large dark eyes. She seems scarcely more than a child. Her hair was very dark and pulled back and tied with string. She wore a drab gray dress covered with a white kitchen apron.

They sat down, Rosa and Sylvia across from each other, and Sister Bathilda behind the girls, but making her protective presence known.

"I am a friend of Officer Nelson," Rosa repeated, watching the girl's face for a clue that she heard. "He thought perhaps you could use a warm coat."

Rosa unwrapped the dark green coat of Mrs. Angelo and holding it up in front of her looked at Sylvia, and when she saw how the huge coat would dwarf the girl, she laughed.

Then quickly looking to see if the girl had taken offense, she said, "Well, I guess I didn't know how big Mrs. Angelo was, or how tiny you are."

Sylvia reached out to touch the coat, and caressing it said, "This is a beautiful coat." Taking the coat from Rosa she held it up to her shoulders and said, "This is not too much too big, I could take it in a bit, I am good with a needle."

Delighted at the girl's interest, Rosa took two dresses from the same package and asked, "Do you think you could do anything with these?"

By the time Rosa left, Sister Bathilda had joined them in a cup of tea, Rosa had told her about her children, about her reasons for coming to America, and about her bakery. But best of all, Sylvia smiled, not once, but twice.

"Thank you for coming, Mrs. Dante," Sylvia said, walking to the door with Rosa. "I'm going to get right to work on the coat."

Rosa heard nothing more from Sylvia until about a week later when Hans told her the girl wanted to see her again. He offered to drive her there.

"In the police wagon?" Rosa asked,

"Yes, in the police wagon, but if you are afraid your neighbors will see, I will bring you a false beard and a big hat to disguise you."

Rosa accepted his offer of a ride, but only if she could meet him a few blocks away before getting into the patty wagon.

Sylvia greeted them in the parlor wearing the coat. Fitting her perfectly, the dark green garment transformed the drab frightened girl into a beautiful frail young woman. Rosa was overcome and could say nothing.

"I will be right back," Sylvia said and hurried out of the room. When she returned, she was caring over her arm, one of Mrs. Angelo's dresses Rosa had given her. She held it up at arm's length, "do you think this will fit you now, Mrs. Dante?"

"Oh, Sylvia," Rosa could hardly speak for the tightness in her throat, "I am so deeply touched." The girl had taken the dress entirely apart and made it over. It suited Rosa as well as if she had picked it out herself.

Officer Nelson excused himself to take care of other business and left Rosa and Sylvia to visit. They talked for a long time, until Rosa looked at the clock, and said, "I must get home now, it is time to get back to work."

While she waited for Hans to return, she told Sylvia of all the orders Peppino was getting for the bakery, and how she would soon have to get someone to help sell in the bakery.

"But at least it is not Friday, Rosa said, Fridays are the worst, people buy twice as much on Fridays, and I end up running all day."

"Perhaps I could help you out on a Friday," Sylvia said, so shyly that Rosa hardly heard.

It was agreed that Sylvia would come on Friday to help. Hans returned, and taking her lovely new dress, Rosa kissed Sylvia on the cheek and left.

Rosa was in the bakery just as the sun rose when she heard someone come into the bakery.

Sylvia stood in the middle of the floor, looking lost and frightened like she had just gotten off the boat from Italy. She was wearing the same drab gray dress, and a black knit shawl, like the nuns wore, over her shoulders.

Her hair was pulled back into a type of bun that made her eyes look even bigger than ever.

"Sylvia, I am so glad that you are here. Come in, you look frozen, here, warm yourself with some hot coffee. Where is your new coat? Why aren't you wearing it?"

"It is too nice to wear every day, I want to save it for Sundays and for special times."

Just then Peppino came in to start helping Rosa, and when he saw Sylvia, he stopped, transfixed.

Rosa introduced them, and watching the look of instant love and adoration in Papino's face, she felt gay, young, and vital.

But Sylvia, so fragile, so vulnerable, was frightened by this handsome young man, and she hung back.

Peppino left to make his deliveries, and Rosa and Sylvia work together, the girl changed back once again from the frightened child to the lovely young woman.

Sylvia came every Friday to help. She arrived early, worked hard, and as the days went on, Rosa could see her features filling out, and now, more often than not, that once frightened look in her eyes was replaced with a smile. She often spoke of her childhood in Italy, but never did she make any mention of her life here in America.

Hans was dropping by once in a while to see her and visit Nina and he remarked how the frightened look came less often to her eyes.

But still, a loud noise or someone knocking at the door would send her off to hide. She gained a few pounds and lost any fear of Peppino she might have had, alas, she seemed to be thinking more of the future than of the past.

On Friday's after school, Angelina and John Edward could barely wait to get home from school to come down to the bakery and see Sylvia.

She had taken some more of Mrs. Angelo's leftover clothes, and brought back a pair of grown-up trousers for John and a dress for Angelina.

The children repaid her with pictures they drew for her at school, and with their unreserved affection.

Sylvia enjoyed being with the children and listened with interest as they told her of their daily adventures and shared with her their treasures.

Angelina showed Sylvia the doll that Aldo had given her, and John Edward told her of their gold mining adventure in Truckee. Letting Sylvia rub the smooth surface of their touchdowns, the children both explained to her how it was used to tell real gold from fools gold.

"Sylvia," Rosa said one afternoon just after the twins had run off to take Paisano for his walk, "you are such a good worker and have been a great help to me, that I wish you could be here every day, instead of just on Fridays."

Listening with interest Sylvia smiled at her words.

"But there is one thing, something that I must tell you…" Searching for just the right words, Rosa was silent.

"You mean about Mr. Orso?" Sylvia said after a long wait.

"Yes!" Rosa was stunned, she already knew the thing that had kept her up at night worried about how to tell her.

"Do you know about Anthony?" Rosa's expression demanded an explanation.

"Yes, one afternoon when you were gone, Nina, I mean Mrs. Orso, came into the bakery and I recognized her. I don't think she knew me, but I remembered her, she was always so kind to me. Then I asked Peppino."

"Oh, Sylvia, I have been worrying so much wanting to wait until just the right minute to tell you, when you were strong and no longer afraid. Oh, I am so glad that you know. Did it, did it upset you when you found out?"

"Yes, Rosa, it did, at first. I almost stopped coming. But Peppino made me feel safe."

Later in the day, Rosa said, "Would you consider coming here to live with the children and me, and work in the bakery?"

For a second Sylvia wide eyes, her face, her posture, everything about her said, "Yes!" But then, just as quickly, a frightened look pulled down over her, everything changed about her."

She said, "Thank you, Rosa, but the sisters, they have done so much for me, I could not leave them, I don't know if they could get along without me, I don't know..." her voice faded into uncertainty.

Leaving the matter for Sylvia to think about until the following Friday Rosa set about preparing a place for her to sleep. She moved John Edward into Papino's room and fixed the bed for her and Angelina's room.

CHAPTER FORTY-TWO

Early one afternoon and late Autumn, Rosa was finishing up her baking for the day when Anna came to the bakery to ask her to go shopping with her.

Christmas was coming and, Thomas, she said, thought it would do her good to get out, to go shopping and look at the stores. All this she told Rosa with a noted lack of enthusiasm.

Leaving Sylvia in charge of the store, the two women headed for the dress shop where Anna was working when she met Thomas.

They had walked less than two blocks, went on the steps and her breathing became noticeably heavy.

"What is the matter, Anna?" Rosa asked, stopping to give her time to catch her breath.

"I don't really know, Rosa. I am just so tired all the time lately. I sleep well at night, even heavily, but when I wake up, I don't feel at all rested."

"It'll be fine. I'm sure Thomas is right, and afternoon shopping would be just the tonic I need."

The owner of the dress store, the woman Anna had worked for, was delighted to see her, but her concern for Anna's health was clear. She took them both into the back room and gave them tea on the pretense of catching up with good old times.

The tea did revive Anna, and as the afternoon war on her spirits improved. Rosa bought a few gifts for Christmas and although Anna showed passing interest in several things she seemed unable to make any kind of decision, and ended up buying nothing at all.

"Thomas said he would look for me in front of the store at 5 o'clock and take me home. We will drop you off, too, Rosa," Anna said.

"Thomas worries about me, he is such a considerate man, and I'm sure he won't mind taking you home."

From Anna's voice, Rosa knew she was not at all sure that her husband would be pleased about her asking him to do that.

Thomas arrived, and not expecting to find Rosa there, tried to hide supplies in cordiality, "It will be my pleasure to escort you home," he said.

"Well, my dear, I do believe the shopping did you good." Putting his hand on his wife, he turned a Rosa, "you know my Anna has not been well lately, don't you think she looks a bit better, Rosa?"

As the buggy pulled up in front of the bakery Thomas stepped out, and taking her packages from her, helped Rosa down.

His hand on her elbow, he walked with her, and just before they reached the door, he stopped her, saying, "Rosa, I am worried about my Anna."

Rosa's back was to the store, and as she looked up at him to see what he meant, he seemed suddenly startled and stared over her head into the bakery. She turned to see what had attracted his attention, all she saw was the back of a figure hurrying into the back room.

"What, what is it, Thomas?" She asked.

"Nothing, nothing," his face white, it took him time to refocus his attention. He smiled, and said, "it is nothing, just a man worrying too much about the woman he loves."

Dismissing his strange behavior from her mind, Rosa went into the bakery calling Sylvia to come and see what she had bought.

Sylvia did not come, and Rosa called her again. Still, she did not come.

Rosa lay the packages down and went to look for her.

There was no one in the backroom, and fear slept over her like a cold chill. Something happened to the children and Sylvia had gone to them. Turning quickly to go to the flat, she heard a sound.

There, in the corner, crouched like a hunted animal, with face buried into her hands, Sylvia cowered.

"Sylvia, what is it? What is wrong? Tell me." The girl's body uncoiled slightly, and cautiously she uncovered her eyes and peaked out.

"Is he gone?" She was trembling and the look of fright and terror she had when Rosa first saw her, was back in her eyes.

"Is who gone?"

"That man, the man you brought home."

"Mr. Page? Yes, he's gone, but why…?"

"It's him, the man who threatened me," Sylvia grabbed for Rosa's arm and held her tight.

"Oh, Sylvia, you must be mistaken. That's Mr.…."

491

"No, I'm not, that's him, I know that face anywhere."

"Mr. Page threatened you, Sylvia?"

"Yes, to keep me from testifying against Anthony. He was the man in the buggy- the one who came to the Sister's home- he told me to keep quiet or- or someone would make me keep quiet."

Rosa helped her up, "Oh, my dear God. Are you sure Thomas was the one? Oh, my God," Rosa exclaimed as she led the shaking girl to a chair.

"Come sit down, tell me."

Rosa poured her a cup of hot coffee, and pulling a chair up close, waited for her breathing to slow down.

"What is this all about?" Rosa asked, "How did you get mixed up in this, please, Sylvia, tell me?"

"Did you know my father died on the boat on the way here from Italy? Yes, he did, and when we landed, I didn't know what to do. With him dead and me sick, I didn't know how I was going to get to my father's uncle in Missouri by myself."

Sylvia told Rosa the now familiar story of how Anthony befriended her at the dock and took her to the boarding house.

"He tried to… He tried…" Sylvia could not finish her sentence.

"He tried to force himself on you, is that right, Sylvia?" Rosa prompted gently.

"Yes," she sobbed and looked up at Rosa begging for understanding. Rosa told her she knew all about Anthony and what he would do.

Reassured, she told how he had let go of her when someone walked in on them, and the next day said he found her a better job and took her in his carriage to a big house and introduce her to Sally.

What she thought was going to be a maid's job for a private family, turned out to be working as one of Sally's girls in a whorehouse.

Sylvia started to cry again, "I was so dumb even when she took me to a fancy bedroom and told me it was my room, still didn't get it."

"Of course you didn't," Rosa comforted her, "it was the last thing in the world you expected. It's alright, Sylvia, just take your time."

"She got me a uniform out of the closet that was nothing but a nightgown you could almost see right through, then she left me there alone, and I heard her lock the door. I went to look out the window and there were bars over the windows. It was about then I began to understand what kind of a place it was."

"She brought me some food later, and there was a pipe on the tray, just like the pipe farmers at home smoke. She tossed matches on the bed and told me to try it, it would calm me down she said."

"Did you try it?" Rosa asked. The girl shook her head no.

"They left me alone, I sat there in the chair for hours just wondering what was going to happen to me.

"I heard people coming and going in the hall, like a lot of men and women talking and laughing, and like someone calling out signals or something. I think they were gambling.

"Then a key turned in my lock and Sally came in with a big man with a heavy black beard. She told me his name and told me to be nice to him. Oh, Rosa, the way he looked at me, made my flesh crawl.

"Rosa, it was terrible. I was so scared! He came at me, I didn't know what to do. He just kept coming, he was awful, he smelled of whiskey and smoke and he kept calling me baby, and coming at me, and his mouth hung open, and all I could see was his big fat lips with spit drooling down his chin. Oh God, it was a nightmare! I kicked him in the shins but he kept coming and he forced me down on the bed. I thought I was going to die, and then he put his hand up to my mouth, and I bit him! He let out one huge scream and slapped me across the face. He cursed me, but he left. I followed him to the door, but just as I got there someone locked it again.

"Sally came back and she cursed me up and down, and told me I was going to earn my keep. And she tried again to get me to smoke the pipe, but the very smell of it made me sick.

"She tried everything, even tried being sweet and motherly, and finally she tried leaving me without food. But I never gave in, anytime she brought a man and I got rid of him. Until one day a man came in and when I resisted him, he started beating me, I guess I screamed, and she came in and threw him out. She didn't care what he did to me, all she cared about was that he shouldn't harm her investment, that's what I was to her, an investment.

"But when she chased him out, she forgot to lock my door, and I grabbed a blanket and ran down the back steps, and just as I got almost out to the street, I heard her yelling and someone coming after me. I just ran, I didn't even know for sure where I was, and I didn't know what to do."

Sylvia broke down again, and Rosa's heart was breaking for this poor child, not too many years older than Angelina. "It's all right, you're safe here, no one can hurt you. You're safe, we are your friends."

"All I can remember is running, I don't even know where I was running to. I didn't have shoes, and the rocks cut into my feet, and it was so cold, it was so cold. And then, they caught me, I was in complete dark, like an alley or something. All I can remember is those two big men coming at me.

"I must've passed out because next thing I remember is waking up on the beach under an old pier. I don't know how I got there or anything.

"All I remember is the cold. I was so cold, and when I moved everything hurt. It was agony. My hands were cut and full of blood, and my nightgown was stained with blood and dirt.

"I guess you know the rest of the story. All I wanted to do was die, and I couldn't even do that right!"

She broke into sobs, sobs that had been bottled up too long. Rosa took her gently by the arm and wrapping her coat around her, led her upstairs to the flat.

While she was bathing the tears from Sylvia's face, flashes of a similar long ago scene darted in and out of Rosas memory. But the little pieces never quite held together.

She shrugged her shoulders and turned her attention back to the present. "And that's when Hans found you and took you to the Sister's of the Holy Family?" Rosa suggested.

"Yes, and they gave me back my will to live. I even became strong enough to tell Hans I would testify against Mr. Orso, until... until..."

"Mr. page came to the Sister's house and threatened you? That is so hard to believe that Mr. page..."

"It's true, Rosa, it's true, oh please believe me."

"Oh, I believe you, it's just that..."

"And you say the Chinese driver told the Sister's there was a lady in the carriage who wanted to hire you as a maid?"

"Yes, and that's why I was so scared the day you came to bring me the coat, and why Sister Bathilda stayed there with us until she was sure you were a friend. I was afraid it was the same story again."

"What did Mr. Page say to threaten you?"

"If I ever told anyone what happened, I'd wish I was dead. He said they wouldn't kill me, just make me pray that they would."

"Oh, Sylvia, I am so sorry, but I promise we will protect you." Rosa turned away. Anthony and Thomas in this together! What else are they into?

"Oh, Sylvia, my poor child, no wonder you were so frightened. But it's alright now, you're safe here."

"No, I am not safe here, I must get away."

"Do you think he saw you?"

"I don't know, yes, I think he did, no, maybe not. Oh Rosa, I don't know if he saw me or not."

Rosa remembered her at the door of the bakery, Thomas suddenly got that strange look on his face, and couldn't remember what he was saying. Maybe he had seen the girl. Rosa turned away not wanting Sylvia to see the fear on her face.

"I must leave because if that man sees me or if Anthony sees me, oh Rosa, they are bad men. I thought I was brave, but just seeing that man today brought back all the terror. I am afraid of them, terribly afraid."

She reached out for Rosa and sobbed. Holding her, trying to comfort her fears, Rosa remembered what terror was.

CHAPTER FORTY-THREE

"Let her rest, Peppino, she has had a bad shock today," Rosa watched the anger and the protectiveness rise in the young sailor's face as she told him of Sylvia's encounter with Thomas.

Peppino paced furiously back-and-forth across the tiny kitchen, "My God, Rosa, you said you had a funny feeling about Thomas. Do you think he knows Sylvia's here?"

"That's what worries me, I am not sure. He saw something but whether he recognized her or not, I can't be sure."

"He must not find out, she must stay out of sight."

Peppino went to Sylvia and Rosa could hear them talking quietly. For the first time, she realized how much time they were spending together. Peppino had become accustomed to going to mass with her at the Sister's home. In the evenings they often played cards and talked. Rosa knew now that he was in love with her.

They came into the kitchen, hand-in-hand, and touching Rosa's arm, Sylvia said, "Thank you, Rosa, I will be alright now. With you and Peppino both looking out for me, I will be alright."

After dinner Peppino sat down at the table with a deck of cards, practicing blackjack, to prepare, he said, for his detective work at the parlor house.

"Where is your partner?" Rosa asked.

"She said she had something to do, she didn't say what it was," Peppino shrugged.

"I can't get over that, about Thomas. I wonder if Anna knows anything about his activities?"

"I doubt it. She probably has no idea. But we can't take any chances, we can't take her into our confidence."

Rosa agreed, "You're right, he is her husband and she worships him."

"He seems so kind and considerate of her, that it's hard to believe he could be so evil."

"Does Sylvia understand how important it is for her to stay out of sight?"

"I think she does, we talked about it, and she has agreed to be very careful so no one will know she is here. But right now," he said, folding up his deck of cards, "I think she's going out for a walk."

"Absolutely not!" Rosa said outraged, "she must not be seen!"

After what they just talked about how could Peppino so casually say she was going out, and not object a bit?

"If they find her, they might kill her and God knows what they would do to us if they knew we had her here. She cannot go!" Rosa ordered, and then, out of the corner of her eye, she saw the figure of a man come into the kitchen. She jumped with fright.

"My God, who...? Sylvia? What in the world have you done?"

There stood Sylvia, wearing men's pants, a men's shirt, and tie. Her long hair clipped close to her scalp, she held her hair in her hand. Her eyes pleaded for Rose's approval.

"Those clothes, where? Where did you get them?" Rosa got up to examine the suit.

"They were in with Mrs. Angelo's old clothes," Sylvia turned hesitantly around to let Rosa see her new outfit.

"Oh, you cut your beautiful hair!"

Rosa touched what was left of her hair. "How could you cut your beautiful hair?"

"It is the only way I can stay safe," Sylvia said, some of the old fear passing quickly across her face, "dressed like this, I can go outside once in a while, and not have to feel like a prisoner, locked up inside the cage."

Peppino put his arm around the girl's shoulder and enjoying Rosa's surprise said, "She makes a handsome man, doesn't she, Rosa?"

"Peppino and I thought this up, do you think I look enough like a man?" She asked.

"Not unless you wear a jacket."

Blushing, Sylvia rounded her shoulders down and at the same time tried to cover her bosom with her hands, "I will not go out without my jacket."

She slipped it on, the buttons were too far apart, and the sleeves hung below her fingertips.

"Let me help you," Rosa said, "those sleeves need to be shortened before you go for your walk," she sent a Peppino off for her sewing basket.

When the job was done, Rosa held the coat up, "Here, Sylvia, try it now."

"Peppino says I should change my name to Serio."

"Serio?" Rosa smiled.

"Yes, Serio," Peppino held his arm, "shall we go?"

"Allow me," she said, "you are older."

Now be careful, Rosa watched them go side-by-side down the long hallways.

Peppino reached for her hand and playfully she threw it away and shook her finger at him. Pretending to pout, he stuck his hand deep into the pockets, and hurrying on, they shared the laughter.

He opened the front door and cautiously looked out to be sure no one was around, then together, the two of them went out for their walk. Inside Rosa's breast, a twinge of envy touched her heart.

The door scarcely closed behind Papino and Serio when Nina and the twins arrived. While the two women helped the children to bed, Rosa listened to all the day's events that had excited their youthful hearts.

Hans arrived soon after, and hearing his voice the children pleaded with him to tell them a story. He told how the men in his village in Norway cut holes in the ice to catch fish in the wintertime.

Then he had to try to convince the children that in San Francisco they would not find any frozen lakes to fish through the ice.

Rosa was impatient for him to finish with the children. She wanted to tell him what she'd heard from Sylvia, and yet with Nina here, what should she do? While she made coffee and put slices of cake out on the table, she struggled to know what to do.

When Hans returned, she told about going shopping with Anna, and how tired and ill she looked. She told how Thomas had driven her home, and what happened when he walked her to the door of the bakery. Then, carefully watching Nina's reactions, she told how Sylvia reacted to seeing him.

Nina sat in stunned disbelief. "Oh Rosa, how could that be true? Do you think she was mistaken?"

How could she tell Nina the rest of Sylvia's story? And yet, how could she not tell her?

Just then Angelina came out for a glass of water, and when Nina took the child back to bed, Rosa hastily shared her dilemma with Hans and together they agreed she must be told.

Slowly, and as gently as she could, Rosa revealed Sylvia's sordid story, all about Anthony and Thomas both.

"How many young women…?" In tears, Nina was unable to complete her thought.

Rosa put her arm around Nina's sagging shoulders. "Why have I put up with him all these years, making excuses for him, crying over him?"

"There there, you did what any good woman does, you trusted your husband, that's all you could do."

"But all these years? I wonder how many girls he has ruined." And then as if suddenly hearing something else, she said, "and what other terrible things has he done? Oh Rosa, why?"

Rosa patted her hand. "All these years I let him make me feel stupid and worthless when all the while he was… Oh, Rosa, how could he?"

501

Hans, who had been standing quietly in the corner, came over and sat down beside Nina. "We want to stop him, Nina, and we will."

"Yes, put him in jail and throw the key away!" Nina's pain made her voice shrill. "Nina, wait," Hans explained.

"We need more evidence than Sylvia's word. If Thomas is involved that means they have friends in City Hall. We have to be very careful. I think the answers to a lot of questions are in Anthony's office."

"Yes! The keys! I will get you the keys now, anytime you want them." Nina spoke resolutely and then side deeply.

"Let's wait until after Christmas," Rosa said, "We must move slowly so that no one gets suspicious. Peppino will go to the gambling hall, and see what he can find out then we will get the keys."

Sorrow turned into anger and indignation, Nina said, "I do not want to wait, I can't spend another night in the house with him. All I've ever done for him is work, work, work and this is what I get."

"Sh-sh-sh," Rosa said, "if you just move out, he will know something is wrong, and we will never find out."

"But now that I know, I am afraid. And he'll see it on my face."

"She is right," Hans said, "I worry about that too."

"You stay here tonight until we figure out what to do," Rosa said.

"Would you consider," Hans asked, "taking in a border?"

"I've never thought about it. I do have that back room. What are you suggesting?"

"Someone should be there with you, just in case…"

"What do you mean?" Nina asked hesitantly.

"Me."

"You? But why would I take in a Norwegian police officer for a border?"

"No one has to know I am a policeman. I could be a merchant, a banker, a delivery man, someone who needs temporary quarters."

"That might be a very good idea, Nina," Rosa said as she poured more coffee. "What would Anthony think about this?"

"I don't know, he's hardly ever around home enough these days to notice."

Nina sipped her coffee and thought it over. Finally she said, "Yes! I think it might work. If Anthony thought it was bringing in money, and as long as it doesn't interfere with him, he'd be happy."

"Then that is what we will do. I will pay you the going rate for rooms. You ask Anthony tomorrow and then I will come in the evening and see about moving in."

"What kind of story should I tell Anthony?"

"Tell him you met me at the market, that I am doing a special project concerning the cable cars and I'll be here in this area for a while and I asked about a room to rent. Yes, that's good, I think I know enough about the cable cars to answer any questions he asks, but then I plan to keep out of his way anyway."

"I won't eat at your house, and I could even use the back entrance. Just as long as I'm in there when he's around. And while you're at the diner, the fishermen, particularly Mario, will be keeping an eye on you."

Rosa saw a look in his eyes she had not noticed before. It was that same concern, that same sense of protectiveness that Peppino had for Sylvia.

"But what about your job?" Nina asked.

"I will still do that. I can change my clothes at the police station. There will be no problem."

"And we will have to be careful about Anna too when the time comes," Rosa said. "She is not well, and she will be in danger too." Rosa wondered if Anna was already in danger.

The front door burst open and the sound of laughter rushed up the steps as Sylvia and Peppino competed to get to the top step first.

They exploded into the room and were surprised, and a bit embarrassed to find Nina and Hans both there with Rosa watching them. Sylvia greeted Nina, and then looking more closely at her, asked, "Are you alright? Are you not feeling well?"

"I've had something of a shock this evening, but I will be alright," and she forced a smile.

"It is good to see you, Officer Nelson," she said.

"But who is this young man?" Hans protested, "I do not know you, sir."

After proper introductions were performed, Rosa teased, "Sylvia I'm sorry I can't say you look beautiful in your new outfit," smiling, Sylvia went off to change.

"If I had not known she was here," Hans said, "I would not have recognized her."

Peppino said, "I suggested it. This way she is safe and she can still work and help you. She wants to earn her own way, and not be a burden to anyone."

"It is good, Peppino, but still we all have to be careful. I have always admired that girl's courage", Hans said, "even after all the terrible things that happened to her, she never lost her spirit, at least not for long."

Peppino approved of their plan to have Hans take a room in Nina's house to protect her. "My beard is almost ready," he said, "when do we start our detective work?"

"Right after Christmas," Rosa said, "we will start in earnest."

CHAPTER FORTY-FOUR

Their second Christmas in San Francisco Rosa decided, would be an American celebration. They will decorate a Christmas tree instead of having the Yuletide log. They would look for Santa Claus to come down the chimney on Christmas Eve instead of waiting for La Befana to deliver the gifts as she did in Italy on the Feast of the Epiphany.

Santa Claus and La Befana were much the same, Rosa reasoned, the good received pretty gifts, the bad got a piece of coal or a bag of ashes.

Like the other children in school, Angelina and John Edward wrote letters to Santa Claus, and on the fireplace, they hung the extra big stockings Nina's knitted them. But just to be safe, they asked Peppino to get a Yuletide log.

They didn't want to take any chances, they would also make wishes as they had done it at least.

Peppino and Sylvia made a nativity scene complete with figures of Mary and Joseph, the three Wiseman, and the shepherds. From old shingles, Peppino fashioned a small barn and lined it with straw from the livery stable.

Though the celebration of Christmas would be American, the Christmas Eve meal would be Italian.

Rosa started her day with a busy morning in the bakery, everyone was buying extra bread. When she finally got away, she left Sylvia, or Serio, to mind the store and hurried home to her own kitchen. Every step she took, Paisano was under her foot. The children had tied a red ribbon around his neck and he knew something special was in the air.

Stepping around him, Rosa prepared the polenta and the baccala and chopped into tiny pieces the candied fruit to make the panettone the children loved. This year, Rosa would try her hand at making Jule cake for Hans.

The Christmas bread that he spoke of with fond memories of his boyhood, was made with raisins, citron, and cardamom spice so dear, Rosa had to send Peppino out to search for it.

Rosa put the last loaf of the sweet bread in the oven and, as so often happened lately, her thoughts flew across the sea to Victor and Dino. The year she promised them was up and she knew that they were struggling to make a go of it. Would she ever see her two sons again?

She missed them more than ever now at Christmas time. Her gifts were mailed so many days ago that now they no longer seem to be part of Christmas at all.

"How would they know she had kissed each gift she sent them? If only she could transport herself back to Italy to see them, to know how they really were.

Her bread baking in the oven, Rosa's thoughts of the past were so strong in her heart that they took her to the bedroom and to her tin box. The side of the box itself caused a torrent of memories to rush out and sweep her back to her life in Viareggio. She held the tiny scrap of Eduardo's tie up to her cheek.

Wife to men, mother of their children, she lay back on the bed and stared at the ceiling. All she could conjure up now were vacant faces, vague bodies of these men she had been wife to. What was it she had felt for them? Was it love she had felt for them?

She carefully unwrapped the flat black stone Aldo had given her and savored the memory of the time they had together.

A touchstone, he said, was to test the quality of gold, to know pure gold from fools gold. Would it help her, she wondered, to know the true will of God?

To recognize false prophets? To know right from wrong?

The odors from the kitchen reminded her of the panettone in the oven. Still holding the stone in her hand and thinking only of the man who gave it to her, she hurried back into the kitchen.

The steam from the oven mixed with the moisture welling up in her eyes. She saw not the bread, but visions of Aldo, the whole person.

She saw every detail of his face, his head, and his heart. She remembered every word in his farewell note, and the scent of flowers he sent was as strong as if she were holding them in her hands.

Would she ever see him again or was he back with his wife?

His wife was beautiful- the daughter of a grand family- Enrico told her that, while she was just a peasant girl.

Why would a gentleman like Aldo from a big city be interested in her? Anthony had taunted her with that often enough.

Overwhelmed with a feeling of hopelessness, a wave of exhaustion washed down over Rosa and she slumped into the chair. As if it held the answers, Rosa looked deep into the shining black stone in front of her.

"Oh god," she said aloud, "bring him back to me."

Letting her head rest on the table, she began, "Hail Mary full of grace, the lord…"

She did not hear Nina come in. "Rosa, what is wrong? Has something happened?"

Struggling back to the present, Rosa said she was feeling homesick for Victor and Dino and all that was left behind.

"I miss them so and I guess with Christmas I miss everyone more. Families should be together and my sons are so far away."

"And that is all you miss?" Nina asked, setting down the cooking pot she had brought for Rosa to use for making dinner.

"No, you know it isn't, I miss Aldo too."

Nina patted her lovingly on the shoulder.

"I try to see his face in my mind but lately it is cloudy, almost as if he's hiding from me. I can't see him clearly anymore."

"It's because I know he is there with his wife and I have no right to even be thinking of him. Oh, Nina, he is never coming back to me. I know I have lost him."

Nina reached into the towel sack she always carried, "I have something here for you. Peppino brought it to me the last time he saw Enrico. It is from Aldo- for you- for Christmas. Aldo made Enrico promise he wouldn't give it to you before Christmas."

Nina looked up at the clock, "The Christ-child would not care if you opened it a little early."

Rosa blew her nose, she took the box in her hand- a box wrapped in lovely colored paper. A plain white card said, "So you do not forget."

Rosa stared at the box.

"Open it, open it," Nina urged.

Rosa wanted this moment to last. She undid the wrappings, slowly and deliberately.

She pulled a long gold chain up out of the box, on the end was a cameo brooch. The face of a woman's profile, surrounded with leaves of gold filigree, and on each was a small diamond. The cameo was set on the top of a gold case. Inside a picture of Aldo looked up at her. Clutching it to her breast, Rosa bowed her head. The tears that filled her eyes this time were happy tears.

"See, Rosa, he has not forgotten you."

"His picture- now I will always be able to see his face."

She held it up for Nina to see. "Thank you for giving this to me now. It has made my Christmas happy." She fastened the chain around her neck.

"It is beautiful Rosa, and the woman's profile looks like you."

"But now I must hurry to the diner. But as soon as I get the fishermen fed, I'll be right back."

"You came just when I needed cheering up." Rosa walked her to the door.

Hans arrived with his arms full of packages, and immediately the twins set about helping him arrange his gifts under the tree.

Sylvia was helping Rosa and while they were putting the food on the table, noticed Rosa's new brooch.

Peppino heard them talking about it and taking his place at the table said, "You just couldn't wait to open it, could you rosa? And Nina, you are just as bad."

"Nevermind Peppino," Nina answered, "this gift was very important. If I had not given it to her when I did, you would have had tears in your panettone."

Everyone ate heartily except the twins, they were too excited to do more than pick at their food.

Hans said it was a grand Christmas feast and had to admit that Italians do know how to cook. He added that even at home in Norway the Jule cake had never tasted as good.

After supper, their patience exhausted, the twins almost dragged Peppino and Sylvia into the parlor.

With blindfolds in place, the laughing children were twirled around and around then set free to find their way to the Yuletide log.

Everyone watched the twins tapping their way around the room, and for each, the wondrous joys of childhood were alive again.

Each, in turn, played the game. And when all the private wishes had been made on the Yuletide log, it was put into the fireplace. If it burned all night, their wishes would be granted, if not…

One by one the gifts were passed out, and as each was unwrapped the others waited and watched.

But the children, too excited to wait to show what they had made for everyone, were permitted to pass their gifts out first. They had something for everyone and for their mother, they had pasted the nativity scene onto a board, "It's for you to hang on the wall," they explained in unison.

Angelina pointed to the nail she had herself driven in the back to hang it up with. Hans brought embroidered handkerchiefs for all the women and a special one with her name on it for Angelina.

Rosa gave Nina a lovely hat trimmed in velvet with colored feathers.

"This is for you to wear to church," Rosa said. Nina tried it on and turned to show the others: "Now Anthony will have to let me buy a new dress to go with this."

Nina's eyes met Rosa's and they both knew Anthony would probably not even notice the hat was new.

"This is for you to wear when you pretend to be a gambler."

When finally the Christmas tree was barren of gifts and the children settled down on the floor to play with their new toys, the others sat around the fire, watching the Yuletide log burn, and they spoke of Christmas's past. Just before midnight, the children placed the baby Jesus child in the manger, and they joined hands in singing "silent night, holy night"

On Christmas morning Rosa was awakened by the cries of the twins telling her to come look that the Yuletide log was still smoldering, and all their wishes would now surely come true.

Rosa sent the children home with Nina after mass and headed out to the hospital to see Enrico. The brooch in her hand, she studied each minutest detail of it, both inside and outside.

She felt happy, Christmas had been a blend of the old and the new, and after all, why should she worry about the future? The Yule log had burned all night.

In the main hall there stood the biggest Christmas tree Rosa had ever seen. It touched the ceiling, and its branches were heavy with colored decorations, glimmering in the light from the windows.

She stopped to wish the nurse merry Christmas and to give them the panettone she had baked for them. She hurried down the hall with her packages to see Enrico.

She was hardly in the room when he said, "I see you are wearing your gift."

Aldo's package had been there for several weeks, and, Enrico said, "I had a feeling that you might need it early, it's easy to feel blue when your loved ones are away from you at Christmas time."

Rosa knew that at that moment Enrico was thinking of his Renata, who had died so young.

"I am so glad you could come today Rosa." Enrico said, "I have been feeling a bit sorry for myself I'm afraid. I was hoping that I could get out of here for Christmas."

Rosa had brought a plate of Christmas dinner for him, and when Enrico finished eating and wiped the plate clean, he said, "Nothing can beat good old Italian cooking. Rosa you have given me the strength to survive longer here in this hospital."

Pleased at the flow back in his face, she handed him a box, "This is for you," inside was a book in California history.

"Thank you Rosa. Over there in the dresser, open the drawer, a few gifts for everyone. I'm sorry I couldn't go out and select them myself, one of the nurses, she is very nice, did it for me. Yours is the one in the envelope. Open it now."

There was a sketch Enrico had made of an Italian fishing boat, and a card that said, "One rug to be delivered after the new year."

"Oh Enrico how lovely I have no rugs."

"Well it is a small rug, one I brought with me from Torino, it was our mother's, and it should be kept in the family. I would like you to have it," he smiled.

Rosa's eyes stayed with Enrico and read to him from his new book.

He had eaten well, and before long he was dozing off.

The winter sky darkening and Hans came in, "I thought you might be able to use a ride home," he spoke quietly so not to wake Enrico.

Enrico stirred, "I'm sorry to have gone to sleep but I did have good dreams, of all of us, someday together. All of us well, all of us happy.

CHAPTER FORTY-FIVE

By early January Peppino's beard had grown full, Enrico's suit altered to fit him, and together, he and Rosa had saved enough money to stake him to a night of gambling.

Wearing the shirt Sylvia gave him at Christmas, he looked older than his years and not too unlike a wealthy gambler out on the town.

Although she tried to hide it, worry showed on Sylvia's face as she said, "Remember, Peppino, you are just going to gamble, nothing else!"

"I will do anything I have to do if it's in the line of duty," he teased and brushed a kiss on her forehead.

"Don't worry, Sylvia, I'll be safe. I'm good at cards, I can spot a cheat across the room. Besides, Hans will be outside. He insists on being there, even though I know I won't need him."

After Peppino left, Rosa and Sylvia settled down to wait. It would be a long Saturday night.

"Peppino said your citizenship teacher had a lawyer look at the contract for you?" Sylvia asked.

"Yes," Rosa said, not at all anxious to burden the worried girl with more reason to fear Anthony.

But she was persistent, "Please, Rosa, I know you're trying to protect me, but if I know the truth I worry less than if I make things up in my head. Tell me what she found."

Bringing two glasses of wine from the kitchen Rosa said, "Well, her lawyer friend thinks that the contract is no good. He says it's probably not valid because the fishermen couldn't understand what they were signing. He said that in the eyes of the law, they had been deprived of their freedom of bargaining by signing a contract they couldn't read."

"But a long time ago," Rosa went on, "even before I came to America, Mario once asked Mr. Page about it, and he said that they signed it so they were bound by it. Then later Hans asked a young law student he said they weren't bound by a contract they couldn't understand, and besides, those men who signed with 'signatures' were supposed to have witnesses sign with them, and so they were no good either."

"The teacher's friend also said that because twenty-four months had been changed to twelve months and wasn't initialed that the whole contract looked real bad."

Sylvia had been pacing the room and stopped to look out the window. "It will all be over soon, Sylvia, and try not to worry about Peppino, he can take care of himself."

The wine calmed her down, but long after they went to bed, Rosa could hear her moving about in her room. It was around 3 o'clock when Rosa heard the front door open. She slipped her robe on and went out in the hall. Peppino looked tired and mussed and smelled of cigar smoke and stale liquor.

"What happened?" She asked.

Peppino put his finger to his lip, "Sh-h-h-h, I don't want to wake Sylvia. Come into my room."

Rosa sat on the edge of the bed and Peppino threw a lot of money down in front of her, then sat cross-legged on the floor looking up at her.

"Well, Rosa, we won, there's more money here than I started with."

"Yes", Rosa gathered up the money, "but did you find out anything?"

"Anthony was there, in all his glory."

"Did he recognize you?"

"No, not at all, he thinks I'm a realtor from Los Angeles looking for investment properties. Well, that did it, it whetted his appetite."

"He invited me into a private poker game upstairs. He told me he owns some choice property around town he might sell if the price was right. He even gave me his card." Peppino pulled it from his shirt pocket.

"There won't be any loose change for Nina in his pockets tonight. I cleaned them out, and I was afraid he would get sore at losing so much. Then I figured it's part of his plan, he thinks he'll get even when he sells me a property."

"We are dead right about Anthony! He's definitely the big boss around here. Sally was checking with him about things all night. Even the dealers kept bringing him receipts or vouchers to sign. I watched them take bags of money into a side room, and then you'll never guess who I saw."

"Thomas Page?"

"Yes, how did you know? He came out of the room they took the money to. I only saw him for a second but it was him, he seemed to be in a big hurry to get out of there. He put his hat on and pulled it way down when he left."

"About that time one of the girls came over and started being really friendly to me. I think Anthony had sent her over, maybe he thought I had won enough. Anyhow she had one of those real pretty dresses, you know, like silk, cut low in front. I think she was real pretty, but she had so much makeup on it was hard to tell."

"Well, she sat on my lap and whispered in my ear, 'my name is Laura' ", Peppino tried to imitate the girl's seductive tones.

"Then she started rubbing the back of my neck and kissing me on the ear. And me there trying to concentrate on poker! Next, they started bringing champagne, and before I knew it, my chips were cashed in and I'm on my way down the back hall with this girl."

"I don't want Sylvia to hear any of this."

"I won't say anything, Peppino," Rosa said praying she wouldn't wake up.

"Everything happened so fast it took me a little while to figure out that I was going to get rolled for my winnings."

"But what could I do? If I backed out, they would know I was a plant. I had to go along with it. She brought the champagne with her and really tried to get me drunk. I pretended I was, but I poured more on myself than in my mouth."

"Are you sure," Peppino said, "that you want to hear all of this?"

Rosa said "Yes," glad that the room was dark.

"The girl was all over me, and she was so obvious about trying to get my bank roll. But I fooled her and hid it under the mattress."

"When I tried to ask her some questions about how she got paid, and things like that, she got mad and told me I was too nosy. Rosa," he said, "the rest of the story you don't want to hear. She couldn't have been more than eighteen. When I left, Anthony was still there, still at the gambling tables, and I figured I'd better get out of there as fast as I could."

Peppino got up off the floor and stretching out his arms and legs, signaling he was at the end of his story.

"Pretty good for a little old sailor, eh?"

"You put in a good night," Rosa said, "you better get a couple of hours sleep, Sylvia will wake you up in time for mass."

All the next week Rosa's mind kept going back and forth over the things Peppino told her about the parlor house. She could not get the picture of that young girl out of her mind, or the sight of Anthony sitting there all night gambling while Nina stayed home alone.

She tried many times to write her letter to her boys, but each time she picked up the pen, her mind snapped back to Anthony, to all the evil things they were learning about him and about Thomas. Her heart ached for Nina, and she worried about Anna and wondered what was going to happen to them.

But they couldn't stop now, they had to go on. They had to get into Anthony's office, there was no other way. If they were ever going to put a stop to all of this, they had to see his ledgers, and soon! If only Nina would get the keys to his office.

Rosa was filled with a sense of urgency, a need to hurry, to rid them of all of Anthony's evil. And she worried about the fishermen, they were becoming impatient, and she didn't know how much longer she could hold them off.

If they confronted Anthony too soon, they would ruin everything.

519

After church that next morning, Mario stopped her and asked what she had found out about the contracts. He wanted to know when something was going to be done. She told him what the lawyer had said about the contracts but didn't tell him about Peppino's night out.

She didn't want him to know they were just waiting to get a chance to break into Anthony's office. Mario was more impatient and she had ever seen him. Could she hold him and the fishermen back long enough?

That evening when Peppino and Sylvia came in from their walk, they ran playfully up the stairs.

"I'm glad the two of you are here, I have a funny feeling about tonight," Rosa said.

Sylvia was in her men's clothes still, and as long as she didn't speak, she could fool almost anyone.

"Are you taking the wagon?" Sylvia asked.

"No," Peppino explained, "we can't take the wagon, it's too risky. It would be recognized, and if we walk, we can stay in the shadows. No one will see us that way."

"You say you have a feeling about tonight, do you think Hans will get the keys?"

"I've been nervous all day, and time is running out. We have to get the evidence soon, the fishermen are impatient, I'm so afraid they may go off and do something on their own, and spoil everything. Even Mario is getting anxious."

"Peppino," Sylvia said, "if you go tonight, I want to go too. I don't want to stay here anymore and worry. I had enough of that the night you went to gamble. I worried all night. I don't want to be left behind again."

"Sylvia, someone has to stay with the children, and no one must know you are here. I know it's hard for you," Rosa spoke softly, "but please be patient, it will not be too much longer, just as soon as we get enough evidence against Anthony, then you can become a woman again."

Sylvia looked to Peppino, but he said only, "You know she is right".

Sylvia shrugged her shoulders and said no more.

Rosa got up, "I'm going to bed early tonight, and I'm going to sleep with my clothes on so if Hans comes with the keys, we won't waste any time."

"Good idea," Peppino agreed, "Anthony won't get home until about 2:30 from gambling, so we should all get some sleep."

Rosa knelt down in front of the children's drawing of the nativity scene. She asked the Madonna to protect them all.

CHAPTER FORTY-SIX

"I have them, hurry up," Hans said as Rosa opened the door. "Get Peppino."

Peppino had heard Paisanos barking and pulling his sweater down over his head as he came out of his room.

Sylvia opened her bedroom door, and grabbing Peppino, pleaded, "Please be careful, you're all I have."

He took her in his arms and kissed her, "I will be careful. Now do not worry, go back to bed."

He picked up the coil of rope that had been stationed by the front door for days, and with a last glance at her, slung the heavy rope over his shoulder.

"Come on, Peppino," Hans yelled. "Got the blanket?" He asked Rosa.

"Stay with the children," Rosa said to Sylvia as she followed the men out the door.

The night was moonless and heavy fog hovered slightly above the ground. The three of them, half running half walking, hurried down to the foot of Filbert Street to the wharf.

Reaching the boarding house, they stopped to listen: The buildings dark, everything was quiet.

Peppino searched the street until he found a good-sized rock and put it inside his jacket. He sprinted across to the wharf, impressing his body close in between piled fish crates, he waited.

Hans and Rosa went inside. Carefully taking each step as if it might be the one to bring the world down upon them, Rosa picked her way behind Hans to the top of the stairs.

She could hear deep breathing and snoring coming from the sleeping rooms. Hans held the bunch of keys tightly in his palm so they would not give off any telltale sound, and tried each one in the padlock.

All the while Rosa stood with her back to him, scanning in the dark hallway, fearful that a light-sleeping fisherman might hear them. When the door finally opened, she backed into the room, and silently closed it behind them.

Standing in front of the window, Hans held up a burning match, let it burn for one second, and blew it out. Then he steered Rosa ahead of him to the far corner of the room. They crouched down and turning away from the window, protected their faces with their hands.

The window glass shattered sending pieces into the room. Something heavy landed on the floor. Then silence, terrifying moments of silence. Have they been detected? Had anyone heard? Rosa held her body rigid, afraid to move, afraid to breathe.

Cautiously Hans stood up and reached down to help her. Stepping carefully across the shattered shards of glass that cover the floor, he went to the window. Afraid, he held a burning match up to the window.

Rosa handed him the blanket and when the window was covered she lit a candle.

Hunched down over Anthony's rolltop desk, Hans was trying to pry it open with his knife. "There must be a key for it on Anthony's ring," Rosa suggested.

"This has got to look like a robbery", Hans spoke brusquely to her, "otherwise he'll know someone got his keys."

"Sorry I snapped at you, Rosa." He said.

When he was satisfied that the lock looked jammed, he raised the roll top. "Here, see what you can find in here," he turned his attention to Peppino who had come noiselessly into the room.

Inside there were half a dozen neatly stacked ledger books. Each was carefully labeled. Rosa picked up the top one and held it under the glow of the flickering candle. In black letters across the top was "S. F. A. House,". another said, "Clay Street Apartment."

The men in the corner looking at the safe, Hans whispered, "The only thing that will get this open will be dynamite or the combination."

"Leave it alone," Rosa urged, "this is all we need, I've got the ledgers, and here's a bunch of receipts, and an address book. Let's get out of here."

"Alright," Hans said, "come in, Peppino, let's get that rope in place."

They tried to open the broken window, but it had been nailed shut. So piece by piece they removed the broken glass cutting out of the window frame. When the glass was gone, Peppino pushed his body through and stood on the outside ledge. Hans held onto his legs as he loosened the rope from its coil. And with the scale of a practiced sailor, threw the rope up onto the roof of the building. Testing it with his weight Peppino swung his body outward.

"Oh my god!" Rosa cried out, realizing for the first time what they were doing.

"Sh-h-h-h," Hans cautioned her looking apprehensively toward the door, "Don't worry, Rosa, it's nothing for a sailor, they climb ropes all the time."

"But why is he doing it?"

"He has to lower himself and leave scuff marks down the side of the building so they will figure that's how the thief got in and left."

"But why the rope up on the roof?" She asked.

"The only way a thief could get in would be to secure a rope to the roof, shimmy up, and swing over the office window. Understand?"

"Be sure to pick that rock up and get it out of here, it's supposed to look like the rubber kicked the glass in with his feet."

Hans watched Peppino slide down the rope until he was safely on the ground. Then helping Rosa with the books, he hurried her out of the office. He locked the padlock and together they went quietly down the stairs.

No one had heard them and no one had seen them. Rosa leaned up against the building and took a deep breath.

"Oh dear God, I do not think I have ever been that frightened before."

Hans and Peppino stopped to catch their breath.

"That was lucky," Hans said, "a policeman is not supposed to commit robberies! If someone had caught me, I would have been ruined. I'm glad that's over."

Knowing for the first time the risk he had taken for them, Rosa said, "Oh Hans, I never should have let you take such a risk!"

"Well, it is over now, and we are safe. After all, someone has to protect Nina's interests. Her husband doesn't."

"I'd better get these keys back to her before he wakes up," Hans started off. "Hide those books good as soon as you get home."

"I'm going to take them to Enrico's as soon as it is light, he can keep them at the hospital. Anthony will never suspect that."

"No, no! Don't do anything different today. If Anthony drives by and sees something different going on, he could get suspicious. Go to mass as usual, and then go to the hospital this afternoon if you want to."

"I will take the books to the hospital myself after I take the keys back to Nina, you can go to the hospital later at your regular time."

Satisfied with his plan, Hans turned the corner and disappeared.

Rosa felt a great sense of relief that the books would be taken care of. They quickened their pace and by the time they reached the flat, the first signs of dawn were trying to break into the fog.

Inside, Peppino went to comfort the waiting Sylvia.

Rosa looked around for a safe place to hide the ledgers. In the parlor, she stacked them behind the sofa. Almost immediately dissatisfied with the hiding place, she was just about to move them to the kitchen when Paisano barked. Hans was tapping lightly on the door.

"Was everything alright?" Rosa asked.

"Yes," Hans smiled, "Anthony had not stirred at all. I told her to go to the diner late to give him time to discover the break-in."

"Now give me the books and I will deliver them to the hospital, and if I can, I'll stop by this evening and give you a ride home."

With his hand on the doorknob, Hans stopped and looked down at Rosa as if seeing her for the first time.

He smiled. "You are a courageous woman, Rosa. It took a lot of nerve to do what you did tonight." He bent down and kissed her on the cheek.

CHAPTER FORTY-SEVEN

Nina walked down the middle aisle holding her husband's arm. She glanced at Rosa. Everything was as usual for Sunday morning, Anthony did not know.

Rosa heard nothing Father Paul said. Her mind fluttered back-and-forth between their adventure last night and the things that could happen next.

When mass was over, she managed to get away before anyone stopped her to talk.

"But we didn't see Nona! Where's Nona!" Angelina protested as Rosa hurried the twins away from the church and took them straight home.

She gave them their meal and changing her clothes sat down to wait until it was the right time for her to leave for the hospital. She tried to read but could not. She picked up her mending and had almost finished darning all the socks when there was a frantic knocking at the door.

It was Anna. Her hat sat crooked on her head, and her hair was windblown. Rosa saw no carriage outside, "Did you walk?" She asked, bringing her inside.

With a wave of her hand, Anna brushed past Rosa.

"Did you hear? Did you hear what happened?"

Rosa's breath stopped inside of her: "No, what's wrong?" She tried to sound calm.

"Well," Anna led the way into the parlor, "after mass, Thomas took me over to visit the Henderson's- they were having sort of a house warming or something- anyhow, then we went home, and just as we got there the telephone was ringing.

"I heard him talking to someone. His voice got awfully loud, he was really mad. Then he slammed the door shut, and I couldn't tell what he was saying, but something was terribly wrong.

"When he came out, his face was beet-red and he almost walked right into me. I asked him what happened, and he snapped at me and told me to shut up.

"Oh, Rosa, Thomas never used to talk to me like that. Anyhow, I guess he felt sorry he yelled at me because then he told me that someone had broken into Anthony's office and taken a lot of valuable books. Then he said something about the books should have been in the safe."

"Did they steal any money?" Rosa asked.

"No, just some books."

"What kind of books are so valuable that they had to be kept in a safe?"

"That's just what I wondered," Anna said, "I asked Thomas if they were first edition. He looked at me with- with disgust- and told me not to be so stupid. He was really angry. I just don't understand."

"Then he hurried out of the house. He was swearing. It sounded like he was cussing Anthony."

"Did he know who did it?" Rosa asked.

"He said something about chinamen, and about a window, and a rope."

Anna was wringing her hands.

"I don't understand why Anthony called Thomas and why Thomas got so furious at him. They didn't even get money. Thomas said the money was all in the safe. But he was swearing worse than I've ever heard him swear."

"I wonder if Nina knows anything?" Rosa asked, "have you seen her yet?"

"No, I came here first."

Rosa wanted to run to the wharf and see if Nina was safe, but she couldn't. Anthony was sure to be in a rage, and if he saw her, he might somehow connect her with the break-in.

Anna kept talking about Thomas and the way he treated her lately. Holding her head in her hands, she started to weep.

"Oh, Rosa I have never told you these things, but I am so worried about Thomas. He has changed so much in the last few years. He used to be kind and gentle but lately, he's distant. I hardly know him.

"He used to be so calm and easy-going, but now his temper is short. I know there's something on his mind. At night in bed, he thrashes around, and sometimes he even talks in his sleep. Something is bothering him, but I can't get him to tell me what it is, I just don't know what to do.

"He stays out late and thinks I'm asleep when he comes home, but I'm not.

"The tea Lu Chin gives me used to make me so sleepy that lately I've been pouring it into the plants I keep on the window sill. You remember, I told you, it's very bitter. But, Rosa, if Thomas is not there to help make babies…"

Anna blushed, "What good can it do?" Anna dabbed her eyes dry. "Sometimes I feel guilty for not drinking the tea."

Rosa was trying to comfort Anna when she heard a carriage stop outside. Through the window, she saw Lu Chin jump and run out the door. Thomas was in the buggy but he did not get out.

"Missy, missy, Mr. Thomas is here to pick you up. Please come, he in big hurry."

Anna gathered up her purse and her hat that had fallen off. She squeezed Anna's hand and whispered so Lu Chin could not hear, "Please, Rosa, forgive me. I should not have said the things I just did. He is just overworked, that is all. Please just forget everything I said."

She hurried off so not to keep her husband waiting.

Rosa watched as Anna got into the buggy and it drove away. She felt sorry that she could not tell Anna the whole truth. But just by being her friend she had already put her in danger.

CHAPTER FORTY-EIGHT

The cable car rattled and bounced as Rosa tried to concentrate on all that had been happening. Anna kept popping into her mind. Rosa knew Thomas loved his wife, but what had happened to make him so thoughtless and rude to her? What part did he have in the ledgers? What was in them? And most of all, she wondered, was there enough information inside those books to force Anthony to make amends?

Her thoughts bounced back and forth in rhythm with the rocking of the trolley car. She must have dozed off for next she knew the conductor was shaking her shoulder asking her if she wanted to get off.

Enrico was asleep with a ledger open across his chest. Rosa quietly slipped one of the other books from the bed and sat down to have her first look at what she had risked her life for last night.

Inside was a piece of paper with Enrico's writing on it. "222 Ellis St: City directory lists as dwelling. Bordello owned by the A & T Co." Inside a circle was written, "A&T Co. = Anthony and Thomas?"

Tucked into a page labeled, "Daily cash receipts" was another of Enrico's notes: "checks and balance with next opening balance." Rosa could not see what that meant.

She picked up the ledger labeled "S.F.A." Another note said, "City directory lists as private dwelling! Same as the 222 Ellis St." One column labeled "Rent Received" and another read "Rent Paid."

Nothing meant much to Rosa, and as she thumbed through the rest of the book, Enrico stirred and turned to see her.

"What a nice picture you are to wake up to."

He adjusted the pillows and sat up in bed.

"Do you know that you have enough evidence there to put Anthony and Thomas in jail?"

"You have taken the lid off a boiling pot. I have been studying them all morning, and the poor nurses I've been running back-and-forth making telephone calls for me to check out the facts. Did you read the notes I put in the books?"

"Yes, but I don't really understand them."

"What you've got here, Rosa is very dangerous material. It's like having a stick of dynamite in your pocket. It could go off at any time."

A sinking feeling passed over Rosa. She felt weak and uncertain.

"I'm surprised these books were lying out on a desk, they are the books of a big business!"

"They were locked inside his desk," Rosa interrupted. "Hans jimmied the lock to make it look like a burglary."

Enrico grunted, then went on, "You see, Rosa, the way they do this is to keep two sets of books, one so that it looks like everything is honest and pure, and the other so that it tells them the true picture."

"That's what we have here – the real set. There has to be a second set of books somewhere. It seems that Anthony and Thomas own a lot of property together."

"Didn't you tell me that Thomas helped close down a whole street of whore houses?"

"That's what Anna told me," Rosa answered wondering what possible connection there could be.

"From what I can gather, that's exactly what he did. Thomas Page was running for supervisor and in order to get himself elected, he made big promises to clean up our city."

"He staged a massive surprise raid on houses of ill repute. They had the police and the mayor, and all the important people there. Anthony was no doubt in on it too. It was a sneak attack.

"Patrons were running out of the houses buttoning their pants. The girls that didn't get away were loaded in the patty wagon and taken to jail. They closed down the street tight as a drum. Then they put all the property up for sale."

Enrico was getting excited, his cheeks were rosy and his eyes sparkled. "Don't you see? This is how they do it."

Gesturing with his hand he was trying to make her understand. "No one would buy the property, it was an eyesore and the city condemned it. No business wanted to go into that part of town. So Anthony and Thomas quietly formed their company, the 'A & T Co', and went in and bought up the whole block including all the houses!"

"Then after waiting a discrete time, they re-opened the houses. But now they were bigger and more elegant than ever. But," Enrico reached for another book, "this is the clincher," he held up the book, "do you know what the S.F.A. stands for?"

Rosa shook her head no.

"It is our Sacramento street bordello! Yes, my dear Rosa, the church owns a whorehouse!"

"Oh my god in heaven," Rosa gasped.

"Surely Father Paul doesn't know this?"

As she spoke she was remembering how the day he denounced the sinfulness of the city from his pulpit he had gone to Anthony's for supper and praised him for his work on the building fund.

"I doubt very much if Father Paul knows anything at all about what the church owns," Enrico said.

"But the funny part, Rosa," he opened the book, "see this, 'rent received' and then this column, 'rent paid' I think our friend Anthony is cheating the church. He receives that figure," Enrico pointed with his index finger, "and he pays the church with the lower figure. That's why there has to be another set of books- the ones he shows the church."

"Maybe they are in the safe?" Rosa suggested, "or maybe Thomas had them in his office at his home. Do you need them too?"

"No, no, these are the important ones for now. Don't worry, no more break-ins for you." He noticed the look of relief on her face and smiled.

"I knew Anthony was up to something dishonest, but never in my wildest dreams did I think it could be this bad."

"And yes, Rosa, never forget for a moment how dangerous Anthony is, and Thomas too."

He studied her face, "Do you really understand how important it is for you to be very careful?" Worry was deep in his face.

"Yes, I do. I will take no chances." Her voice reassuring.

"That is one of the reasons my brother loves you so, he saw that quality in you, he spoke of it many times."

"That quality?" She asked.

"Yes, the openness of your soul, your honesty, and your spirit- your undying spirit."

"What good do those qualities do me when he is in Italy, and I am in America?" Suddenly overcome with a longing for Aldo, she fought back tears.

As if reading her thoughts, Enrico said, "He loves you, he will not forget. Rosa have faith."

The nurse came in to bring Enrico his dinner.

"Is it getting that late," Rosa said, "perhaps I should leave?"

"That's alright, you're good for him, just make sure he eats all his dinner," the nurse said.

Enrico was finishing the last bite of his bread pudding when Hans came in. He shoved the tray hastily away and said, "Come here, Hans, grab those books and let me show you. You and your detective friends uncovered a boiling pot of crime."

Rosa listened to the two men talk, Enrico going over all the evidence with Hans. She sat back in the chair and closed her eyes.

Overwhelmed with what she knew must lie ahead, she felt the urge to go home, to scoop up Angelina and John Edward and hug them to her breast. She wanted to know peace, to feel safe. Unconsciously fingering in the brooch, she wished Aldo could be at her side.

She heard Hans say, "Of course, so simple, the closing balance here in the beginning balance for the next months don't match!"

"Anthony has not only been cheating the church, he's been cheating Thomas too! One crook cheating another." Enrico laughed.

Rosa broke in, "What can we do now that we have all this information? What are we going to do?"

"Well, whatever we do," Hans said, "we are going to be very careful, these are dangerous men. This is not a child's game."

"Hans, you say the police just turn their backs to the brothels and the opium?" Enrico asked.

"Yes, the laws against them are seldom enforced." There was sadness in his voice.

"What can we do? I thought I would be happy when I finally got the goods on Anthony, now I am more scared than ever," Rosa said. Between the two of them, they have ruined hundreds of lives, and God knows what else they have done!"

"That is it!" Rosa stood up.

"What?" They both looked at her.

"God will help us."

"What do you mean?"

"Tomorrow, I will go to Father Paul and tell him everything. The church will be our way to get Anthony."

"Now wait a minute, Rosa", Hans cautioned, "we have to be careful who we tell. Are you sure you can trust Father Paul?"

"He is the church! If we cannot depend on the church, then what is there at…"

"Well, alright, even though you trust him, he could inadvertently say something to someone."

"You send Father Paul to me." Enrico said, "I will explain everything to him, and show him the books."

"Good idea," Hans said, "Do you feel well enough to do all of this Enrico?" Rosa asked.

"I feel fine. Look at me, I am as fat as a pig. The nurses and the doctors said today that they have not seen such a good color in my cheeks for a long time. I have something to do, I am not bored. I feel fine."

"Now Rosa, you bring Father Paul tomorrow. But don't tell him what this is all about, we don't want him to approach Anthony in any way. Let's just think of him as our ace up our sleeve," Enrico smiled with satisfaction.

"We have to move quickly, the longer it takes, the more chance there is of Anthony finding out who broke into his office. Speed is essential!"

CHAPTER FORTY-NINE

When Hans' buggy rounded the corner, Rosa saw a strange carriage parked in front of her flat. Her heart jumped heavily against her chest, she knew something was terribly wrong. The horse barely stopped, Rosa jumped out and hurried up the stairs.

Sylvia ran to the door saying, "It's Nina, she has been hurt. The doctors with her. She fell at the diner."

Pale and frightened, Nina lay on the bed. A doctor was wrapping her leg.

"What happened, what is wrong?"

"I'm alright, Rosa, do not look so worried. Down the stairs at the boarding house." Nina's voice was weak and thready.

"She'll be fine in a few days," the doctor confirmed. "A little bruised, she may have sprained her ankle. But it's too swollen to be sure, I don't think it's broken." The doctor closed his bag, "she'll have to stay completely off that foot for a few days, but she'll be good as new in no time. I gave her something to help her rest."

Sylvia and Peppino and the twins huddled together in the open doorway. Hans had towered over them all.

Rosa picked up Nina's hand, "What happened?"

Nina looked toward the door and to the twins said, "Come here, give your Nona a hug, I'm fine, do not worry." She kissed them both. "Now run and get ready for bed, and say your prayers."

Nina tried to sit up, "Here let me help you," Rosa propped the pillow up behind her, and winced as she noticed the dark-colored puffiness around her left eye.

"Did Anthony do this to you?"

" No, not really".

"What do you mean, not really?"

"I will tell you," Nina inhaled deeply- summoning up the effort needed to tackle an unpleasant task.

"Anthony discovered the robbery," as Nina began, Rosa beckoned Hans and he came in quietly and sat on a stiff wooden chair in the corner.

"Anthony was upstairs in his office," Nina continued, "he was on the telephone. He was really mad, he was yelling at someone. I went upstairs, the office door was open a crack, and I heard him say something about 'a dumb wop'.

"Then he hung up the phone and before I had a chance to move, he came out into the hall, and when he saw me he was furious.

"I tried to be calm," Nina said, the fear coming back into her eyes. "I asked him what had happened, he was hardly making any sense at all, he said we've been robbed, and he said something about a Chinaman- Thomas' Chinaman.

"I asked him why he didn't call the police, and then he got really mad! He snarled at me, he sounded like a caged animal, and he came at me.

"At first, I thought he was going to hit me, but he just pushed me out of his way. That's when I fell."

"He did push you!" Hans said, unbelieving rage in his voice.

"I don't think it was deliberate. He just pushed me aside and I fell."

"Nina, when are you going to stop defending him?" Rosa asked impatiently. Then, in a more gentle tone, she added, "He doesn't deserve the loyalty of a woman like you."

"The habits of a lifetime…"

Nina looked back up at Rosa and gave her hand a little squeeze.

She continued, "When I landed at the foot of the stairs Giuseppe came running in and Anthony told him it was alright, but for him to get a wagon and take me home. Then he told me again that I was alright, and he left.

"I made Giuseppe take me upstairs to the empty room instead, I want it to be around to find out what I could, and my leg didn't hurt that much yet.

"After a while, Anthony came back and Thomas was with him, and they went into the office and closed the door. I could hear them arguing, and I'm pretty sure that's who Anthony was talking to on the phone. They were in there for a long time and then I heard the door open, and Thomas said something about being more careful, and Anthony called him some kind of a city official, I didn't get the word, but it was no compliment.

"They both went out, and by that time my ankle was beginning to hurt, and I hobbled down the stairs and Mario brought me over here.

Peppino, who had been sitting on the floor asked, "Do you think they have any idea who broke into the office?"

"Anthony seems to think it's the Chinese. He would never think we had brains enough to do something like that".

Sylvia came in with a cup of soup and a piece of bread for Nina, "She needs to rest now, the doctor said."

"Yes, Nina, you eat and rest, we will leave you be." Rosa stood up.

"No!" Nina grabbed her arm, "don't go until you tell me what Enrico said about the books!"

Rosa looked to Hans for help. How much should she tell Nina? Sooner or later she was going to have to hear it all, but now? Now when she is lying here in pain?

Hans came over, "You must try not to get yourself all upset, Nina," he said.

"Tell me! I will get more upset if you don't tell me. Is it bad?" She asked, her voice timid, revealing her fear of knowing the worst.

Together, as gently as they could, Hans and Rosa told Nina what they knew of Anthony's criminal activities.

"I would give anything to be able to spare you this," Hans said as he patted her hand.

"There's just no easy way," Rosa said, "for a woman to hear these things about the man she has spent her lifetime with."

Nina slid down in the bed, and Rosa straightened the covers around her.

"I can remember," she said, "when we first came to San Francisco. We were young and we were happy. We had very little money, and we saved every cent so we could to buy that first boat. Anthony was a good man in those days, and a hard worker. Then we got a boat, and then another, and he seemed to change somehow. We bought the diner, and… Well, you know, Rosa, a little money meant more money, and that's the way it went, he was never satisfied."

"That's enough, now, try to sleep," Rosa said.

As if she had not heard, Nina went on, "He said that all he wanted to do was 'show those people', I never did know who 'those people' were. But he wanted to have lots of money so he could go back to Italy and show it off."

"He always said the way to get rich was to be the middleman, the middleman makes the money, he'd say. Well," Nina said, her voice falling to a whisper, "Anthony is rich and he is the middleman alright, he's right in the middle of everything."

Rosa arrived at church just as Father Paul was finishing his last mass of the morning. She waited for him to come out of the vestry.

"I must talk to you, Father, I have something very important to tell you."

The priest waited.

"I want you to come with me to French hospital…"

"Who is sick?"

"No one is sick, not really. But there is someone there who wants to speak to you. He is ill, but that's not what he wants to see you about."

"Is this person Catholic?"

"Yes Father," Rosa said hoping her disappointment did not show, "he is Catholic, but what he wants to talk about concerns you and the church, and it is really urgent."

Father Paul studied her face. "I don't understand, but if you think it's important, I'll have the buggy around, and we can go now."

CHAPTER FIFTY

Father Paul held the heavy hospital door open for Rosa and hurried to keep up as she walked briskly down the hall.

"What's wrong?" A young nurse called to them, "Has something happened?" She fell into line behind them.

Realizing how they must look, Rosa slowed down her pace and turning to the worried young nurse, assured her that it was no more than a social call.

She slipped quickly into her mask and gown and helped Father Paul tie his in place. Enrico was sitting up in a chair in front of the window, a broad ray of morning light at his back.

"Thank you for coming, Father. This is a very delicate matter I must discuss with you. But first, if I may, I'd like to ask you a few questions."

Father Paul nodded his agreement, although the look in his eyes showed more a mixture of irritation and curiosity.

Skillfully Enrico posted general questions about churches and cities to Father Paul, and as the priest relaxed, and focused the questions in on the church's building fund, and the men who directed it.

"And what is the building fund money invested in?" He asked most innocently.

"An apartment building, I believe," Father Paul said. He explained that the building fund books were kept at the rectory and that Anthony picked them up once a month, in time to give the monthly report.

Father Paul expressed his pride at having two such bright and successful men as Anthony and Thomas on his building fund committee.

Enrico paused to drink the glass of milk the nurse brought in for him.

"Are you going to tell me what this is all about?" Father Paul asked.

"Yes, yes of course," Enrico assured him, "but it is not a pretty story."

Rosa sat back in her chair and listened as Enrico unfolded the story. She watched the color drain from the priest's face and saw his head tilt backward in a hard unmistakable attitude of disbelief.

A cold bath affair swept over Rosa. She had not counted on any resistance from the priest, but Enrico appeared undaunted.

He went on talking quietly and confidently. Selecting a ledger from his nightstand, he laid it open on the bed for Father Paul to see.

Rosa and Enrico silently exchanged glances as the priest studied the books.

Finally closing the ledger with a heavy sigh, he took his glasses off and sank back into the chair.

"What can we do?" He asked with total resignation. Then not waiting for an answer, he went on, "My church owns a building of ill repute?"

"When the bishop and the people of the parish find out how I have allowed the church money to be invested, I will be the laughingstock! All of it is sin money." The priest buried his face in his hands, his shoulders rocked back-and-forth.

Rosa said, "I will get some coffee." When she returned with a tray, Enrico brought out a secret cache of brandy to add to Father Paul's cup.

When he had drained his cup, Father Paul said, "I will have to go before my bishop. He must be told immediately. And the parishioners- they gave their savings- they too must be told." He stood up to leave.

"No, wait!" There was alarm in Enrico's voice, "we must be very careful, if Anthony and Thomas even suspect we have these books, they might- well, I don't know what they might do."

Father Paul sat down.

"I have thought of nothing less all night," Enrico said. Setting his coffee down, he pointed to the stack of ledgers and said, "We could give all this information to the newspaper. The bulletin would love to cover a story like this, particularly about Thomas Page and Anthony. It would give them a good story, and we could let the outrage of the city take care of them both."

"No, no," Father Paul said, "I could not permit parishioners to read about this in the paper. First I have to go to the bishop and tell him, and then Sunday in church I will announce it to the whole parish," Father Paul's voice betrayed the reluctance in his heart.

"No! We cannot wait that long," Rosa said.

"If Anthony should find out we are the ones who took his books. We will not be safe- Nina would be in great danger!"

The sudden image of Nina's swollen blackened eye made her shudder.

"We cannot give Anthony the slightest warning. Yes, that's it! We must all come down upon him at once- before he suspects anything," Rosa's voice became louder as her confidence in the idea increased.

"How could you say that Rosa?" Father asked.

"Father, you are the key to this. If you meet him face to face and tell him you know how the church money is invested..."

"Oh, if only I could get out of here, how I'd love to confront Anthony!" Enrico interrupted.

"Rosa is right, we cannot afford to wait, but he is too dangerous a man for one of you to face alone. There is safety in numbers. Face him as a group, and soon. Anthony and Thomas too, are no doubt right now trying to cover their tracks," Enrico said, "we must set up a meeting with everyone as soon as possible."

"How can we get Anthony to come?" Father Paul asked, looking somewhat like a lost child.

"This is where you come in, Father. Somehow you must convince him to come, tell him it's church business or whatever you need to say, but get him to come."

"Tomorrow Father, tell him tomorrow at 3 o', clock. Offer to come to the diner to meet him," Rosa added.

Father Paul remained motionless, he seemed to be thinking this over. Rosa and Enrico exchanged glances, and agreeing on the priest's lack of decisiveness, Enrico said, "Father perhaps it would be best if you called him from there."

"And ask if Thomas could get there too, but don't insist upon it. Just get Anthony to say he'll come. Try to be casual but make him feel it is important," Rosa said.

Father Paul stood up, "I don't have a telephone at the church house."

"Father," Rosa said, "we need your help. Call from here. The bishop will be pleased to see that you were already correcting the wrong that has been done."

A bit restored, he left the room, and standing up, Rosa took a deep breath, "he is the key man."

"I hope he won't panic, he is confused, he might fall apart."

"No, I don't think so," Rosa said more strongly than she felt, "he is in shock like we were yesterday. But as soon as he realizes the seriousness of all this, how many lives have been touched, he will come through for us."

Rosa silently prayed she was right. Father Paul reached both Anthony and Thomas.

"I told Anthony we had some more church money to invest and I wanted to see him and Thomas about it. I mentioned how well he had done with our other investments." Looking up at the ceiling, father Paul made a sign of the cross in atonement for the lie.

"And Thomas, what did he say?"

"Thomas is busy, he was very polite and said he was sorry but that Anthony could handle it and that they could meet later. I told him that it was important for me, that I really needed a legal mind but I did not want to become too insistent and told him that I understand he was a very busy man. He then said that he would come if he could rearrange his schedule."

"I will see that the fishermen are there," Rosa said.

"Be sure they understand they must not let a hint of it slip out," Enrico said.

"They understand about things like this," Rosa said, "and I will see Hans tonight, he will be there, and Sylvia, she will be there, and Nina of course. We will all be there." Rosa said.

Father Paul walked to the window, and picking up the book from the sill asked, "What is this one? You did not show me this one". He read the title, "Jones Street apartment. Is that another one of the houses?"

"No, that really is a private dwelling." Enrico looked at Rosa. She shrugged her shoulders. "That is the apartment house where Anthony keeps his mistress."

Again the look of disbelief crept onto the priest's face.

"How do you know that?" He snapped.

"We are sure, Father," Enrico spoke gently, "this has all been verified. We have checked records at City Hall. The building is owned by Anthony Orso and a Miss Dolores Porter lives there."

"Miss Dolores Porter", Father Paul said, "is a sinful woman, and she too will be punished."

Hearing the priest's uncompromising judgment of this woman, Rosa felt strangely drawn to her.

She pitied the woman who, like herself, loved a married man. Was there that much difference between them? She thought, if I had given myself to Aldo, as I often wished I had, I too would be the other woman, the mistress.

And Aldo would be here with me instead of in Italy with his wife. I would have someone to lean on. Instead, I am alone.

Whatever lies ahead, I shall have to face it alone.

Father Paul interrupted her thoughts, "I must go, I must hurry to the bishop. Shall I take the ledger with me?" he asked.

"No, that would be too risky. They are the only proof we have, and they are safe here. But if the bishop needs to see them himself, have him come see me."

"I am not going anywhere." He laughed.

"I will tell him," Father Paul said accepting Enrico's decision. "Come early tomorrow, before the meeting, and we will plan."

After the priest left, Rosa said, "Will Anthony believe us? When we confront him will he believe we have his books? He might think we are bluffing, trying to cash in on his burglary."

Enrico thought about this, and then tearing a page from two of the ledgers, he handed them to Rosa, "Here, Rosa, is your proof!"

She folded the pages carefully, "Oh how I wish you could be there with me."

"I wish I could too," he said.

"I've never been involved with anything like this before."

"Do not forget that one cornered, Anthony will be more dangerous than ever. Hans knows, he will stand by you, and Father Paul will help."

"Remember, Rosa, two brothers love you." He smiled his wonderful warm smile and for a moment Rosa forgot what lay ahead.

CHAPTER FIFTY-ONE

Pulling back the curtains from the bay window, Rosa watched the street for Father Paul. He had promised to come early to tell her what the bishop said and to plan how best to confront Anthony. Now there were twenty minutes left and no sign of him.

"Dear God, she said aloud, please help me through this day."

Telling Peppino to go ahead with Nina and Sylvia in the buggy, Rosa decided to walk. With every step, she prayed that Father Paul would overtake her.

But she had turned the last corner before the priest's buggy pulled in front of her. She stepped out briskly, and he tipped his hat to her, took her by the arm, and said, "I hope we're not late."

She stopped and pulled him to a halt: "Father, what did the bishop say? We've not had time to talk, to plan…"

"Sh-h-h-h, there, there, now don't you worry your little head about it. I'll take care of everything," he tried to move her on toward the diner.

She desperately wanted to put her trust in this man of the cloth and believe that everything would be taken care of, but there was something in his tone, in his manner, that made this impossible.

"What did the bishop say?" she repeated, "did he see Enrico?"

"Yes, yes, we went there this morning. Now, now, do not worry, everything is taken care of."

The priest's voice had become stern, and the pressure on her arm increased. They were at the diner. Father Paul held the door open for her.

The room seemed empty. In the corner, silent and motionless, a group of fishermen sat huddled together. The window shades were drawn, and the room was bathed in an eerie, foreboding silence. None of the usual sounds of cooking came from the kitchen nor any of the familiar smells.

As if they were one physical bean, the group of men looked up but remained silent. At the long table up against the wall, Nina sat flanked on either side by Sylvia and Peppino. The three leaned back, their arms resting on the table before them.

Hans came in. He was wearing a dark blue business suit. Nodding to Rosa and the priest, he went straight to Nina's side.

The room was deathly quiet, with only the sound of the sea outside. There was no noise coming from upstairs, dear God, she thought, what if he's not up there?

"It is time, Father," Rosa said, "for you to go up and bring Anthony down."

The door from the street opened and an older woman in a blue cape over a white dress looked in. She seemed familiar, but Rosa could not think where she had seen her. The woman stepped into the room, and behind her was a tall, well-dressed man in a gray suit. He removed his hat and look straight at Rosa. An electrifying surge of excitement sped through her! Aldo! Clapping both hands to her mouth, she muffled a cry.

But no, it was not Aldo. my God, she thought, it is Enrico! She knew the woman – from the hospital- she was the nurse. The woman took a seat at the far corner of the room, and Enrico made his way to Rosa.

Father Paul came down the stairs and stepped into the room. Behind him, Anthony paused one foot on the bottom step. He surveyed the room. A mixture of surprise and anger covered his face.

Mario moved to block the doorway.

Tension filled the room.

Rosa looked to Father Paul. He did not meet her glance.

"What is going on here?" Anthony asked.

No one answered. Again Rosa looked to the priest, and again he evaded her.

Anthony strolled arrogantly around the room. He studied every face and stopped in front of the man he did not know.

Enrico bowed slightly and said, "Good afternoon, sir."

Ignoring his greeting, Anthony turned his back and asked, "what's going on here?"

No one answered.

At the far table, Father Paul sat uncomfortably, as if in a chair of thorns. He looked out the window.

Rosa looked to Enrico. He leaned down and whispered, "We had better not count on him."

A dryness in her throat like sand, her stomach burned.

553

She felt a strange mixture of excitement and fear. She heard herself say, "Sit down, Anthony, Father Paul has something to say."

His face white, and looking like a trapped animal, Father Paul shook his head no. His hands moved back and forth in front of him trying to make her go away.

"Father, please!" She urged.

Reluctantly he stood up, and avoiding Rosa's eyes, went to the front of the room. He spoke in a barely audible voice.

"We are all proud to be part of the splendid congregation of our fine Saint Francis of Assisi church. As I look about before me here today, I recognize almost all of these faces- some I see too seldom."

He paused for the polite ripple of laughter.

"In these troubled times, we must always be ready to reach out and help those of us less fortunate, and we should count on our blessings, to be here next to this beautiful sea, a sea of plenty, where all we have to do is drop in our nets and God provides…"

Enrico whispered, "He's not going to do it. The bishop must have told him not to say anything, afraid of the publicity. You'll have to be the one to do it, Rosa."

Enrico was right, Father Paul had his chance, and he let her down. She looked at the smug expression on Anthony's face and listened to the sanctimonious phrases flowing glibly from Father Paul's mouth.

Holy mother, Mary of Jesus, she thought, if I don't do something, everything will be wasted. All our efforts, all the wrongs, will stay and Anthony will go on his merry way!

Rosa stood up and filling her lungs with air, pulled herself up as tall as she could. She moved to the front, and placing herself in front of the priest and next to Anthony, she turned to face the room:

"Anthony", she started, "each person in this room has a grievance against you."

Everyone gasped.

"First of all, the contracts you have with the fishermen are not fair, and we know that they are also illegal."

Mario stood up. "Damn right!" He said, pulling a bunch of folded papers from his back pocket. "These contracts here are no good! You made us sign pieces of paper we didn't understand! They are worthless."

Holding them high above his head he tore them in half and let the pieces flutter to the floor.

Anthony sneered at Mario. "Do you think that tearing up the copy of those contracts is going to change anything? Well, it won't. I have the originals you signed, and you still owe me money, and there's no way you're going to get out of paying."

"Excuse me, sir," Enrico stood, "you are mistaken. These contracts have been declared invalid, and as far as the law is concerned, these men are no longer in your debt."

Anthony glared at Enrico. Then turning away from the taller man, he looked down at the seated fisherman, "You ungrateful bastards, I'll take every one of your damn boats away and you'll never sell another catch around here! You'll have to sell to the chinks."

He stared at Mario, trying, without success, to intimidate him.

"Alright, Mario," Rosa waited while the sturdy fisherman took his place among the others.

Anthony started to leave.

"Please wait," Rosa said.

"There is more?" He's sneered but sat down again.

"Not only have you cheated the fisherman," she said, "but you have sold your own countrymen into slavery".

Anthony mocked her, "slavery?"

Alfredo, the carpenter, stood. He took off his hat and holding it in front of him, said, "I would like, I have something to say," his voice trembled.

Anthony spit on the floor. "You expect me to sit here and listen to some stupid Italian who can't even read or write?"

Mario stepped forward threateningly, "you have been doing all the thinking for years, now you listen."

"Go on Alfredo," Rosa said softly.

"Mr. Orso, here," Alfredo continued, "he arranged for my passage. I come from very poor village. Very poor," he repeated, "and this agent he come one day to our village."

"He say he will pay our passage to New York and train trip across America too. Then, he says, when we get to San Francisco this Mr. Orso will meet us and give us jobs building boats, and then after we work for him just a little while to pay back passage, then will be free. Just like that," Alfredo snapped his fingers. "I think that was a good idea. I bring my sister with me. We both come, that was five years ago. I still owe for passage. I never get enough money to pay back."

"Why don't you quit then, Alfredo?" Rosa prompted.

"He," and he looked at Anthony, "he says if I don't pay, he will send me back. Things are bad over there in Sicily, so every month, I owe him more money." Alfredo looked as if he might cry, "and I don't even know where my little sister is."

"What happened to her?" Rosa asked.

"I don't know. Anthony says he gave her a job, but I never see her again. All I know is she is in the valley working. She can't read or write, me neither, so I don't know how to find her. Maybe she is dead. I do not know."

"I was supposed to send money for my brothers, but I have no money. I am good Carpenter, I work hard, but," and he shrugged his shoulders.

Alfredo pointed to the three other men Rosa did not recognize. "This here is Antonio, Roberto, and Pietro. They are working for him too, same thing, he bleeds them dry."

The three men shook their heads yes, and like a huge wave on the ocean, I dawn rolled across the room.

"That's just the beginning," Rosa raised her voice, "there is more."

"We all know about your house on Sacramento Street, and the ones on Ellis and Pine. Yes, we know that your so-called apartments are really houses of prostitution!"

Again the noise rose up like a swell in the ocean, until Mario, with arms raised, came to the front of the room and quieted the men.

"We all know about the gambling and the opium," and she signaled Peppino to get up. He faced Anthony, a smile on his lips.

"I'll be damned! You said you were a real estate broker from Los Angeles. You bastard!" Anthony cursed.

Peppino laughed and the room buzzed with approval.

Rosa said, "And we know about the slavery, selling innocent immigrants into prostitution."

Hans and Peppino stood up in unison, studying Sylvia between them. No longer hiding her identity behind men's clothes, Sylvia was dressed in a pale lime green dress which hung loosely on her frame and provided a sallow background to the reluctance in her eyes.

Anthony studied the girl for what seemed a long time, and when finally a sign of recognition crossed his face, he sloughed it off and said, "Just another whore."

With murder in his eyes, Peppino lunged at Anthony, but Hans' quick grasp held him back.

Recognizing Hans as his border, Anthony said, "Jesus Christ! You're in on this too, who the hell are you, another lawyer?"

"No," Hans answered, "I am Officer Nelson, San Francisco police force."

Anthony turned to Nina. "You knew he was a policeman! You did this to me, to your husband. You will burn in hell for this!"

Instinctively Nina cringed. Then from some long silent inner source, a strength flowed into her. She straightened up and looked him right in the eye, "I am not the one who will burn in hell."

Sneering, Anthony tilted his chair backward onto two legs, "Talk is nothing, you can't prove a thing." It was more a question than a statement of fact.

"We have all the proof we need," Rosa reached into her pocket and pulled out the carefully folded sheets torn from the ledger. Smoothing them out, she held them up for Anthony to see.

His face drained of all color, he stood up. Mario placed a heavy hand on his shoulder and pushed him back down into his chair. Beads of perspiration broke out on his forehead, the smug look disappeared from his face.

"Where did you get...?"

"From the ledger of the A&T company..." Rosa started.

Anthony jumped up, the chair fell to the floor, "You damn slut, you robbed my office. You are the thief. It was you, you bitch!" He grabbed for her.

"Sit Anthony!" Mario commanded, "and shut your damn dirty mouth. You are here to listen."

Rosa sensed victory. She had broken through to Anthony! No longer afraid, her voice became strong and steady.

"All your activities are known to us. We know about Thomas Page too, and his part in all of this!"

"We know too that the church building fund is a fraud," Rosa looked at Father Paul still hoping that he would say something, but he sat in silence, his lips pulled tight. A pulse pounded in his temples.

"The bishop has been told. He knows where you and Thomas invested the church's money!"

Anthony interrupted, "I didn't hear the church complain when they took the money," he scolded at Father Paul.

"Well, they're complaining now," Rosa said, "now that they know you invested their money, the church money, in a whorehouse!"

The fishermen were on their feet. Loud talk, curses, and threats against Anthony turned the room into angry confusion.

"One more thing," Rosa said raising her voice above the noise, "we invited Mr. Page to be here today, but he declined. We know that you have been cheating Thomas too, and..." The sudden bravado on Anthony's face belied his fear.

"... And when we show him these," she waved the ledger sheets at him, "he will have plenty to say to you."

"You don't scare me..." Anthony snarled at her, "what do you think you're going to do about it? Slap my wrists?"

"We have made up a list of demands," Rosa spoke in a calm, controlled voice. "We're giving you a choice Anthony, if you agree to what we ask, we will do everything we can to help you, but if you do not agree..."

"There's nothing you can do to me!" Anthony spoke with the self-righteousness of a guilty man.

"If you do not agree, then," Rosa went on, "we will turn you over to the police, and these ledgers will go to the newspapers. These books will tell the whole story." Anthony listened.

"Here are the demands. The fishermen's contracts are to be torn up and considered paid. The houses are to be closed, and the girl's given train fare back to wherever they came from."

"No more selling opium, no more gambling houses or selling liquor, nothing illegal."

The fishermen stood up and cheered.

"Is that all?" Anthony struggled to stand up. The hatred in his eyes was frightening.

"The choice is up to you." Rosa inwardly recoiled from the intensity of his anger. "You either agree to these demands, or we will turn you over to the police."

Anthony suddenly stood up and stared at Nina, "It is you! You are ruining me," and to Rosa, he said, "your aunt will end up in the poorhouse, and you'll be begging for bread."

Nina pleaded, "Anthony, we could start over. We did it once, we could do it again, please Anthony," Nina held both arms out to him.

Anthony glared at her, "Start over with you? You are nothing but an embarrassment to me. You're an ignorant peasant, I should have left you in Italy."

All hope sucked out of her, Nina slumped back down into the chair.

"You will regret this day, the day you turned against me! I have power," Anthony was screaming, "I have friends in high places! By tomorrow all of you, the whole damn bunch will be out in the street begging. Not one of you is worth a damn thing without me. You are all nothing but a bunch of damn wood. Damn dumb dogs!"

Screaming and straining against the hands that held him, Anthony's eyes filled with rage and hate, and the veins on his temples stuck out. Sweat poured down his face.

"And you, you damn whore," Rosa did not back off, "I will kill you!"

He spit in her face.

Nina who, unnoticed, had come forward, stepped in front of her husband and with the fingers of her tiny white outstretched hand, slapped him hard across the face.

Stunned by the attack of his mate, he focused his rage on Rosa, "This is all your fault!" Lunging, he pushed her to the floor. All the men rushed to help her, and in the confusion, Anthony escaped out the door.

CHAPTER FIFTY-TWO

The door to the diner burst open onto the street as Mario and all the fishermen crowded through in pursuit of the fleeting Anthony. He leaped into a waiting buggy. Snatching up the whip, he snapped it mercilessly across the back of the waiting horse.

The startled animal bolted. Lunging out into the busy street, he crashed head-on into an oncoming brewery wagon. The two screaming horses reared up words, eyes wide with terror.

The heavy beer wagon climbed up over the broken buggy while frothing streams of beer and ale spewed out of splintering barrels. The driver of the beer wagon was thrown up into the air, and landing upon his feet, sat dazed on the stone street.

A loose wheel wobbled crazily off across the roof cobblestones. Broken wagon parts flew into the air, and pieces of wood and metal showered down upon the wreckage. The brewery horse broke away and ran.

Anthony's horse fell over backward splintering the shaft and landing dead center on top of the shattered buggy. The twisting harness held him tight between the broken shaft.

His iron shod feet flailed about as he tried desperately to get his footing. But each frantic motion of his hooves grabbed not the

Stone Street, but the unconscious flesh of Anthony Orso pinned beneath the wreckage.

Nina hopped on her good foot, frantically trying to reach the wreckage.

Rosa caught her, grabbed her by the shoulders, "Stop! Nina! No! Don't go in there!"

The sound of a gunshot exploded through the confusion and everything stopped in a vacuum of silence. From his hidden holster, Hans had taken his service revolver and with deadly aim, had placed one bullet into the brain of the threshing animal.

The nurse reached Anthony first.

"Is he dead?" Nina screamed. The white skin of his face, turned upward toward the ground, was bloody. His neck and chest pinned beneath a broken shaft. The nurse knelt beside him, and raising a hand, said, "he's alive, but barely."

Father Paul, his prayer book in his hand, knelt to pray over Anthony's unmoving form.

Men came with ropes. They bound the horse's hind legs together and slipped lines across the animal's bloody chest. Cussing and panting and pulling together on the ropes, the men moved the carcass from the wreck, while others rolled the remains of the buggy off Anthony.

Curious drivers stopped to see what happened. Men climbed up into the nearest wagon and began throwing his load out to clear space for the injured man. The driver, ready to fight to protect his cargo, jumped to the street only to be stopped dead in his tracks by the sight of Anthony's blood-soaked body.

Taking control of his horse and wagon, he started shouting orders. The nurse knelt down beside Anthony while Hans and Peppino slid a canvas under his body. A man at each corner, they lifted his motionless form and placed him in the waiting wagon.

Others helped the nurse up into a place beside him. Hans swung himself up alongside the driver, and turning back to Rosa, said, "Follow us- St. Mary's hospital."

Their buggy following close behind, Rosa and Enrico held onto Nina whose eyes never went straight from the wagon in front of them, not knowing whether her husband was alive or dead.

Rosa squeezed Nina's hand, and whispered, "He'll be alright." But Nina gave no sign of hearing. Rosa felt a hand on her shoulder and looked up into a reassuring glance from Enrico.

Father Paul, followed closely by Sylvia and Peppino, rushed into the hospital waiting room, and as soon as he found out where they had taken Anthony, he rushed off, muttering something about last rights.

For a long time, they waited in silence, Peppino and Sylvia, Enrico and Rosa, each wishing they could spare Nina the pain they knew she was going through.

The door to the emergency room opened and Enrico's nurse came out.

Her clothes wrinkled and bloody, she looked exhausted. Enrico hurried to her side, "Here, Mrs. Larson, sit down for a minute", he helped her to the bench.

"I should get you back," she said in a breathy voice.

"How is he, what are they doing in there?" Nina stood above her.

"They are doing everything they can," she said,

Peppino brought some coffee for her, and taking it with a grateful smile, Mrs. Larson said, "I'll just take a sip, we must get back."

"In a moment," Enrico spoke gently, "give me a minute, you rest."

He signaled Rosa. A few steps down the corridor, he said, "I don't want Nina to hear, but I must tell you about the bishop."

"He came this morning, you know. He listened to the whole story. Then, when I finished and looked to him to tell us what to do, all he said was that no one must hear about this. He wanted no publicity on the matter. If Rome would find out about this, he said, he would be transferred. He said the church would handle the matter quietly, in their own way. I argued with him. I told him there was more involved here than the church, but he would not budge."

"Then he said he was going to see Anthony and Thomas! I pleaded with him not to give away our hand, and he finally agreed, reluctantly, saying he would let Father Paul handle the whole thing. Well, I knew we were in trouble right there."

"How did you ever get them to let you come?" Rosa asked.

"I had no way to get hold of you and time was running out. I went to the front desk and told the nurse it was a matter of life or death that I had to get to the wharf before 3 o'clock. They said absolutely not."

"Oh, Enrico, did you come without their permission?"

"Well, I told them I was going to go no matter what they said, and finally the nurse talked to the doctor and he said I could go if Mrs. Larson went with me and if I promised to be back before supper."

Rosa studied his face and for the first time realized how pale he looked, and noticed circles under his eyes.

"Oh, Enrico, and all this is too much for you, let's sit down."

"I suspected Father Paul would have instructions to avoid a confrontation at all costs and to try to smooth matters over. I was

565

also not sure that the bishop wouldn't go ahead and see Anthony or Thomas and blow the whole thing. I just had to be here in case you needed me."

"I don't know what I would have done without you when Father Paul didn't follow through, I thought for sure the whole thing was lost."

"And, Rosa, there is something else…" Enrico stood. The lines on his face appeared to deepen. He said, "I gave the story to the newspapers." He waited.

"But we were going to give Anthony a chance to make things right…" Rosa looked at him for a reason.

"I know," Enrico explained, "but remember, there I was at the hospital, no way to reach you and not knowing what the bishop was going to do, I figured we just couldn't afford to take a chance. If the bishop had gone to them first, or if Anthony or Thomas found out – the whole thing would have been ruined. There was too much involved here to take the chance."

"Yes", she said, after thinking it over, "I can see that, and now the whole thing is bound to come out anyhow."

"And Rosa, there's one more thing. You better get Thomas's wife down here and tell her about the newspaper story. I think it's going to be a terrible shock."

The revived Mrs. Larson came toward them.

Enrico went to Nina and holding out his hand said, "I am sorry but I must leave. If there is anything I can do…" Nina smiled weakly at him.

Rosa walked to the front door with him, "When I find out how Anthony is, I'll let you know. I'll get a message to you at the hospital."

When they had gone, Rosa sat down next to Nina. Taking hold of her shaking hand, she tried to comfort her.

Nina looked at her dumbly. "He put himself above the church, above God, and now he may be dead." Her voice faltered.

Hans came toward them.

Nina asked, "Is he dead? Why won't they let me in?"

Rosa broke in, "Is he… Is he?"

"He's alive," Hans said, "he's hanging on."

"Will he die?" Nina asked, with no emotion in her voice.

I don't know, Hans took Nina's hand and held it. They sat in silence.

Finally, the doctor came out, and hurried Nina toward him, "How is he doctor?"

"Sit down, Mrs.Orso. Your husband is fighting for his life. He's unconscious. He has a concussion, the horse's hooves struck him on the temple, and we have no way of knowing how bad it will be. His neck has been crushed, and his larynx is severely damaged."

"His larynx?" Nina repeated.

"His voice box," the doctor explained. "The part of the throat that lets him talk. I'm afraid he will never be able to speak again. Maybe in time, he will be able to make some noises but nothing that could really be understood."

"Will he live?" Rosa asked.

"I cannot say, the doctor answered. We are doing everything we can possibly do for him. It's in God's hands now."

"Can I see him?"

"In a little while, the nurse will call you when you can go in. If you would like something to eat, Mrs. Orso, speak to the nun at the front desk and she'll get something for you."

"Go", Rosa said, "you have to keep up your strength, Nina."

Rosa asked the nun for a tray, and coming back, she noticed the door to the chapel. Although she felt no desire to pray for Anthony's life, she went inside.

CHAPTER FIFTY-THREE

Standing before the statue of the Madonna, Rosa blew out her match and watched the tiny flame of the votive candle fight for its life. She bowed her head. *Because of me, Anthony is fighting for his life. Because of me, Nina may be left all alone.* Rosa fingered her rosary beads. *Dear God, forgive me for all the pain I have caused.*

A muffled cough and Rosa realized she was not alone in the dark in the chapel. In the corner, Father Paul got up and made the sign of the cross as he turned to leave. Seeing her, he stopped, but not wanting to intrude upon her privacy, remained silent. The pain in his face, in his eyes, cried out to her for forgiveness.

He looked so tired and so old, that a twinge of pity shot through Rosa.

She followed him. At the holy water font, they spoke. "Are you all right, Father?"

They sat in the back of the chapel. His voice barely audible, he said, "Rosa, I am so sorry for what happened."

Thinking he was referring to Anthony's accident, she was surprised when he added, "I let you down. I let all those poor fishermen down. I let myself down."

The disappointment and anger she had felt for him when he failed to stand beside her and face Anthony, turned to pity.

Beside her now, sat not a godly reproduction of Christ, but a flesh and blood man, whose spirit had been crushed by the folly of his own humanness.

He was talking ",… You, a mere wisp of a woman standing up in front of all those men…courage… facing evil…"

Rosa's Thoughts drifted back so many years ago. She hurt again, the anger in mother superior's voice turning her out of the convent because she did not have 'the calling.'

Was mother superiors anger as Rosa had always thought, the disappointment of God? Or was it perhaps, more simply, the anger of a single flawed human being?

Blowing his nose, Father Paul continued "… My silence, my lack of courage, as simple as Anthony's… As guilty as any sinner."

"We take vows of obedience, but not until I looked at this altar with Christ hanging on the cross did I remember that I have only one divine being to answer to. And I, like Peter, denied him."

He got up and without a word walked down the hall. He reached into his pocket and wiped his eyes with his handkerchief, "I must look in on Anthony," he said.

Outside was a dark, moonlit spring evening, and Rosa felt a great need to breathe deeply of the cleansing sea air. But she turned instead and went back to be with Nina.

A nurse came out of Anthony's room, "You may go in now, for just a moment, the doctor has given him a sedative, do not stay too long."

She laid a bundle of clothes on the empty chair. "This is everything he had."

Nina shuddered as she looked at the bloody bundle. Rosa stepped forward, "These clothes are worthless, I'll discard them." On top of the clothes was an envelope with the contents of Anthony's pockets, his bills folded, a bunch of keys, his gold watch and chain, and his diamond stick pin. She handed them to Hans, "Please, hold these things, take care of them for Nina."

"Come with me please, Rosa. I am afraid."

A small light hung above the bed. A deathly quiet filled the room. Only the rasping sound of Anthony's breathing could be heard.

Nina spoke softly and touched his arm. His eyes fluttered open, and when, finally, he recognized his wife, he opened his mouth to speak. No sound came. Anger colored his face and his whole body struggled against his fearful impotence. He tried to raise his hand, but wide leather straps kept him from tearing away the bandages and the tube in his throat.

Exhausted, Anthony lay back. Expressionless, his skin gray, his eyes sank deep into their sockets.

The nurse stepped silently into the room, and seeing Anthony's closed eyes, took his pulse and signaled them to leave.

Outside she said, "You should go home now, Mrs. Orso, and get some rest. We will let you know if there is any change."

Rosa and Hans walked with Nina toward the front entrance. They arrived while Peppino was tethering the horse. Anna was not with him.

On the way home, he told her he had gone to get Anna, and was met at the door with a belligerent Thomas.

"I told him that I would like to see Mrs. Page, that I had a message from Mrs. Rosa Dante. He was gruff. No," Peppino reconsidered, "he was downright rude."

"He told me she was asleep, that she was not well, and could not be disturbed. He offered to take a message. I thought it best not to say more. I told him that Mrs. Dante would contact her when she was feeling better."

"He practically slammed the door in my face. He definitely did not want to stand there talking, that was obvious."

Peppino pulled a horse to a halt in front of Nina's flat. She would stay the night with Rosa and stopped only to pick up her night things.

They all helped her in. Rosa opened the heavy drapes in the parlor. When the beams of moonlight lit up the room, she wondered if from now on there would be darkness or light in this room, in Nina's room, in Nina's life.

Wandering idly around the room, Hans', attention was drawn to the mantle by moonlight glimmer on a silver picture frame. Picking it up, he stepped to the window to examine it more closely. "This is a beautiful piece of silver carving," Hans said. "Not like the crude wood carving I like to do."

In the kitchen, they could hear Nina talking. "Here, this is what I wanted." In one hand she carried her bundle of clothes, and in the other, a crystal decanter. She handed the bottle to Peppino, "Take that, I think we will all need it when we get back to the flat."

Holding the picture, Hans came into the kitchen and asked, "Nina, what are these numbers on the back?"

"Anthony told me that they were reordered numbers. Why do you ask?"

"It seems strange somehow."

Rosa came over and looked at the numbers. "Look," Hans said, putting the picture face down on the kitchen table, "23-14-17-0-5."

"They don't look funny to me, just numbers," Nina added.

"That's exactly what's funny about it," Hans said, "no name or address, just numbers. It is odd."

Unconcerned, Nina said, "I am ready," and started to leave.

"Wait!" She called out, hobbling back to the parlor, she put Anthony's picture back on the mantle and enclosed the heavy green drapes. The room was as it had been before.

The twins, already in their night clothes, heard the buggy drive up and were waiting for them at the top of the stairs.

Shyly, unsure of how they should act or what they should do, they looked up to Nina for a hug. "How is uncle Anthony?" They asked.

"He is very sick," their mother said. "We will have to wait to find out how he is."

Sylvia made a pot of stew and smelling it, Rosa realized how long it had been since she had eaten.

They ate in silence.

After dinner, Rosa poured Nina a small glass of brandy, "It will help you sleep," she said and helped her aunt to bed.

When Rosa came back, the others, still sitting at the table, were talking over all that happened that day. Hovering over all the talk was a sense of tragedy, and almost disbelief in the way things have turned out.

Again beset with worry that she should not have stirred things up, Rosa became quiet.

573

Seeming to sense her mood, Peppino stood up, and said, "Let us look at the brighter side, at the successful break-in we staged."

He raised his glass, "We do make a pretty damn good combination!" He raised his glass of brandy to his lips.

Hans jumped to his feet. "That's it!" He yelled, "Of course! How stupid of me! That's it!" They stared at him in silence.

"These numbers! I knew I had seen numbers like this before! This is the combination to the safe, to Anthony's safe!"

Hans patted the table with delight, "How clever he is to keep this at home, in broad daylight, too."

"Of course," Rosa said, "come, let us go now and try to open it."

She got up, "this will be easy, this time we have the keys."

"Wait until morning. Wait until morning," Peppino said, getting up to dry the dishes Sylvia was washing.

Hans said, "No, in the morning I have to be at work. I have already missed today, come on Peppino we will go down now."

Hans stood, "Rosa, maybe we should ask Nina, or should she come with us?"

"No, there is no need to disturb Nina. She has had enough for one day." She added, "and I will stay here and help Sylvia with the dishes. I'll try to fill in for Peppino."

CHAPTER FIFTY-FOUR

"**S**tanding here with you doing this simple, everyday job of washing dishes," Rosa said, "I can hardly believe all the terrible things that have happened this day." A sadness closed in upon her.

Sylvia put her hand on Rosa's arm. "Do not be sad, Anthony is not worth it."

"I am not sad for Anthony, but for Nina, and for Anna. What is going to happen to them?"

"I often wonder why it is that good people like them get hurt so much."

"God is punishing Anthony, Anthony, and Thomas both. They hurt so many. We'll never know all the lives they have ruined. I wonder how many girls there were, how many girls weren't lucky like me?"

"If it hadn't been for Hans... I owe my life to him, and I don't think I ever really thanked him."

"It is thanks enough for him to see you blossom the way you have done. I am sure that is enough for Hans."

"And you and Peppino have helped me more than I can ever tell you. For him to understand as he has... If he hadn't, I would never have come through all this."

Silently Sylvia scrubbed the pan she had cooked the stew in.

When it was put away, she turned shyly to Rosa, and began, "Even now," and her face reddened, "I dread the thought of a man touching me. I do not know if I will ever..." And her voice faded away.

"I love Peppino, but I don't know if I will ever again feel like a whole woman."

Rosa's mind saw an instant image of Father Joseph groping at her, and even now, after all these years, she shivered. But to Sylvia, she said, "The time will come. When you are with someone you truly love, it will be alright. Do not rush it. I know Peppino truly cares for you. You will know when the time comes."

"Thank you, Rosa. You are good to me. You are like a mother to me."

She hung up her dishcloth and left the room.

Rosa sat heavily down at the table. Paisano wandered over and positioned himself at her feet, his nose on her lap. Unconsciously she stroked his head.

The pure, unconditional love in his eyes made Rosa feel very much alone. Paisano started barking and Rosa heard Sylvia hurry down the hall to the door.

Hans and Peppino came into the kitchen with two metal boxes.

"That was the combination," Hans replied. "We got it right open."

"There were lots more things inside," Peppino said, "but we just brought the most important."

Nina hobbled into the kitchen, pulling her robe closed around her. "I heard Paisano barking, what is the…?"

Questioningly she glanced at the two men with their coats still on.

Explaining their mission, Hans helped her across the room, and pulling a chair out for her, asked, "Do you need something to rest your foot on?"

The concern in his voice did not go unnoticed. Peppino left the boxes on the table and Hans handed Nana the keys.

"These belong to you, you should be the one to open them." The key in her hand, Nina hesitated.

Rosa could see the doubt, the fear, in her eyes. To open Anthony's private papers, and without his permission? A fearful thing for a woman born in Italy and raised under the doctrines of the Catholic Church.

Reassured by those who waited silently, Nina turned the key. Inside were six tightly packed, bound piles of paper money. She lifted one stack out and set it on the middle of the table.

Peppino let out a long, soft whistle. Ruffling the edges of the paper money with his thumb, he said, "My God, it's all hundreds!"

As if in shock, they all remained silent while Nina replaced the money in the box and turned the key in the lock.

The second box was filled with official looking papers all neatly folded. "What are these?" Nina asked. Seemingly overcome with the enormity of their find.

"Legal documents," Rosa said, "you're going to need help to understand all of this. You'll have to find someone to manage Anthony's business until he gets well."

"Yes", Peppino said, "some of these things can wait, but you should have a man down on the wharf to run the fishing fleet, someone who knows the business."

"These are deeds to property," Hans said, "here's one in the name of the A & T Co. There are so many," he spread the documents out on the table in front of him. "These will take some study."

Handing one to Peppino to look at, he opened another.

Oppressed by so many new and unfamiliar responsibilities, Nina sighed heavily. From the bottom of the box, she took a small package of hand-addressed letters.

Nina looked up at Rosa, and hands, trembling, removed a letter from his envelope. "Dolores Porter, that's her, isn't it?" Nina asked, knowing the answer.

"It's been going on longer than I thought," she said, her voice devoid of emotion.

Gently, Rosa took the letter from her, and replacing it in the box said, "Later, Nina, there will be time for that letter."

Peppino had opened another package. There were receipts from a dress shop and for furniture. There was also a man's gold watch. Inside the back cover, it read, "Anthony from Dolores. Christmas, 1879."

Mechanically handling each item, Nina said little. She took a dainty gold chain from its velvet case. On the end was a teardrop shaped lavaliere, its center lavender stone surrounded with small sparkling diamonds.

The full force of her husband's infidelity came down upon her at once, and barely able to control her fingers, she tried to put the pendant back into its case. Hans got up and taking it from her, returned it to its case.

"Anthony may have known stones, but he surely did not know women."

He rested his hand gently on her shoulder.

Nina looked up at Hans, gratitude lessening some of her suffering. Rosa handed Nina a heavy chamois sack from the bottom of the box.

Untying the drawstring, she turned it upside down. They stared. Gold coins rolled out across the table. Nina picked up a single gold piece, and holding it between her thumb and index finger, said, "Someday, we will all have supper at the palace hotel."

In the morning, when the last loaf of bread was finally on the delivery truck, Rosa sat down for the first time.

She heard Nina approach. Still favoring her ankle, her gait was unmistakable.

They sat together at the little table behind the store, and looking around, Nina said, "You have done well, here, Rosa. From nothing you have built up a good business."

"Not alone, Nina," Rosa said, "I have had many people helping me."

"Yes, and now I need help," Nina said. "All last night I lay awake wondering what I am going to do. I know nothing about running the fishing business. I know nothing about Anthony's other businesses. I have made a decision. I want you to send for Victor and Dino."

"Send for them?" Rosa repeated needing time to fully comprehend.

"You promised them a year on their own, you said, and that year is more than up. Am I right?"

579

"Yes, of course, you are right," surprise had turned to excitement. The thought of having her two sons close to her filled Rosa with a giddiness.

"You say they are good boys? Yes? Well, they had their try and now it is time for them to come. Write and tell them we need them. I want them to take over the fishing business for me. Do you think they can do it?"

"Yes. I know they could. They are hard workers, and very smart, you will see, they are good boys. I will write to them this evening," Rosa said.

"No! Write now! I want you to get go see Mr. Fugazi and arrange for their passage. And I want you to bring them here first-class!" She set a bundle of paper money down in front of Rosa.

"I do not want them sweating down there in the bottom of the ship the way Anthony brought me here, and the way you and the twins came. No! They are to come first-class."

"You do that right now and then you write to them."

Inside a building that looked like a bank, Rosa waited in Mr. Fugazi's office.

A stout, balding little man, he came in and tossing his newspaper on his desk, looked intently at Rosa.

She introduced herself and reminded him of the time they had met through Anthony one Sunday after mass.

"Can you arrange for my sons' passage to America? They are in Viareggio, near Lucca. Can you bring them here?"

"Yes, I can help you." Taking paper from the cubby holes in his large rolltop desk, he began asking Rosa questions.

"I want them to come first-class," she said.

"That will cost quite a bit more, Mrs. Dante." He looked at her doubtfully.

"I am quite prepared to pay for it," she took the money from her purse which Nina had insisted she take because, as she put it, the boys were coming to help her.

"I will let you know as soon as everything is settled."

"How long will this take?"

" I should have everything arranged in a few days."

She got up to leave. "No, I mean, how long before my sons arrive?"

"My agent in Genova will contact them as soon as they get my message. He will arrange with them. You should see them in about 2 1/2 to 3 months."

Disappointment was clear in her face, is something wrong, Mrs. Dante?

Oh, I thought they could be here sooner. With Anthony hurt, we need their help at the wharf but…"

"Anthony hurt? What happened?"

"I'm sorry. I thought you knew, news travels so fast here in North Beach. There was a terrible wagon accident yesterday." Rosa told him the story.

"I'm sorry to hear that, what are his chances?"

"Not very good I'm afraid," Rosa answered. "The doctor said he has a fifty-fifty chance."

Shaking his head sadly from side to side, he said, "It is good you have sons to help run his business while he is sick. It will help his recovery if he is not worried about business."

Mr. Fugazi picked up the newspaper and said, "Two nasty accidents one after the other. You have heard about Thomas Page?"

"No, I have not heard anything," Rosa said assuming that he was talking about the story Enrico released to the papers. Wondering how the story could be published so quickly, she took to the newspaper.

"His poor wife must be in a state of shock." Rosa opened the folded newspaper. In bold headlines across the top of the front page,

THOMAS PAGE FOUND SHOT TO DEATH.

Rosa's heart jumped against her breast bone, "Oh my God, dear God!"

Sitting down, she read:

"Thomas page, longtime city attorney, was found slumped over his desk at City Hall. The one time candidate for supervisor was found dead from what appeared to be a self-inflicted gunshot wound. Earlier in the day, when asked by a reporter from his newspaper to comment on a story linking to his activities with Mr. Anthony Orso, Mr. Page had angrily slammed the door."

According to the story, Mr. Page, once responsible for closing down several houses of prostitution, had later became part owner, with Mr. Orso, of the same properties.

"The same reporter," the story continued, "had in his possession, evidence of Mr. Page's part ownership in the A & T company, thought by some to be involved in diverse illegal activities.

The final line of the story was: "Mr. Page is survived by his wife, Mrs. Anna Page."

Rosa lay the paper down on her lap. "Dear God, this is terrible. I never dreamed something like this might happen. Poor Anna, dear Anna."

"Is all of this true?" Mr. Fugazi asked, and not waiting for the answer, "Anthony's accident? Was his accident connected to this? I never suspected that Anthony was involved in anything like this. He seemed like such a good, God-fearing man, helping out the church, and bringing all of those people over here from Italy. I helped to bring so many over. He was so kind. Why, he even helped you and your children come to this country."

"No, Mr. Fugazi, he did not help me. I paid my own passage. He liked to tell everyone he paid. I let him talk. He didn't ask you to arrange my passage did he?"

"No, but somehow he gave me the impression that he had sent the money directly to you," he said, "but now that you mention it…"

Rosa could see the understanding come slowly into his face. She asked, "Did you keep any sort of record of the people he did help come over from Italy? I would like to find them, and see how they have fared."

"I'm sure I have records somewhere, but it will take some time to get together. Anthony has been doing this over the past ten years, I will get them to you."

He walked with Rosa toward the door, "When I know what ship your sons will be on, I will contact you."

They shook hands and Rosa asked, "Could I have that newspaper to show Nina?"

"Of course," he said, "and don't worry about those boys of yours, I will see that they are well taken care of."

583

CHAPTER FIFTY-FIVE

As she approached the wharf, Rosa saw Mario talking to a strange man. He was gesturing as if upset, and when the buggy brought her closer, she heard angry words. The stranger walked away, writing in a notepad.

"Who was that, Mario?" Rosa called to him.

"A reporter from the newspaper. Asking about Anthony."

"Did Nina see him?" Rosa asked.

"No, she's not back yet. Her and Sylvia went to the hospital. She asked me to watch things while she went. I told her I'd handle it, but then this here fellow comes asking all sort of questions."

"Like what Mario? What did he ask?"

"He wanted to know where Anthony was. I told him I don't know nothing. But he kept right on asking questions. He asked about some company called A&T. I told him to go away and to leave me alone."

"I have to go now, lots of things to do." His weather-leathered face was red with frustration, "No time to stand around talking."

"I am a man of the sea. I go out in my boat, I am happy. I help Nina until she find someone else because you are both good to me. But I only want to be boss of my boat, only boss of my boat," he repeated as he started to cross the road. "Here comes the boss lady now," he called back over his shoulder.

Sylvia helped the exhausted Nina down out of the buggy.

"Come into the diner, and I will make us all some tea," Rosa took Nina's other arm. "We must get you off that foot, it is still bothering you."

Somewhat revived by the tea and biscuits, Nina said, "Anthony is hurt bad, very bad. And he is frightened. He is having trouble breathing- you knew they put some kind of pipe in his throat? He is in a lot of pain. Groggy, he kept fading in and out, Rosa," Nina said taking her hand, "he thinks he is going to die, and he is scared."

"When we got to the hospital," Sylvia said, "there were reporters waiting in the hallway. They were awful. They asked awful questions."

"The police were there too", Nina added. "I think they'd like to throw Anthony in jail, even as sick as he is. They are like vultures."

"Poor Nina", Sylvia said, "the reporters were no better. They didn't seem to care what they said. They talked to her as if she didn't have any feelings."

"I got so flustered, I didn't know what I was saying. Oh Rosa, it was terrible. They treated me like I was a criminal. Then the doctor came and ordered them to leave the hospital. And they said that Thomas Page was dead, that he killed himself, is it true?"

"Yes, it is true." Rosa opened the newspaper and read the headlines aloud.

"I am worried about Anna. I must go see her."

I want to go with you," Nina said, "but I have to fix supper for the fishermen. And I don't want to be there alone, those reporters might come back with more questions."

Rosa asked, "Where is Bianca? I thought you were going to ask her to come in and help until your ankle mended."

"That is another thing," Nina said, her shoulder sagging even more.

"I spoke to her before we went to the hospital. The man had just brought the fish to her and she was greeting her stand ready for customers. I asked if she would come in and help me with the cooking for a few days.

"She said she knew all about what had happened to Anthony, and it serves him right. She said she hoped he would die! That's what she said, Rosa, just as mean as you please, she hoped he would die!

"Later Mario told me that Anthony was padrone to her. He paid for her and her son to come to America. The son was supposed to help her pay off the passage money, but he ran away three years ago and she hasn't seen him. She blames Anthony for driving him away.

"All this time that she has been selling fish on the wharf, she has hated Anthony, and now, with everything that has happened, she hates me too. Because I am Anthony's wife she thinks I am bad too.

"I told her she was free, that she didn't owe him any more money. I told her she could go, but she didn't have to worry about being deported. She took off her apron! Just like that – without a word. it was like she thought I'd change my mind and she wanted to get away before it was too late."

Nina buried her head in her hands. "Oh Rosa, all the terrible things he has done – that poor old woman – what will become of her?

And now she thinks because Anthony did bad things, that I am evil too."

Rosa patted her on the back. Let her cry, maybe that was good for her. "Dear God, Rosa thought, every time we turn a corner, another of Anthony's victims is there. Where will it end?"

"Nina, I must go to Anna. Come with me, Peppino will help Sylvia, you don't have to worry about the fisherman. They will take care of them."

"Nina looked to Sylvia, and receiving an encouraging nod, said, "Alright, I will go with you."

The buggy took them up the streets of Russian Hill. Both women were silent for a long time, then Rosa said, "I am anxious about Anna's feelings towards me. I hope she will not blame me for- for all that has happened – for Thomas's death. I never wanted to hurt her, she has been a dear friend. I cannot bear it if she turned away from me."

Nina padded Rosa's arm, "Right now she will know only her grief – but all things will come in time."

Worried and tense Rosa walked through the gate and up the Rose bordered path to the door. She hesitated.

Forcing a smile, Nina rang the bell.

No one answered.

She rang the bell again.

The door opened, and Rosa recognized the little Chinese boy she had seen working in the kitchen.

He peeked out nervously through the slender opening.

Rosa said, "We have come to see Mrs. Page."

There was no reply. The door did not move.

"Please let us in. We are her friends."

Seeming to finally recognize her, the Chinese boy opened the door, "Missy upstairs, she sick, Missy no get up."

Hurrying up the broad stairway, Rosa called back, "Please help madam, she has a bad ankle."

She knocked on Anna's bedroom door. There was no reply. Her insides seized with a dread of what she was going to find. Rosa turned the doorknob and slowly entered the room.

The room smelled of sickbed. Closed windows and doors shut tight. The shades were down, and all Rosa could make out was a vague form laying on the bed.

The blankets pulled up around her neck, only the chalky white face could be seen. "Oh, my God! She's dead!"

Rosa took her hand out from beneath the blankets, and as she rubbed the limp flesh, Anna moved.

"Oh thank God!" Rosa turned to Nina who had just come into the room.

"Open the shades," she ordered.

Rosa knelt beside the bed, "Anna can you hear me? It's Rosa. Anna, Anna, please talk to me!"

No color in her face, her eyes were lost in the dark circles of her sunken cheeks. Anna moaned.

Rosa turned to the boy who was hovering nervously about.

"When did Mrs. Page last eat?"

"I bring her tray but she no eat it. She no will eat." There was an untouched tray of food on the night table.

"She sick, very sick. Tea make her sick." He took a jar down from a high shelf in the bedroom closet.

"Tea, no good, make her sick. No make babies like Lu Chin says, take babies away. It is bad tea. Lu Chin and Mr. Thomas give it to her. Make her sick."

"What are you saying? That the tea is poison? Let me see that."

He handed Rosa a jar of leaves in powder. "That is Shui yim. It is bad old Chinese medicine."

"Where is Lu Chin?" Rosa asked.

"He run, he scared. He do not want to stay. He take buggy, he take horse, he run. Me not scared, me do nothing bad. Me likes Missy, Missy good."

"Will this kill her?" Rosa asked just beginning to realize the urgency of Anna's condition.

"She is very sick, very sick."

Nina raised the window shade, and the sun poured in, onto the row of plants on the sill. Rosa cried out, "Oh my god, the plants, the plants are dead. They are dead!"

The soil around the plants was damp. "The tea! It's the tea! Anna didn't like taking the tea. She told me that when Lu Chin and Thomas weren't watching she would pour it on the plants. Dear God in heaven, the plants are dead."

Rosa took Anna's limp form by the shoulders and shaking her gently said "Anna, Anna, wake up, speak to me."

Anna's eyes flooded open, "Is that you, Thomas?" she whispered.

"We've got to get a doctor", Rosa said, "Nina, come here, try to keep her awake. I'll call the doctor."

"Where is the telephone?" Rosa asked running down the hall, the Chinese boy trotting behind her.

"Mr. Thomas keeps the door locked, the phone inside, door locked."

"Well go get something to break the locks, I have to use the phone, hurry, hurry."

He came back with a hammer and a pic from Anna's garden. "What is her doctor's name?" Rosa asked while he pried at the door.

"Dr. Spinosa, he just down the block."

"Alright, I'll call Dr. Spinosa, and what is your name?"

"Missy call me Sam."

They hammered and pounded and pried until finally, the door flew open.

Rosa picked up the unfamiliar black instrument, looking around for something to turn on. A woman's voice asked her what number she wanted.

"It's an emergency", she shouted into the mouthpiece, "I must get Dr. Spinosa right away."

With Sam stationed at the front door to wait for the doctor, Rosa went back into Anna's bedroom. Nina was wiping her face with a damp cloth, and Anna seemed a little more awake.

Within minutes, the sounds of footsteps taking two steps at a time announced the arrival of the doctor.

He did a swift examination, and closing his bag, said, "We have to get her to the hospital, now right away."

With the help of the driver, the men managed to get Anna into the buggy, while Nina hobbled along behind carrying blankets.

Keep her warm, the doctor ordered as he climbed into his own buggy to follow them to the hospital.

Wrapped in blankets, Anna sat propped up between Rosa and Nina. From time to time her eyes open unseeingly, and sometimes she mumbled.

Her eyes appeared more sunken in, her skin even paler than she had seemed inside. The two women, their arms around the shivering Anna, tried to pour the will to live back into her body.

Anna wheeled into the emergency room on a gurney, and Rosa gave Dr. Spinosa the jar of tea and powder.

"This is what they've been giving to her to make babies," she said. "It's called Shui yin, but Sam says it doesn't make babies, it takes them away."

The doctor took the jar in his hand, and shook his head, "Those Chinese think they have herbs for everything! It's a wonder so many of them live!"

He walked away still shaking his head. Rosa followed. A nurse stopped her and pointed her toward the waiting room.

Stunned with all that happened, Rosa and Nina sat silently in the deserted room. Sam went outside and walked up and down in front of the hospital, smoking one cigarette after another.

Getting her bearings for the first time, Rosa said, "This is Enrico's hospital, I must go tell him all that has happened. I will let the nurse know where to find us."

CHAPTER FIFTY-SIX

"The doctor has given me good news, he says I can leave the hospital."

Enrico told Rosa and Nina after they had brought him up to date on all that happened. "But he wants me to remain in San Francisco for several months so that the doctor can keep a close check on me."

"How wonderful," Rosa and Nina spoke in unison. "Where will you live?"

"I don't know yet. I have to find a place and get a nurse and someone to cook for me. The people here at the hospital are helping me, they are keeping their eyes open for a flat or a house I could rent."

"I cannot wait to get out into the world again. I have been so miserably bored, forced to lie here all day after day, doing nothing."

A young Filipino boy peaked into the room, "Mrs. Dante?" He asked, "the doctor says you come now to Mrs. Page." He disappeared as quickly as he had come.

"How is she?" Rosa whispered to the Doctor who was just leaving Anna's room.

"She is suffering from malnutrition," his tone showing his impatience with anyone who didn't eat proper food.

"She is also disoriented. But her vital signs are not too bad, considering. She's having severe abdominal pains and I have given her something to relax her. She will sleep soon, do not stay long."

"Will she, will she recover?" Rosa asked, almost afraid to speak the thought.

"I will know more after I talk to the house boy and find out how much of that tea they are giving her. That Shui yin is a Chinese abortion medicine."

"An abortion medicine?" Rosa and Nina looked at each other in shock.

"And poor dear Anna, all she wanted in the world was a baby!"

Silently they looked down upon the fragile figure of their friend. Breathing heavily, her long black hair hanging across her shoulders in a loose braid, Anna looked a little more like a child, so pale, so frail. When Rosa spoke, Anna opened her eyes briefly but seemed not to know who they were. As if in fear, she turned her head away.

"Mrs. Dante," the nurse said, "Do you know Mrs. Page's relatives? Do you know who to contact?"

"I know she has a sister," Rosa answered, "I am sure Sam can give me the address. I will call and tell her to come."

Thomas's funeral was simple. The church looked upon suicide as a sin. No mass could be had. A handful of people watched the brief graveside service in the tiny cemetery at Powell and Lombard Street where he laid to rest in unholy ground. A plain stone marker read, Thomas C. Pagenelli 1840- 1882.

Anna's sister, Theresa, came immediately upon receiving the news. Very large with child, she arrived with her husband, Carlo Covella, and their three sons. With the same black hair and round dark eyes, Theresa looked like a younger Anna. Her skin was tanned, and her hands calloused.

Carlo owned and worked a small vineyard in the valley, where he kept a few dairy cows and some sheep. His hands and arms were tan and his face showed one strip of white skin across the top of his forehead.

After the service, Rosa and Nina rode with the Covella's up the road to Anna's house.

Sam brought them coffee and laid out a simple meal on the dining room table for them. Theresa fussed over the children, and several times got up to help Sam. He would nod politely and say, "No, Missy, I do. You sit, you eat."

Carla went down the hall to the guest bedroom and came back with a straw wrapped bottle. "This is my wine." He poured some for everyone.

"Thomas would never drink my wine, he thought wine was no good unless it came from Napa," Carlo lifted his glass, and sadly said, "and see where he is today."

Draining his glass, Carlo said, "I'm going outside to smoke my cigar. I know you ladies want to talk." He stopped to pat his wife on the shoulder and plant an affectionate kiss on her forehead.

"Tell me, Theresa, how is Anna?" Rosa asked.

"When I saw her last night the nurse said she had eaten a little. Some of her color is back. I am going to see her this afternoon."

"Today will be hard for her, that is if she realizes Thomas was buried today. Sometimes she seems to know what happened, and at other times, she sits there, just waiting for him to come to get her."

"Yesterday she was talking about her rose bushes, just like she thought she was at home. And that medicine they were giving her!" Theresa said.

"The doctor decided it was a Chinese abortion potion with quicksilver in it," Rosa said.

"Quicksilver? That's terrible stuff. I've heard it can do terrible things. Make your head- makes you go sort of crazy."

"Will she get well? Will she be alright in the head like she used to be?"

No one knew. They could only shake their heads and worry.

"Was he trying to kill Anna or just making sure she never had children?" Theresa asked.

"I don't know. I wonder if Thomas even knew himself."

"Anna told me," Nina added, "that Thomas made her drink the tea whenever he came to her in bed."

"It looks like he told her it was for making babies! And by doing that, he broke her heart and almost killed her."

Rosa said sadly, "We will probably never know what he was trying to do."

Sam came in to remove the dishes and restraining her impulse to help him, Theresa went with the other two women to the parlor.

"Carlo has to return to the vineyard tomorrow." She said. "He will take the boys with him, and I will stay until Anna is well enough to travel."

"I want her to come home with me and stay until she gets her strength back."

"What about the house?" Nina asked looking around at Anna's China closet and all her lovely things.

"I don't know, we'll have to find someone to look after it," Rosa suggested.

"Anna has never seen our place. Thomas never wanted to bring her."

"When is your baby due?" Nina asked.

"In about a month," Theresa patted her stomach and smiled. "We're wishing for a baby girl. I hope I can be home before she arrives." Theresa smiled fondly at the bump under her dress.

Carlo returned from Anna's yard with an arm full of roses. He laid them on the table, "Take these to Anna, when you go, maybe they will cheer her up."

"Did you know Thomas very well?" Theresa asked Rosa.

"No, not really. Anna became a good friend, but we saw Thomas only on special occasions. Did you?"

"I knew him better than Carlo," Theresa said glancing at her husband who responded with a look of disgust and sat down. The look was enough to answer Rosa's question.

"I always had the feeling he thought he was better than me," Carlo replied.

"I must confess I had mixed feelings about him," Theresa said. "When they were first married, he couldn't have been sweeter."

"He acted sweet in front of you, but he was a phony."

"No, not at first, Carlo. At first, I believe he was a good man, and then he started to change."

"Let's forget about him, he is dead and gone and Anna is better off, even though she doesn't know it yet."

Rosa looked at the people around the table and thought of all the lives that were now in turmoil. Anna ill, Thomas dead, Anthony dying, and Nina so strangely quiet- so humiliated.

Dear God, Rosa wondered, why are so many good people being made to suffer for the sins of a few? Was it my meddling that caused all these terrible things to happen? Rosa felt frightened and alone.

Theresa and Carlo went to the hospital to see Anna and Nina and went to be with Anthony.

"Come with me, Rosa. I am afraid the reporters might be there. I will not know what to say to them."

A man was waiting at the door to Anthony's room. It was the same man that Mario had been arguing with at the wharf.

"I represent 'La Voce del Popolo.' May I ask you a few questions, Mrs.Orso?"

"No, no," Nina replied, she tried to hurry by him. "I must see my husband."

"Just one moment of your time please, Mrs. Orso."

"Alright, one question that is all," Nina said.

His voice soft and comforting, and looking benevolently down at Nina he asked, "What will happen to your husband's business now that he is so ill?"

Her hand already on the doorknob, Nina replied, "I will take over the business until he is well." Closing in on her he asked, "Were you aware of the full extent of his activities before the accident, Mrs. Orso?"

"No, no, no more, you said one question," Rosa helped Nina into Anthony's room. Once inside, Nina paused leaning up against the door. Rosa could feel her shaking.

The room was growing dark, and under the single light, Anthony lay very still.

"Anthony," Nina whispered to him, "it's me, Nina." Anthony looked up at her, his eyes cold and expressionless.

"Are you feeling any better? Can you eat anything?"

He stared at her. His forehead wrinkles and his eyes grew dark. His lips moved, but the only sound was a faint raspy noise from his throat. Fury and frustration in his eyes, he pulled against a leather strap that held down his one good arm.

"Do you want something to drink?" Nina asked, becoming frightened.

Anthony rolled his eyes to the ceiling.

Patting his arm, trying to quiet him down, Nina asked no more questions. Instead, she told him all the things that were happening at the wharf.

She told him about Mario helping, how he was doing the buying. She told him of Rosa sending for her sons to run the fishing fleet. Nervous at the anger and frustration she could see building up inside Anthony, Nina spoke quickly.

He turned his head away from her and closed his eyes.

Embarrassed, Nina said, "He fell asleep."

Rosa came to the side of his bed and looked down on Anthony's pathetic form. Tears rolled down across his face. Rosa wondered if they were tears of regret, or tears of frustration and rage.

In the hall, they met Anthony's doctor.

"How is my husband?" Nina asked.

"He is having considerable trouble breathing and swallowing. His lungs are becoming congested. It's pneumonia we have to worry about. I don't know if he would be strong enough to fight it off. We are doing everything possible. Only time will tell."

CHAPTER FIFTY-SEVEN

Rosa had just taken her hat off and was hanging up her coat when Hans arrived. Dressed in his uniform, his walk was heavy, and his face lined with worry.

"How is Anthony?" He asked, sitting down at the Kitchen table.

"Not good. His lungs are getting congested. They are afraid of pneumonia," Nina answered turning away, shamed by the memory of the hatred she saw in Anthony's eyes.

Hans looked to Rosa. She explained, "He gets very agitated because he can't talk. Tonight, when we were there, it was very hard on Nina, he is so angry."

Rosa placed some cold meat and bread on the table and made coffee.

"What is bothering you, Hans?" She asked.

"Well I suppose I might as well tell you, it's all going to come out soon. Down at the station, I am in trouble."

"How?"

"They found out that I was there at the meeting when Anthony ran out and got run over. They are trying to fire me but first, they have to dream up some kind of legitimate reason to give me the sack."

"How did they find out?" Rosa asked.

"Oh, that was a simple matter. After all, I was at the hospital with Anthony- in my civilian clothes- there as a friend of the family. And besides, there are spies all over. I was even mentioned in the newspaper article."

"By name?" Nina asked.

"No, but they know I know Nina, and they knew about Sylvia. It didn't take many brains to figure that out. The sergeant called me in today and suggested that I stick to my own beat."

"Will you lose your job?" Rosa asked, almost afraid of the answer.

"I could very easily. It depends on what happens next. It's like I told you, this is a dangerous business. There are lots of big important people involved here. There's a big machine working here, many palms getting greased."

"Nina, and you too Rosa, will have to be careful. There's a lot of money in San Francisco and the towns run by powerful men."

"'Blind Chris' is one of them, and he is ruthless."

"Who is blind Chris?"

"Is he really blind?"

"Yes, they say he lost his sight from drinking bad whiskey. But there's nothing wrong with his mind. He came from New York in the mid-70s. He was part of Tammany Hall and he learned his lessons very well there. He controls the Democratic Party and pretty much rules the city politics. He thrives on kickbacks and bribery."

"See, in the setup, Anthony and Thomas had going, many palms were greased all up and down the ladder. The police looked the other way, so when an operation like this gets shut down, a lot of people are affected. And they don't like that, not one tiny little bit."

"I hear that blind Chris is very unhappy, and this not only involves the police but also city officers. Nina, I have decided it's best if I move out, I'm going to have to stay away from here until it all blows over."

He looked at Nina with a sadness that transcended friendship.

"But the police were at the hospital," Rosa said, "they were talking like they wanted to put Anthony in jail and throw away the key. Why would they do that if they were taking kickbacks from his crooked dealings?"

"That Rosa, my dear, was strictly for the newspaper. This is the only reason the police were there at all. You will not see them anymore."

"The ones who really benefit from the sin money are the liquor dealers, the pimps, and the opium dealers."

"And there are plenty of the city officers and some police who don't want to see crime cleaned up, not all but some. The ones who make the money don't want things to change."

"We have opened a real can of worms. What next, what next?" Rosa asked.

Hans got up, "I must get my things and go."

"I will miss you, Hans," Rosa said.

"I will come by when I can," and he reached over and patted Rosa on the back.

"Nina, you try to be brave," and he kissed her on the top of her head.

Pad and pencil in hand, Rosa was making her morning check of bakery supplies when Nina burst through the door brandishing a newspaper.

"What is it, what is wrong? Is it Anthony?"

"No, no. Look at this," Nina thrust the paper into her hands. "Look at what it says! I will never be able to show my face again!"

The article read:

"The wife of Anthony Orso told this reporter that while her husband lies critically ill, she will carry on all his activities as usual. Does this," the article asked, "mean that Mrs. Orso will continue to operate the houses that this newspaper has been trying for years to close up?"

"Dear God in heaven," Rosa said, reading the rest of the article which referred to more of the same about Anthony and Thomas and their illegal activities.

Nina demanded, "What are we going to do about this? The paper makes it sound like I am going to run the whorehouses."

"You heard what I told the reporter. I only said I was going to continue with the business. I meant the fish business, not all that other stuff, not the whorehouses."

Rosa looked at the despair on Nina's face. At least when Anthony was around Nina had been spared any public ridicule. But now it was all falling on her, and just because she was his wife.

"This all started so simply," Rosa said, "we just wanted to make Anthony be fair with the fisherman. Then all the other things came up, the building fund, the liquor, and opium, the whorehouses. Now that he's hurt, everything has stopped, except the houses, and that's what the newspaper is writing about."

Rosa studied the cup of coffee she held in her hand and was silent for a long time. Then, finally, as if having made a great decision, she said, "they must be closed down!"

"Otherwise the newspaper will keep right on crucifying you. And, since Anthony can't do it, it's up to us. We will have to close them ourselves!"

"No, Rosa. What could you do about it? No, no," Nina protested. "The newspapers are going to keep on printing the stories and we will have no peace. What if Sylvia's story leaks out? She would die."

Pacing back-and-forth," Rosa was deep in thought. "First thing, Nina, we must take some of the money from Anthony's safe."

Nina waited.

"I am going to the parlor house, the one Peppino went to. I am going to talk to the girls." Rosa sat down again, "We wanted Anthony to give them a train ticket home and money to start a new life. He can't so I must do it."

"You cannot do this alone, you will need help."

"Who? Tell me who?" Rosa replied sharply. "Hans can't, Sylvia certainly can't, Enrico can't. Who? Peppino? They know him and will not trust him." Rosa was already combing her hair and putting her hat on.

"You are crazy, Rosa. You cannot go alone," Nina argued. "You do not even know where all the houses are."

"But he does," and Rosa pointed to the driver of Anthony's buggy parked outside. "Do you have Anthony's keys, Nina? I should take them."

CHAPTER FIFTY-EIGHT

Recognizing the house from Peppino's description Rosa told the driver to wait. She walked to the door and suddenly felt panic. The show of confidence she had mustered up for Nina's sake deserted her. But before she could retreat, the door opened.

A tall blonde woman, about forty, appeared at the door. Rosa knew who she was.

"Yes, honey what can I do for you?"

"I am Mrs. Rosa Dante."

"Are you looking for work, sweetie?"

"I am the niece of Anthony Orso," Rosa said offended by the woman's tone.

"I want to speak to you." The woman clearly did not believe her. Taking Anthony's keys from her purse, Rosa held them up, hoping her fear did not show.

The woman opened the door wider and looked up and down the street. When she saw Anthony's carriage she said, "Come in. How is Anthony? I hear he is in pretty bad shape."

"He is fighting for his life," Rosa followed her into a large elegantly decorated room. Tables from Italy, chairs from France, velvet Crimson drapes, a Rosewood bar across one wall with mirrors the length of it, and glass shelves filled with bottles and glasses.

Above the bar was a huge painting of a nude seductively posed on a red velvet couch holding a bunch of grapes that hung to the floor.

"That is me, sweetie, in my younger days," the woman was smiling at Rosa's reaction. "One of my old beaux's couldn't pay his bar bill, so he gave me that."

"Come sit, what can I do for you?" She led Rosa to a small table and chairs in the corner of the room. There was a curious acrid aroma, a bitter smell, and Rosa wondered if that was the lingering odor of opium.

"I read in the newspaper that Anthony's wife is going to carry on his business as usual," the woman smiled.

"That is why I am here, but what can I call you, what is your name?" Rosa felt awkward in front of this woman so definitely in charge of the situation.

"Everyone calls me Sally," she said, still smiling.

"The story in the paper was wrong. Mrs. Orso is closing down all the houses."

"Tell me you're joking, sweetie! You can't just close down a house. These girls don't know anything else. They'll end up in the Barbary Coast in those drives down there. Have you seen some of those places on Clay Street or Pike Alley? Listen, sister, don't start anything you can't finish."

"Let me tell you a little story, sweetie. You sit still and you listen good," Sally spoke with authority. "You're a housewife, probably a house full of kids, maybe had a few miscarriages. And you have a pretty face, but some of the other girls, God was not so good to them! All some of them ever saw was poverty. They watch their mothers working from morning to night, bearing one child after another, and putting up with husbands who beat them.

"For most of my girls, that is where they came from. I have girls coming here, maybe sixteen, seventeen, they want to work. They looked around at the poverty, and they didn't want that kind of life for themselves. So they come here. They have nowhere else to turn to."

Sally went to the bar and poured two glasses of wine, "Here," she placed one glass in front of Rosa, "drink that up and relax sweetie."

"My name is Rosa," she tried to sound firm and confident.

"Alright, Rosa. These girls have a better place and some of you out there who are casting stones at us. After all sweet…" She corrected herself, "after all, Rosa, us girls are no different. We sell ourselves, the only difference is we get paid for it. You give it all away for free, we are all sisters under the skin."

Rosa watched while Sally drank her wine, nearly draining the glass. "I know about the slavery that goes on here," Rosa said. "I know all about that. I even have a list of names," she was lying but hoped it did not show, "I have a list of all the girls that Anthony brought here," she repeated.

"Listen here Rosa, there's no lock on their door, no bars on the windows."

"That is where you are lying to me Sally. I know for a fact that you have locked girls in the room," Rosa was thinking of the story Sylvia told her, and she cringed remembering the tear it left in the girl.

"Well, miss do-gooder, if you don't believe me, why don't you just go talk to the girls yourself? They're just having their lunch now, right in there, go ahead, go ahead and ask them yourself."

Rosa followed her to a big open dining hall. 15 women, dressed in robes or negligees, their hair in rags or tied up in scarfs, sat at a long table, eating a meal. Talking and laughing, none of them wearing makeup, they were just like any other group of young women having an informal meal at home.

A tall large-boned black woman was serving soup from a cauldron at the foot of the table. She smiled at Sally when she opened the sliding door and brought Rosa in.

"Company for lunch," she said looking Rosa over from head to toe.

Rosa declined Sally's offer to try the soup. "Well, go ahead, then," Sally said, "they're all yours, go ahead and talk to them."

"After you've talked to a few of them," Sally said, "her voice loud enough for everyone in the room to hear, you'll find that my girls are all pretty content here."

"Yes, I want to do that," Rosa could see the way the girls looked to Sally for their cues, "but without you present. I'd like to talk to them upstairs in the office."

"I don't know…" Sally was showing her first signs of doubt.

"If the girls are as happy as you say, then you shouldn't care. If they want to leave, they should be free to make that choice, without you sitting there."

Sally came closer, and spoke in a hushed voice, "Some of them might say they want to leave, just to see what they can get out of you. They might try to cheat you."

"I'll take that chance. At least they'll have the choice."

Displeased at the turn of events, Sally unwillingly lead the way upstairs through the wide upper hallway filled with green felt-covered gaming tables. Sally waited while Rosa fumbled through the tangle of keys and finally found the one that opened the door marked "private."

Inside the large cluttered room, were two heavy wooden desks, one at each end. The desk nearest the door was covered with papers, and on the top was a silver frame much like the one on Nina's mantle. It held a picture of a woman whom Rosa recognized as Anthony's mistress.

Sally saw Rosa look at the picture. "She used to be one of my girls until she took permanent residence with the boss." She added. "I guess she's out in the cold now. She will have to go back to work."

The other desk on the far wall was neat and bare. On top was a small calendar, a pen holder, and a picture.

It was of Anna and Thomas at their wedding day. Anna looked beautiful and Thomas was smiling a friendly confident smile. She held it up and looked at Anna lovingly. So many things have happened to poor dear Anna.

Rosa drew the curtain aside letting the sunlight in through the big window. Sitting at Anthony's desk waiting for the first girl, she wondered if Sally was right.

Maybe none of the girls would want to leave. Fear weld up inside of her. She had no one to reach out to for advice or help. She was alone. She had no alternative but to go through with this. She must have faith that she was doing the right thing.

Yvette was the first. Her complexion was sallow and listless, her walk was defiant. Rosa thought her not as old as she looks.

Refusing Rosa's offer to be seated, she said, "If you think I am leaving this place, you're crazy. I have all the freedom here I want and I consider you a medellin do-gooder. Leave us all alone. We do not need the likes of you poking your nose in our business."

Before Rosa could stop her she walked out.

The second girl came in immediately. Without taking the time to close the door behind her, she repeated almost word for word what Yvette had said, and turned and left.

Rosa went to where Sally was waiting at the poker table. "I thought you were going to be straight with me," Rosa said.

"What do you mean?" Sally asked, innocently.

"You sent me two heavy users, and I'll bet my bottom dollar you told them that if they didn't behave, you would see that their supply was cut off. Am I right, Sally?"

Sally turned away, "Why don't you just go back home and leave us alone?"

"Yes, that's just what I am going to do. I came here to try to help your girls, give them a chance before we locked up the house. But you spoiled that. The house will be locked and they will have to shift for themselves."

"Rosa, maybe you speak for the landlord's wife, but he was not the only one I paid. I have to pay the ward boss, the policemen on the beach just for the privilege of staying open. You close this house and you upset a lot of people."

"Who are you worrying about, Sally? The girls, the politicians, the police, or yourself?"

"I am trying to keep my business open, like any other businessman. And I will keep it open, either here or somewhere else."

Rosa remembered what Hans said about so many 'palms to be oiled', and knew that Sally was right, she had to stay in business.

Rosa got up and put the keys in her purse.

"You are leaving?" Sally asked.

"Yes, there is nothing more to do here now. I will have the men come and put locks on the doors. I'll give you forty-eight hours to be out of here."

"Now, sweetie, I mean Rosa, don't be in such a big hurry."

"I see now that you are a straight shooter, just tell me what you want. I care about these girls too, just tell me what you want to do."

Rosa studied her, wondering if this was just another trick. Deciding to take a chance that Sally meant it, she said, "all right, let me go in there, all alone, talk to them altogether. Let me give them a chance at a better life, will you let me do that?"

"Come on then," Sally said taking Rosa by the arm, "almost all of the girls should still be in the dining room. I'll have the rest sent down to you. I'm betting you won't get very many girls to say they want to go, then what will you do, Rosa?"

"All I am concerned with, Sally, is that each girl gets the chance. What she does with it, it's up to her, or up to you, please I beg of you as one woman to another, let them have this one chance!"

Sally said nothing, but Rosa knew she had touched her heart.

Rosa waited outside while Sally stepped into the dining room. She told the girls to listen to Rosa. Calling her a straight shooter, she told them to trust her. When Sally came out, Rosa took her hat off and, preparing for a struggle, went inside.

611

CHAPTER FIFTY-NINE

They watched and waited for her to say something.

"My name is Rosa, Rosa Dante," she started, "I'm here to make you an offer."

They didn't care.

Rosa knew she needed something to grab hold of them, to get their interest, to forge some kind of bond with them. It was not enough that they were all women.

Then she remembered Sally telling her that many of these women have been beaten or abused.

"When I was a young girl," Rosa spoke hesitantly, her voice faltered, "I was sent to a small fishing village in Italy, to a church house, to take care of the priest."

I had been there several months when one night a traveler came to the church house asking for food. The priest, Father Joseph, went to bed and told me to feed him.

Rosa sensed their interest rising, I gave him a good meal of fish and pasta, and then, when he had eaten every crumb, he got up, and I thought he was going to leave, but instead, he grabbed me, he threw me down on the floor and tried to rape me.

Rosa worried about the changes she was making in the story, but there was something strong inside of her that would not let her malign a man of God, no matter what he had done. And now, at last, they were listening.

He pulled my clothes off and tried to rape me. But I was lucky, I got away from him. I don't think I knew what was happening. I was very young and naïve. I'd been raised in a convent, I didn't even know what he was trying to do."

The girls were snickering. "I just knew that he was hurting me and I was terrified. I ran down into the village, it was late at night, and everything was dark. There was only one light shining anywhere in any of the houses, I ran there and pounded on the door.

"I was lucky, a very kindly woman took me in. She treated me like her daughter. I didn't have anywhere else to go- my parents were dead, my only relative was thousands of miles away, here in America. But if this man had raped me, my life in Italy would have been ruined.

"I know that now, I didn't know it then, but no man would have married me, even the women would have scorned me."

The girls were listening, some were shaking their heads in agreement. She went on,

"In Italy, virginity was the most important thing for a man looking for a wife. It made no difference that the girl wasn't responsible for the rate. No, no Italian man would have married me if I had been raped."

They were listening. Some were crying, some looked resentful, and others stared off into space.

"I had no place else to go – I had no one to turn to. If it had not been for that woman who took me into her family," she continued, "that woman who gave me a chance – I might have been thrown out into the streets to shift for myself."

"That's why I am here today. I want to give you all another chance."

They were mumbling. She heard moans and a few tears from the girls.

Yvette stood up, "Oh, come on lady you think you are some kind of saint or something?"

"No, Yvette, I don't think I am a saint – far from it – but I can help you. If you want to get cured of your habit, I can help you."

There were murmurs, and many turned to look at the standing girl.

"See, Yvette, even you have a choice. But no one can do it for you. I can only give you the chance."

"What does Sally say?" A voice in the back asked.

"Sally and I have talked, she knows why I am in here. You are free if you want to be."

"I will give you money to start a new life."

At the mention of money, a surge of excitement passed over the room.

"I will try to find you jobs. Or, if you want to go back to where you came from, I will give you a train ticket. If you want to start a new life somewhere else or go home to your family, you can do that. The choice is yours. It's alright with Sally. She will not stand in your way."

A plump dark-haired girl stood up.

"What is your name?" Rosa prompted.

"Rosita." Her eyes were beautifully big and brown, but they were filled with fear and sadness.

"Where are you from, Rosita?"

"Mexico. The same thing happen to me, in my little village, I was no good anymore. No one wanted me, so I run, I come here."

"Do you want to go back home?"

"No, no! I can never do that, but I like to be free, but I don't know nothing. I don't know how to do nothing."

"I can help you. If you want to be helped, I promise I will do my best. Anyone else?" Rosa asked.

Louisa stood up but kept her head so low Rosa could hardly hear.

"I come to America with my brother. A man brought me here and told me I had to stay here until I pay for my boat trip. Does this mean I can go?"

"Yes, yes," Rosa said. "You can leave. You are free. What man brought you here?"

Louisa looked around apprehensively.

"Don't be frightened, tell me. No one will hurt you."

"The man who met us at the wharf. The man my brother works for. I am afraid for my brother. I am afraid," and she started crying.

"What is your brother's name?"

"Alfredo."

"Alfredo, the carpenter and boat builder?"

"Yes, yes, that is him. Do you know him? Is he safe?"

"Yes, yes, Louisa, he is safe, I will take you to him. He is free too now. You have nothing to fear."

For the next several hours, Rosa listened and talked to the girls. When she went back to the main hall, Sally was sitting at her desk.

"Well, any luck?" Sally asked.

"More luck than you thought I would have, and less than I wanted to have." Rosa sat down and looked across at this woman with the bottled blonde hair and the seductive black gown.

Suddenly she smiled. Sally smiled back. They understood each other.

"How many girls want 'their freedom' as you call it?"

"Five, only five."

"Are you surprised?" Sally asked.

"Yes, I thought more of them would."

"Well then, Mrs. Orso, still owns a whorehouse. What are you going to do about that?"

"It will have to be sold. You'll have to find another place."

"Will you sell it to me, Rosa?" Sally asked.

Two days after the meeting between Sally and Rosa, Anthony died.

Nina was with him. She had rushed to the hospital in the middle of the night and never left his side.

His breathing came with terrible effort, and from time to time he stirred and opened his eyes. For a moment he seemed to recognize Nina, and as if wanting to tell her something, and with barely enough strength, he reached out to her.

A priest came silently into the room and standing at the foot of the stark white hospital bed, prayed for the repose of his soul.

When Anthony's eyes opened and settled upon the solemn black clothes figure, his whole body tense, a terror filled his eyes.

Anthony died just as the sun was rising.

A requiem mass was said, Father Paul's brief eulogy was more for Nina than for Anthony.

At the gravesite, a handful of people watched. Peppino held the twins' hands, Hans and Rosa stood by Nina, trying to give her strength.

In the distance, a carriage stopped and watched the service. Rosa thought she recognized Sally's blonde hair and wondered if the other woman was Dolores.

How sad, Rosa thought, a love so illicit that even in the face of death it must be hidden.

Rosa could not cry for Anthony. The sorrow she felt was not for the dead but for the living. In the weeks that followed, Sally negotiated with Nina's attorney and bought the house.

Yvette went into the hospital to be cured. Louisa reunited with her brother and went with Rosita to work for Nina in the diner.

Rosa and Sally took three of the girls to Oakland to the train station. Rosa gave them their tickets and Sally gave each a motherly goodbye kiss. On the way home, she said to Rosa, "Maybe if someone had given me a second chance when I was their age, I'd be somebody today."

Rosa smiled at her, "You are somebody, Sally."

Nina insisted upon going with Rosa to the Sacramento Street house to pick up Anthony's personal belongings and leave the keys for Sally.

Her curiosity overcoming fear and shame, Nina said, "After all, Rosa, he was my husband, and this was a side of his life I never even knew existed."

It was early in the morning and the girls were still asleep. The cook let them in. Looking around nervously, Nina recognized a small table that had once been in her parlor. She nudged Rosa and said, "I told Anthony I didn't like that table, and he said he would get rid of it for me."

When she saw Sally's picture above the bar, she whispered, "Isn't that terrible?" She tried not to look at it, but Rosa watched as she looked up at something else and then quickly glanced back up at the picture and away again.

Opening the door to Anthony's office Rosa remembered she had not removed the picture from his desk, but Nina had already seen it.

"Do you think she's pretty?" Nina asked. Without waiting for an answer she put the frame face down on the desk and said, "this frame matches mine at home – the one on the mantlepiece."

She removed the picture from the frame and tossed it into the wastebasket.

A small slip of paper floated down toward the basket. Rosa grabbed at it before it could land, and holding it up, said, "Here's another combination, Nina."

"Now, we won't have to blow it open with dynamite!" Nina said.

The two women sat on the floor in front of the open safe. They had found gold coins, two locked metal boxes full of paper money, and the "last will and testament of Anthony Orso."

Together they read the will. Everything was left "to my dear wife, Nina", except the house on Jones Street. That was left to Miss Dolores Porter.

"Well, I guess I can't evict her," she said.

"It is just as well, I don't think I'm ready to meet her face-to-face anyhow."

Rosa gathered the rest of the papers from Anthony's desk and put Thomas's belongings in a separate box with Anna's wedding ring on top. Rosa locked the door and leaving the key in the lock, they left.

Rosa and Nina rode with Peppino to take Thomas's things to Anna's house. Anna was still recovering at her sisters in the Central Valley, and Enrico and his nurse were staying at her house.

Rosa had not seen Anna since the day they took her to the hospital and feared she held her responsible for all the terrible things that happened.

Enrico, who saw her every day at the hospital, said she was very confused, and often didn't seem to know where she was. In her few lucid moments she seemed to know Thomas was dead and feared she had no money and would starve to death.

Other times she worried about someone stealing her house from her, and yet she refused to go back there.

Most of the time, Enrico reported, she wouldn't talk about Thomas or anything that had happened. They could never be sure when she thought he was coming to get her, or when she knew he was dead.

Rosa had written several letters to her at her sister's, but Anna did not answer. Rosa knew then she felt betrayed and could not forgive her.

Peppino waited with the wagon while Rosa and Nina rang the bell. Sam answered the door and Enrico soon appeared.

"Come in, come in, ladies come in, come in, ladies," Enrico said.

"Here is the last of Thomas's things from the office," she handed Enrico the box. The wedding picture was on top.

Turning the box over to Sam, Enrico picked up the picture and said, "A beautiful woman, isn't she?"

He led them into the sitting room. To Rosa, he said, "I have not heard from Aldo, but I did receive a letter from Theresa today."

"When I sent the rent money, I wrote that I had engaged an attorney for Nina and asked if she wanted to have the same man look after her affairs. Theresa wrote back telling me to talk it over with you and do whatever was decided is best. Anna seems not to understand or care, she said."

"She still will not speak of Thomas, Enrico paused. "Anna is going to have to face the things that he did before she can go on with her life. But right now, from what Theresa says, she is so sad and confused I don't know what will happen to her."

They decided to hire the attorney for Anna, and Rosa told him of the money they found in the safe.

"Perhaps," Rosa said, "when Anna hears of this, it will ease her worries about being penniless."

They put the boxes on the table, and after he had looked through most of them, Enrico said, "I will contact the attorney and have him handle the police investigation, too. Anna doesn't need to be bothered by that."

There was a strong tone of protectiveness in Enrico's voice.

"Will there be much of a problem with the police?" Rosa asked.

"No. With both Anthony and Thomas dead, it's all pretty much a closed book. It's Anna and Nina who will suffer. They are the innocent victims. But, with time, everything will settle down, and then, perhaps, we can all get on with our lives."

Walking them to the door, Enrico said, "Father Paul came to see me yesterday. He tells me that he is out working the streets, trying to help some of the girls."

"He disguises himself, pretends he's a writer or a businessman. He tells the girls that he is not interested in women, not interested in what they have to sell. He says he gains their confidence before they know he is a priest. He's already helped a couple of girls break away from that life."

"He is also trying to open a home for wayward girls of all ages. He's lined up an order of nuns to move in to take care of them."

Enrico laughed and said, "It seems that the bishop may be transferred, and then Father Paul will be free to do a lot more."

"So Father Paul has been able to make something good out of all this," Nina said, a certain sense of wonder in her expression.

"When you write to Anna," Rosa said, "send her my love. She is a dear friend and I miss her."

CHAPTER SIXTY

Rosa woke early. Today was to be the happiest of days for her-one she had often feared would never come.

She dressed carefully and looking at herself in the mirror, wondered if she had changed very much. Would they recognize her? She placed her new hat on her head and looked at the clock. It was yet too early.

While she waited until it was time, she sat on the edge of the bed and picked up her black tin box. One more time she would look through its precious contents. She took out the brooch Aldo had given her, admired it, and put its golden chain around her neck. Settling back against the headboard, she again unfolded Dino's last letter.

Dear mama,

When you left, you said we had many choices, that fishing was not the only work we could choose. Since then, I have spent many hours thinking about that, thinking about what I would do with my life.

I have made my decision, not in haste, not without advice and counsel, and not without prayer. I spent a great deal of time with Father Michael and the bishop of Lucca. When your letter came, and you asked us to come to America, my heart knew right then what my decision was.

I leave soon to study for the priesthood. I will join the order of the Salesian and will begin my studies in Rome.

Please do not be sad mama, Father Michael and the bishop think that because I know English, that you drilled into us for so many hours, I might very well be sent to America. Then, mama, you would see your Dino, not as a Fisherman, but as a priest. Please pray for me and pray for my vocation. Victor and Guido leave soon. The Rosa I has been sold, and the new owner has promised to take good care of her.

It will be good for Guido to come to America. There has been so little left for him since Maria died, he started to grow very old. Victor said to tell you they should arrive sometime in June and he will write you the exact date.

Before I leave for Rome, I will walk one more time to the graveyard and say a prayer for my father Giovanni, and for Eduardo and for all who stay behind.

Your devoted son,

Dino

Rosa sat on the edge of the bed. It was hard for her to think of her son, Dino, entering the priesthood. She could not help thinking of him as a little child, and now he is a man and has chosen to give himself to God.

Rosa knew this was not an easy decision for him. Her thoughts took her back to the convent in Lucca. To that day Mother Superior told her she had been chosen.

If she had taken the veil, Rosa wondered, would God have spared her loved ones from the sorrows she brought into their lives?

623

Maybe if she had become a nun, everyone's lives would not be in such turmoil. Rosa felt a sudden grip of guilt.

Rosa, Rosa, she said to herself, stop! Today is a happy day. Today is the day Victor and Guido arrive. Putting the letter back in her pocket tin box, she went to the kitchen to wait for Nina and the twins.

The children often stayed overnight at Nina's.

Since Hans had moved out, she was lonesome and found frequent excuses to have them stay with her.

Nina stood panting at the top of the stairs after trying to keep up with the twins.

"You look beautiful, Rosa," she said when she caught her breath.

"And so do you and Angelina, and you, John, you have grown so much I wonder if your brother will recognize you."

"Is everything ready for the party tonight, Rosa?" Nina asked.

"Yes, we will have enough for a grand celebration! All the baking is done, and Sylvia will set up the table for us. The fishermen will bring their instruments. Even Enrico and his nurse will be here. Tonight we will have a real party for Victor and Guido."

The ferry boat pulled out into San Francisco Bay, and Rosa stood at the railing looking toward the Berkeley hills. It pained her to think of Aldo being so far away in Italy.

And sometimes, in the last few weeks, she played a game of make-believe. She would close her eyes and pretend that when Victor and Guido came down that gangplank, Aldo would be right behind them.

But when she wasn't pretending, she couldn't get it out of her mind that he was back with his wife and she would never see him again.

It was her own fault, she knew that now. If only she had not been so self-righteous.

And Enrico was no help. When she asked him, he would explain that Aldo was taking care of some business for the hotel. Then he would say something like, "Be strong, Rosa, have faith", and change the subject.

The ferry boat glided into its slip and stopped with the groaning sounds of moving piles. They hurried down the ramp and followed the crowd to the trains.

She could hardly believe that finally, after all these months, she would see her son again. But would Victor be happy here, in this new life? Was he really going to be able to take over the fishing fleet? Was he ready for this kind of responsibility? Has she done the right thing in bringing him here?

They heard a whistle in the distance. The train came so slowly into the station, so slowly Rosa was afraid it would stop before it got to them.

She hopped about nervously, trying to see every person who stepped down from each car of the very long train. John Edward and Angelina stood up on a bench to watch. Rosa spotted Guido stepping down out of the train, and behind him, Victor. So grown up and handsome, Rosa gasped, he was the image of Giovanni. So filled with maternal pride, she could hardly call out to him.

"Victor, Victor," the children shrieked and started running towards him, Rosa and Nina close behind.

"Mama, mama!" Victor shouted as he saw them. He dropped his bag and hugged her so tight she could not breathe. The children hopped up and down pulling on him.

Rosa could scarcely see through her tears of happiness. "Guido, Guido," without letting go of Victor she reached her hand to him.

You look even more handsome than I remember, she said, and she beckoned to Nina.

The twins spoke shyly to their brother as if they feared he had forgotten them. Victor scooped up Angelina.

"Little princess, I have missed you so, and you, Porko! How you have grown, Porko. Soon you'll be as big as me." John Edward looked up to the top of his other brother's head. There was both wonder and envy in his eyes.

Rosa stood back and watched the scene. At last, her family was almost complete.

The morning fog lifted, and a brilliant blue California sky looked down upon the ferry boat headed west. A flock of seagulls escorted them back across the bay, screeching they're welcome to the newcomers.

"Mother you look beautiful. You are dressed like a fine lady. America agrees with you."

"And you, Victor, look more like a prosperous businessman from Genova than a fisherman from Viareggio."

"You have grown so. You are at least six inches taller than I am now," Rosa pushed him from her so she could admire him. "You remind me so much of your father."

"Yes mama, it's been too long. It was good we had time alone in Italy, but now I am glad that I am here in America with you."

The twins held onto Victor's hand as if they feared he would get away from them, and Nina was keeping Guido busy asking him questions about Italy.

"How did Guido get along on the trip?" Rosa asked quietly, "He has aged so, and he looks very tired."

"Well, at least we didn't get seasick, like you did, Mama. Old sailors don't get seasick. But it was hard for Guido to leave Italy. He was sad because of Maria. Every day he went to the cemetery to visit her grave. I think he was mad at her for dying and leaving him. He bought her the most expensive casket he could find. He had her buried in a new dress."

"It is funny, Mama," Victor said, "because all they did was bicker. 'The soup was too hot, ' 'the soup was too cold, ' ' this was wrong, ' 'this was right. ' It got so that Dino and I would sneak out and sleep on the boat just to have some peace. Then, when she died, he almost died. I was afraid to leave him."

"I am glad you brought him. He will like it down at the wharf. He will have a nice room. He will like it I know."

They walked to the bow of the ferry boat, and Victor stopped to light his pipe. He looked so like his father, the strong square jaw, the silky brown hair, and heavy square shoulders.

"You have grown very handsome. Did all the girls cry when you left?" Rosa teased.

"Not as much for me," he smiled wistfully, "as for Dino. Remember he favored Eduardo, and there was something about his quiet, thoughtful ways that the girls loved. But he was not interested in them, his mind was on the priesthood, it had been for a long time. "

"How did he seem?" Rosa asked.

"Very happy Mother. Maybe I should have prepared you that he was thinking about the priesthood, but I didn't really know for sure, myself. I was surprised. When he finally made his decision, everything seemed to fall in place for him. The decision was a good one. He will make a fine priest. "

"Now tell me all that you have done," Victor said as they sat on the bench on the top deck of the ferry boat. Rosa told him all that had happened.

"Was it all right for me to send for you, to bring you halfway around the world because we needed you here?"

He put his arm around her and said, "I am glad you sent for us. We are family, and I want to be part of this new world."

The buggy turned the corner and the children pointed proudly to the bakery. Victor said, "Mama, you have done so well! You have a house and your bakery. I'm proud of you, Mama. But what is that sign 'RO-ZAH-TU?'"

Rosa told him how Hans had made the sign for her. "He has become a dear friend to us all, and you will meet him tonight. I call this my American sign."

That evening, everyone gathered to celebrate the new arrivals. There was music and dancing, and food and wine. There was talking and singing, there was laughing and arguing. Everyone was happy. There was the spirit of a new beginning.

Rosa went into the parlor where Enrico and Hans were having a serious conversation. She poured them more wine, and Enrico said, "Hans tells me that he is thinking seriously of retiring from the Police Force, and I have just offered him a job."

"He is exactly the man I need. Soon I will be able to go back to work, and I'll need a good man I can count on, " he looked to Rosa for agreement.

"That sounds good to me, Hans," Rosa said.

"Let me think about it. The only thing is that I really do not want to move. All my friends are here in San Francisco."

"Well, think about it, and I will take you there to see the place. It is so beautiful, and not too far from San Francisco either," Enrico said.

"We will take Nina and Rosa with us. They have not seen the hotel, we will make a day of it."

"Let me think about it," Hans got up, "Now, it is time to dance." He walked straight to where Nina was sitting.

"I do need him," Enrico said, "Jensen wants to go back to New York, and I need a good man I can trust."

Enrico leaned his head back. "I know Aldo would approve of Hans."

"I am sorry, Rosa, I should not have mentioned Aldo and made you sad. Today you should be happy, your son is here with you, and he is a fine looking young man, and I have spoiled it now talking of Aldo?"

"Come, let us dance," he stood up. I am allowed only one dance tonight, may I have it with you?"

The music changed to a waltz- to the one she had danced with Aldo, that evening on the wharf.

"What is wrong?" Enrico asked as Rosa's stiffened. He stopped dancing and looking down at her, said, "am I that bad a dancer?"

"No, no, it" she held back tears. "It is all the excitement of the day. You dance beautifully," and she hugged him.

They finished the dance without speaking. Rosa closed her eyes and pretended she was dancing in Aldo's arms. She felt safe and no longer alone.

Victor, finished a dance with Angelina, reaching out for Rosa said, "From what I hear, from the fishermen and Nina, you didn't tell me everything that has been happening."

"Well," she laughed, feeling better, "then we are even. I am sure you didn't tell me everything that you were doing either."

CHAPTER SIXTY-ONE

Victor was seldom at the flat. He spent all his time out in the boats with the fishermen, or at the wharf. He was eager to learn from anyone who would take the time with him. He followed the brokers, spent hours with them and when he came home he was filled with all sorts of ideas to talk about.

"Mama," he said, "this place is a miracle! The boats are full in no time, and there are so many people eager to buy, it is not like at home where we had to cart our fish out into the little villages to sell it."

"Yes," Rosa said, "Anthony was not a stupid man. But he was a greedy man."

"This is a virgin bay," Victor went on with joy in his eyes and happiness in his voice. "Even the fish are bigger here, it's like they followed me here to America."

As the weeks went by, Victor became the acknowledged boss. The men naturally turned to him when there was a problem or a decision to be made.

His quick mind and warm heart combined with a quiet wit to make him well thought of by all.

He decided to move to the wharf where he would be closer to everything. Mario was happy to get back to the sea again, and recognizing the same longing in Guido's eyes, took the old man on as his crew.

Rosa worried about Guido's health and urged him to take it easy, to lie back and enjoy the sunshine. He would pull his old wool cap down over his ears and tell Rosa, "What do you take me for, an old woman? No, I am a fisherman, I want to be out at sea, doing the job I know how to do, not basking in the sun like some damn loaf of bread."

Some time after Victor arrived, Rosa received a letter from Theresa Covella. It read:

Dear Rosa,

I write because I worry so much about Anna. She is the dearest sister anyone could have. But she is not getting better. She does not eat much and has not put back any of the weight she lost. She grows more quiet and distant every day. She sits for long hours out in the grape arbor, rocking and saying nothing.

We named our baby after Anna, thinking that would give her an interest and cheer her up. But instead, it seems to have made her more distant. She does nothing in the house, and doesn't even take pride in herself.

Sometimes she asks about Thomas, and tells me she is expecting him to come and get her very soon. I don't know what to do. Could you come and see her? I know that at first you worried that seeing you might upset her. But please come, she is not getting any better, I feel like she is slipping away from me.

Please try to come. Help me to know what to do for her.

Your friend,

Theresa

Distraught over Anna's worsening condition, and hoping Mrs. Larsen could give her some advice, Rosa took the letter and went to see Enrico.

The rosebushes and summer flowers lining the path to Anna's front door were struggling to bloom without their usual care.

Sam opened the door. "Missy Rosa come in, come in, nice to see you, Missy Rosa."

Sam shuffled down the hall bowing and smiling.

"I'll get Mr. Enrico, you sit down and wait."

Rosa smiled at his constant excitement about everything.

"It is good to see you, Rosa, Enrico said as he came into the parlor."

"Please, sit down. We shall have tea, whether we want it or not. Sam insists that for every cup of coffee I drink, I must have one cup of tea."

"What is it Rosa, you look worried." He leaned back in the chair.

Rosa gave him the letter. "This came yesterday, and the more I read it the more I worry."

Enrico was already reading it before Rosa had finished speaking.

"Dear God," he said as he laid it down on the desk. "has Anna seen a doctor since she left the hospital?"

"I don't know. All I know is what's in the letter. Has Theresa said anything to you in her letters?"

"No, no mention of it. Her letters to me are mostly about business things- about things the lawyer wants to know."

Sam arrived with a tray of cookies and a large pot of tea which he set on the desk near Enrico.

Pouring them each a cup, Rosa said, "I want to go and see Anna, but I don't know how to help her."

"I thought perhaps Mrs. Larson, being a nurse, could tell us what to do and what not to do to help Anna."

"Excellent idea, Rosa. She is not here right now, but perhaps we could both go with you to see her. Could we go on Saturday?"

A huge weight lifted from her shoulders, Rosa said, "I could have Sylvia and Peppino look after the bakery. But will it be alright with your doctor?"

"Yes, no problem. As long as I have my nurse with me, and get my rest." Sipping his tea he added, "Mrs. Larson is an excellent nurse as well as a compassionate woman, I think she'll be able to help with Anna."

Saturday morning the five boarded the train to Stockton.

Rosa had a bag of Anna's clothes and personal belongings for her, including the wedding picture from Thomas's desk. Mrs. Larson carried a large bouquet of Anna's flowers for her, and Sam sent along his tea cakes that Anna loved so much.

Angelina and John Edward were excited about going to the country especially about playing with the Covella boys.

Carlo met them at the train station in a large buckboard.

Apologetically he explained that he had made arrangements for Enrico and his nurse to stay in town at the hotel while Rosa and the children would stay on the farm.

"I wish I had enough room for everyone," he explained.

Mrs. Larson graciously agreed, "it's best for Mr. Martinelli to stay at the hotel, where he'll get his rest."

After a short trip to the farm, the children exchanged excited, noisy greetings, and then off they went to play.

With little Anna in her arms, Theresa led them into the big white farmhouse, stopping to put the sleeping baby in her cradle in the screened-in porch. Theresa poured tall glasses of lemonade for them all and apologizing for the heat of the day, assured them that the cool summer evenings would make up for the hot afternoons.

"Anna is sitting out under the grape arbor," Theresa said.

"I try to bring her into the house when it gets so hot, but as soon as I turn my back, she picks up her chair and goes back out. I worry that she could get heatstroke out there, but she just can't seem to stay in the house for long."

"I am really worried about her. The doctor from town came out to see her. She hardly uttered a word while he was there, and all he said was that her heart was broken, and I should see that she got lots of good healthy food. But of course, she will hardly touch a thing."

"I am afraid that she has lost touch with reality, and has lost all interest in living. She sleeps very late in the mornings, sometimes she doesn't even get up before noon. I try to get all my work done so that I can spend the afternoons with her, but she'll only stay with me a little while and then goes to sit outside. She seldom ever says anything."

"Offering more lemonade, Theresa went on, when we named the baby after her, we hoped she would take an interest in her, but she hardly looked at her, she has never even asked to hold her."

635

From the kitchen window, Rosa could see Anna sitting under the grape arbor, she was sitting very still. "Does she take any interest in the garden?" Rosa asked, "she took such good care of her plants at home."

Once in a while, she will get up to pick a dead leaf off the vine. But then she just lets it drop to the ground, and goes back to her chair, and sits down.

"The baby's crying makes Anna very nervous- she gets agitated, so I try to keep little Anna quiet."

"That must make it very difficult for you," Rosa said, noticing the lines of strain around her face.

Holding her arms out to take the baby, she added, "Anna wanted so much to have babies." She cuddled the sweet-smelling bundle to her breast.

"Do you think she knows that the tea they were giving her was really to keep her from having babies?" Rosa asked.

"I am not sure. It is very hard to know what Anna knows and what she doesn't. Sometimes she talks to me like she thinks I am our mother."

Theresa sat down at the table, her head in her hands she gave way to a moment of desperation. Carlo, who had been standing at the far wall, silently rested his hand on her shoulder.

"I have seen patients like this before," Mrs. Larson said.

"Sometimes after a terrible shock, when the body is ill, the mind is able to digest only a little piece of truth at a time. When the body is ailing, the human mind can be a fragile thing, and Mrs. Pages body has been through a major illness."

"Perhaps, Rosa, you should go and talk to her. Do not try to push her, just talk to her like you used to, and maybe that will break through the wall that surrounds her, and stir some memory."

Handing the baby back to Theresa, Rosa picked up two glasses of lemonade and started for the garden.

CHAPTER SIXTY-TWO

"Anna," Rosa held out a glass of lemonade, "it's me, Rosa." Anna turned toward her but there was no sign of recognition. She excepted the glass placed in her hand and listlessly drank from it. As she raised the glass, she looked at Rosa.

"I know you, don't I?" She asked in a flat voice.

"Yes, Anna, you know me, I am your friend, Rosa. Do you remember the classes we went to together, and how you used to visit me in the bakery?"

For one moment Rosa felt Anna trying to grab hold of her memories, only to be locked out again by confusion. Her mind returned her to the distant scene known only to her.

"Come," Rosa said, "let us take a walk, you can tell me all about the things that grow here."

Anna got up slowly and followed Rosa through the arbor and out towards where the endless rows of grapes were planted around the house.

"What are those black grapes growing there, Anna?" Rosa asked.

"Carlo called them zinfandels." Anna walked beside Rosa as an obedient child, she said no more.

"Let us go look at the flowers, Anna," Rosa said, desperate to get a response from her, "you used to love your plants so much". Silently Anna lead Rosa to Theresa's garden, eyes seldom raised from the ground, she spoke no words.

Sighing deeply, Rosa turned back toward the house, "There is another friend here to see you, Anna."

Enrico stood up and took her hand in his, "it is so nice to see you again, Anna. You are looking beautiful today. Here, sit down," he pulled out the chair next to him. Anna sat down, and for the first time, she smiled.

As the train departed the next morning, Rosa kissed Theresa goodbye and boarded the train with Rosa, Enrico, Mrs. Larson, and the twins.

It had been decided that Anna should return home.

In familiar surroundings, near her own doctor and Mrs. Larson, they would be able to bring her gradually back to reality. Making no objections to the decision, Anna followed dutifully on the train.

Rosa saw Anna frequently and watched her gradual improvement as well as her growing closeness with Enrico.

Sam stayed on to take care of the house. He moved Anna's things out of the bedroom she shared with Thomas and set up a bright sunny room for her on the first floor, so she could look out on her garden. He hovered over her like she was a starving kitten, and prepared all her favorite foods, and soon got some weight back on her.

She still had bad days but they came less often and lasted not as long. Under the watchful eye of nurse Larson, Anna and Enrico took long, leisurely walks in the garden.

Being an easy man to talk to, like his brother, Enrico helped Anna understand and accept what had happened. When the attorney finished examining Thomas's and Tony's records, and the case against them was finally closed, Anna learned that Thomas had provided well for her.

He had taken out two large insurance policies and had bought several properties in her name alone. She would never have to worry about being hungry.

Gradually Anna came to know that Thomas had indeed loved her very much, and that, at least in the beginning, he was a good man.

With time she came to understand and forgive the weakness in him that had made him turn bad.

For Nina, the scars Anthony left upon their marriage, and upon her as a woman, healed more slowly. Striving through the oblivion of exhausted sleep, Nina worked herself from morning to night.

With Rosita to help her, she continued to run the diner, and when she hired Louisa, she found herself doing less of the hard, everyday work of cooking. Hans helped her understand the business side of running the diner and boarding house, and she slowly took over the management. She became, as Hans dubbed her, "executive director."

Nor did she want for company. The twins loved to stay with their Nona, and often Victor took his meals with her. On Saturday evenings Hans often came to visit.

Hans was now the general manager of Enrico's hotel in Berkeley. Since resigning from the police force, he seemed to be his old self again, the strain gone out of him.

When he visited Nina, he brought her fresh fruit or wildflowers from the hills around the hotel. He often told her how beautiful it was, and how eager he was for her to see it.

"When the doctor lets Enrico go home, that will be plenty of time for me to see it," she said, fearing that a more positive response would be unseemly for a woman recently widowed.

For all of them, the fall was filled with happiness.

Peppino and Sylvia, their love for each other a secret from no one, finally decided to get married.

Father Paul celebrated a solemn high mass at Saint Francis Assisi church, and the celebration following the nuptials shook the wharf. More than a wedding between two well loved young people, it became a symbol for the future– a symbol of prosperity and happiness.

But with the happiness, there came sorrow, the new world had not been the answer for Guido.

He died while out at sea, his heart just stopped beating. Perhaps his was heartbroken by the death of Maria, or by a long life of hard work. Victor knew that his old friend's last wish was to be buried in his beloved Italy next to Maria.

They passed the hat among the fishermen and the next ship that sailed for Italy took him home.

For Rosa, that fall brought pleasure in her children and satisfaction in the success of her bakery. She had so many orders for her bread, that she decided to move to a bigger building.

And now that Peppino and Sylvia were married, they would live in the apartment above the store and run the bakery.

But even with all this in her life, for Rosa, there was a void, an emptiness.

CHAPTER SIXTY-THREE

Locking the bakery door behind her, Rosa felt very much alone. Everyone was away, they had all left early that morning. Nina and the twins had gone with Enrico, and Anna to visit Hans at the hotel in Berkeley.

Newlyweds Peppino and Sylvia, still living in their own romantic paradise, had not yet rejoined the rest of the world.

The November nights had begun to taste the chill of winter, but today, Rosa felt that special warmth and beauty of an Indian summer afternoon.

Walking toward her flat, under the rich blue cloudless sky, she could not bear the thought of spending such a day inside. She put some food in a basket and calling Paisano, she headed for the beach.

It was a windless day, and as they neared the ocean, and made their way down the hill past the Cliffhouse, the sky above the distant horizon turned to haze.

Rosa trudged across the sand and out to the water's edge.

In silence, she looked over the ocean as she has countless times before from a different shore across a different sea. Paisano dropped a stick at her feet and panted and whimpered at her until, reluctantly, she picked it up and tossed it for him. Each time he brought it back she threw it as far as she could hoping he would not find it and again intrude his game upon her mood.

Finally, the stick was lost to the grasp of a wave. She watched the waves rushing onto the shore and flowing back out to see. Hypnotized by the endless repetition, she stared:

Wash in, wash out, she thought, just like the people in my life. They come and they go, and I, I end up alone.

Rosa and Paisano shared a lunch, then satiated, he stretched out in the warm sand and slept. Rosa leaned back on her elbow and watched a young couple walk hand-in-hand along the water's edge.

She felt a surge of envy for these unknown young people, for the love they shared. They were together. They had each other. It seemed to Rosa that everyone was paired up, two by two, like those boarding Noah's Ark.

Rosa watched a gull fly overhead, his flight graceful and effortless. Where, she wondered was he going in his solitary flight? Was he content to fly alone?

She thought of the many times in her life she had been left alone, by the mother she had never known, the father who went away to fight for the freedom of Italy, and by her aunt Nina taken away to America. She thought of how the nuns turned her out of the convent for not having 'the calling', and how Father Joseph's betrayal had closed another door for her.

And she remembered the death of Giovanni and Eduardo. They had both left her.

Rosa walked along the edge of the water. She stopped to watch an old man, his clothes dirty and little more than rags. He searched through a can of garbage and shaking his head and grumbling himself, shuffled off along the beach.

A gentle gust of wind blew against her face, and she breathed in deeply of the fresh salt air. Paisano circled in front of her, and laughing at his antics, she picked up a stalk of dried seaweed and threw it for him.

She thought of the day Aldo gave the puppy to the twins on their birthday. She thought of Angelina and John Edward, and how they had grown into strong and healthy young bodies with bright, clear minds.

Looking back over her shoulder at the old man now almost out of sight, she thought of all God had given her; health, family, friends, and even success. And yet, it was not enough. There was something missing. In all that she had, there remained yet an emptiness, an aloneness.

Aldo. That was it. In all her life, there had never been a love like his before. She knew now that the one thing she craved, the one thing she hungered for, was love.

No matter what else she had in life, she yearned for and had always yearned for, that unconditional, that all-consuming love.

Aldo. Yes, his was the love she craved. But this, God's law denied her. It was her own fault. She knew that. She should never have permitted herself to fall in love with him.

She knew he was a married man, and that nothing could come of it. But yet, she did love him, and there was nothing she could do to change the way she felt for him.

Rosa sat down on the warm sand and drew her knees up under her chin. Paisano snuggled close and watched her with loving eyes. Thankful for his unquestioning, uncomplicated love, she stroked his head.

Why, she wondered, was her love for Aldo and his for her, imprisoned behind a web of man-made rules? Were they forever to be kept apart by his mockery of a marriage? Was he never again to be permitted to feel the blessing of true love?

Was this the will of God?

Rosa looked around at the beauty which he had created on the small section of the earth. There was the beauty of the sea air, the warmth of the sun, the sky with its tiny wisps of clouds, and the water, and the almost endless stretch of sand.

Why would the same God who created the earth with such beauty, dangle the temptation of happiness in front of her only to snatch it away?

This could not be the true will of God. Perhaps it was the rules made by flawed human beings in the name of the church.

She thought of the pain she had suffered from imperfect human beings acting in 'the will of God': The cruel coldness of the convent nuns, the lust of Father Joseph, the cowardice of Father Paul. These were all no less human than those who for centuries had been telling others the will of God.

No, she could not accept a petty and vengeful God. But where was the line to be drawn? How was she to know what was real and what was false? She reached into her pocket and took out her touchstone.

Shining and black and smooth, the stone looked back at her, and almost as if she could hear its voice, it said, you will know, Rosa, have faith.

On the ride back home, Rosa surrendered to her feelings of loneliness. Her heart ached for Aldo. Why she wondered, had she been so foolish to drive him away from her? She knew he loved her even as she loved him, and yet, she had to let him go. Only her stubborn adherence to the rules of the church had kept her from giving herself to him. Had she been righteous or foolish?

With Paisano standing guard out over the back of the buggy, the horse pulled the wagon slowly along the rough streets. Paying little attention to where they were, Rosa was listening to two parts of herself which were inside her, fighting for control of her soul.

As if with a voice of its own, one part of her spoke, "have faith, Rosa." While the other said, "faith in what? In man-made rules? Are these the true will of God, or are they the creations of flesh and blood men whose only desire is to control?"

Does God really want me to spend a loveless life alone, she wondered.

Rosa recognized the first voice as the one she had heard so often as a child, the voice of the nuns and the voice of the priests. It was the voice of the church, and it came gently back to her: "Rosa, God's rules are right. You have lived by his rules all your life, you cannot deny them now."

But the other voice, which was all that was new and different in her life, she hardly recognized. It thrusted itself upon her: "God sent Aldo to you, a good man and full of love. But you drove him away." The voice became stronger, "so now, you haven't heard from him in weeks. He has probably found someone else, after all, he is only human. Rosa, you are a fool."

"God's plans are not always known to us," the familiar voice said, "he often tests us to see if we are worthy. Do you not see that meeting out there was no chance occurrence? Put your faith in God."

Back-and-forth they went, Rosa couldn't stop the voices in her head. All the way home they tormented her. She felt she had no control of her mind, that the two voices raging between themselves were oblivious of her existence.

Home, inside her flat, she put her palms up to her head and squeezed her temples. She wanted to scream! Anything to stop the voices! She ran to the bedroom, took off her clothes, and drew a warm bath.

Letting her body relax in the warm water, she tried not to think. But she could not control her mind and the voices started again.

"Rosa," one voice said, "do something if you love this man go after him, fight for him. Pay no attention to the foolish man-made rules of the church. It is only God you must obey. Unless you want to be alone for the rest of your life, do something. What is wrong with you?"

The voice from the past said, "Now be calm, Rosa, do not doubt your faith. Have a nice relaxing bath. Have faith."

"Faith?" Scoffed the other voice, angry. "Do something Rosa, or it will be too late, and then a warm bath will be your only comfort. Write to him, tell him of your love for him. Tell him before it is too late."

Rosa lifted her body out of the bath and rubbed the towel hard across her wet skin. Paisano, who had curled himself up in a ball on top of her discarded clothes, opened his eyes, wagged his tail, and followed her into the bedroom.

She slipped her nightgown down overhead, combed her long hair, and let it fall loosely down her back. There was no need for a robe, she thought, it is warm, and who is here?

She poured herself a glass of wine and sat at the kitchen table with writing paper and her pen. She stared at the blank paper before her. The old, familiar voice in her head said: "Go ahead, Rosa, write him a nice friendly letter. But be careful, don't compromise yourself. He is a married man, and you know the rules of the church."

The new voice came back, "why bother to write if you're not going to say something that matters? He hears all the news from others. What he wants to hear from you is how you feel about him. Why not, Rosa, tell him of the love in your heart."

"Careful, Rosa", the familiar voice said, "he has a wife, and you have no right to him."

"You love him, don't you?" The new voice asked and added impatiently, "and do we not know that God is love?"

"Yes," Rosa said allowed as if she were speaking to another person, "I do love him!"

She started,

My dearest Aldo. I write to tell you of my love. I have been afraid before to reveal my heart to you. But I can no longer bear living an ocean and a continent apart from you. I should never have let you go without first letting you know the depth of my love. It is forever. If you still want me, I will be yours, on any terms. If you cannot return to me, I will come to you. Without you my life is empty. My love reaches out to you."

She signed her name, and setting down her pen, went into the parlor. She crossed the dark and empty room and pulling back the curtains looked out onto the bay. Her yearning for Aldo was so great she could almost feel herself out across the ocean and into his arms. She closed her eyes and could feel his touch. Imagined him standing there, holding her in his arms. A warm flutter went through her body.

But then she became aware of another feeling, something uncomfortable inside her. An uneasiness was gnawing at her. She reread what she had written. She heard the voice from her past: "you know you cannot send that, Rosa."

She paced across the kitchen, and the new voice taunted her, "go ahead, Rosa, you wrote it, you meant it, didn't you? Why would God want you, one of his children, to suffer for nothing? So now go ahead, put a stamp on it and mail the letter before it is too late and you end up with nothing."

She threw the letter down. "Shut up, shut up!" she screamed into the empty room. Suddenly becoming self-conscious, she knew it was only herself she was yelling at.

But the voice from her past said, "don't send the letter, Rosa. Think of your son, Dino, a priest. How would you feel if you were the cause of his shame, you, the mother of a priest, mistress to a married man?"

She pressed the letter to her breast, then tearing it in half, she slumped down into a chair, her feelings numb within her.

"You had your chance, and you let it slip past you", the new voice tormented. "Now all you have to look forward to for the rest of your life is a warm bath and a glass of wine at night to help you sleep."

Rosa rested her head on the table and tears of all her sorrows and all her years of wanting poured out. The comforting voice of the past whispered, "you have done right, Rosa. Obey the laws of the church, you must have faith."

Something nudged her leg, Paisano's sad brown eyes looked up into hers. She patted his head. He always seemed to know when she was blue.

"Come, it is time for bed," she said.

She put the torn letter in her tin box, and as she started to close the lid, a flicker of light reflected from her wedding band. She slipped it off her finger and held it in her hand. Giovanni and Eduardo are gone – they are no more than memories from another world.

And Aldo, whom I love as I have never loved before, can never put a wedding ring upon this finger. I am alone. I shall always be. I have only myself to depend on. She opened her hand and let the ring fall into the box.

"Good night, Paisano," she crawled between the covers and pulled them tight around her. She lay there in silence. The new voice did not speak. The voice of the past was still. She had silenced them both. She felt a sense of peace, a strength which she had not known before. No longer frightened or abandoned, she felt strong and confident.

Rosa looked around the room and smiled at the nativity scene the children made for her at Christmas. She thanked God for all that he had given her. She had her health, a loving family, a comfortable home, friends, and success. Truly he had given her much. She prayed for the faith to understand his will in keeping Aldo from her.

She drifted off to sleep, her thoughts returning to the man she could never have, the man whose simple gesture of putting his arm around her waist stirred her senses and delighted her soul.

CHAPTER SIXTY-FOUR

After a short time, Rosa woke up, and sleep would not return to her.

She stared out at the night, out at the stars in a moonlit sky. Her thoughts kept rushing back, back to the letter she had written and then torn in two. Has she done the right thing? All her life she had tried to live according to his will and the rules of the church, and now she had to give up this very special love. Was she really strong enough to live by the decision she had made?

Paisano, sound asleep on the foot of Rosa's bed, woke up suddenly.

Ears alert, he listened, then jumped down from the bed, and tail wagging ran toward the front of the house.

The doorbell rang.

Fearful images of children sick or injured children flooded into her mother's mind as she pulled her robe around her and hurried her after Paisano. At the door, the dog jumped about excitedly, his tail wagging. The outline of a man showed through the door curtain.

Cautiously she opened the door. She almost fell faint. She didn't believe her eyes. Lifting her hands to her mouth, she stifled a cry.

"Aldo, Aldo, is that you?" She threw her arms around his neck and embraced him.

"Yes, it's me, Rosa, my beautiful Rosa." He held her tight. He kissed her.

Rosa could say nothing. No words were needed. He was there, in her arms, and that was all that was important. She returned his kisses with a passion that she hardly knew she had, a passion that had never been aroused in her.

She held him close. Her body trembled with excitement as she clung to him. She wanted to never release him, not even for a moment.

When finally they drew apart, she took his hand and led him to the parlor. "Why didn't you tell me you were coming? When did you get here?" Rosa asked.

"This afternoon. There was no one here, the bakery was locked, even Enrico was gone! So I went to the Palace Hotel, and got a room, and came right back again, and here I am. But where is everyone? Where are the children?"

Rosa explained about their overnight trip with Enrico and Nina. Smiling that smile that only he had, his eyes sparkled, and he kissed her again and ran his hands through her long black hair.

"I have missed you so, Rosa. Do you know how many hours and days I have done nothing but think of you, just waiting for this moment to be with you again?"

"Oh Aldo, I know. Never a day went past, never an hour, that my thoughts were not of you…"

"Oh, my dearest,.." Aldo pulled her to him.

"But why didn't you let me know you were coming? We would have been there to meet you."

"I wrote, but I guess too late. Well, no matter now," he lifted her head in both hands and smiled down at her.

"I am here," he said, "and that is all that is important." He kissed her and hugged her close to him.

Silently they embraced. Her head against his chest, she could hear his heartbeat. Merged together with the pulse of her body. They became as one. Time, rules, voices, and even God's word stood still for them.

Rosa was filled with such happiness she thought she must be dreaming. But Aldo was there, he was real, his touch was real, this was no dream.

His nearness thrilled her as it always had. Their separation had changed nothing. A rainbow around them drawing them close while seductively his hands caressed her. Her whole body responded a warm wave rushed down upon her.

"Rosa, Rosa," he whispered, "I have missed you so, I have so much to tell you, so much!"

She stood back from him, and strangely afraid to hear what he was going to say, released him reluctantly. "Let me build a fire. Yes," she said, "we do have so much to talk about." She felt like she was running into the parlor, and the voice within her said, "don't be frightened, Rosa, listen to him."

She could feel him watching her every move as she prepared the fire. When she stood, he smiled down at her and reaching out his hand, pulled her to him.

Suddenly she thrust him from her.

"What is it? What is the matter?" He asked, "the color draining from his face."

"Your wife..." she looked at him with pleading in her eyes.

He wrapped his arms around her and pulled her close: "I am a free man," he whispered.

"Free?"

"Yes, free."

"What do you mean, you're free?"

"I mean I'm free," he laughed out loud and twirling her around and about, repeated, "I'm a free man."

"Free?" She said again and again, delirious with joy, but not understanding why. "Tell me, tell me, quick, what do you mean?"

"I mean I am free to marry." Laughing with sheer joy, he put his arm around her, and together they collapsed onto the sofa. "Let me tell you the whole story."

"I know it was hard for you the way I left," and he explained about the letter Enrico had received from Isabella. "With that letter proving that Isabella had no intention of having children, I had enough evidence to ask for an annulment."

"An annulment?"

"Yes, an annulment. But at first, Isabella tried to deny she had written the letter. Then I located the doctor she went to in France, the one she saw before we were married. He gave her a 'golden button', it's an ancient kind of thing that keeps ladies from having babies, it's something the French have used for years."

"When you told her this did she agree to the annulment?"

"Yes she did, but for a while, I thought her father was going to oppose it. Then he found out she was seeing a French Count. He was afraid of a scandal."

Aldo smiled as he added, "She always liked nobility."

"When I returned from France," he picked up Rosa's hand and held it, "I had to find an advocate to represent me before the Ecclesiastical Tribunal of Torino. I had to present all my evidence to the three judges, all priests."

"They granted me the annulment, but when it goes automatically on appeal to the next court in Mondovi, I don't have to be there, and they promised it wouldn't be too long before we got word the appeals been granted. The rest is just formalities."

He reached to kiss Rosa.

She pulled away, "Why in God's name didn't you tell me, Aldo? It would have made all this waiting bearable," she felt angry for the first time. Walking to the window, she said, "I thought I had driven you off with my strict sticking to the rules of the church. All this time, I have blamed myself."

Her voice was filled with regret.

"Rosa, if I had told you there was a chance I would be free, and God knows I wanted to, you would have waited, and maybe done nothing but wait."

"You had to make a life of your own, and find your own strength and independence. This is what you came to America for, wasn't it? You needed to find out that you are a strong woman capable of making a life for herself, not a woman who can only do what a man tells her to. I know that about you, and I wanted you to have the time to find out for yourself."

Aldo stood behind her, "I knew we were friends who could be lovers. But you didn't see it that way, you saw yourself as a mistress, a kept woman. If it had worked out that I came back still married, I needed to know that you were going to be ready to make the decision for yourself. If you chose to come to me, then I needed to know it was because you wanted to not because you, as a woman, thought you had no other choice."

Rosa turned to face him. The moonlight shining upon his face, she had almost forgotten how handsome he was.

Suddenly the room was a make-believe world, she could hardly believe he was actually there with her and telling her he was free. She touched his face.

He laughed at her.

"Didn't I always tell you I would come back, that god willing I would return? That was the only hope I had the right to give you. If I were not to succeed in getting the annulment, then it would have been up to you. And every day I prayed that if that happened, you would know you could trust my love."

Rosa turned and kissed Aldo, "I never doubted your love, what I didn't know was if, in the eyes of God, it was meant to be."

He looked at her so deeply she felt she could see his soul in his eyes. He kissed her.

"Rosa, it is meant to be. I want to be with you, to love you, for the rest of my life."

He kissed her lips, her throat, and caressed her breast. She felt his hand move down her leg. She was overcome with a wave of excitement and longing that she had never known before.

We will have our own life together. Tonight, Rosa, we will build our dream. He lifted her in his arms and carried her to the bedroom. He placed her on the bed and bent down and kissed her.

Rosa woke early and looked over at the sleeping Aldo laying next to her. Overcome with a surge of love for this man, she feasted her eyes on his presence.

Carefully she lifted herself out of bed to try not to wake him. But he stirred, then rolled over and opened his eyes. He lifted his hands towards her, and silently, easily, she was back in his arms.

It was late in the morning when they got up. They sat in the parlor, drinking their coffee and looking out the window at the bay and at the bank of fog hovering over the hills. They said little.

Watching him, Rosa had to try hard to convince herself that he really was there with her. She smiled with sheer happiness of his nearness.

He watched her watching him, and laughing at her, he put his coffee down and took a small tissue-wrapped package from his pocket.

"This is for you, something I ordered when I first got to Torino. Open it, go ahead, open it,"

His eyes sparkled with excitement as he watched. She removed the paper carefully from the dark blue velvet box. Inside was a white gold wedding band set with rubies.

She could say nothing. He knelt at her side and lifted her hand. "Rosa, my love, you know how much I love you, will you accept this wedding band from me?"

Tears of happiness flooding her vision, she nodded her head, "I cannot imagine a life without you."

When Nina and the children returned from their trip, they were thrilled to find Aldo back, and when Rosa told them they were going to be married, they were beside themselves with joy. They threw their arms around Aldo and Angelina asked, "Does this mean you will never leave us again?"

John's question was of a more immediate nature, "When you marry will mama get a new name and us a new papa?"

Aldo sat down, one child on each knee. He told them he would be proud to give them his name. But, because he knew they loved their own papa, he would understand if they wanted to keep their own name. With a hug for each, he assured them, that either way, they would always, truly be his children.

That night, sitting at the kitchen table, the twins practiced. John wrote, 'John Edward Martinelli'. Angelina chose 'Angelina Maria Dante Martinelli'. Nothing could have delighted them more than to have the "old man" from the boat, their new, true papa.

When Aldo's final annulment was granted and the banns for marriage were posted at the church, Nina decided it was time to treat everybody to dinner at the Palace Hotel. When Aldo protested that he should be taking everyone out to celebrate, Rosa told him of the bag of gold coins they found in Anthony's safe, and of Nina's promise.

On their way to the celebration dinner, Rosa told Aldo, "It is not easy for Nina to do this. To use one of Anthony's gold coins in this way is against everything she has ever been taught, and it is against the way she and Anthony lived all those years. I hope she can do it."

"Yes, I hope so too," Aldo said, "Enrico remarked just the other day how much change has taken place in her. He seems to think that Hans is sweet on her, is this true?"

"I wouldn't be surprised," Rosa laughed, "and did Enrico happen to mention a certain gentleman who is sweet on Anna?"

Helping her down out of the carriage, he said, "Oh? I was wondering what had put that gleam in my brother's eye."

Nina was wearing a lilac organdy dress and looked years younger. Her hair was in soft folds around her face. She seemed happier than Rosa had ever seen her, but still, there was a tenseness, a nervousness about her.

Fit and healthy, Enrico brought Anna, and Sylvia and Peppino followed together still looking very much like honeymooners. The twins came in on the arm of their brother Victor, handsome in the suit he bought in Genova.

They walked through the upper marble floor with its glass dome court filled with statues and growing ferns that transformed it into a king's courtyard. Smiling pleasantly at passersby.

Through the large dining room the color of peach blossoms, Nina followed the maitre d. He escorted them to a large round table with a gleaming white cloth of Irish linen set with Bavarian China and Italian crystal.

As Rosa took her seat opposite, she saw that Nina was not completely at ease in such elegant surroundings.

Looking around the room admiring the decorations, Rosa's glance stopped on a woman sitting with an elderly man at a small table directly behind Nina.

A sense of dread coursing through her, she squeezed Aldo's hand under the table. "What is wrong?" he whispered, "you look like you've seen a ghost."

"That woman over there is Dolores, you remember, Anthony's mistress?" Whispering she tried not to look in the woman's direction. But Rosa's surprise had not escaped Nina's attention. She turned to look. She too recognized the woman.

Rosa looked at Nina, her eyes silently asking her if she wanted to leave.

Without warning, Nina got up. She moved so quickly she startled everyone, and was at the woman's table even before Aldo could get up.

What was Nina going to do to this woman, to the mistress of her husband? What scene would she create? Rosa glanced nervously at Aldo, he shrugged his shoulders helplessly.

Everyone watched Nina. What would she do?

They saw Dolores look up, and as a sign of recognition crossed her face, her mouth dropped open, her face turned deathly pale. With extreme effort, the man got to his feet, and with perspiration showing on his forehead, he waited nervously to see what would happen.

Rosa could not hear the word spoken but when Nina turned away from the stunned woman there was a smile on her face.

As Nina took her seat, Dolores rushed out the dining room, her portly escort lumbering behind her.

With a confidence in her eyes, Nina spread the napkin on her lap. She lifted her champagne glass and said, "A toast to us all, and especially to you, Rosa, you have freed us all."

Lifting the dress of apricot iridescent silk from its bed of tissue paper, Rosa slipped it down over her head, she fixed her hair up in a swirl of loose curls to frame her face. She dabbed on the perfume Aldo brought her from France. One dab behind her ear, one at her throat, and smiling, she touched each breast. Feeling beautiful, she was basking in happiness when the doorbell rang.

Victor smiled as he came in, "You are not ready yet? I expected to see you all dressed and waiting."

"I have been waiting for this day all my life, and I want to savor every single moment."

Fastening the buttons on the back of her dress, he said, "You look beautiful, mama." The bodice fit snugly about her, showing her figure to its full advantage. "You look sixteen." he turned her around and hugged her.

"Your carriage awaits you."

Rosa picked up her bouquet of forget me nots and took Victor's arm. He helped his mother into the carriage, careful not to step on the hem of her dress.

As they entered the church, Rosa saw Aldo and Enrico waiting for her at the altar. In the first pew, Nina and the twins turned in their seats watching. The organ played, and, on the arm of her eldest son, Rosa walked down the aisle.

Dressed in his full vestments, open Bible in hand, Father Paul smiled down on her. For one brief moment, Rosa saw Dino standing there in front of her.

Rosa felt such happiness she feared her heart would burst, she looked at her children, Nina, and finally at Aldo. Her life was starting over once more. She had a new beginning. She had kept her faith in God, and now, confident in herself, her fear of abandonment was gone.

The touchstone in her heart told her that the unconditional love she's been searching for all her life, was there for her- had always been there.

It was God's mysterious grace.

Made in the USA
Las Vegas, NV
27 August 2021

29110884R00392